# couchwarmer

### a laundromat adventure

# greg kramer

The Riverbank Press

Cover illustration: Ian Phillips
Cover and text design: John Terauds

Canadian Cataloguing in Publication Data

Kramer, Greg, 1961-
    Couchwarmer

"A laundromat adventure".
ISBN 1-896332-02-1

I. Title.

PS8571.R356P87  1997          C813' .54          C97-930472-5
PR9199.3.K72P87  1997

First published by
The Riverbank Press
10 Wolfrey Av.
Toronto, Ontario, Canada M4K 1K8

Printed and bound in Canada

Dedicated to:
*The Speed Queens of Victoria*
*Michael 'Plunder' Doward*
and
*Mr Clark Render*

with all my admiration and jealousies intact

Primal editing by Jeffrey Aarles


BIG FUCKING THANKYOU's TO:
Everyone in my phone book
Lawrence Seguin, MaryAnn Camilleri, Sheila Chevalier, Joseph Attison,
Attila Berki, John Terauds,
Dean Gabourie, Psychic Judy, Margaret Lamarre,
Kerry Wadman of the Canadian National Institute for the Blind,
Morgan Holmes of the Intersex Society of North America,
Melanie Kurzyk of the Ontario Lottery Corporation,
Edward Roy, Ellen-Ray Hennessy, Patricia Wilson,
James St Bass, John Hastie, Toby Rodin
Open Stage Sundays at Buddies in Bad Times Theatre,
University of Toronto Reading Series,
Tim Egan, The Toronto Gay and Lesbian Archives, Richard Robert Leroux,
John Muir, Michael Sinelnikoff, Liza Soroka, Amy Wilson,
and
Dear Mistah Turner

Quotes from the Psalms are taken from *The Holy Bible*
(King James Version), New York Bible Society, 1955.


## DISCLAIMER

The lottery organization described in this book bears no administrative resemblance to any existing lottery organization known to the author. Similarly, the names and effects of certain drugs have been modified to annoy the inexperienced. Some medical conditions and treatments have been simplified for the sake of clarity or plot. Finally, anyone wishing to identify themselves with any character (other than the deities) may do so at entirely their own discretion. No such flattery was ever intended.

# couchwarmer

# A ... in the hole

'Tis the last shopping day before Christmas and a tiny, red, so-called lucky money spider just crawled across the table, curled up, and died. Flat on its back with its legs in the air: a miniature star getting tighter and tighter until it's nothing more than a point of blood.

This is not a fallen eyelash. This is a dead spider and it has to be a sign, an omen. But of what?

SHE's in the neighbourhood, that's what it means.

She who?

Our Lady, Santa Calamity d'Oopsidaisy, patron saint of the inattentive and clumsy, that's she who. Lady Luck's ugly twin sister, Baba Yaga, Lilith or Lachesis, Kali or Loki, Little Miss Fortune, call her what you will, she's getting closer – she may even be at the end of the block by now. Don't just sit there staring wide-eyed and shocked at that dumb, dead speck of a spider on the kitchen tabletop; the warning couldn't be clearer!

Praises be to Our Most Gracious Bitch of the Moment, Santa

Calamity, Whore of Mammon, Provider of Riches for Trivial Intentions. The Lady in Red. She who digs her virgin potholes in the paths of innocent travellers and hides behind the bushes, snickering at their approach. She who requires the ritual burning of tobacco incense at her altar and the quaffing of cocktails at her communion. She who will reward the faithful with the required two dollars and fifty cents for black-market Marlboros – it's not that much to ask for, surely? She who will provide.

Watch out! Those eyes may seem enticing, but at twenty paces, one of her glances can set a Christmas tree ablaze, cause a pileup on the freeway or crush a beggar with a falling safe. Listen up! From a block away, the vibrations from the hooves of the beast whereon she rides can lull you into a zombie-trance and hypnotize you into handing over your wallet. Even from across the park, the Bitch can flip the channels on your TV set and shake the silk out of a spider. Her power is not to be underestimated.

Perhaps she's in a generous mood this year and will reward her faithful fucked-up children with something more than the usual punch in the pocketbook or slap in the fates. She is, after all, in control of the board. Santa Calamity tilts the roulette wheel, stacks the deck, rattles the dice and fogs the magic eight-ball. Best to send up a prayer or a curse – heck, *incinerate that spider* as an offering – let her know you're one of the True Believers. Got to do something: things are getting desperate.

Look it. The holiday coffers are empty, the days of Cuban cigars and Russian Sobranies are long gone. No matter how much you try to pretend otherwise, seven fag-ends rescued from the ashtray never quite make a real cigarette. That sorry, bedraggled excuse for a handmade butt is never the same as one freshly pulled, tailor-made, pristine, from the pack. Admit it. Tobacco doesn't taste the same secondhand. There's always that burnt flavour, ashes in the mouth, a hint of desperation, regardless of how well you fool yourself that poverty is fun. Hey gang! Let's play Roll Your Own. Line up the stubs in the ashtray like wounded soldiers in the field; count 'em, measure 'em and classify 'em. Chop off their charcoal-filter heads, wrap 'em up, three to a shroud and burn the remains. One more stogie until the inevitable, until there is nothing smokable left in the apartment other than sandalwood joss sticks.

Or dead spiders.

Cigarettes may well have gone down in price but that makes no difference when you're broke. It's time to plunder the couch again for dust-encrusted dimes and pennies, to go through the lint from the bottom of pockets, to boldly explore the crud balls atop the refrigerator. Count on sacrificing at least one fingernail in the process.

Bah, humbug! Deck those halls, just deck 'em.

For those who call themselves Moneyed Christian, the annual festival of Santa Calamity d'Oopsidaisy is basically unknown, though all will feel her influence to some degree. Ostensibly, now is the time to celebrate the birth of the Messiah, a time for family, joy and goodwill. For others, however, for whom these holy days are nothing short of a mandatory prison sentence; now is the time when liquor stores are only open for weird, unpredictable hours and it's almost impossible to find a taxi without being charged extra or freezing your falsified tits off. It's a challenge just to get through the week without spending the rent or electrocuting yourself on somebody's fairy lights. The miracle of the baby Jesus is simply not relevant. During this week, those who call themselves Impoverished Heathen must be careful to remember just whose parade they march in.

Oh yes. Santa Calamity rode into town on the back of her Gilded Calf this morning. She was wearing her scarlet cape and her fur-trimmed hood of invisibility, so her arrival went more or less unnoticed except for a slough of twisted ankles in her wake. She's come for her winter festival: the Long Night of the Reckless Spenders. From Christmas Eve to New Year's Day her reign will be a celebration of mishap and greed. And she'll corral the lesser beasts – the spiders and the wasps, the trolls, the pixies and the pigeons, the worms, the moths, the gnomes and the roaches – she'll whisper her instructions to them all and send them out on their assignments.

With a flick of her handmaiden's tail, cash and catastrophe will dance hand in hand through this sunless week; her victims will crash into festivities, unaware of the cause behind their apocalyptic behaviour, stubbornly ignoring their imminent doom.


'Tis the season for accidents. Downtown is an abattoir of consumer desperation. Late-night shoppers grope along the treacherous sidewalks, heads bent against the snow, woolens wrapped, collars turned, blinders in place. Christmas lists may as well be pasted on foreheads as the hypnotized unfaithful make their pilgrimages to perfume counters and toy departments. Every so often someone will – mysteriously – lose their footing on the ice and take a tumble amid splatters of fresh purchases. Vehicles plough laboriously through slush, horns a-tooting and headlights a-blazing through a veil of flakes a-falling. Streetcars play Slaughter-The-Pedestrian as they rumble by, packed to the ventilators with steaming overcoats that are mere hazy bundles of colour through the condensation-choked windows. Tow trucks make a killing while ambulances wail their approval. Outside articulated window displays, tinny speakers blare the funereal theme song of the season – *God Rest Ye Merry, Gentlemen* – with no explanation as to what God, what gentlemen, nor indeed what kind of advice this might be. No one seems to heed it anyway. 'Tis the last shopping day before Christmas. Urban Carnage.

Unable to quit smoking cold turkey and finally having scraped together enough coinage from around the apartment, Cherry Beach (not her real name), one of the world's postgendered omnivestites (she'll wear *anything*) braves the elements and the fickle wrath of her personal deity to prove her worth as a True Believer. The taste of burning spider is still in her mouth, spurring her on to the corner store three blocks away in search of a fresh pack of black-market cigarettes. $2.50 as opposed to $3.75; it makes a difference.

Slim as she is, she waddles down the street like a giant pregnant beaver, clutching indiscriminately at passersby to maintain her equilibrium, thankful for her unnaturally long fingernails – or what is left of them. Her six-inch crepe-soled platform shoes splat through the slush, avoiding the slippery death-trap down the middle of the sidewalk where some foolhardy maybe-Asian maybe-Hispanic maybe-woman is trotting much too quickly towards her. Cherry angles her mohair bolero jacket sideways to avoid collision as the bundle rushes by, an overall-green blur of urgency with a white balaclava and coke-bottle spectacles, hurtling toward a future as another statistic, another notch in the crucifix for Santa Calamity.

Survival. The air is thick with it. For most, it is the survival of the season, these last few hours before the Big Gift Swap, the Hated Family Gatherings and the nepotistic blessings of He Who Carves the Turkey.

For Cherry, however, survival is a constant factor. Christmas doesn't change the picture, it just adds another colour to the mix. Out-by-Christmas. Another weapon to be used against her. A convenient date, six days earlier than the usual Out-by-the-end-of-the-month.

The cold wind prickles down her neck and up the back of her pantyhose. This isn't an evening to be out, but cigarettes are essential if she's to get through the night. Alcohol would be nice, but she's not working this evening and unless she stumbles across a friendly Saint Bernard in the two and a half feet of frozen shit that lines the sidewalks, she's out o' luck. Out o' cash. Ha! Understatement of the season. She who rides the Sacred Bovinity may provide, but not that much to the likes of Cherry Beach. As it is Cherry's going to have to peel open another tin of tuna for supper. No, for alcohol, she'll have to wait until tomorrow. After all, that's what staff bar tabs are for. Why else would anyone want to work in a nightclub?

Well, it's not exactly work; she's doing it as *a favour*. Helping them out. Gone are the days when Cherry could pay off a bar tab with a smile and a shrug, when some nice gentleman with a platinum AmEx would step in to rescue a would-be lady in distress. Gone. Now she's shackled to the dishcloth and forced into slave labour without so much as a contract of employment, just a veiled threat and a nod at the mop and the bucket standing in the corner. Six hours of work is about equal to two vodka tonics.

Cherry Beach has been "helping out" at the Kennel Klub for about a month, giving them the benefit of not only her scrubbing skills, but also her screwdriving and electrical talents. Little Miss Fix-it. She started off by patching up their sound system and look where it's gotten her. Now she is blamed for every conceivable wrong that befalls the establishment – along with a few inconceivable ones. She's solved the electronic riddle of the pinball machine (a swift kick to the tilt mechanism), managed to open the cash register when no one else could (acrylic fingernails have their uses), twisted the mirror-ball back onto its motor and, as far as Cherry's concerned, has kept the place from falling apart in return for alcoholic credit.

Admittedly, it can be fun. She likes to think of herself as the club mascot, a role of endearment that management is loathe to encourage. Left to her own devices, Cherry's self-appointed unofficial duties include hanging out with Lady Liberty at the door, checking the guest list, chatting up potential cocktail targets and, once the evening has gotten under way, stumbling around, pissed out of her brainbox, creating "atmosphere." Supervised, however, she'll sulk herself into a morose drudgery and whisper to herself that she's the Secret Illegitimate Queen of the Ashtrays as she scrapes the gum from the bottoms of tables, slops the dregs from boozy buspans, or steams her face over the evil glass-washing machine behind the bar.

It won't be for much longer. The Kennel Klub, a crumbling disco dinosaur, is in the final stages of extinction. It's only open on the weekends now and the staff are living off their tips while looking for alternative employment. Sad. Rumour has it that the governing Bloor family are hoping Grandpa will kick the bucket before the end of the tax year and thus solve all their problems. If that happens, according to Whatserface, the club's accountant, then everyone will get their due, along with a Christmas bonus.

Ha! Pay day? Chances are it won't happen, thinks Cherry, as she negotiates her way around an arguing couple in the doorway to the smoke shop. Grandpa Bloor is too tightly sprung to shuffle off his mortal coil in the immediate future, and chances are that Cherry's bar tab will be blamed – once again – for the inevitable payroll shortfall. Typical.


It's warm inside the store, if you don't include the freezing glare from the girl behind the cash who, ever since an unsuccessful bid for a free pack of smokes, has greeted Cherry with undisguised hostility. The load of coins spilling over the counter from out the upended toe of a nylon stocking doesn't improve their relationship, but Cherry isn't into social niceties tonight. It's all there, she's counted it twice, just give her the fucking Marlboros and she'll be out of there.

"No Marlboro. Camel only."

Cherry's heart sinks. Camels. It's not just a bad sign, it's a harbinger of doom. Those damned ships of the desert always seem to appear in her life when it's time to move on. Camels. They're an intro to the theme of packing her bags – a miniature caravan in her purse, taunting her with the promise of an oasis just around the corner, over the horizon, on the lee of the sandstorm. So far in her travels, Cherry has set up camp in an inordinate number of mirages. Camels.

"Thank you so very much," she quips, swiping the cigarettes out of the girl's hand almost before they've emerged from their secret drawer beneath the counter. "Merry Christmas and a Happy Caucasian New Year to you too."

The door bangs rudely against her buttocks, pushing her out onto the street. Mission accomplished – more or less. She pulls her collar back up against her ears, flips the blond nylon locks out of her eyes and snarls at the gusts of snow blowing in her face. Yuck! Frosted lipstick went out Halloween Weekend.

Homeward bound and hours to go before Cocktail Mama gets back from her family shindig. Hours of claustro-domesti-phobic torture trapped between a cantankerous, ancient invalid and a sugar-intoxicated seven-year-old. The task of gramp and baby-sitting seems nothing short of lunacy, but "looking after" them was part of the arrangement. The things you have to agree to nowadays to get a place to crash. Ah well, it's only an emergency stopgap. Another mirage. At least she now has smokes, which takes the edge off the agony. A parking meter provides a momentary crutch of stability as she cracks the cellophane, extracts and lights a cigarette before resuming her laboured three-block trek from the corner store back home – back to the crumbling hovel of an apartment balanced atop a secondhand bookstore. She pulls on a deep lungful of contraband Camel, and continues to scale the north face of the street.

Splat, splat, splat. Three weeks sleeping on the couch at Cocktail Mama's are three weeks too many. It's time to find another place to crash, and stash the gowns, cosmetics and wigs. Time to flip through her mental Rolodex for an address that isn't crossed out, burned, wise to the game, or otherwise non-virginal. There aren't many left to choose from. Liberty Hanna and Rose St James want money (cash!) before they'll even consider letting Cherry in through their warehouse door. And Zachary requires at least twenty dollars towards his phone bill. No, for the time being, she's stuck where she is.

It isn't that great a deal. Cocktail Mama's may well be expedient, but Cocktail Mama's is overcrowded: four humanoids in an apartment designed for the occupancy of a family of postwar squirrels. The place should be condemned; it's little more than a tree house, a ramshackle cubbyhole. The roof leaks, the electricity crackles, the television reception (now that the cable's been cut off) goes on the blink every time a taxicab goes by, and the hot-water faucet runs brown. Above and beyond these horrors there are the inhabitants themselves, the unwanted residue of the infamous Bloor Family, the banished branch of the great nightclub empire, the Kennel Klub embarrassments: Grandpa, Cocktail Mama and Brock. What with the kid going through her stuff whenever her back is turned and Grandpa hurling Bible passages at her whenever it isn't, the only sanctuary Cherry can find from this giddiness is in the bathroom – as long as someone else isn't "powdering their nose" in there, that is. Cocktail Mama has been spending three-hour soaks in the tub of late: candles, aromatherapy, bottle of whiskey, coathanger, *the whole bit*. Oh yes, it's time to find a new couch.

For the past fourteen years or so, Cherry Beach has been living off the hospitality of other people's sofas in return for household repairs or karma brownie points in future incarnations. Got a broken toaster? Look out. You may end up with more than you bargained for setting up a Bedouin tent on your couch.

The concept of sleeping on a *bona fide* mattress is an alien one to Cherry. Fourteen years of cushions, foamies, foldouts, canvas cots, divans, inflatables, hideaways and – yes – futons have left their impressions on her sleeping habits. Even her dreams are nomadic. There have been brief periods of honest-to-goodness mattresses, but these have either been shared with others or of the institutional, rubber-coated variety. Never alone and never in a room dedicated to Cherrysleep.

The chief problem with couches, however, as Cherry well knows, is that they have a slender shelf life, apt to turn sour at the mere appearance of a telephone bill and, consequently, Cherry often has half a dozen forwarding addresses (with accompanying pseudonyms) within as many months. It doesn't take long – a few seasons of living out of plastic shopping bags – before survival techniques naturally evolve: screwing on the tops of cosmetic bottles firmly at all times, keeping a separate bag for soiled laundry, knowing exactly where the important papers are hidden, etc. etc. After more than a decade, the effects of this lifestyle on a person are more subtle, a calcified resistance to permanence sets in, a jealousy of stability that masquerades as a belief that one is so genetically different from the rest of the human race that this nomadic existence is not just the only way to live, but in some way healthier. It certainly keeps you on your toes. Splat.

The gods were looking the other way on the day that Cherry Beach was born. Some intergalactic crisis grabbed the entire pantheon's attention and – despite having spent too much time drinking at the waters of Lethe, the river of forgetfulness, in preparation for her next stint on earth – Cherry was early for the first and last time in her life. She rushed headlong into this existence a good two weeks ahead of schedule, much to the surprise of her good-for-nothing mother, who was watching television at the time and only just made it to the superintendent's door before Cherry broke her waters and made her entrance in the hallway.

"It's a little boy," said the smiling super to his wife, pleased at his first home delivery.

"No, Albert," whispered his wife. "Look. It's a little girl."

"It's a freak!" screamed the good-for-nothing mother. "A freak! I don't want it! Take it away!"

So Mr and Mrs Metcalfe were faced with a decision. Moved by what they deemed to be their civic duty in the face of such vehement abandonment (and unilateral desertion by the Gods, had they but known), they carried the baby into their grease-glazed apartment, closed the door and laid it ceremoniously on their couch. Two hours later, the baby, blue in the face, was still screaming and screaming while Mrs Metcalfe sat dumbfounded, smoking cigarette after cigarette while she stared and stared at its genitalia.

"Hand me my needlework basket, will you, Albert?"

A practical woman, Mrs Metcalfe.

The baby settled down somewhat after that, afraid perhaps that its mouth might get sewn up as well. The damage done, thimble still on her finger, Mrs Metcalfe named it Frank, after Albert's father, and for six years or so raised an erstwhile son as her own.

Rumours of a virgin birth eventually died down as the baby became another fixture. The good-for-nothing mother vanished without a trace from her bachelor apartment and the spots on the carpet in the hallway became indistinguishable amongst the everyday flurry of Axminster roses. Life went on.

Mrs Metcalfe's stitching held its own. Had she but known that her belovéd Frank's profusion of sexual apparatus was due to a lack of attentive ministrations from Mars or Venus at the critical moment, she may not have taken the child in, either literally or figuratively; her Catholic sensibilities were steadfastly opposed to anything that smacked of the Heathen. As it was, her prayers were filled with doubt (steeped in the blood of Christ) as to whether or not she had done the right thing. She finally galvanized her resolve. She told herself it had been nothing short of Duty for her to sex the young Cherry, so to speak. And, if the truth be known, the needle had been a more attractive solution than the scissors. By the time the universe noticed the subterfuge it was too late: the child fell under the jurisdiction of Santa Calamity d'Oopsidaisy, and that was that.

Young Frank was a strange baby. He never grew any hair. Not even eyelashes, which caused him to blink continually as if the world could only be viewed in fleeting samples. In his crib, his legs remained crossed, perhaps in imitation of the stitches that kept him in place. As a toddler, he never seemed able to stand upright, his torso angled astonishingly forward – as if his diapers were swaddled far too tight. He would careen, pigeon-toed, down the hallways after his father.

"He's such a *clumsy* child," complained Mr Metcalfe.

"Oops!" sang his wife, swooping young Frank into her arms after another collision with the coffee table. "Oopsidaisy!"

They kept him secret. He didn't go to kindergarten or to school. Mrs Metcalfe taught him to read and write, albeit in a haphazard, distracted manner. Young Frank spent most of his time on his own, poring over illustrations in *Every Child's Book of Greek and Roman Mythology* and in a garishly coloured picture book that depicted the Stations of the Cross and the Pains of the Christian Martyrs. It was hardly surprising, therefore, that deities and saints got a little mixed up in his mind, cross-pollinated, as it were.

The Catholic image of the bearded God the Father, sitting on his cloud amid his choirs of angels, was remarkably similar to that of Zeus. Christ ascending to the heavens bore a striking resemblance to Hermes flying through the air. Mary Magdalene and Medusa merged into one, and everyone wore sandals.

Gods and Saints were all the same to the young Frank, distant familiar figures who, he felt instinctively, had overlooked his existence. They certainly didn't send him anything on his birthday. He knew their names but they didn't know his.

couchwarmer

Cherry's memories of her first parents are superimposed over an image of *American Gothic*: Albert Metcalfe, plunger in hand, with his wife standing next to him, brandishing her needle. That her earliest role models were involved in fixing things goes a long way to explain Cherry's persistent fascination with the very same activities. That she actually knows little or nothing about electricity, plumbing or sewing is a sad reflection of the gullibility of those who perk up when she says "I can fix that!"

Perhaps if the young Frank hadn't been forcibly removed from the Metcalfes on that traumatic afternoon – perhaps if he'd had a chance to actually practice some of the trade – there might be fewer permanently damaged stereo systems and VCRs in this world. But then, Dr Meadowlands had been adamant; the Metcalfes were, in his words, barbaric criminals. Frank was better off out of there, regardless of whether he'd learned how to replace a fusebox or not.

And the Glebe Institute was not the kind of place where a little girl would learn plumbing or household electronics.


Group homes, foster homes, surgical rehabilitation units, experimental farms (both legal and not), cottage hospitals and plastic prosthetics from the Pacific Rim have long since faded into the cavalcade of Cherry's history. Once she passed the magical age of adult responsibility she had to fend for herself. Official care and concern evaporated when it was realized that in societal terms, Cherry was a loose peg in a tight hole. *Lost to followup.* It wasn't so much a case of slipping through the cracks as being magnetically repulsed. There was only one place she could possibly fit: out of the real world. Thus, she found herself on the other side of the mirror, living in a through-the-looking-glass land of the habitually insane: the party circuit.

Considering the odds against her, Cherry has done remarkably well for herself, somehow managing to prevent the complete implosion of her morale by moving on to the next campsite whenever things – inevitably – start to deteriorate. After so many years of floating from one living room to the next, she has finally learned the trick of removing herself before her bags are thrown out the window. The trick is not so much knowing when you're no longer appreciated, as it is knowing when you're no longer tolerated. There is about a three day difference. And the reason why Cocktail Mama has tolerated her longer than the usual "couple of days while I sort myself out" is that Cocktail Mama is, once again, two weeks late with her period and is trying to scotch another mistake like Brock.

Splat, splat, splat.


A municipal snowplough emerges out of the evening traffic as if from nowhere. It's a monstrous yellow cow of a machine with a flashing blue halo and a tiny howdah cabin way up high in which the ghostly image of the driver's red coat can just be made out through the dirty windshield. It ambles along the gutter, mooing its horn, shitting its slush dung behind it as it goes. Cherry jumps out of the way to avoid getting splattered.

Following the snowplough, as if in procession, comes an ambulance. Its siren is off and, as Cherry watches, it douses its beacon. They obviously aren't in any hurry. Two dough-white paramedic faces turn as one to glance at Cherry and then, embarrassed, back to the road ahead of them. Blank.

The next second, Cherry feels that stomach-lurching panic as her weight-bearing leg slips out from beneath her. Her cigarette goes flying into the crowd, and Santa Calamity d'Oopsidaisy claims another victim. The six foot three inches of Tragic Glamour Puss that is Cherry Beach resigns itself to the decidedly unglamourous fate of wiping out. Instinctively, she clamps one purple-taloned hand over her two carefully packed breasts and the other over her pageboy wig. Wiping out is one thing. Wiping out and losing your hair and tits into the bargain is an unnecessary embarrassment.

Curses.

She sits sprawled in the snowbank for a while, estimating the bruisage to her hips, mourning the loss of her cigarette and glaring at her shoes. *Faux Pas*. Perhaps six-inch platforms weren't the most sensible fashion choice given the weather, but damnit, this is the city, isn't it? Sensibility is for the suburbs. Disoriented, she checks around her: towering buildings, street lights, concrete and cubic distortions of civilization, all seen through a curtain of soft, wet snowflakes.

People continue to shuffle by like mechanical turtles, each focused on their own drama, not a single one breaking away from the beaten track to come to Cherry's aid. A stalled streetcar a few yards away is getting more attention than she is. Transit officials buzz around in the slush like maroon flies. What's the point of wallowing in self-pity, thinks Cherry, when the audience isn't interested? Out of spite, she considers staying where she is for the rest of her life as a monument to the heartlessness of the times, letting the snow bury her body in a curbside grave, to be discovered come the Springtime thaw. Poor little matchgirl.

Clumsy little matchgirl. Clumsy, elephantine, mis-matched girl who wasn't looking where she was going. If only she'd pay more attention in life, then she wouldn't keep getting into these scrapes. If only ...

... If only someone hadn't carelessly dropped that *Scratch'n Win Lottery* ticket still stuck to the crepe sole of her shoe, she wouldn't have slipped up on it. How dangerous. Santa Calamity (who must be giggling herself into an epiphany behind the snowbank) is getting inventive. That the road to gambling Hell is a slippery one has oft been mentioned, but Cherry has never quite seen it as the physical equivalent of the cartoon banana peel. Well, this banana has a silver lining. Finders keepers.

The *XXXmas Lottery* ticket is a gaudy, metallic wonder, resembling the label to some fancy new pine-scented cleaning product. The design features a Christmas Tree, with ornaments to scrape away, a golden star at the top and a crimson bonus pot at the bottom. One out of every four tickets is a winner. Reveal three matching symbols to win – anything from a free pop to – how much is it? – a cool quarter of a million dollars, if one is to believe the blinding type across the top of the ticket. Cherry squints. It seems to her that the ticket sends out shafts of light, spreading its multicoloured promise into an otherwise monochrome world. Win! Win! Win!

Last year, she seems to recall, there had been a similar game. She'd given it a bash half a dozen times and never won a cent, her luck never being strong around this time of year. Oh well, who knows? Perhaps her fortunes have turned and her standing with She who holds the pursestrings of the insta-wins has improved. It's worth a try.

Cherry presses a nail into service and scrapes away at the play area of the ticket. That old familiar gambling sensation of Expectation-versus-Reality gives her a slight heart tremour. After scratching only four of the ornaments from the Christmas tree she realizes that – yes, indeedy – this little Norwegian Spruce is a winner. She has a triple match. Two bucks.

Hey, it's better than nothing. She tucks the ticket into her purse and is just about to winch herself back up onto her bruised legs when she spots another ticket across the sidewalk. That's right, another *XXXmas* tree flapping against a snow-coated brick. For a moment, she wonders about who might have dropped these tickets and how much they might miss them. For a moment. Then she stops wasting time pondering such trivialities and starts crawling across a stream of side-stepping pedestrians toward another crack at hitting the jackpot before someone else grabs it.

She needn't worry. The general population pretends not to notice what they would consider a lone, scavenging drag queen sprawled in the street. Everyone continues their same private shuffle at their same private pace, if anything speeding up to avoid the moral dilemma of having to deal with someone of such obvious sexual ambiguity. Some-one even pushes her – rudely – out of their way. It's a sneer from on high which, although not lost on Cherry, is hardly anything new and thus deserves no response.

Typical, she thinks as she feels the wetness soak through to her knees. Here I am again, in the gutter, ruining my pantyhose. When will I learn?

Ticket number two turns out to be the unexpected bonus of two tick-ets stuck together by the snow. The first gives her another two dol-lars, while the second yields nothing but a free pop and a growing gully of silver scrape-goop underneath her nail. She almost tosses the free pop ticket back into the street but decides not to at the last moment; you never know when you might need a beverage. Perhaps she could apply it to her bar tab at the Kennel Klub.

Still, all three tickets are, technically, winners. Three out of three ain't bad, much better than usual, even if they are all at the bottom rung of the prize ladder. She starts back towards the corner store to cash them in, and pick up a bag of chips or maybe a chocolate bar. She knows that the two-dollar tickets are supposed to be reinvested into the gambling addiction but that philosophy only ever appeals to her when she's drunk.

She doesn't get farther than three yards before she freezes in her tracks. There's another ticket on the ground. And a little way beyond that, another. And still another. The trail continues as far as the falling snow will allow her to see, back in the direction of the smoke shop.

It's a trail of glistening bread crumbs in the slush, flashes of gold, metallic green and red. A string of jewels. Or beads of dew, sparkling on a spider's web.

She scrambles into action. She slips and slides from one ticket to the next like a demented slalom skier, magically swooping them up with a fa-la-la-la-la and a Merry Fucking Christmas to one and all ... *five ... six, seven ...* she is giddy with Fortune. The Earth slips away from beneath her feet ... *ten ... eleven ...* buildings swing by like a carousel ... people ... snow ... stores ... *thirteen, fourteen tickets!*

She comes to a standstill. That's it. The *Scratch'n Win* magical-mystery tour has ended up outside a Laundromat – a Dixie Wash 'n Dry Coin-Op Laundromat, featuring (presumably) Dixie, a cartoon bulldog with a slobbering snout who grins in faded 1950's cream-and-blue styling from the marquee. Cherry looks around, searching for more tickets but can't see any. By the flickering neon light, she examines her hoard, straightening it up and aligning the trees in the same direction, as if the tickets were bills in the cash register – an unusually anal gesture for her – more to get her breath back than to put the world into any semblance of order. Some of the tickets are warping with the damp while others are as crisp as if they've just rolled off the foil press. She steps out of the street, out of everybody's way, and shelters against the blue-tiled wall of the Laundromat before applying her lucky fingernail to the game at hand.

Two bucks, two bucks, a free pop, free pizza, *ten* bucks, two bucks and a movie pass for two redeemable at any Cinescreen complexity in the city. They're all winners. Each and every one so far – and there's more to scratch.

Ten dollars, *twenty*, pop, pop, pop, a free CD and – on the stubbornly damp play area of the last ticket in the pile – *fifty* joyous dollars in a triple match that appears beneath her fingernail with such simplicity, such inevitability, that Cherry is aware of her breath turning to steam on her lips.

One hundred dollars in cash and a barrel of goodies. Not bad, considering the fact that half an hour ago she was fishing pennies out of couch cracks. Already she feels taller, her spine more capable of carrying her weight, her feet sturdier. Almost human.

The moment doesn't last. In spite of her sudden windfall, or maybe because of it (she cannot tell), she finds herself sighing, verging on anger and frustration. This is a gift from Santa Calamity – obviously

– and gifts from that Bitch always carry a nasty hidden caveat. She feels like tossing the tickets back into the street, back into the stream of shoppers from whence they came. One hundred dollars. A cab to work, a couple of cocktails, a game or two on the pinball machine, a gram of weed and breakfast at the greasy spoon … it'll all be gone in the flutter of an eyelash, sucked back into the urban economy and scattered around the city into that invisible river of cash that runs through wallets, pockets and purses. One hundred dollars is a mere drop in that river, especially when her bar tab stands at – what is it now? Two hundred dollars? Five hundred?

She rests her head against the Laundromat window, not caring that the nylon strands of her pageboy wig cling to the glass. Someone has cleared a little porthole in the steamed-up window in order to see out. Fluorescent light illuminates tatty linoleum and a flank of washing machines. Superimposed on this dim interior scene are images, reflected in the window: harsh reds and whites of the traffic, shadows of bodies passing, snow that seems ephemeral and the ghostly image of her own face lit by the neon marquee. A mirage of an oasis.

Lost for a while in the double-exposure diversion of trying to figure out whether that *XXXmas Scratch'n Win* ticket lying on the floor is inside the Laundromat or outside in the street, or even as it appears to her, coming out of her own reflection's nose, Cherry takes longer than expected to realize that yes, it's on the inside and yes, it is another ticket. It could mean another free pop, if she dare accept her assignment and go inside to claim it. Never one to back down from a challenge, least of all from one posed by herself, Cherry opens the door and steps inside.


The place is deserted except for a few bottles of bleach and boxes of detergent. Flattened corrugated cardboard boxes soak up dirty puddles of melted snow on the floor; there is the vague scent of warm laundry soap and mildewed socks. *Welcome to Dixie's* says the professionally brush-scripted sign on the back wall, alongside another portrait of the darling bulldog, this one somewhat cross-eyed. Less detailed but nonetheless still recognizable metal, die-stamped dog-heads brand each and every machine in the joint. Dixie washers, Dixie dryers. The omnipresent canine.

Red and green hand-crayoned notices are scattered on the walls

– reminding, chastising and warning – all written in glorious pidgin-spel. PLEASE NO SITING ON THE WASHER'S and DO NOT OVERLOAD SOAP.

There are, in fact, *seven* more tickets strewn along the linoleum tiles between the washers on the right and the dryers on the left. Feeling particularly blasé now, Cherry saunters down the aisle collecting them. When she stoops to pick up the second one, she is startled by a sudden mechanical whir behind her.

*Bzzzzz.*

It's the clock above the door, a sturdy old electric clock with a bunch of dusty wires sticking out of it and the buzzing's getting louder as the second hand mounts towards the twelve.

*Bzzzzz. CLUNK!*

A locking mechanism triggers, shaking the door frame, and an amber light springs to life beneath the clock. Just as the sign says: DOOR CLOSE AUTAMATICLY 8 PM – LAST DRY. THANKUO. Hopefully this means that she can still get out; presumably she has as long as it takes to dry her pantyhose before steel shutters slam down, trapping her inside. One thing's certain: no one can now get in.

The trail of tickets leads to the last dryer on the left, the one with the OUT OF SERVISE notice taped over the coin slot and, cruelly, over Dixie's snout. The one that has trapped another damned *Scratch'n Win* ticket between the lip of the door and the machine. Now that couldn't have fallen there. Someone must have shut the door on it for it to be caught like that.

Something very weird is going on here.

She looks up questioningly at the OUT OF SERVISE-muzzled Dixie as if to ask permission to continue. Assuming silence to be a "yes," she confronts the inevitable, tweaks the ticket from captivity, adds it to her growing stash, and flings open the door.


Oh dear.

Inside, in the shadowy recess of the dryer, sitting with an air of warm, vinyl innocence, is a shabby green sports bag. A spray of lottery tickets escapes from its half-open zipper, spewing forests of shiny evergreens onto the dark metal hole-punched drum. It's just sitting there, waiting for someone to come along and scratch.

Praises be and joy to all mankind, to womankind or otherwise – especially She!

Scary, though. Cherry's heart starts to pound uncontrollably, her artificial breasts shake, the backs of her knees pulse. It's like being propositioned. Look at all these sexy tickets!

She tentatively reaches in, pulls out one of the small stacks nearest to her and thumbs through a two-inch thickness. *One in four's a winner.* In her addled state she can't even begin to do the arithmetic, but knows for certain after just a couple of seconds that in this one fistful alone, the odds (considering she hasn't yet hit a single losing ticket) would give her well over a thousand dollars, easy.

And what if the big one's in there? The $250,000 jackpot ...? A quarter of a million dollars ...

She feels faint. It's hard to breathe. Vague thoughts of peril flit about in the nether regions of her brain, overwhelmed by much more concrete thoughts of living in the lap of luxury. She closes her eyes. Stretch limousines roll across diamond-studded landscapes on the inside of her eyelids. Snake eyes, blackjack, royal flush and BINGO! Triple Cherry combo on the slot machine. She opens her eyes. The green vinyl sports bag is still there.

Take the bag and run. *Take the bag.* Zip it up, clutch it close to your foamcore tits and saunter out of the Laundromat to a smart cocktail or twelve. Worry about the consequences later. On the other hand ...

A guilt-demon masquerading as a survival-angel whispers uncomfortable questions in Cherry's ear. *What about those consequences? Where did this come from? Isn't the Lotto company going to miss so many tickets? What kind of person leaves a bag of scratch and wins lying around in a Laundromat anyway?*

A futility-imp joins in the argument: *The tickets are stolen, the serial numbers are no good. There's a homing device in the bag. It belongs to the drug-dealing Hell's Angels arm of the Laundromat Mafia and if they ever find out who took it ...*

Cherry glances about her. The door is locked; no one can get in. The windows are steamed up; no one can see in. There are no security cameras. Oh boy. With shaking hands, she lights a cigarette to smoke out the voices of Santa Calamity's henchmen. Then she smokes another, sparking the second from the embers of the first. Calm down, she tells herself. Calm down, girl ... chill, cool ... *Think.*

It's the chance of her fractured lifetime. Say goodbye to the old, drab, survivalist Cherry Beach, the one who hauls beer crates to pay off bar tabs and sleeps on crusty couches in a never-ending tour of city after city, name after name, waiting for things to take a turn for the better in a world that never could, never would. Say hello to a green vinyl sports bag, with the promise of change as she has never known, not ever. The bag doesn't have her name on it – not even one she no longer uses – but try as she might, she cannot quell that feeling of having had a page in the scrapbook of her life saved, empty, waiting until now. It had to happen sometime. Fate. Destiny. Looking at it from that point of view, she feels decidedly better.

Halfway to the filter, Cherry stubs out her third cigarette in the handy-dandy cylindrical ashtray. She's reached a compromise. To appease the Bitch Inside, she's going to conduct a test. If the next, randomly pulled ticket from the bag proves to be another winner, she'll take them. Otherwise she'll call it quits and leave the Laundromat as if nothing had ever happened. Yeah, right. As if. But Cherry Beach, if nothing else, is a stickler for appearances and a champion for pulling the wool over her own eyelashes. She reaches in, closes her eyes to ensure true randomness and pulls a ticket.

It's a winner, all right. Two hundred dollars. Take the bag.

It's a lot heavier than she expects, although surprisingly easy to pull over the transom of the dryer door. She stuffs the loose tickets back inside the bag and zips it up. No shaking hands, no sweat, the palpitations have vanished. The swag was obviously meant to be hers.

Time to leave. The door to the street, thankfully, can still be opened from the inside. Cherry turns for one last look at the hallowed Laundromat.

*KA-KATHUGGGGG!!*

With a shuddering bolt, the lights go out. Time's up.


Cherry hurriedly closes the door behind her and steps back out into the street, the green bag slung loosely over one shoulder, her purse over the other, a whistle on her lips. An image floats in her brain – an image from the moment when the Dixie Wash 'n Dry Coin-Op Laundromat turned itself off and plunged itself into darkness. She had seen something on the wall. With the sudden transition of light it had seared itself onto the shadows and onto her retina, throbbing repeatedly fainter over the cold and silent washing machines until it faded into the slowing click … click … click from the lights as they cooled down. It was more than an omen, more than a confirmation that

Santa Calamity d'Oopsidaisy was happy with her work tonight. It was a sign. In spidery green crayon.

*NOT RESPONSABEL FOR ARTICALS LEFT IN MACHINE'S.*

# 2 ... jumPin' jupiter

Mrs Metcalfe's needlework, of course, couldn't last forever. Half-way between young Frank's sixth and seventh birthdays, something shifted within him and, despite the constant warnings *never to touch himself down there*, he found himself scratching uncontrollably, guiltily locking himself in the bathroom for hours and picking away at the itch between his legs. It seemed to be weeping a clearish liquid. A few weeks went by and it got worse. Sometimes it felt as if he were actually peeing through his skin, as if his tubes had gotten tangled and had burst inside him before anything could stream out of his "little faucet," as his Dad, the superintendent of the building, called it. In point of fact, he wasn't that far wrong. As Dr Meadowlands later explained, his "waterworks" had shifted – a plumbing analogy that would not have been lost on Albert Metcalfe. The fishing line, which had stayed in place for nigh on seven years, couldn't be expected to hold back half a dozen bladders of urine a day.

The technicalities of what had actually happened were more

complex than any doctor at the Glebe Institute could either diagnose or explain – it was beyond them. The child had an extra five mutated chromosomes of shifting classifications, along with twenty-three pairs of autosomes instead of the usual twenty-two. They called it intersexed "mosaical," which was another term for "we don't know." Identifiable gender was a knife-edge issue that teetered first one way then the other, throwing Dr Meadowlands into a moral quagmire that would last until Frank left the system of his own accord. *Lost to followup.*

Oblivious to his internal mechanisms, the six-and-a-half-year-old Frank thought he was enduring divine punishment for touching himself. Mrs Metcalfe had managed to instill in him a fear of the Holy Mother's wrath with stories a good deal more bloody and vengeful than the usual Catholic parables. The way she told it, you'd think that Jesus had a divine army working for him – soldiers equipped with swords and stones – to root out the unclean and safeguard the holy sanctity of heaven from contamination. The crucifixion was nothing compared to the punishments awaiting those who left the tops off toothpaste tubes or who wouldn't eat their greens. Above and beyond these simple domestic threats, Frank was cautioned that his soul would shrink if he violated the golden rule of *no touching*. A shrunken soul meant a shrunken after-life and, as Mrs Metcalfe made clear, no number of Hail Marys, pure thoughts or bleeding be-Jesuses could ever restore his soul to its original size. The warning made its impression, but try as he might, the young Frank couldn't keep his meddling hands away. He certainly didn't dare question anyone about what was going on with his body. Instead, he'd perch himself on the edge of the toilet in the bathroom, amid the stink of cooking smells and detergent, tears rolling down the side of his nose while his fingers relieved the pressure of his urinary tract. He dribbled into the bowl while his soul shrunk away to Purgatory.

The day the stitching burst *in veritum* he could hide it no longer. Before he passed out, he screamed loud enough for the police *and* the Humane Society to be summoned by a neighbour who was convinced that another cat had been desecrated by the local hooligans. Mrs Metcalfe, who believed that doctors and priests are interchangeable, fell to her knees on the Axminster roses and confessed her wrongdoing to a surprised paramedic. That was the last Frank ever saw of her.

He was whisked off in an ambulance to the Glebe Institute Children's Unit for emergency surgery with no more than a teddy bear stuffed between his legs to staunch the flow. He didn't even have time to pack a toothbrush.

"I'm leaking!" he screamed. "I'm lea-ea-eaking!"

Dr Meadowlands was inspired by the challenge young Frank presented. Here was an interesting specimen! He'd come across intersexed babies before (usually those with ambiguous genitalia: an oversized clitoris or an undersized penis, undescended testes, etc.), but never one with a complete inside-and-out double set. Frank had what analysis confirmed to be four *ovotestes*; a gonadal anomaly that the doctor had only previously read about and had dismissed as fiction or something that only appeared in snails or crayfish.

The main problem was a legal one. The law required that a human being be either male or female to exist. Frank was both, the only clue as to which side of the fence he should have been sitting on was his urinary tract which – at the time – favoured the female. Dr Meadowlands was averse to performing a castration, it was too final and ruled out any future research possibilities. So instead, he opted for cosmetic surgery which satisfied the legal requirements but left the organs intact, although disguised.

A smart nip and a tuck performed under general anesthetic transformed Frank into Frances (or *Little Frannie* as "she" came to be called) and when Frank awoke in his hospital cot two days later, he found himself surrounded by nurses who kept calling him a *brave little girl*.

The worst of it all was that he could no longer pee standing up, a trick which had taken him so long to master in the first place and which he was loathe to abandon just because he'd lost his little faucet. That he would not be returning home was the least of his problems. Her problems. She was a little girl now. Little Frannie. Her soul had obviously shrunk beyond redemption. She was plonked into a dormitory with the "three little pigs" – a trio of obnoxiously mutilated little girls (who had, much to her surprise, *always* been little girls) – and visited three times a day by Dr Meadowlands and his ever-changing entourage of friends. No one ever gave advice on how Frannie was supposed to adjust to her new state of affairs. They merely observed the effects of their experimentations, somehow expecting Little Frannie to respond without actually being told *how*. This had to be Purgatory.

"I'm a friend of Dr Meadowlands," they'd say, pulling on their rubber gloves or preparing their syringes.

"I'm not," Little Frannie would reply, sullenly. "Dr Meadowlands is always touching me *down there. Where's my little faucet?!*"

A so-called anatomically correct stuffed doll was used to show Little Frannie what had happened surgically: a pillowy penis was pushed backwards into a buttonhole vagina and then held in place with a Velcro strip and a collar of pink satin. One of Dr Meadowlands' students, Jamie, had gone to great pains to adapt this eternally smiling doll for Little Frannie's educational benefit. As well-meaning as this gesture may have been, the doll was no favourite and ended up being abandoned in the kitchen garbage along with potato skins and leftover baked beans.

"I don't know. I lost it." Frannie was learning how to lie. "I want to go *home.*"

"I'll ask Dr Meadowlands," Jamie promised her. "We'll try to get you put on the foster home program."

The hoard of doctors, social workers, experimenters (and, Frannie suspected, the plain old *curious*) continued to visit. Crowded around her bed, they talked of her as if she wasn't there, filling her ears with talk of *the preservation of the neurovascular bundle* and serving up baby-blue pills that would, she was told, help her to *stay a little girl forever.*

Mr and Mrs Metcalfe were referred to as barbaric criminals and Frannie couldn't quell the disconcerting suspicion that somewhere on the other side of town, her erstwhile mother and father were paying for some crime committed upon a person none of them knew. Jesus' soldiers were crucifying them, stoning them, carving them up into little pieces, sending their bleeding souls to Hell.

"I want to go *home,*" she wailed. "I don't want a vagina!"

"The sooner you adapt to your new surroundings, the better," said one.

"You have to put that behind you," said another. "Why don't you play with your new friends?"

"The foster program has a ten month waiting list," said Jamie.

"You're such a *pretty* little girl."

One day, while waiting in the examination room, her legs kicking distractedly off the edge of the gurney, little Frannie was surprised by the sudden, breathless entrance of a small, crumpled old man with a camera, who took a couple of rapid snapshots of her operation scars before vanishing as quickly as he had appeared. All that remained was the smell of his body odour and the echo of his raspy breathing.

couchwarmer

Little Frannie, at that stage in her life, didn't have the sense to ask what all the fuss was about. She kept hoping that her penis, along with her soul, would grow back.

"There's nothing wrong with your vagina!" exclaimed Dr Meadowlands. "It looks like a million dollars!"

... Boy, if ever I had even a quarter of a million dollars ...

New friends! A new world! Toss the old one into the garbage and look at the difference money can make! Little Miss Hostilla at the corner store transforms. Now she's Little Miss Happy Fortune Cookie and even helps out with the skill-testing question, she is so smile-agog. She checks her answer on a calculator, proudly showing Cherry that her solution to the math question matches the electronic one. Everybody loves a winner and Little Miss Happy must be on commission.

"Lady lucky," she beams, counting out Cherry's two-hundred-dollar win in twenties. "Just in time for Christmas." Cherry nods and smiles in agreement.

With her winnings (just in time for the long haul between Christmas and the New Year), she buys a carton of Camels, half a dozen candy bars, a pint of frozen fudge, a box of liquid ginseng capsules and a bottle of Ukrainian two-hundred-proof-poison-wood-alcohol that, with a pinch of lime, could pass as vodka. She tips the girl ten bucks in gratitude for solving the math and foxtrots half a block further west to the next store.

Little Miss Happy's evil twin sister at the Smoke & Shop is too busy trying to prevent a gang of street urchins from ripping off the porno mags to pay much attention to Cherry. She refuses to cash in more than one of the tickets on the grounds that there's "one win per ticket only." The stubborn woman can't be made to understand that this refers to the limit on each ticket, not the limit on how many tickets can be redeemed at once. She doesn't care; she's too preoccupied with keeping tabs on her *Big Boobs* and *Bad Boys*. Cherry cashes in a free pop and gives it away to one of the kids, who must be all of eight years old.

Three stores later, she's still trying to cash in more than one ticket at a time with little success. She barks out the answer to the skill-testing question – *fourteen* – as soon as she slaps her winners, totalling a hundred dollars, onto the counter. The middle-aged man examines them suspiciously, turning them in his hands and sniffing the dry goods and provision-scented air.

"You buy these here?"

"Oh, no," says Cherry, truthfully. "But I will. Give me a couple more, I'm feeling lucky."

The trick works. It's worth the four dollars to get the ninety-six in return. She scrapes her two new tickets ostentatiously at his counter to demonstrate twisted proof of her loyalty to his store. When they come up losers, she shrugs her shoulders, buys a childproof lighter and makes her farewells, somehow convincing herself that she's done the guy a favour.

Doubling back, she avoids walking past the darkened Laundromat by stopping at a pizza store around the block. In the window they have a giant promo cutout of the XXXmas tree, which is covered in slices of cardboard pizza (not to be confused with the real thing). The display is dog-eared – as if it's been kept in damp storage for a year – which it probably has. The tree does its job though, ensuring that the world is reminded of the tie-in promotion.

"Gimme the gourmet deluxe with extra anchovies."

Her *Free Pizza* ticket is accepted with respect, demonstrating employee familiarity with the current campaign. There is no reason to suppose that the world is yet on the lookout for Cherry Beach, the scratch 'n win bandit. The green bag over her shoulder feels, nonetheless, like a monkey on her back. She gets her free gourmet deluxe pizza; in fact, she gets two for the price of one. They are served up in tandem, pulled from the oven on a double-headed wooden spatula and then slid, side by side, into the box. Twins. They give her a red plastic-net bag of golden chocolate doubloons as a token of their festive camaraderie.

"Happy Holidays, sir – er – madam." A hint of a giggle.

Fuck you, thinks Cherry, automatically. I'm the one with the free pizza.

Outside the apartment, snowflakes float like narcoleptic butterflies; cabbage-whites on valium. In the window of the pawn shop next to the second-hand bookstore is a rack of instruments: silver trumpets, electric guitars, a trombone, a dusty old tuba fallen lopsided against the velvet curtain. Cherry contemplates buying the pearl-inlaid accordion as she juggles pizzas, bags and keys to let herself in through the crappy brown door set into the wall between the two stores.

The staircase inside is, for all intents and purposes, vertical, rising on a steep incline that threatens to tip her up and send her hurtling back down to the bottom on her head. It's hard to see, the only light comes from a humming orange bulb way at the top. Cherry's going to miss climbing these stairs almost as much as she's going to miss looking after that brat and walloping the old man's television. At the door at the top of the thirty-nine steps, she stops, has difficulty finding the right key, and after a momentary attack of vertigo, lets herself into the notorious Bloor Psychosis.


Families have appeared throughout Cherry's life like traffic accidents glimpsed out the corners of her eyes. Mangled wrecks of personalities in blood-drenched gene pools, observed from a distance, from the end of the street. She's never encountered a family in which she was made to feel entirely welcome. She's always the outsider. A family is something that happens to other people. Not to her.

There have been enough of them. Once she'd started on the circuit (thanks to the petitioning of Jamie, the student doctor) it was difficult to stop. Nuclear families, extended families, military, left-wing, right-wing, academic, government-funded, poor, struggling, rich, satisfied, do-good, bleeding-heart, malignant, grumbling and exploding-in-transit families, families, families. All of them fading into a soup of memory where some can only be recalled by the colour of wallpaper in a guest room or a lonesome synapse firing off somewhere in Cherry's brain when she orders a particular curry in a restaurant.

There was the incomprehensible Laval family, who seemed to be ruled by their giant, neutered calico cat, Maloney. There were the Bronsons, the Kingsways, the Rideaus, and the Outrements. Ultimately, at the point when she could bear the foster shuffle no longer, there had been the suburban sprawl of the Monaghans, who refused to call her Frank; "Jumpin' Jupiter, we've already got one of *those*." Families mean children, adopted or otherwise. Families mean rules just begging to be broken. Families mean idiosyncrasies so strange that Cherry's fluctuating hormones, extra chromosomes and hairless body seem positively tame by comparison.

She'd thought she'd rid herself of siblings and parents, aunts and uncles and the rest of that tangled overgrowth when she'd left the Monaghans that cold December evening, stuck out her thumb on the highway, headed off to the Big City and left them all behind her. She'd thought she'd never again have to graft herself onto another genealogical tree.

But here she is fourteen years later. With the Bloors.


"Cherry! What are you doing in there? I have to use the washroom. *Cherry!*"

"I'm having a bath. Go away!"

"You are not! I'm hungry. I'm *fuck*-ing starving!"

"Eat your pizza."

Cherry turns on the hot water to drown out Brock's sugar-cracked soprano objections to anchovies and turns her attentions back to her fingernail. She's fed the little bastard, hasn't she? A two-for-the-price-of-one (free) pizza, and if he doesn't like it he can scream until the cows come home. He should think himself lucky he hasn't been enlisted into child slave labour – scratching tickets.

She could use the help. One ticket may be fun to play, half a dozen are exciting when you're riding a winning streak. Any more than one hundred, however, and a severe medical condition sets in: Gambler's Nail, where the curvature of the acrylic actually changes shape – flattens out, splits, starts killing nerve endings. At two hundred, a numbness creeps up the arm to the nub of the shoulder blade. After five hundred tickets, the entire surface of the hand turns silver from latex residue which can't be blown or wiped away. Now, at over one thousand scraped tickets and counting, the mess is everywhere, clinging with static persistence to Cherry's arms and knees, shoulders and ears, as if she's been tarred and feathered by some alien experimenter. Some of it has even gotten into her eye. It's an ugly business, this gambling.

For more than two hours, Cherry has been sitting on the toilet seat in the bathroom, the door locked, a "vodka" cocktail and a slice of pizza at her elbow, the bag of tickets between her feet and sorted piles of winners stacked along the lip of the bathtub. There are stacks of ten-, twenty-, hundred- and two-hundred-dollar winners – thousands of dollars' worth. In her purse she's put a couple of five-hundred-dollar babies. She keeps telling herself she needs to stop and think, take a breath, figure out what the hell is going on. Her internal Cassandra is screaming doom and gloom with every ticket. *Warning! Warning!* But all she can do is scratch.

And win. And win. And win.

The odds of hitting so many winning tickets are much the same as a tossed coin landing on its edge – ten times in a row. It's making Cherry's temples throb. She's freaking herself out. The mathematics involved are erasing whole sections of her memory banks. Soon, she'll forget who she is (which isn't such an unusual occurrence). She's spinning into an arithmetical tizzy; numbers, numbers, everywhere numbers. Dollar numbers, security numbers, serial numbers, winning numbers, lucky numbers, telephone numbers, digits, figures, fractions, odds and evens. If this excitement keeps up, she's going to have a nose bleed.

"He loves me … He loves me not …" she chants, amusing herself.

He loves her. Definitely, whoever he is, he lo-oooves her.

Suspicious? No kidding. In more than a thousand play areas and bonus *XXXmas* tree pots, she hasn't yet come across a single dud, not one – there's always at least a free pop. Her first thought had been that the "one in four" winners meant that the losers were the two buck re-plays and the promotional merchandise: the pops and pizzas, movie passes and CDs. That this was a friendly Christmassy game where every ticket was some kind of a winner.

Then she remembered the two losers she'd picked in the store earlier on. No. Something fishy is going on with this particular bag of tickets.

Chance has taken a back seat to inevitability, the initial glee has worn off, and now it's getting tedious. She's hardly made a dent in the bag. There's at least another fifteen pounds to go. By Cherry's frantic calculations, there are upwards of a quarter of a million tickets wedged into the bag.

"He hates me … He hates me not …"

Her arm is giving out on her. Switching to scraping with a coin instead of her nail provides only temporary relief. The same muscular tremors are required; the same pressure – if not more – is called for to prevent the loonie from suddenly slamming flat against the ticket and squeaking away more of her broken nails. Maybe there'll be a complimentary manicure somewhere in here. Maybe she'll rub up a magic genie who will save her the trouble and show her where the quarter of a million dollar ticket is hiding. It has to be in here somewhere; she just hasn't found it yet. It's only a matter of time, she's convinced of it.

What she needs is a long, hot soak in the tub, a chance to scrub this evil silver residue from her life, call up Liberty and put a couple of hundred dollars down on the warehouse space. It's time to bring this scratching to a halt and call it a night. Her bath is almost ready – she'll stop as soon as the tub is full. Yes, that's what she'll do. Absolutely. One more ticket, maybe two more, and then she'll relax in the hot water, make a few phone calls.

And she's got to stop biting her nails, for Chrissakes. The cuticles taste awful.

One more ticket …

… Ten thousand dollars … Ten thousand dollars … Ten thousand dollars! Three times ten grand. Triple match!

Yes!

Unable to contain the expanding emotion in her chest, Cherry screams her good fortune into a towel until she gives herself a headache.

Ten thousand dollars!

Yes!!

*Thank you for calling the Provincial Lotto Centre. The offices are closed for the holidays …*

Curses.

Of course, they're closed. Typical. Cherry lights a cigarette, balances the ashtray on the edge of the bathtub. The *Seabreez* bubbles are doing their job, soaking the silver film away from her skin. The hot water coaxes the muscles from her bones. Aaah. She turns her attention back to the phone that's tucked between her shoulder and her chin.

The perky recorded voice continues to inform anyone who cares to listen that over the next week, the Lotto Centre will be open at a whole range of hours that seem to be negotiated around the weekend, statutory holidays and employee schedules. If one has a winning ticket, one is advised to store it somewhere safe – say in the icebox – until one can get into town at a time when the centre will be open again.

This is both good news and bad. Bad, because Cherry can't cash in any of the big winners for another three days and by that time, the theft of these winning tickets (for now she's convinced that they've been stolen) may well have been discovered by the authorities. Good, because for the next three days there will be no communication with the Lotto people, leaving the corner stores and other scratch 'n win outlets ripe for the plundering. She has hundreds of dollars' worth of small prizes to cash in. If only she could be certain of not getting herself busted in the process.

*Winning tickets are valid for one full year – redeemable at Lotto outlets throughout the Province …*

Cherry hangs up.

The Gods are playing an evil game. After a lifetime of negligence, they have turned around and cursed her with just enough good fortune to get her into Big Shit. Santa Calamity is going to get a gold star for pulling this off and the Olympus crowd are going to be rolling around on their clouds in hysterics. Hercules' Labours were nothing compared to this. To clean up the mess in the bathroom alone is going to be worse than mucking out the Augean stables.

And she's still no nearer to knowing where all these tickets have come from.

The simple explanation is too complex to face. These are the winning tickets. All of them. The randomly distributed *one-in-four's-a-winner*s have ganged together, folded in upon themselves and collapsed like a dark star into the green vinyl bag. Somehow, they found their way into the OUT OF SERVISE dryer in the Dixie Laundromat. Stolen, they have to be. Or forged, counterfeited, printed on the sly by Kriss Kringle's mischievous elves. Depending on which of Cherry's paranoid mixamythologies she chooses to believe in at any given moment, there is also the distinct possibility that the whole thing is a setup. Just for her. A test of character by Zeus and his gang to see if she'll do the right thing and take the bag to the nearest police station and hand it in. In which case, she fails, and she will always fail.

Fuck it. If she can turn her find into real money, she's going to do it. If she ends up in prison, then so be it. A chance to spread her wings like this comes along only once in every twelve lifetimes. This time around she isn't going to fuck up if she can help it.

It could get dangerous. She needs protection: a safe place from which to operate, which the Bloors are simply not going to provide. She runs through her mental Rolodex, punches in Liberty's phone number, adjusts the inflatable bath-pillow behind her head, flips the telephone cord out of the bubbles and waits for an answer.

"Liberty, hi, it's Cherry. Guess what? My boat came in." She impersonates frantic cash register noises.

"Wa-a?" Liberty's voice is blurred, nebulous.

"Two hundred dollars, right? For the deposit on the space."

"Oh, right." A pause. "I'm sorry Cherry, it's gone. We couldn't wait any longer."

Cherry chews her lip. "All right then," she suggests. "How about two-fifty? Tell your new roomie you made a mistake."

"Well, I don't know, it's hardly fair to Phoebe." Liberty sounds unmoved. "How come you have money all of a sudden? You rob some pensioner of their Christmas bonus?"

"Look, I could sleep on the couch. I can't stay at Cocktail Mama's any more, they want me out in a couple of days."

Silence on the other end of the line.

"I said, I could sleep on the couch, it's only for a couple of days until I ..."

"Uh-huh, I heard you." Liberty is brusque. "I have to get to work. I'm late."

"Lib ...?"

The phone goes dead. Some bath water probably got into the receiver. Cherry hangs up, leans back in the tub, and smiles. Liberty has swallowed the bait. And Liberty's the best protection money can buy; she's Cherry's *Get Out of Jail Free* card. Liberty's a born intimidator, which is why she's one of the most sought-after bouncers in the city. One look at her and the underaged, uninvited, unwanted and unruly turn into meek, obedient ducklings. With the leather-clad, spiked and aftershaved Liberty Hannah to ward off the evil elves and Lotto bogeymen, Cherry even has a chance of cashing in her big winners through sheer intimidation. And then – aaah – what she could do with that ten thousand dollars ... twenty thousand dollars ... maybe she'll find that jackpot ...

"Che-e-rry," whines Brock from the other side of the bathroom door. "I'm bo-ored."

He bangs on the door, a volley of fisticuffs. The wood around the lock starts to heave and crack. "What are you *doing* in there?!"

... Frank! ... Murray! ... Frannie! What are you doing in there?! ...

"Frances, will you get yourself out of that tub before you turn into a prune!"

The strident voice echoes along the corridors of time, and surfaces with a splash of soapy water in the ceramic bathtub with the spreading stain around the plug-hole and the overflow drain. Beneath the water, clinging like a second skin to the bottom of the tub are a million tiny bubbles that rise in a cloud when disturbed.

"I will remember this as long as I live. As long as I live, I will remember ..."

Eight years old and in the bathtub, cowering from Madame Rideau's wrath, trying to escape into another existence, wishing she could swim away and join the sea-monkeys at the bottom of the ocean, never to return. Holding court in the undersea castle, lounging about all day with Aquaboy and Flipper. Playing with that strange new protrusion *down there* that had started to appear a month or so after she stopped taking those little blue pills. The purple fleshy bulb that, when touched, grew painfully engorged. One stroke would send bubbles to her head, make her brain swirl in confusion – catapult her off to another continent. We can't understand it, Madame Rideau, the girl seems to have vanished into thin water. Another unexplained mystery. It would serve them all right.

"Frances! What are you doing in there?" The door handle rattles. "Frances, why have you locked the door? I can see you through the keyhole, Frannie. Why? Why can I see you through the keyhole? What have you done with the *key? Frannie*?!"

Why doesn't she just shut up! The key is where Frances left it, in the soap rack. It had been fun for a while, playing with that obscene bar of pink soap that has the magnet embedded in it, waving the key like a magic fairy wand, letting the soap dangle until gravity overcame inertia and the bar would splash into the water. Now it's forgotten, abandoned in the wire rack that hooks over the side of the tub. The fleshy bulb, responding to the splashings in the bathtub, pokes its arrogant little head out of her million-dollar vagina, doubling backwards upon itself through years of scarring and stitching, demanding attention ...

"I will remember this as long ..."

The injustice of it all, coupled with the guilt of having a secret penis, is certainly something to remember. The bathroom was a dungeon, the room of banishment, the place where Frances was sent when she'd become too much to handle. *Get that stuff scrubbed off you this instant.* Why couldn't she just be left alone then, to enjoy her punishment, her solitude, her clandestine masturbation? But no, the foster-parental urge to control follows her to the cell and bangs on the door.

"Frances, do you *want* to be sent back to the Glebe?"

Not-so-little Frances crouches in the tub, her lips just below the water, at bubble-blowing position, at tea-sipping level. The inside of her mouth is exhausted from the taste of medicated soap. Madame Rideau's coral lipstick won't come off as easily as she'd hoped. It won't come off, it won't. The Glebe Institute sounds like a welcome escape, something to work towards.

"... as long as I live I will ... Boy, if ever ..."

*"Frannie, you're not playing with yourself in there, are you?"*

"... if ever, if ever ... "

Cherry flings open the bathroom door just before it splinters. Brock stands there like a Child of the Damned, his eyes gleaming with curiosity. His mouth and hands are smeared with chocolate and ice cream. A Camel cigarette is hanging from his lips – lit. A half-eaten stick of a nougat-peanut bar is in one small fist. Cherry's favourite *Smoky Sunset* lipgloss, blunted and damaged, is in the other.

"Are you wrapping my Xmas presents in there? Are you?"

Cherry adjusts the turban-towel around her head, knots the waist-tie on Cocktail Mama's robe. She smells of avocado scrub. She surveys the damage that Brock has wrought in the living room and counts to ten. The little shit ...

"You poisonous tadpole."

He's been through her stuff again. It's all over the couch, melted fudge ice cream and milk chocolate rubbed into the cushions and glossed over with layers of *Smoky Sunset*, mascara and panstick. Jackson Pollock, the younger. Cocktail Mama's going to have kittens. Maybe that's what she's been trying to drown in the bathtub over the past few days. Or perhaps (if she had any sense) she's been bleaching her ovaries or scouring her uterus. The girl has such a fertile womb, she could tie her tubes in twelve places and *still* get pregnant. That's probably what happened with Brock, that knotted, twisted, screaming, smoking, Satanic proof of her fecundity. The identity of the Great Paternity is always carefully avoided, as if a hex would descend at the mere mention of his name. It's too late, the curse has already landed.

"Give!" Cherry extracts the burning cigarette from his mouth, then pries the dead lipstick from his clutch.

"That's not your robe, you know that?"

"You shouldn't be smoking at your age."

"Who cares?"

It's true. Cocktail Mama is unlikely to be shocked by Brock's progress along the road of nicotine addiction. She might even be pleased that her child is finally showing signs of maturity. If he's old enough to smoke, he's old enough to fend for himself. He's already the reject of the rejects, the lowest of the low in the Bloor family hierarchy. Which isn't saying much. To be ostracized by the likes of his uncles Bob and Al is an honour.

The family rift is such that even though there is a superficial invitation for everyone to join in the Christmas Party at the Bloor homestead, everyone knows that there'll be Hell to pay if either the old man or the kid turn up. There's a lesson in all of this. Something to do with the gratitude of families and the foolishness of providing for them. Feeding hands that get bitten, etc., etc.

Candy wrappers litter the floor. The bag of golden chocolate doubloons has been looted, ransacked. The frozen fudge is no longer frozen and is fudging from its pint tub all over the kitchen counter.

"Who gave you permission, you little fuck, huh? Who?!"

"They were in the fridge. It's not your fridge you know."

"They were in the freezer. The freezer is for grownups."

At least he hasn't drunk all the vodka. He's taken a slug – Cherry can tell from the milky daubs all over the opened bottle – but a Highly Acquired Immune Tastebud System is required to stomach the stuff. Even with his experience, Brock still has a few years to go.

"The woman who calls herself my mom says that you're a freak of nature. Is that true?"

"Yes, my little gargoyle. That makes two of us."

If Brock is going to take after his genetic roots, he'll be ready to commit his first felony in a couple of years. What is he now, six? Seven? Whatever. He's going to be dead if he doesn't sit still while Cherry transfers her Travelling Beauty Parlour into the bathroom – bag by bag – where she can give it an autopsy in peace and quiet.

"Are you going out tonight?"

"What does it look like?"

"You have to pay the rent, remember."

"I paid it." She slams the door and starts sorting out the corpses of eyebrow pencils, lipstick casings, and powders in the bottoms of the plastic bags.

"Guess what?" Brock's voice pipes through the keyhole, "I heard that when you lie, your soul shrinks."

Cherry stops, her hands full of cosmetics.

Out of the mouths of chocolate-smeared children. The little bastard, hitting her with something like that. She tries to ignore the idea but it won't go away. Even though she has long since vanquished her childhood fears, Mrs Metcalfe's threats included, enough belief remains for Cherry to be wary of fucking up her soul. She's going to need it for her next incarnations. Not that she ever thought that fibbing could do it any damage; if that was the case, it would be well atrophied by now. It's just that now she actually has money – for the first time in this life – so the karmic forces must have undergone some re-adjustment, and she could, conceivably, be doing some damage. Not by lying – she'd sooner work her way through purgatory than give *that* up – but by being cheap. She'd hate to be accused of being a tightwad when she actually has the readies.

She opens the door a crack.

"There you go. Now you be sure to give this to your mother."

"But it's been *scratched* already."

"That's right. A hundred dollars. Rent."

"It's not a real ticket! Gimme one that isn't scratched. *Gimme!*"

In a fit of pique, Cherry pulls out an unscratched ticket and wings it at him as she would a bar coaster. Its flight pattern is as erratic as a June bug's.

"I hope you choke on it."


Kids are Evil. Children do the most obnoxious things. Boys and girls alike; it's in their nature. Filling the plastic lemon with urine. Defecating on the slide in the playground and covering the turds with grass. Dolloping jam into a waiting shoe to attract the wasps. Bugs in the catsup, snails on the window. The meadow provides a wriggling, creeping, crawling source for all the wrongs yet to be committed against the prize of childhood.

The worm, though. That was the worst.

Frannie had been returned to the Glebe and was a few weeks shy of her ninth birthday. They'd gotten up early – the whole dormitory, the three little pigs, even Julian in his wheelchair – and gathered in secret around the sewage pipes at the building site across from the Institute. Someone had bought a bottle of detergent to squirt on the mud to make the worms rise to the surface, gasping for air. They'd pulled them, wriggling and blind from the clods of earth, collected them in a blue plastic bucket, the kind used for building sandcastles and which on a summer's day stinks of warm piss.

"A pee-nis for Fran-nie!" A giant specimen raised its thick, bulbous purple head like a soggy yo-yo. "D'you think it's big enough?"

The reasoning behind the dawn mission became clear. Little Frannie ran. She'd gotten as far as the rise leading down to the ditch before they caught up with her and pinned her to the grass, the farting, plaid-skirted rear end of Catherine O'Connor in her face, unseen little pig trotters scrabbling at her panties.

"See! Frannie has a pee-nis! A pee-pee penis!"

"There's a hole! She's got a vagina as well!"

"Not Fair! Not Fair!"

Two weeks later, the not-so-fair nor not-so-little Frannie was just able to walk again. She was in a foul mood. The three little pigs had squealed to Dr Meadowlands about Frannie's secret penis and so Dr Meadowlands had wheeled her into the operating room once again to practice his backstitch. It had taken him a long time and he left a lot of damage in his wake. It wasn't merely that he'd had to chase the worm (which was still alive when he extracted it); on his way he'd discovered that, thanks, in part, to Frannie's self-deprivation of estrogen, her penile tissue and testes were now cramping her urinary tract.

In a rare moment of clarity, Dr Meadowlands made a decision that was to have far reaching consequences: he decided to leave everything inside intact and turn Frannie back (at least superficially) into Frank. It is quite possible that he acted with the best intentions in the world.

"What do you mean? You're saying that I'm a *boy* now?"

"You mustn't tell your foster families about your operations, Frank. We'll tell them you had testicular cancer."

"I should be so lucky."

Dr Meadowlands was to change his mind three more times before Frank/Frances was finally *lost to followup*. There was so much scar tissue that not only was all sensation lost, but also growth was stunted, maturation impeded and trust in surgeons destroyed forever.

It also laid the foundations for Dr Lyndhurst's surgery years later.

Oh yes, the worm was the worst.

Kids are Evil. Cherry has discovered why the phone is dead. Brock, the little crustaceous wart, has ripped the cord right out of the wall in the living room. That does it.

"My mom says you're not to make any more calls until you pay the phone bill."

"Into solitary with you, young man."

Cherry steers him by the ear, up to his grandfather's room, where the television hisses its snowstorm petitions for money in the name of Jesus. Hallelujah. She pushes Brock onto the bed and stands guard for the required thirty seconds while the room forms a claustrophobic straightjacket around him.

Grandpa Huntley Bloor lives, eats, sleeps and rots away in this one small windowless room, the central burial chamber of the apartment. The place is jammed with artifacts the old boy has accumulated over his life and which he obviously has every intention of lugging along with him into the next: a high-mattressed bed with a carved headboard, a rosewood dresser, a tallboy, a mottled mirror with the silvering peeling away, and watercolours of Scottish glens and hollyhocked cottages. The numbing stench of embalming medications wafts from a side table that's crammed with bottles dribbling chalky pinks and whites. The air is so thick with death, so anticipatory, that when the priest arrives, all he will have to do is turn off the television.

Grandpa Bloor slowly turns his sunken eyes on the intrusion. His focus goes beyond, missing its target.

"Finally," he croaks at the wall. "My bedpan needs changing."

"Who do you think I am!" grumbles Cherry, locking the door behind her as she leaves. "You haven't had a bowel movement in twelve years. Why start now?"

… Boy, if ever I had a quarter of a quarter of a million dollars … Just think …

It's too cold out not to wear a wig, but Cherry's been living in the blond pageboy for the past few days and she's getting tired of it. She needs a new look to go with her newfound wealth. More important: if, by any chance, she was spotted leaving the Laundromat with the bag over her shoulder, she'd better change her appearance.

Red. Namesake red.

Red is the colour of action. Any assertiveness-training infomercial can tell you that. Cherry has to find a new pad for herself and her belongings, she has to coax Liberty onto her side, she has to cash in a few more tickets and she needs wheels to get to all those corner stores. So much to do, and this time, it's for real. Things are going to change, the orchestra is playing the overture to the next act and she is the conductor of her own Destiny. Fuck it, she's the Ringmaster. Red.

Half an hour later, she's at the appraisal stage. The shiny black pudding-basin wig hangs in a solid Cabaret around her ears – flawless. Purple metallic eyelashes. The poppy-red pant suit, however, has a small soy-sauce stain down the front … not to worry; it'll vanish under the right light. She ties a burgundy scarf around the throat; a gash of blood to match the ensemble.

"You look like a Holiday Inn whore," her reflection in the bathroom mirror snarls at her. "A two-bit, backstabbing whore."

The spent casings from the chocolate doubloons make the best earrings – two arching saddles of foil punched through with a stud. They're symbolic, they don't have to be real; in fact, fantasy is preferable. They can always be thrown away at the end of the night. Toss 'em away. Change your plans.

If Liberty doesn't come through, there are plenty of other options. Heck, Cherry's rich now, isn't she? She could jump on a plane and claim a free Vegas breakfast. If she doesn't want to risk crossing any borders with her loot, she could always stay in town, take over the Penthouse floor at the Chateau Fusspot, or move into some split-level downtown ranch, fall in love, get a fake suntan and vanish forever into the designer-drug rave circuit. Most likely, however, she'll end up renting a cheap room for a couple of weeks. The Belt 'n Buckle is right above the best speakeasy in town and within crawling distance of three others. Prime location. Maid service, free soap, clean sheets and coffee in the morning, all included in one low price.

The Camels are calling. *We Three Kings* …

Coincidentally enough, it was around Christmas when the seventeen-year-old Frank finally left his childhood and the continual hand-me-over-to-another-family scenario behind him. The sprawling Monaghans, with their small-town ways, pushed him over the edge.

"We can't call you Frank. We already have a Frank."

"So? Now you have *two!*"

"Jumpin' Jupiter, what's wrong with Murray?" Charlotte Monaghan wrung her hands. "Murray's a *dandy* name."

Jupiter doesn't jump; he expands and he looks like God. When he calls himself Jove, he laughs and great guffaws of jollity spread throughout the universe. Wave after wave courses through the heavens, a roaring, bellowing racket of delight. He sits on his cloud and chuckles over his children – his thousand and one gods and goddesses – for Jupiter is the Father of All. All, that is, except for those who manage to slip through his fingers when he isn't looking.

Jupiter: the Father of Luck, the Master of Chance, the celestial juggler. When he closes his eyes, he becomes a form of Fate. Sometimes, when he falls asleep, his nightmares don a scarlet dress, mount a lumbering beast and go exploring in the world of men, weapons drawn and ready. Shhh! Don't wake him up!

Oops.

"Don't you get all high and mighty with me, young man. It's just an expression."

"Jupiter doesn't jump. I bet you a million dollars that Jupiter doesn't jump."

"You're just being an asshole, Murray," whined Frank – the Frank Monaghan Frank, Frank-for-ever-Frank, Frank of the top bunk, Frank as in "Douglas, Cameron and Frank" – the third and youngest child of the Monaghans. "Anyway, you don't have a million dollars. You don't even have ten dollars. You've had your allowance docked, remember?"

The bathroom door made a satisfying slam. Lock the door. Run the water. Sulk.

"Murray!"

*This town ain't big enough for the two of us.*

A decision had to be made. For seventeen years, Frank had been shoved from family to institution to household to bunk bed. His name had been changed to Frances, Little Frannie, *Laviolette, Marie,* back to Frank and, in the case of the military Bronson family, not even a name – just a *number.* Murray? *Murray?* What kind of name was that? It was time to stop other people making the important decisions. Something had to be done. If he couldn't be Frank with the Monaghans, he'd go elsewhere. Somewhere where he could be whoever – *what*ever – he wanted to be.

"Jumpin' Jupiter, indeed!"

In the safety of the bathroom, Frank mimicked Charlotte Monaghan in a hoarse whisper. He undressed, folding his clothes and piling them on the fluffy pink toilet seat before carefully stretching the elastic of his swimming goggles over his skull and then lowering himself into the water. At the last moment, something caught his lashless eye.

"Jumpin' Fuckin' Jupiter!"

It was in his underwear. Right there in the gusset of the Y: a blob of blood the size of a quarter. Holy menstruating Jesus.

Oops.


It came as no surprise to Frank that he had begun – albeit a few years later than most girls he knew – to ovulate. It wasn't something he could have stopped, even if he had wished to. In many ways, he was glad. He had the best of both worlds. In the captivity of the Monaghans, however, he knew that he would have the benefit of none. Charlotte Monaghan wouldn't know how to handle it; an official explanation wouldn't help. Since Dr Meadowlands had retired by then, he wasn't available to explain to anyone why Frank, at seventeen, had started to bleed. Regardless, with the onset of womanhood, Frank discovered a new strength.

When Mr Monaghan returned from work that evening, a scene erupted around the family Christmas tree. Charlotte Monaghan, already familiar with the content of Frank's briefs, sat in the corner of the living room, nursing a half-empty bottle of her best Christmas rum.

Her husband took one look at her and launched into his kangaroo-styled judicial attack.

"What the blazes have you been up to then, Murray, m'lad!"

Murray-Frank was prepared and gave it all his worth. The family suffocated him. Suburbia cramped him to the point of bleeding. Then there was the issue of his name, a thousand and one complaints of mild and sundry natures (mainly aesthetic objections to the Monaghan Taste) and eventually, just when Mr Monaghan thought he could see his way through to a workable resolution, the bloody briefs were produced.

They landed on the miniature crèche on the veneer sideboard, where they draped, bloody side up, over the camels.

"What the hell is this?!"

"Frank had his period, dear," explained Charlotte Monaghan in a surprisingly clear voice.

The proximity of scandal horrified the Monaghans. In their overly bylawed existence, they'd never encountered a creature like Frank. They had thought they were fostering an underprivileged survivor of cancer, not embarking on an adventure of sexual dimensions. Heavens, they had *children* in the house! Next time, they'd surely ask the Institute for a child with an obvious, socially acceptable problem – no legs, perhaps. Or a black child. Yes, a little black child would be *dandy*.

In the silence that followed, Murray-Frank excused himself from the walnut-panelled courtroom, walked into the kitchen, and out the back door.

He hesitated in the garage that still smelled of lawnmower and grass clippings and swiped a box of frozen pizzas from the deep-freeze. He walked casually out into the street, hit the highway, stuck out his thumb and headed south, to the Big City. Civilization. Anonymity. Called himself Pat.

Freedom and the holy pursuit of identity carried Pat through fourteen years, dozens of pseudonyms and a thousand couches, to arrive – if not full circle then at least full spiral – in front of a mirror at midnight on the last shopping day before Christmas, smelling the approach of a lifestyle he can finally call her own.

At the last moment, Cherry decides it's too dangerous to continue lugging around the green vinyl sports bag. She finds a *Louis Vachon* bag, a cheap designer knockoff, at the top of Cocktail Mama's closet and transfers the tickets.

The additional ballast plus all her other bags of memorabilia are a difficulty, but not an insurmountable one. She hoists everything up around her like a pair of clown pants, takes one last look around the hated Bloor apartment, grabs one of Brock's half-nibbled slices of pizza and makes for the door.

Down those steep stairs she goes, in a complex, balletic *pas de problem*. The descent is slow. Care must be taken, especially since she's laden with enough bags (coincidentally enough) to fill a taxi. Halfway down, she loses her grip and, in the ensuing juggling act, her scarf somehow becomes unravelled, streaming over her shoulder behind her. She shakes it loose. She's learned the lesson from Isadora and won't let an opportunistic garrotting prevent her escape. The Bloors can keep the scarf as a souvenir of her stay.

At the bottom, she takes a bite of pizza. Cold, rubbery topping. Chewy crust. She opens the door to the street, negotiates her way over the transom, takes a deep breath of uncompromising night air and launches herself into the snow in search of the welcoming, jovial glow of a taxi light.

Liberty awaits.

# K ... of the dump

You know what?! The woman who calls herself my mom (code name: Welfare Cheat) still hasn't come home to give me my supper. I reckon I've been left on my own now for over sixteen hours without an authorized baby sitter and we all know THAT'S ILLEGAL!!! Not a sign of her. The Welfare Cheat has abandoned me for THREE DAYS NOW! not even a phone call so she must be still at her party with Victor her Boyfriend. Cherry Beach (the evil monster Hun-Queen IT) has finally left the house packed her bags and down the stairs GONE! HALLELUJAH! and I think that Grandpa Huntley (the Quilted Troll) is just about dead or will be soon because they're always talking about it and anyway he SMELLS DEAD! Everyone's forgotten all about me I bet three million dollars.

How come I've been left alone for so long? It's because I'm an UNWANTED CHILD I'd be an idiot not to know this because I'm always being told so to my face and even in front of strangers casually, like it's a general description of me along with my hair or the colour of my eyes or my height OH YES WELL YOU KNOW BROCK WAS AN ACCIDENT!! Well! This information finally sunk in by the time I was five so I'm used to the idea by now OK so I'm a bit slow, give me a break. Too many people hate me as it is, like the Welfare Cheat treats me like I turned up on the doorstep uninvited, like I'm a bad word or a shit on the carpet or like I caused all the problems of the world just by breathing and taking up space.

When we had a meeting at the social services last year, Bob's My Uncle left the room in one of his tempers. WELL, I KNOW WHEN I'M NOT WANTED he said and got up and left. IT'S NOT FAIR!! I can't do the old Get Up and Leave no matter how much I'm not wanted because I'm locked in prison with the Quilted Troll and it's NOT my idea of fun!

However.

I'm giving the Welfare Cheat another hour or so and then I'm breaking the door down and I'm outta here! I'll run away and get a job in the flea market or I'll get my picture put on a milk carton like Wade Lansdowne. That'll teach 'em.


As I said, the Quilted Troll is going to die soon if he isn't dead already but I can't tell because his TV is the liveliest thing about him. Oh he moves when you prod him and he comes out with all those rerun stories of how he won the war in Egypt or how he started up the Roxy Club or how no one's grateful for anything and he didn't even get an invitation to the Xmas Buffet but it doesn't fool me. A dead person could still pull that off no problem.

The TV is stuck on the God channel and it won't change I TRIED! All this Virgin Mary swaddled clothing in a manger story over and over I swear that if this keeps up I'm going to turn into a lowly cattle shed. It's so GAY. YEUCH!! I dare anyone to try sitting through *Today's Revelation* with a full bladder. No cartoons and no gunfights and nothing but boring old tight-skinned orange faces yacking on and on and on world without end AMEN ALREADY! School would be preferable to this torture hour after hour but schools are CLOSED FOR XMAS NOW! until next year so I am a prisoner in my own house and I'm forced to watch the 24-hour fucking prayer line without a telephone.

SAVE ME SANTA!

The truth is that the Quilted Troll's nothing but a wheezing old bag of stale air. It turns my stomach GAG! All this fuss about changing his bedpan when there's nothing in it to change just the SAME LITTLE TURD that's been there for ever and ever rattling around like the black Cheery-Wheaty in the box. His lucky shit he calls it and you can't throw it out or flush it down the toilet or SUFFER THE CONSEQUENCES!

SUFFER THE LITTLE CHILDREN that's what they keep saying on TV and it's true. First it was Bob's My Uncle and sometimes Uncle Al and then it was the Welfare Cheat and then the evil monster Hun-Queen IT for a while so you can see it's been a LONG LIST! Now it's the Quilted Troll which has to be the WORST OF ALL! I warned him one more whack around the ears and I would call up the child-abuse line again I'M NOT JOKING! I swear. That trick got me out of Bob's My Uncle's and it could get me out of here at the snap of my fingers if the phone was working.

Problem is I need proof. I learned that one the tough way the last time because I had to hit myself over the wrist and legs with a block of wood to get those bruises which would have worked fine if they hadn't caught me at it. EXCUSE ME?! Privacy is what I need, like for instance my own bedroom for a start and NOT some curtained-off area and a foamie in the lounge NOT some itchy cushion on the end of the Quilted Troll's bed or NEVER AGAIN NOT! the plastic mattress in the social services with the video camera.

I wish he would hurry up and croak I really want to see him dead before I leave I've waited long enough. AMEN! I want to see if his soul leaves his body like they said on *Today's Revelation* because I suspect that it was all a load of crap and NOTHING WILL HAPPEN but I want to see it anyway. I'll give him half an hour until the Gospel Choir comes on and then if he's still alive I'll give him another whack on the head.


Wade Lansdowne went missing about two years ago. He had curly hair and had a front tooth missing and he was a regular standard at our breakfast table on the side of the milk carton. He didn't look too unhappy for a missing kid in fact he told me once he was very pleased being a runaway. Yes, I used to talk to him on the carton! We shared a few good jokes mostly about my cousin Martin (the GAY DRIP) and Wade would always laugh.

"Dad! *Daaaaad!* Brock's doing it again!"

That was the Gay Drip screaming at Bob's My Uncle who never liked to be disturbed from his zombie state before the hand of noon struck twelve never ever ON PAIN OF DEATH!!

"Martin, shut the fuck up." Bob's My Uncle's arm appeared over the top of the couch in the sunroom where he was relaxing having his morning smoke of skunky weed, the DRUG ADDICT! Thirty-four hippopotamus seconds later the penny dropped and Bob's My Uncle managed to reenter the earth's atmosphere and coordinate his mouth.

"Whassa?" Bob's My Uncle's fat alien head poked up where his arm had been. His moustache stuck out in clumps from his chewy old lip. "Brock?! Did you wet yourself again?"

"Nooo Uncle Bob."

"Great. All right then. Great. You guys eat your fucking breakfasts."

I hadn't wet myself. I had peed with amazing skill and accuracy into my plastic juice glass using the table as cover! I put the glass of pee back in front of Martin and I dared him with my eyes to say another word. I even turned the milk carton around so that Wade my Best Friend Lansdowne's smile was right next to mine and together we stared down the Gay Drip!

"Daaad!"

What a loser! Of course, when Bob's My Uncle dragged himself off the couch and came over to the table to see what all the fuss was about, I denied everything NO NOT ME I WOULD NEVER DO A THING LIKE THAT! and before it turned into a major incident I drank my piss juice down to prove that there was nothing wrong with it at all. Yummy bum-holes! as Victor the Welfare Cheat's Boyfriend would say.

Wade and I would smile a special missing-children smile and we won every game we played. Ha-ha-HA! We made the best team we did especially against Martin. Sometimes I wonder if Wade is still out there FREE AS A BIRD missing and laughing somewhere or whether he really did get murdered by SOME SICKO AND DUMPED IN A DITCH LIKE BOB'S MY UNCLE RECKONS. I DON'T THINK SO!


At least the evil monster Hun-Queen IT has finally gone. HALLELUJAH! Well! That took long enough let me tell you! The Hun-Queen IT had the temporary use of our couch for what was supposed to be forty-eight hours NO LONGER but turned into a more than fifteen day siege! I mean the lounge is MY bedroom and having to share it with the Creature from the Lost Mudpak is criminal.

You should see the crap that the Hun-Queen IT kept in those plastic bags. A few days ago I found a can of something that called itself a vaporizer but it was a complete trick PHONY LIAR! it didn't vaporize at all. It was just another stinky aerosol! The pepper spray however was MAXIMUM EFFICIENT as I soon found out but I wasn't expecting to be treated like an axe-murderer for defending my territory. UNFAIR!

I was beginning to think that an A-bomb wouldn't get rid of the Hun-Queen IT. When I complained to the Welfare Cheat about my territory being taken over all that I got told was that I had been given the choice of sleeping with the Quilted Troll and I'd turned it down. THEY WONDER WHY?!!

Anyway the problem is solved. The evil monster Hun-Queen IT packed IT's bags and O-U-T OUT! down the stairs and gone GOOD RID-DANCE! I bet there's still a mess left in the bathroom but I'm not cleaning it up before I go NO WAY!!


I never should have shown my winning ticket to the Quilted Troll because I should have guessed he would be dead set against gambling the way he is with his Christian Prayer Association and all that. You'd think with starting up the Roxy all those years ago there'd be some fun in him but NO. That's all behind him now he says REFORMED whatever that means. Sinners the whole damn bunch of them he likes to say THE DEVIL'S WORK which of course means ME and I'm sure that's got something to do with why Bob's My Uncle, Martin and my Uncle Al live in a nice big house with the Toothy Fairy while we get stuck with this pathetic old dump. That's where the slippery road of gambling can lead you. In quarantine with Grandpa Huntley and the evangelists. SO HELP ME JESUS!

Soon as Grandpa Huntley saw that Yours Truly the youngest in the Bloor family had taken to gambling he grabbed MY winning ticket and he wouldn't let go for Love Nor Money! Somewhere along the family tree we must have a branch of pit bull terriers because I couldn't even bite his fingers off from MY ticket his grip was that tight.

There was nothing I could do except give the Quilted Troll a taste of his own medicine. He loves to clip me round the ears mostly for no reason not even for trying to change the channel and I warned him what might happen if he kept it up! So! There we were tugging away at MY winning ticket and he tried to give me a few swipes around the head when with my free hand I reached into the Twilight Black Hole Zone beneath his bed and pulled out his stupid bedpan. It made the best noise when it hit his skull BONG! It's a good thing he's bald because I'm sure hair would have spoiled the music. BONG!! End of argument!

The fucking ticket's MINE. It was given to me fair and square I scratched it myself so the way I figure it I GET THE PRIZE! I get to visit Santa at the Pearson Centre Mall it says so right there in the bonus play area even I can read that! FINALLY! I get a gift for Xmas and I'm going to claim it AS IS MY RIGHT. If the Welfare Cheat isn't back by the next prayer-a-thon I'm out of here dead Quilted Troll or no dead Quilted Troll because I deserve an Xmas don't I?


Xmas is for us kids, like everyone knows that. Santa Claus and GIFTS beneath the tree and stockings filled with more GIFTS. *Today's Revelation* makes a big deal out of SANTA being an anagram of SATAN and they seem to think that this explains everything! So what about all the other SANTAS? the Rosas? the Marias? the Monicas? Are THEY all agents of the devil too? I DOUBT IT. The only proof I have that SANTA is the Antichrist is that so far this year I have written a total of FIVE letters to him and I haven't yet received ONE SINGLE REPLY and time is running out! After this weekend Santa will have left the Pearson Mall and I have to have a word with him before then or I'm toasted cheese!

My question for Santa is WHERE WAS HE LAST YEAR?!! Not even a fucking lump of coal like Bob's My Uncle and the Toothy Fairy threatened. There had better be a good explanation for nothing OR ELSE!

My cousin Martin maintains that there is no Santa and that Santa doesn't even exist and that Santa's really only Dad Dressed Up but since I don't have anything that even remotely resembles a Dad Dressed Up, the Gay Drip can suffer in his ignorance. Myself, I'm prepared to give Santa the BENEFIT OF THE DOUBT as my Auntie Marg (the Toothy Fairy) always says, even if I suspect that Santa hates me and that he's crossed me off his list. Well!

Two years ago when I was living with Bob's My Uncle and the WANTED branch of our family tree, Santa came for sure NO QUESTIONS ASKED. There was no overlooking THAT house with all those lights on the roof! No chance of a blip on the reindeer radar there because Bob's My Uncle and the Toothy Fairy know how to do Xmas properly. The Xmas tree was so huge we had to move the couch AND the TV out of the way to make room for it! The decorations alone would have attracted any Xmas elf because Bob's My Uncle wasn't taking any chances! There were bells and balls and breakables and untouchables all over the house and everywhere thick ropes of tinsel and the Xmas Buffet and one kind of fake snow on the mantelpiece and another kind of fake snow all over the windows and an advent calendar and blinking fairy lights and stockings with all our names on them and a plate of cookies left out with a carrot for Rudolph that was certainly munched by SOMETHING when we saw it in the morning! I sent a letter to Santa that year I did because I remember mailing it and getting a reply on Santa's Personalized Note Paper! Also in my stocking and underneath the tree I got the gifts I wanted so don't tell me that Santa isn't real or Dad Dressed Up!

These days though, I'm inclined to agree with the Quilted Troll that the world is falling apart WE'RE DOOMED! We don't even have any stockings not a single one! No tinsel and no sparkles just a couple of pathetic twigs painted white and stuffed into an industrial soup can in the corner of the room IT'S SO GAY! There are three plastic balls hanging on these twigs, one red, one blue, one gold. Three for a dollar. Count them: one two three. There is no fairy and there is no Star of Wonder. And NO XMAS GIFTS!!!!

Well! I searched everywhere for anything resembling a gift that may have been hidden away, like even in the Twilight Black Hole Zone underneath the Quilted Troll's bed or even up in the Welfare Cheat's DO NOT TOUCH drawer but I couldn't find a thing! Well! I've got something now! I've got a Free Visit With Santa!


OK that's it. TIME'S UP!!


Well! I'm not sorry that's over and done with because it had me worried for a minute. I couldn't hit him with the bedpan again since I'd used it to relieve myself in earlier on, there's only so long I can hold my horses. So I searched around for a substitute until I found out the most AMAZING THING. I discovered that he had an OFF SWITCH! Right there on his pacemaker thing was an off switch all tubed into his chest. Handy.

OK so it wasn't that simple because I had to keep pressing down on the switch for the length of an entire gospel song before anything happened and my arm was starting to get tired and I was beginning to think WHAT A CHEAT IT'S NOT A FUCKING OFF SWITCH AFTER ALL! There was nothing but a funny clicking sound coming out of his throat and certainly no Light at the End of a Tunnel or any Holy Singing Choirs of Angels and no Ghostly Entity floating out of his body special effect and I was watching REAL CLOSE. The TV reception came in a bit clearer but that is ALL!

I felt a bit sad for him then, like the only time his favourite program with that woman in the red dress ever came in without any static and there was my Grandpa Huntley unable to enjoy the experience! So I pushed the TV set closer to the bed so that his hand could reach the screen and then I left it there with *Today's Revelation* running up his arm. I may have knocked a few ornaments off the top, like the photograph of him and his war-buddies in Egypt and a brass plate or two but WHAT DID I CARE?! Then I got the door open. The wood around the hinges was almost rotten anyway so it didn't take me too long just a bit of a bruise on my shoulder but I cut my leg trying to pull off a Killer Ju-Jitsu Nazi Death-Kick on the door and now there's blood everywhere! COOL!


I'm out! HALLELUJAH! I don't know what time it is or what day it is either to be honest I hope I haven't missed Santa! Every time I move my head to the right my left eye closes up and I've got this wicked bruise all the way down my side. Those stairs are fucking LETHAL even without that booby trap halfway down them and as it was I almost broke my neck! Someone's going to pay for leaving that scarf there AS IF I DON'T KNOW WHO but in the end it turned out to be good luck! because I wrapped the scarf as a bandage around my leg and stopped the bleeding!

For a moment it was WILD! WILD! WILD!! I saw the orange light bulb swinging away in a space beneath my feet like ANTIGRAVITY! and I saw this long band of red material because I didn't know at that point what it was I saw it wrapping around my shoe, like a killer boa constrictor! Xtra Cool! But it was scary because all my hopes for freedom went spinning away from me and I thought OH, NO! Oh shit. This IS IT!! GAME OVER. The only Life Flash that I saw was the smiling face of Wade my Best Friend Lansdowne on the milk! I swear I saw the red-and-white carton and the picture of the cow on the side I'M NOT MAKING THIS UP! I actually saw Wade's face floating in the air, sort of in my head but not really and I thought that he seemed to be giving me the old Silent Encouragement and he was letting me know that this flying through the air number was only a minor setback.

I don't remember much after that for a while because THERE'S NOTHING TO REMEMBER THAT'S ALL, OK?!!


It was dark outside in the street and so by my calculations it must have been past five o'clock which meant I didn't have much time. I got on the subway by grabbing the hand of a Grown Up to get through the turnstile it was THAT EASY! no questions asked but finding the Pearson Centre Mall once I got downtown was a lot harder. I knew the way to it was underground but I wasn't expecting so many other stores and miles and miles of shopping mall that all looked the same in every direction with NO signposts or NO arrows to follow! I mean GET WITH THE PROGRAM! you'd think they'd at least name some streets down there because people could get seriously lost! I asked directions from a thousand different people and kept getting funny looks and a thousand different answers. Down there or to the right or up there or to the left and through the double doors. I swear they were sending me just far enough away so that they could be LONG GONE by the time I returned to confront them with their lies.

By the time I finally got to the Pearson Centre Mall it was closed. Fucking Cocksuckers.

OK so I saw it coming. As I got nearer to Santa's Castle I saw the stores around me all pulling down their metal gates and turning off their lights and going home for the night! Everywhere around me Xmas was vanishing! There were only a few stragglers left in the mall along with me, like a couple sitting on a bench and a guy walking fast to catch his bus or his train and a group of Grown Up women dressed in pixie outfits sitting in the Smoking Section of the Food Court. There were giant cardboard snowflakes floating on fishing line above them otherwise the PLACE WAS EMPTY! So it was no real surprise to me when I found that the Toy Fort and Santa's Castle had been shut up solid for the night SORRY! CLOSED!! NEXT CHANGING OF THE GUARD AT TEN O'CLOCK TOMORROW?!!

Well! I wasn't going to take no for an answer. I mean I'd come all that way for NOTHING?!!

It wasn't that difficult to get into because the water in Santa's Moat didn't have any crocodiles and it wasn't really very deep at all and anyway the castle was completely open around the back. There was a great big barrel of stupid teddy bears and a throne covered in purple material but no sign of Santa, like he doesn't sleep in his own castle?

So I sat on his throne for a while with my feet not quite reaching the floor and dripping on the carpet. I played King of the Castle for a while until I got bored because I wanted to send all my Captured Enemies off to the Torture Chambers but there weren't any Torture Chambers or even any Captured Enemies and there's only so long that anyone can survive on their IMAGINATIONS ALONE!

FUCKING SANTA!! Where was he?! Where had he gone to when I needed to talk to him about getting NOTHING not even a lump of coal in my stocking last year and he'd better make the difference up to me this year OR ELSE! I'd show him! He was going to be SORRY!

Guess what?! I left him my own Xmas Gift right there on his throne! It wasn't as tough or as small as the Quilted Troll's but it still looked very much like a lump of coal. THREE lumps of coal to be exact! HA! HA! HA!!! I wiped my ass on the purple material draped over his throne and then I got out of there before anyone could catch me red-handed. Or should I say BROWN-handed?!! Ha-ha-ha!

Then I sat on the edge of one of those fuzzy green carpet-covered platforms and I almost fell asleep right there.


"Got a problem, sonny?"

I was woken up by a fucking Pearson Security Guard! His uniform didn't fit at all well because it was kind of baggy where it shouldn't be and his pants were turning shiny at his knees, like he was much too old and UGLY! He put the Quilted Troll to shame in the Ugly Department!

"I won a free visit to Santa," I said and I showed him my ticket for proof.

"Santa's gone, kid."

"oh."

"Where are your parents?" he asked me and he looked around as if my parents would cyber-transport and materialize out of the shadows. "You all alone?"

Well I didn't feel like answering him did I? I didn't like his tone of voice and so I shrugged and I thought some more about how I'd missed Santa. My head hurt, my leg hurt and my bum felt itchy. The

Pearson Security Guard wouldn't leave me alone HE WOULDN'T! He kept repeating his stupid Parent Question and he reached for his walkie-talkie.

"Spare a cigarette?" I asked him because I could see the packet in his pocket. Anything to stop him calling for back up.

"You're too young to smoke."

"What? Are you my FUCKING SOCIAL WORKER?!"

I got up to leave because I knew that if I stayed around any longer this Pearson Security Guard would radio for back up and then the whole game would be OVER! I'd get taken to the Pearson Security Room which I'm well acquainted with THANK YOU and I'd get the third degree, like why was I out by myself so late without a Grown Up? and I'd end up in the social services again. NO WAY! FUCK THAT SHIT!! So I walked towards the Underground Parking as if I knew where I was going.

"What's the matter with your leg, son?" he called after me.

I stopped and I gave him THE EYE but it didn't shut him up.

"What's your name, Bub?"

"Wade," I told him. "Wade Lansdowne."

He didn't follow me through the door to the stairwell. EXCELLENT! I don't know why I lied about my name because it just came out of me without me thinking about it at all and I'd told another lie! Who says that lying doesn't get you anywhere? It got me away from the Pearson Security Guard didn't it?

HALLELUJAH! He didn't follow me into the Underground Parking but even though I'd won that round I was worried just a bit and with every step I took going down the stairs to P-2 and then to P-3 I felt my soul shrink and I was getting closer and closer to the CENTRE OF THE EARTH and I was feeling more and more like something that looked like my Grandpa Huntley's lucky shit in the bottom of his bedpan. I was IN FOR IT I could tell because now I was never going to get to play with Jesus in heaven for telling lies and because I'd taken a shit on Santa's throne.

Well! FUCK YOU JESUS! AND FUCK YOU TOO SANTA!!

Guess what?! I've found an EXCELLENT hiding place FINALLY! All those hallways and stairs and doors made me think that I was going around and around in circles. I swear an explorer could die down here and NOT ONE PERSON would ever know!

I don't think anybody's been down here for centuries except for the birds because there's bird shit everywhere and I can hear them scratching and cooing in the roof. There are bins of broken dummies and painted plaster heads and arms and legs poking out and all of it is covered in dust, like I'm in the Tomb of the Pharaohs or something. There are shelves and boxes everywhere and SUMMER SALE! and 50% OFF!! notices so I know I must be in the Deepest Darkest Depths of the Pearson Centre Mall. There's a corner filled with plastic palm trees and sand dunes made out of burlap which are way too hard and uncomfortable to lie down on. It's pretty warm though so I must be close to a boiler-room and the pipes sure make enough noise!

There's a life-size nativity scene which has been dragged out and only half assembled. Whoever had been working on it clearly gave up and I would have too. Nativity scenes are so gay, like the one in the Social Services which is SUCH A CHEAT because the whole thing fits onto a tabletop and the Star of Wonder just has a pathetic flashlight-bulb in it and I don't know anyone who thinks it's cool let alone EXCELLENT! These days you have to compete with jolly workshop elves and marching soldiers if you want to make any impression at all. No wonder they abandoned it!

The cattle shed smells of airplane glue and there are life-size shiny statues of Mary and Joseph and the shepherds and real straw on the floor but not enough to lie down in comfort which is TOO BAD I could do with somewhere to lie down. Mary's halo is broken and her eyes have fallen out and she's covered in PIGEON BOMBS! The three wise men have stumps for hands and peeling faces where you can see that they've been painted and repainted in different skin colours over the years they must be ANCIENT! One of the sheep is lying on its side it's been DECAPITATED and you can tell that the cows would nod in their stalls if you plugged them in.

My left eye has almost completely shut CLOSED! SORRY!! COME BACK TOMORROW! I have to sleep. I can taste the back of my nose dripping down my throat and it's warm, like blood but I'm not surprised. I hope I didn't do myself any SERIOUS DAMAGE when I fell down the stairs.


Guess what? The baby Jesus won't come out of the crib! He's fixed in there with a LENGTH OF CHAIN! I can push him out of my way though so that he hangs over the edge of his crib and there's a well-made bed beneath him of soft padded material, like this stupid doll needed comfort? I DON'T THINK SO! But I'm not complaining because it's perfect for now, like EXCELLENT! It smells the same as the bottom drawer of my Grandpa Huntley's wardrobe or is that just the blood in my nose? I can't tell.


There's a fucking BIRD in here who won't leave me ALONE! For real! It's an ugly old pigeon and it's up on the pipe over there and it keeps looking down at me with its ugly pink eye! I threw a few dummy arms and legs at it to chase it away but it's too smart. I think it's got it in for me. I think it wants my WINNING TICKET! Seriously I swear it knows exactly where it is! That scrawny bird gives me the fucking HEEBIE GEEBIES!

I'll deal with the fucker tomorrow after I've had my BEAUTY SLEEP!

Tomorrow. Right now I have to get some sleep before my head throbs off my neck so it's NIGHTY NIGHT TO YOU JESUS I'm sorry about kicking you out of your bed but the way I see it I need it more than you. After all you're just a doll right? You don't even have a wang because that was the FIRST THING I checked.

That fucking pigeon had better not do its business on me in the night because otherwise we'll be having ROASTED BIRD for breakfast tomorrow! For sure …

I wonder what pigeon tastes like? Could I live off of it I WONDER?! Would a pigeon be Nutritious and Healthy full of Vitamins in every Mouthful? …I think maybe I could stay down here forever … or at least maybe for a couple of days … until I find myself some New Parents … nnn …


… night everyone! … sleep tight! … and don't let the bed bugs bite!!

# 3 ... operation cash flow

"**Y**ou have to look on this as a military exercise, Cherry. Treat it like war."

"Huh?"

Liberty Hanna's face pushes into Cherry's for an extreme close-up; it's a battlefield of scar tissue, craters and trenches, with an accompanying stench of acrid chemicals. Cherry is more than halfway through her second celebratory bottle of vodka, so her vision is decidedly blurred. The back of her neck prickles hotly; she may have to puke soon. Liberty has mixed up a special blend of airplane glue and carpet-cleaning solvents in her snorting bag, so she's barely coherent. The two of them are communicating on an intuitive level.

"You gotta plan this strategically."

"Whassa matter with Rose?" asks Cherry, concentrating on her breathing. "You'd think she doesn't want me to stay here."

"She doesn't."

"Too bad."

Meaning "Too bad for Rose, Tough luck and Too late." Cherry's already moved in. Her bags are through the door, her cosmetics are in the washroom and she's arranged a Chinese folding screen around the *chaise longue* for a modicum of privacy. Liberty has two hundred dollars in her pocket. For the next month, at least, this is Home.

"You gotta treat this like war."

Cherry isn't sure whether the "this" Liberty is talking about is Rose or the *Louis Vachon* bag of lottery tickets currently on Cherry's lap. Or even, quite possibly, the Kennel Klub's imminent closure. War could easily describe them all and a few more topics besides. Cherry decides the "this" is Rose, Liberty's long-suffering partner, Rose the bar-squirrel Rose, whose cut-off is still crackling in Cherry's ears.

"You can't stay here and that's final. We've already rented the room to Phoebe."

"I'll sleep on the couch."

And that's where the argument has stayed, both sides under the impression that they've won, both sides digging in their heels until the next offensive, which will, in all likelihood, be tomorrow morning, along with the hangovers and the damage assessments of this evening's binge. As things stand, there are too many revellers around, too much of an audience for anything other than a bitch fight, which, as everyone knows, is mere entertainment and never accomplishes a thing, no matter how much street credibility it lends to your party.

Cherry knows all about parties. Slow parties, fast parties, parties where the police turn up and parties where the drugs turn into powdered sugar and wallets walk from coats in the bedroom. A party, regardless of its premise or success, is always an event. Cherry's social life, ever since she hit the Big City all those years ago, has been not just eventful, but chock-a-block.

Most of it's a blur. A mulch. Once you've danced on half a dozen tables, snorted coke in a score of bathrooms and tumbled down a mile of fire escapes, events have a tendency to bruise together. It all becomes one large barrel o' fun, a fermentation of jubilance out of which only a thimble-sized snifter of pure vintage experience can ever be distilled. Faces mostly. Tear-stained, booze-streaked, rubber-lipped faces pushing to the foreground in overlapping multiple exposures, the laughter indistinguishable from the howls.

"Wa-ay to ga-augh!"

This party is hunkering down for the night. The dominatrices have taken off their boots and the skinheads are putting on their tuques. Tonight wasn't really so much a party as a wandering snowball that had started out at the Kennel Klub, which was empty enough to appear closed. After a few shooters, Cherry shanghaied Liberty from her redundant post at the door, and moved on to club after club, hitting a few choice after-hours spots, gathering momentum and celebrants as they went. Her Uncle Jericho on the West Coast had died, Cherry maintained, and she had come into a mild inheritance. Now, at around four o'clock in the morning, everyone who is capable of blowing a trumpet to help celebrate the fall of Jericho has wound up at Liberty and Rose's studio. There are a dozen or so reliable party freaks clumped in wilting groups of twos and threes around the warehouse – mostly in the kitchen area, where a broken window lets a refreshing winter's breeze into the otherwise overheated space. Rose has sequestered herself behind a slammed door (with, it must be noted, the new roomie) while Liberty and Cherry are having a council of war behind the Chinese folding screen. For some strange reason, it seems the Oriental factor has rubbed off on Liberty.

"*Loo-wee-wa-chon!*" she chants.

"Huh?"

"The bag." She caresses the outside of it. "*Louis Vachon.* The closest I ever got was a really cheap imitation. Some little export store in Chinatown. *Five dollar. Loo-wee-wa-chon.*"

"That's not funny," gurgles Cherry. "You're beginning to sound as racist as Jane Finch."

"Don't show this bag to Rose. She'll have a bird." Inexplicably, Liberty starts to laugh. Then she has to strip the mucus lining her nose with a snort from her glue bag to help herself get over her humour. Eventually she calms down.

"Who else have you told?"

"Huh?"

"The tickets," Liberty says with exasperation. "Who else have you told?"

Cherry shifts her brain. Concentration is difficult. Perhaps she shouldn't have had that extra pizza slice, she can hear it splooshing around in her gut. Liberty is the only person Cherry has dared entrust with the true story of how she'd found the lottery tickets.

"I gotta plan," she burps. "Trust me on this one, Lib."

"Attagirl!" Liberty slaps her – hard – on the back with assurances of her undying faithfulness. Cherry's stomach churns. She reaches for an empty beer.

After a decade and a half of hard and fast partying, Cherry Beach has mastered the fine art of puking into a beer bottle. The process involves rolling the tongue into a tube, inserting it into the neck of the bottle and then letting Nature take its course, keeping the lips in an tight embouchure, inserting a fingernail at one corner of the mouth to regulate the airflow. Rather like playing a delicate tune on a clarinet. Gloss lipstick helps, as does a Zen-like breathing through the nose, keeping a rigid control of the diaphragm to avoid any pressure build-ups or sudden bursts of air with their annoying subsequent explosions. Executed properly, the whole operation can escape detection, can almost be passed off as a genteel flourish whilst pretending to rummage for cigarettes in one's purse.

"You're lucky I did a stint in the Army," says Liberty. "I know how to plan a strategic attack."

"Please," sighs Cherry, casually placing the pizza-filled bottle by a leg of the *chaise longue*. "Don't talk to me about the Army."


"The first three Principles of War are … Mass! Objective! Offensive!"

The leader in the black fatigues screamed at the drizzling rain, his voice ringing through the park. It was late September on the West Coast, which means a wetness, a dampness that soaks through to the bone. A night mist hung in the evergreens while high overhead, a seagull, disturbed by the noise, screeched a circle above the small group before winging its way back toward the salt-winded ocean.

There were three of them – three guys in army gear and purple berets. Two of them dragged their mud-covered prize between them. The third stood beneath the dripping overhang of a small barracks cabin – no more than a hut, really – shouting his orders into the park. A high-powered searchlight cut through the drizzle, turning the strange little group into glistening shadows.

"How y'doin' there, Talisman?" one of them jeered.

Their victim – their "talisman" – didn't answer. Couldn't answer. Her arms were pinned behind her shoulder blades and one of the captors had a tight grip on her nose, having failed to keep a hold of her when he'd grabbed at her wig. She was winded from her fall, bruised, scratched, covered in mud and livid with rage.

Mass. Objective. Offensive.

That had been their plan, and they'd followed through on it. Earlier that evening, they'd gotten together with a crate of beer (mass), decided to go downtown and pick themselves up a trophy (objective) and when they'd arrived at the first hotel on the strip that happened to have a strangely gendered front-desk clerk – yup – they'd been really offensive.

Nicola Beach, still pretty green to both the city and her name, wasn't prepared to be kidnapped and taken forcibly from her place of employment by a trio of baby Pongos. Army cadets. The youngest was only barely peeking over the edge of legal drinking age while the others couldn't have been much older. Nicola herself was only twenty-two at the time, but five years of hard and fast living had given her the comparative experience of Methuselah. She'd fallen for their ruse, however: a promise of cocaine and a quick fifty bucks for servicing the servicemen.

They took her by taxi to the park, the four of them crammed in the back seat making it look like a load o' fun for the driver's benefit. She knew something was wrong by the way they'd grabbed hold of her wrists and stuck a service revolver in her ribs. She knew enough not to argue with a gun. Then they'd piled out of the cab at the northern entrance to the park and frogmarched her straight into the undergrowth.

The cabin stunk of urine and beer. Only part of the floor had boards across it, the remainder was exposed earth, worn flat and hard. In one corner was a foldout couch and an upturned crate. Half a dozen pairs of ripped and torn panties were hung on the wall. Trophies. An aluminum pail collected rainwater that dripped through a crack in the roof. Pornography and stubby beer bottles littered the floor along with cigarette butts and – the not-so-green Nicola Beach couldn't help but noticing – lengths of thin cord, the kind used for guys on tents.

"Tie the Talisman up!" shouted the youngest, his freckled cheeks flushed. Drops of rain clung to the ginger moustachlette he was cultivating on his upper lip.

Like eager Boy Scouts, the other two obeyed, pulling the couch a few inches away from the wall before they bound Nicola securely to it. She had to give them credit, they knew their knots. In minutes they had her spread-eagled, her wrists and ankles tied to each corner, a broomstick across her throat. The crease in the couch ran down her spine, threatening to fold her open. The sharp edges of springs pushed into her.

"Any of you cocksuckers got a cigarette?" she managed to spit out before she was gagged.

"A cigarette?" The youngest seemed pleasantly struck by the novelty. "The Talisman wants a cigarette?"

The never-again-so-green Nicola cursed herself as she shook her wigless head in disagreement. It was too late. She should never have put the idea into their heads.


"I am so glad to be out of there, Lib, you cannot believe."

"Hmmph."

"That whole family's fucked, if you ask me."

"Hmmph."

"Hey, pull over! Convenience store at two o'clock. I'm dying for a smoke."


The Great White North, it has been said, was built to the war cry of tires spinning in the snow. It's a familiar noise, the rising whine, the frantic repetition, as if some animal were caught in a trap, the persistence of the hopeless. It can be heard throughout the long winter months, from as early as October to as late as March or even April, reassuring one and all that other people have their troubles too, stuck in their individual dramas, wheels spinning, late for the Rotary Club Casino, unable to meet Aunt Stephanie at the airport on time, accepting the inevitability that they'll get there when they get there, which might not be ever and that's just too bad. A nation founded on a contingency principle: not everyone might turn up. Or get the joke.

The back wheel of Liberty Hanna's battleship-grey Plymouth Fury is behaving in a truly patriotic manner, whipping around and around in an ice gully, obstinately preventing the auto from being mobile. Parallel parking is no mean feat at the best of times; in the winter it is a challenge for the expert. Getting stuck is a nightmare that can easily become a waking reality, as it now is for Liberty, and for Cherry, who is spinning her own wheels in the passenger seat.

Nicotine calls. There are some cars you can smoke in and some you can't. Liberty's is one in which you never even dangle a cigarette out of the window because it's too dangerous. The interior of the Fury must be marinated in gasoline, butane and carbon tetrachlorides. After five minutes in the car, Cherry feels dry-cleaned. She daren't light up. She daren't even say anything: the wrong word might cause a spark and blow the car to Kingdom Come.

"I just love winter," growls Liberty, turning off the ignition, plunging the engine into silence. She reaches for her glue bag and has a snort to bolster her morale.

Along with Cruella DeVil, Ida Lupino – and surely Catherine the Great if she'd ever lived long enough – Liberty Hanna is one of the original gals in a big car. She fits behind the wheel like a doll in a highchair. A compact flyweight lesbian, Liberty tips the scales at just over one hundred and ten pounds, five feet, but she makes up for her lack of stature with attitude and a missing middle finger from her right hand, which – depending on the story you care to believe – is the result of an argument with an ice-skate, an elective surgical procedure, or an industrial accident in a sheet-metal pressing factory. The missing digit gives her a vaguely Napoleonic air, if Napoleon could ever be confused with a vegetarian, glue-sniffing dyke with a penchant for thrash punk, mosh pits, and big cars.

The back seat of the Fury is filling up with crap. Chips, chocolate bars, cans of pop and *Liter-Gaz*, dollar-store junk and other treasures bought with the proceeds of the afternoon. One of Cherry's earliest purchases of the day had been the mother-of-pearl piano accordion from the pawnshop below the Bloor's apartment. She has since added a camera tripod, a makeup mirror with three adjustable light settings, an *Aqua-Relax* footbath, and a whole bucket of cosmetics. Money is a powerful thing.

In the grip of a solvent-induced mind-warp, Liberty attempts to get her vehicle moving again. It lurches, it coughs, splutters, spins its wheels into a gyroscopic dynamo but refuses to budge. Liberty swears.

"Scrambled fuckin' tofu!"

Cherry says nothing. There is nothing to do in these situations but to send good vibes to the driver. Liberty has been very kind. At the risk of jeopardizing her relationship with Rose, she's been driving Cherry around town all afternoon, carrying out Operation Corner Store in return for a mere hundred bucks and a negotiable percentage of the final haul. With such a faithful partner in crime, it's wise to overlook the occasional addiction.

Be that as it may, the fumes threaten to strangle Cherry's brain cells. The chemical compound is turning her world green at the edges.

She opens the door. She's not getting out to push. She's getting out to smoke. Fresh air, so to speak.

Dusk is falling like a bad velvet painting, the colours all running together against a darkening sky. A few snowflakes the size of head lice skitter through the air. They're some miles north of downtown, outside a small strip mall.

To suit the location, Cherry is dressed in what she considers to be suburban unisex camouflage. A baby-pink anorak, matching tuque (with appliquéed strawberries), clashing orange scarf, denim overalls, sneakers and bubble gum lipstick. If she thinks that she blends in, she's wrong.

In her left pocket she has a stack of two-dollar replays; in her right, she has the high winners under two hundred dollars. The kangaroo pouch of her overalls has a growing stack of duds, with their corners torn off for ease of identification. After four hours of this game, they've got it down to a fine art. They're cleaning out convenience stores in an ever-widening radius from the city centre. The enterprise has a distinct heist flavour to it, an edge of danger. Thelma and Louise, Bonnie and Clyde, Butch and Sundance.

"Fuck it."

Liberty clambers out of the Fury, abandons it with its back end sticking out into the road. She slams the door and leans against the car while she breathes into her chemical lung. Liberty needs all the encouragement she can get.

"C'mon, Lib," says Cherry, "I'm freezing my tits off."

"You don't have any tits."

Liberty horks in the direction of the stuck wheel as she joins Cherry at the curb. Together, they scuttle across the ice floe to the salted sidewalk of the mall. Liberty stuffs her evil bag into the pocket of her leather jacket as they approach the first convenience store. Her eye is still twitching. Her lips are growing gummy crystals at the corners.

Cherry opens the door. "Ready?" Liberty nods, loosely. "Here we go then."

Operation Corner Store works like this:

Cherry and Liberty enter the convenience store and buy chips, candy bars, *Triodent-with-Pepsodent*, whatever, it's just an excuse. Casually, as if as an afterthought, Cherry asks for a couple of *XXXmas* tickets to be added to her purchase and moves out of the way to scratch while Liberty asks for an obscure pack of cigarettes or yesterday's paper or anything to grab the attention of the clerk. Under this cover, Cherry swaps the tickets just bought from the store with a couple of winners from her pocket: a high roller and a replay.

"Hey! I won a hundred bucks! I can cash that here, can't I?"

With the replay, under the guise of feeling lucky, another ticket is bought and – heck, why not? – a few more. Much to Cherry's giggling surprise, these turn out to be winners, too.

The whole game's played over and over until the store runs out of either money or tickets. Cherry's kangaroo pocket fills up with un-scratched tickets while Liberty acts as a diversion at the door to cover the crucial swap, yelling things like "C'mon, Susie, we'll never make it to Ma's in time for dinner if you don't hurry up!" or "Honey, did you pay the baby sitter?!"

For her part, Cherry gets in a few hours of orgasm-faking practice.

"Oh, o-o-o-o-o-o-o, OH!! Two hundred dollars! Aaaaw, Right Oooon!"

It's difficult not to cackle in the clerk's face as they clean out the cash register.

Operation Corner Store is a success.


They kept their Talisman bound to the foldout couch for three days, during which time they'd exhausted the variations of torture and – truth be told – bored of their games. Under cover of night, they let her out into the park on a leash to relieve herself. They fed her on fried chicken and beer, and the chubby one, Mackie, slipped her a few multi-vitamins when the others weren't looking. At least they had the humanity to smoke her up before their sessions with her. They probably thought of it as part of the degradation, but to her it was the only escape she had. Their weed was excellent.

She had a phalanx of circular scars marching up her inner thighs, tiny buttons of scorched skin. The later, more aggressive burns had pained her much less than the earlier, more tentative approaches. Indeed, as the game had wound down, she had smiled to herself through her purple-tinged vision at the sight of her own flesh adhering to her tormentors' cigarette embers. The pain developed into some-thing soft – enveloping – once the initial trauma wore off. The first time, however, she wet the couch with the shock.

"The second three Principles of War are … Surprise! Economy! Movement!"

James, the leader, with the shorn red hair and freckles, would keep a running commentary of military dogma, as if to remind himself as much as to instruct his mates. His constant referrals seemed to sanction their activities, as if keeping a bound and tortured prisoner was somehow part of their official training and that their superior would put in an appearance and grade their efforts.

There were hours during the day when she was left alone with nothing but the ants for company. There was a nest of them in the far corner of the cabin, from whence they would forage out to the spills of beer and crumbs of fried chicken. Once, she thought she could feel them crawling over her and the itch became unbearable, but she was unable to tell whether or not she was hallucinating; she couldn't lift her head further than a few inches from the couch on account of the broomstick. At one point she started praying but, as usual, the gods weren't listening.

Only the ants reminded her that she was alive.

A figure came to her in her dreams, in her moments of unconsciousness, an angel of indifference who laughed at her predicament and taunted her for being so stupid as to have fallen into this particular trap. Over and over she replayed the scene at the front desk of the hotel. She should have reached for the phone, called the police, called for the manager, ignored the temptations of a cocaine high and an easy fifty dollars. Should have this. Should have that. The apparition always seemed to be moving away from her, face turned, a retreating entity that gave out such a strong sensation of belonging that it overwhelmed any complaint. Things were as they should be. This was her lot.

Santa Calamity d'Oopsidaisy was no fly-by-night. She was with her for the long haul.


"Where did you get this ticket, eh?"

"Whaddya mean? I bought it here." Cherry fakes bewilderment. "You just saw me buy it!"

"Not with this serial number, I didn't."

The man in the convenience store is inquisitive and opinionated: a dangerous combination. He had immediately gone on the alert when Liberty and Cherry entered his store. It was probably their outfits that aroused his suspicion. He wanted to watch Cherry scratch her ticket from start to finish. It was all Liberty could do to pull his attention away for the all-important exchange.

"It's a winner, isn't it? Two hundred dollars. It says right here that I can cash it in at any lottery outlet. This is a lottery outlet, isn't it?"

He screws up his face, convinced that something's wrong. Shakes his head firmly.

"The numbers don't follow," he says. "They come in batches. Consecutive numbers."

"Maybe they lost count?" suggests Cherry.

"Do you have a problem?" suggests Liberty.

One look at Liberty approaching the entrance to his sacred behind-the-counter cul-de-sac and he reaches for the phone.

"I'm calling the police."

Liberty, unflustered, walks right up to him, snatches the receiver from his hand. "Let me call a tow truck first. My car's stuck in the ice."

The moment of puzzlement is enough to open a chink in his armour. He is caught between being a good citizen helping Liberty free her car and being a good citizen calling the police. He wavers for a second and then swallows his prejudices against the freaks of nature who've just walked into his store.

"Need a push, then?"

Liberty and Cherry exchange a winning glance. The two-hundred-dollar ticket remains uncashed. The next store is bound to accept it. Or the one after that.

They drive back to the city – laughing, hooting and hollering – having amassed thousands of dollars. The back seat is buried in junk and Liberty is only an hour late for work. Behind them, tossed out the window into the snowbank along the main road is a paper-chase of tiny, glistening torn-off triangles. Seven-thousand-four-hundred-and-some-odd dollars are jammed into Cherry's purse, looking like a paperback novel that's been dropped in the tub and dried on the radiator. That's a lot of stores. That's one very smart cocktail.

⁕

One of the disadvantages of knowing your bartender is that personal problems can – and so often do – get in the way of a drink. Such is the case with Secret Agent Rose who, for some reason tonight, has a pickle up the proverbial.

"I'm sorry, Cherry, I don't care what Lib told you, but there's no way you can stay another night at our place."

"I'll just sleep on the couch again, Rose. You won't notice me, I promise."

"No can do. That's not cool with our new roommate."

Bullshit, thinks Cherry. Phoebe, the new roomie, hadn't said a word and there had been ample opportunity that very morning. Cherry had been awakened to the smell of burning rubber and the distressed bleatings of Phoebe.

"It's the kettle!" she'd warbled. "The kettle's gone psycho!"

With her eyes still misty from the *vino collapso* of the previous night, Cherry had been able to fix the sputtering and smoking kettle in less than thirty seconds. Someone had left a dildo in it. The rubber bludgeon was well and truly sterilized now. Part of it was even beginning to melt where it had pressed against the element.

Phoebe had been both relieved and bemused.

"That was quite the party last night. Are you still alive?"

Cherry had groaned something approximating an affirmative and gone back to sleep. A while later, something hot and stinky was shoved under her nose.

"Would you care for a cure for anusitis?"

"I beg your pardon?"

"Your itch, remember? You were telling me all about it last night." Phoebe perched herself on the arm of the *chaise longue* with her own steaming cup and cast an eye over Cherry's bags. "You must be doing the Grand Couch Tour of the city, right?"

"Uh-huh."

Cherry didn't bother to tell Phoebe that her itch was as far from anusitis as a monkey's tit, or that she had been enjoying her particular Great-Grand Couch Tour for more than fourteen years now and counting. She didn't think it pertinent. Phoebe had bubbled on and on about how relieved she was that her own two-week stint of crashing on friends' couches had finally come to an end with her moving into the studio, and Cherry had smiled politely. The herbal concoction had tasted of licorice and, as Phoebe put it, was going to attack every single living cell in her body, and wipe out that pesky morning scratchy bum. Cherry discreetly abandoned her cup next to the stinking beer bottle by the leg of the *chaise longue*.

No mention had been made of any horror at having Cherry stay there. No screams of appropriation. No leases waved in the air – *No pets, no garbage in the hallways and no intersexuals on the chaise longue.*

Rose must be mistaken.

"Phoebe and I had a great chat this morning," says Cherry, casually lighting a cigarette. "She seemed fine about it then. Has she changed her mind?"

"We can't have you staying with us, Cherry. I'm sorry, that's just the way it is. Nothing personal."

Cherry slaps a fifty dollar bill onto the bar. There's one way to find out how nothing personal it is, she thinks. Raise the stakes.

"Give me a vodka then, if you'll be so kind."

"And I can't serve you until you pay off your tab. You've got the cash." Rose holds up the soda gun. "I can get you a pop if you like."

"No, thank you." Cherry prepares herself to expose the whole hypocrisy. "But tell me: why don't you use the fucking deposit money for your studio space that I gave Liberty to pay off my bar tab? Then we'll be Even-Steven and I can get a drink."

Rose huffs. "You should know better than to give money to Lib."

She tosses her ponytail and moves to the far end of the bar where a gaggle of chiclets and gerbils are clamouring for mineral water. She must have gotten her wrists slapped pretty hard by Cocktail Mama or – more likely – Whatserface over last night. What is the world coming to? It wasn't as if any terrible crime had been committed. Cherry had just done a little celebrating, that's all. Not too much – she'd been ultracareful about splashing the cash around. Fuck it, Rose had encouraged them all, lining up the shot glasses on the bar and pouring free shooters, hadn't she? The stupid rule about Cherry not being allowed to buy any drinks until her tab was cleared up had come from Cocktail Mama. Rose is just being a nazi asshole.

Cherry shrugs and puts away her money. The Kennel Klub can suffer without her custom and Rose, the secret-agent party-line bar-squirrel, can go chew nuts. No cause for concern. The Chinese screen will be good for another three nights, possibly four. It's really most infuriating, especially since Cherry *likes* Rose. This stoppage of alcohol, however, is a serious problem. There's a nasty, dry sensation in her mouth and something has to be done.

She considers reaching over and helping herself to a spritz of *C* for cola but decides against it. Instead, clicking her tongue against the roof of her mouth, she fishes a small bottle of *jalapeño* pepper vodka from her purse, removes the cap in one easy twist and knocks back a hit. She swooshes the liquid around her gums and teeth and, after sterilizing her mouth with this flesh-puckering cocktail, she squirts a stream from between her teeth into the gap between the wall and the pinball machine. The Phantom Dilophosaurus strikes again. With her mouth freshly rinsed, she takes another swig, this time for swallowing, savouring and putting a spark o' life back into the ol' false eyelashes.

That's better. The club looks almost habitable, now. One could almost imagine fitting right in with the practical butch decor and peeling linoleum. The Kennel Klub has been a mainstay of the alter-no-thrash-fag-dyke circuit for as long as anyone can remember. Rumour has it that originally, way back in the days when it was the Roxy, it catered to the travelling-salesman and secretary crowd, the cheap dinner-theatre set, but without the dinner or the theatre. Maybe an exotic dancer or two, cigarette girls, padded coasters, the whole bit. You'd never guess it, now.

According to the Bloor family, who run the joint as a poor cousin to their other much more successful and snooty Empire and Palais clubs, the place is a festering boil, a liability. It may be popular, but it doesn't make enough money. It's always filled with kids who would sooner spit at you than buy a flashy ten-dollar cocktail. The Kennel Klub is described in all the local gay and not-so-gay guides as *funky* and *alternative*. Basically, this means that the police are always being called in and the local residents live in fear of finding a leather fairy having a bad acid trip in their backyard.

From the outside, the place looks like a Nissen hut – a concrete block with lighting fixtures that are functional at 600 feet below sea-level. Inside, however, the belly of the beast is rotting. Liquids have been flowing for so many years that the floor has gone spongy, the bar is growing mystery bubbles under its formica and you can follow your nose to find the washrooms. Remnants from the Roxy days gather disgust behind the bar: signed publicity photographs of jazz muses, nicotine-ravaged newspaper clippings and exotic liqueurs in coloured bottles that have sealed themselves shut.

Since its name has been changed to the Kennel Klub, white cartoon bones have been stencilled all over the walls, fighting for attention with graffiti, ancient peeling band posters and notices for political rallies. The bohemian cannibals have moved in. Bow-wow-Bauhaus.

Tonight the club is humming with the groovy alternative sounds of Rajah Sultana and his whistle-blowing entourage. Groove is an excellent description – he seems to have gotten himself stuck in one. The repetitive pounding is relieved only by the occasional shriek or whistle-toot coming from the enthusiastic dance-floor contingent. Everyone is having a fine old time, working up a sweat to rival the Ecstatic gleam in their eyes, knocking back the mineral water and roving around the bar in couples or groups, looking for that elusive something or somebody. Christmas Eve is nowhere to be seen, it's been shaken off with the snow and Liberty Hanna at the door.

Cherry's booked off work for the night. She's sorely tempted to throw in the towel for good and tell them all to go *phphuq* themselves, but she daren't. Other than Liberty, no one knows about the *XXXmas* tickets and she'd like to keep it that way. *It's an inheritance – not much, my Uncle Jericho on the West Coast died and left me a couple of bucks.* She's lying low for a couple of days. On the one hand, she's telling herself that she's saving her energy for the heavy party week ahead. On the other, she's shit-scared of getting caught and landing herself in major Trouble. What she's doing with the tickets has to be deathly illegal; she'd better carry on as normal, pretend nothing's happened. Which means putting in an appearance at the Kennel Klub. But work? Screw that shit. Her excuse is a twisted ankle, which nobody believes, but Liberty backs up the story which, of course, keeps changing.

Despite the big crowd, there's very little actual work to be done. The kids are on drugs; they don't need booze as well. They'll buy one bottle of mineral water at the top of the night and keep ahold of it, running to the washrooms to replenish it whenever they need rehydration.

Rose is running the bar solo, with the sporadic assistance of Cocktail Mama lording it over the cash register. Coady, bright little spark of gutter-slut muscle-Queen that he is, is slowly bussing. Nobody has been paid yet, and it shows.

The Bloor's company accountant, Whatserface, is hiding up in the so-called VIP lounge, doing the books – whatever that means. Odds are that it's not the payroll. Most likely she's hiding in the VIP lounge since it's the quietest place in the building. Whatserface is petrified of this hard-edged groove-rave thing, grasping it only to the extent that it attracts the biggest crowd of the week and the smallest revenue at the end of the night. She can't understand it. She will never understand it. But she still spends a lot of time at the Kennel Klub.

Coady suddenly appears, smiling, at Cherry's elbow. He greets her as if she were a drag queen, his hands twirling like propellers.

"Dah-ling. Queen Isabella requests your presence," he announces. "Something about a bar tab and an inheritance, I do believe?"

"Queen Isabella?" says Cherry, innocently. "Oh, you mean What-serface, right?" Coady nods as Cherry steels herself. The summons has come.

If there is one Golden Rule that Cherry Beach has learned in her thirty-one years of accidental existence, it is that "Telling the truth will always get you into trouble." No matter how strong the appeal of honesty, it can never atone for the damage it does, nor break beyond the limit it imposes. There are many other well-worn maxims to modern living, rules of hard-learned experience that Cherry has acquired over the years: "Never apologize," "Drugs won't pay the rent," "Bad boys get spanked," "Never drink more than your friends can afford," "Pizza is breakfast," "Vitamins are addictive," etc., etc. – but "Telling the truth will always get you into trouble" stands at the top of the list as the axiom to remember at all costs, especially where money is concerned.

She can easily pay off her tab, it's not as if she doesn't have the moolah to spare, but something stops her – every man-made fibre of her being balks at the idea, wary of the intense suspicion it would throw upon her if she coughed up. Much like "Telling the truth," "Paying off all your debts" is bound to invoke discord, upset the nat-ural balance of power, draw attention and create a mutiny of alliances better left unrealized. No, for the time being Cherry has decided to leave her slate slopping over the high-water mark. If the truth be known, she resents giving the Bloor family any more money than is absolutely necessary. She's paid the rent, hasn't she? She left a hun-dred-dollar ticket with Brock? Surely that shows enough goodwill.

She strides across the dance floor, the club kids parting before her, adjusting automatically. The flashing disco lights fuel her journey, pro-pel her up the tricky wrought-iron circular staircase. Cherry is aware of the mass of dancers falling away beneath her. She moves to the beat of the funk as she winds herself into a confrontational frame of mind.

Up in the DJ booth, the sound is not so much quieter as more dis-persed – heavier, duller. Rajah, the DJ, dances alone, one hand holding onto his earphones, the other holding onto an album jacket, oblivious to Cherry's intrusion. To his right is a girl on a stepladder, operating a tri-beam spotlight that shines through a cut-away in the glass to the booth. Behind him is a wall of equipment, including a stretch of tightly packed records – Cocktail Mama's collection that guest disc jockeys are not allowed to touch on pain of having their drink vouchers withdrawn.

Warm cracks of light shine through this wall from the sacred VIP lounge that Whatserface and Cocktail Mama have lately claimed as their den, their warm and cozy refuge from the harsh world of Clubland. The rack of albums provides soundproofing from the very tunes they contain. Cherry doesn't bother to knock on the cheap veneer door to warn the occupants. She is expected.

What a picture of domestic bliss.

Isabella – Whatserface – is hardly doing the books. She's watching a black-and-white portable television that is on her desk. There she sits, with her smart legs curled up beneath her in a tan leather armchair, her blue patent pumps lying crisscross on the floor. Her Chihuahua perks up its head from its snoozing place on her lap as Cherry enters the room. It jumps to the floor and yaps around at ankle level. A half-empty bottle of tequila and a Tupperware jug of mix stand guard next to the television, the trademark margarita hangs from Whatserface's claw. If she could hold her liquor, she might be a class act. As it is, she can't and she isn't.

"Help your selfish," she says, proffering a plate of sausage rolls to Cherry, then laughing at her own joke with her grating cackle.

"You wanted to see me?" Cherry glares at the dog who, cowed, returns to its Mistress' lap.

"Pauline, Cherry's here," drawls Whatserface, her eyes and nose screwing up into a lump of TV-lit sourness. Her loosely scrunched wine-red curls constantly get in her way. Every drunken move she makes is unnatural; at some point in her deep, dark past she's spent a couple of bucks on plastic surgery. The cheap kind. Her demented little hamster eyes glisten from behind strange folds of skin, and every time she laughs that horrendous cackle of hers, her cheekbones slip around beneath the surface. Hence the moniker "Whatserface," even though everyone knows it's Isabella Sherbourne.

"Pauline, Cherry's here. Wake up. Be nice."

Pauline – aka Cocktail Mama – is flaked out on the couch next to

Victor, the club's favoured chemical magnate. Cocktail Mama looks like a beached walrus, while Victor, slumped over the couch arm, looks like he always looks: a collapsed puppet. Joe Ninety or Howdy-Doody in broken spectacles. One glance at his cracked lens and Cherry can tell that he's flying high on something expensive. There are remnants of a turquoise powder smeared over a mirror on the coffee table.

Cocktail Mama has a lumberjack shirt thrown over her head. An oversize black T-shirt with the logo of an orange happy face with X'd out eyes envelops the rest of her body. Her legs, in their nondescript nylon slacks, rest on the arm of the couch near Victor. She has lost one of her thongs. Cocktail Mama wears those ugly beach thongs all year round, except at home, where she wears men's slippers. She paints her toenails red.

"*Pauline!*"

Cocktail Mama groans, pokes her head out from beneath its cover. Her dark, bobbed hair has been pinned back with a pink plastic unicorn. There is a shaved section of scalp across the back of her neck, a line running from ear to ear that gives her that pig-ready-for-execution look. She rights herself on the couch, wipes her mouth with the shirt, finds the lost thong. Victor slips into a crack between the cushions and hugs his knees.

"No arguments, all right, Cherry?" drawls Cocktail Mama, reaching for one of her high-tar non-filter cigarettes. "I'm not in the mood for arguments."

"And a Merry Christmas to you, too," responds Cherry, seething with *faux jolité*. "How can I help you beautiful people tonight?"

"We hear you came into some money recently."

Cherry denies it but Cocktail Mama stops her.

"Why didn't you pay off your bar tab instead of buying more alcohol?"

Cherry hates to point out the obvious but realizes she has to. "Because I wouldn't have been able to drink anything then, right?"

Cocktail Mama takes a grim pause and launches into her spiel. Three hundred dollars is the limit, she explains through a cloud of nicotine, and if Cherry wants a drink, she'll have to make good on her Outstanding before normal service can be resumed. Cocktail Mama must have been a telephone slave for a collection agency in a previous life. Her language is so brittle and impersonal, shunting along a prepared line of attack, making codified assumptions as she goes. Part of her is still out cold. If Cherry is hard up, she argues, then some arrangement – as always – can be made, but if Cherry should, say, come into a couple of hundred bucks, then Cherry's priorities should lie with clearing up her debts before frittering it all away. A celebratory drink is understandable, maybe even one for her friends, but first things first, yes?

"So, I'm sorry, Cherry, but I'm cutting you off and docking your pay."

Docking her pay? What pay? Has the long-awaited ship come in? Grrrr.

Cherry feels a forgotten store of testosterone surge through her body, marching through her veins like an army of soldier ants. She can feel the familiar tensing of the shoulder blades, the prickling along the spine. Testosterone always appears with confrontation, chemically sluicing Cherry's body in preparation for some macho battle that – inevitably – will reunite her with her long-standing fighting buddy, Trouble.

The solution to the bar tab problem is right there in her purse. Three hundred dollars? It would be so easy: reach in, pull out a wad of cash and plunk it on the coffee table. *Here. Go get your moustache waxed.*


The final three Principles of War, according to James, were … "Unity! Simplicity! Security!"

Five years after her experience with the Pongos, Cherry had revisited the West Coast, once again calling herself Nicola. Time had mellowed her memories, certainly it had smoothed the scars into shadows on her thighs. She even entertained the fantasy – if only out of perversity – of harbouring some affection for her captors. Not so much the harsh trumpet of James, nor the pudgy meekness of Mackie. The quiet one, Nigel – the one with the long eyelashes. Now he had had possibilities …

The cabin had been torn down but she could see the hardened patch of earth and the discolouration in the grass where the walls had stood. Someone had lit a campfire there recently, cooked up corn, wieners, and baked potatoes, the remnants of which were now overrun by an army of ants among the ashes.

She stood for a while, staring up at the sky, willing it to rain. Then she squashed an ant beneath her shoe and walked away from it all.

At the edge of the park she flagged a cab back to her latest couch. Sitting in the back seat, toying with a cigarette and looking at the mountains through the taxi windows, she managed to convince herself that it was the very same driver who had taken her to the park in the first place, all those years ago.

When she got out, she tipped him seven bucks in Great Northern Hardware Dollars she had stashed in her purse for a rainy day.


"Are you finished?" asks Cherry, pulling a face at Whatserface's lap dog, which is following the conversation with great interest. "Is that it? Three hundred? I don't have it."

"Of course you don't," snarls Cocktail Mama. "You never have it, do you? And now the bar's still out three hundred dollars. What am I supposed to do? I'm not even going to mention the fact that Grandpa and I are still owed two hundred for the rent and twenty for the phone bill." She stubs out her cigarette. "There's got to be gum in those ashtrays out there. I suggest you get back to work immediately if you know what's good for you."

That's Cocktail Mama – always looking out for what's good for other people. Trouble nudges Cherry's elbow and whispers in her ear. *Pay them off. It's only a few hundred dollars. Pay them off and you'll never have to look at their ugly faces again.*

"I paid your fucking rent," snaps Cherry. "I left it with Brock."

There is a pause as something makes a connection in Cocktail Mama's brain.

"Aren't you supposed to be baby-sitting?" she asks eventually, her eyes narrowing. "Aren't you supposed to be looking after Grandpa?"

"That was when I was staying there. In case you hadn't noticed, I've moved out."

Victor chooses this moment to have one of his coughing fits. As she watches Cocktail Mama give Victor a version of the Heimlich assault, Cherry wonders – for merely a fraction of the second – who the heck's looking after Brock if Cocktail Mama's right here? *She hasn't been home, yet. She's been out partying for four nights solid and forgot about him, the irresponsible cow.*

Victor settles down and the questions continue.

"So tell me, what's stopping you from working tonight?"

"I can't," offers Cherry in a tone of voice that implies that she'd love to if she could, "it's my friend's birthday. I promised." She remembers her earlier story. "And I twisted my ankle."

Cocktail Mama sighs, her cheeks puffing with exaggerated sadness. Whatserface dips her face into her margarita, surfacing seconds later with a sparkling upper lip. The dog watches television. Victor looks like a smiling store-window dummy. Cherry counts the ceiling tiles, wishing she had some of whatever Victor is on.

"We're disappointed in you, Cherry," says Whatserface at last, from behind the salted rim of her drink. "We're heartbroken, truly. We've always done our best to help you out, you know that, Cherry. We consider you part of the family, isn't that right, Pauline?"

Family?

Pauline shakes her head gravely, meaning yes, that's right, they've welcomed Cherry with open arms, yes, they've invited her into the inner circle of loved ones, yes, given her a place to stay only to be abused, and, yes, considered her part of the family, like some jailbird uncle no one dare talk about around the dinner table.

Family? *The Bloor Family?!* That does it. Call the Fire Department! The Jaws of Life are going to be needed to extract her from the wreckage.

The ants march a little faster through her veins. They must have smelled some formic acid coming off of Victor.


The God of War – Mars, Ares, Shiva or Woden, take your pick – the red-haired, tight-muscled commando of the pantheon marches to a drumbeat a few milliseconds faster than the average heart. His is a blunt and direct force all the more effective because he stays a quarter-step ahead of the masses. When invoked, he strikes to the quick with minimal fuss. Protocol having been observed with declarations, warnings, counterchallenges and oaths of allegiance, he enters the field with one clear goal: to destroy.

Mass, Objective, Offensive, Surprise, Economy, Movement, Unity, Simplicity and Security. Nine parts of the whole. One aim: to destroy.


Cherry delves into her purse, takes out a fistful of bills and starts counting them off, tossing them carelessly onto the table ... fifty dollars ... sixty ... seventy ...

All eyes follow the bills as they fall like leaves. Victor suddenly springs to life and moves the drug mirror out of the way. The dog jumps from its perch, scampers over to get a closer look, and puts its front paws up on the edge of the coffee table. It follows the fall of each bill with its perky little head and perky little eyes, threatening to give itself a perky little hemorrhage.

"One hundred and forty ... one hundred and sixty ..."

Cocktail Mama cannot stop herself from tidying up the cash, sorting the denominations, pretending to be practical when all she wants to do is get her hands on the lucre, to dirty her fingers, to touch it to make sure that it's real.

"Two-twenty ... two-thirty ... fifty ..."

Whatserface cannot stop herself from rising out of her armchair; the momentum from her raised eyebrow is too strong. Feigning nonchalance, she pours herself another drink, but the muscles in her face betray her interest, swivelling around beneath the flesh to get a better view of all that money.

Cherry loses count but she doesn't dare stop the rhythm of her onslaught – that would involve losing face – so she starts tossing bills in handfuls, confetti-style, into the air.

"There's your rent as well!" she crows. "There's the phone bill! The glass I broke last week!"

Everyone except Victor is standing now. The dog chases after the falling cash, yapping and jumping in the air, running around in frantic circles. Whatserface and Cocktail Mama look like newlyweds emerging from the church, the expressions on their faces a mixture of horror and delight.

"And I hope you'll be very happy together!" proclaims Cherry, suddenly reaching into her kangaroo pouch and pulling out a handful of *XXXmas* tickets – the ones with torn corners – duds.

"I quit!"

She lobs the tickets into the air and storms from the room before she can stop herself. They can all go screw themselves. Begone, malignant spirits!

How much had that cost her? Four hundred, maybe five at the most, and worth every dollar. There's plenty more where that came from. She's actually beginning to enjoy herself.

She descends the spiral staircase *à la* Norma Desmond, to the cheering of her fans below. The disco lights become the flashing bulbs of photographers; the music, the swelling soundtrack of the finalé.

She is transported on a cloud of exuberance. She holds her head up high, her shoulders comfortably back; her eyes glisten with the joy of having discovered a world where retribution falls naturally into place. Her well-turned legs negotiate the vortex of the wrought-iron steps as smoothly, as perfectly as did the tap-dancing Ginger in *Roxie Hart*, arm-in-arm, with her new-found travelling companion, her consort for the evening, her new partner in crime: Trouble.

"**H**elp your shell-fish!"

I don't know whether Marg had slipped on her tongue after one too many eggnogs, or whether she was actually making a joke about the crab paté. It sure was funny, though, and we laughed until the boys in the poker room yelled at us to cut it out. I was being given a guided tour of the fridge. Help your selfish, indeed. It was like an Aladdin's cave in there.

More food than people, that's Marg's secret to a good party and she's done the family proud, I have to say. I've never seen so much fancy party stuff: mince tarts, shortbread, fruitcake, brandy snaps, coconut truffles, cookies, and those red-and-green marshmallow-krispie-squares. Tupperware has taken over the kitchen. The fridge is full of salads and sauces and dips. Cartons of eggnog in the milk bin and milk-chocolate Santas in the egg rack. There's a giant – and I mean giant – Yule log hogging the freezer. And that's only the half of it all. Out on the tables in the dining room there are chestnut purées, cocktail wieners and shrimp soufflés, around a centrepiece that might be a gingerbread house under all those smarties. Marg has mixed her killer punch, a cloudy brown brew that stinks of cloves. No one has touched the two figgy puddings, the curdled English trifle or Sy's chili. Everywhere you look, it's food, food, food. And most of it is sugar, sugar, sugar. Christmas at the Bloors. Try the crab paté – it's excellent. Help your shell-fish. Ha-ha-ha! Did I mention turkey? No? That's because there isn't any. Turkey was Thanksgiving. The Bloor family's weird about that.

On top of the TV there are pretzels, chips, chips, chips (ruffled, plain, pan-fried, shoestring), peanuts, walnuts, hazelnuts and something fishy in a little Dresden china bowl that came from Al's aunt who's visiting from the Old Country. I think she said it was jellied eels, but her English isn't that good and I daren't risk it. Besides, it's getting warm from the TV.

I'm not a fan of all this rich food, I must confess. I tried to fix myself a simple sandwich, but the only bread to be found was a raisin-malt-cranberry loaf and I really had to rummage in the cupboards to rustle up a can of tuna. Marg came into the kitchen to pick up some fresh beer for the boys. She laughed at me when I asked for some honest white bread. By the time I'd made the mistake of spreading rum butter on my burnt slabs of fruit toast I was in a foul mood. So I tossed my thwarted snack in the garbage, mixed up another margarita and called it a night. I'll chew on a few peanuts.

Luckily there's no shortage of booze, but that's to be expected when you're in the hospitality industry. Just pennies a glass, and I should know. I do the books for them. Even so, the tab is running pretty high. These guys sure know how to knock it back. Al reached his limit about three days ago and he's been searching for his car keys ever since. I'm pretty sure that Marg's got them in her purse but she's not handing them over. She likes to think that she's being protective, that she's brimming over with concern for her man, when in reality, its an excuse to be a bitch and torture the poor guy.

"Well, *I* don't know where they are, Al. Have you tried looking in your pocket? Ha-ha-ha!"

It's quite the party. Bob's kids are spending Christmas with their mother this year, so this is an adult affair. Gifts were swapped weeks ago, leaving everyone to enjoy themselves without pressure or guilt. No big sit-down dinner, just this eternal buffet. There's the traditional poker game going on in the den – for pretty high stakes, I believe – but the cigar smoke's too heavy for me. Not that I'm not welcome. Anyone who can afford the ante can get in the game. Come as you can, when you can, as often as you dare. It's been going on for at least four days now, in strange shifts. People will arrive, stay for a while, drink their faces off, pick at the food, lose or win some money on the cards, leave, come back again maybe a day or two later and repeat the process. Family, friends, and hangers-on. Somewhere in there came Christmas ... Jeez, it might even be today. At least there are no hypocrites in the Bloor family. They look upon this week as a good excuse to socialize, nothing religious about it at all, and ain't that a relief in this day and age?

Despite a wicked hangover, I managed to get some work in yesterday, doing the rounds of the clubs and spending time with Pauline at the Kennel. I like it there. It gives me a chance to escape, to put my feet up. I feel like I actually own something, you know? Yes, it's a dump right now, but you can feel the history in those walls. Both Bessie Smith and Billie Holiday sang there, they say. Besides, there's a lot of work. Pauline left the books in a complete mess, so I've made sorting out the Kennel Klub my very own pet project. Well, it keeps me occupied.

The family's been good to me, I have to admit, even though I'm not a true blood relative. It's the old boy network. They took me in when Charlie went to prison last year, gave me a job and a room in the basement. Carlo and I are very happy there. We have our own private entrance, so I can come and go as I please. There's a park nearby for Carlo, where I can let him off the leash in the afternoons provided there aren't too many big dogs around. Those large breeds can't stand him and he will keep going up and teasing them. In that respect, he's much like me. Always attracted to the ones who'll do us in.

Charlie's out now, on good behaviour; he has been for a couple of weeks but I haven't dared call him. Marg keeps pushing me to get it over with, tells me that the family would always give Charlie a muscle job if I needed something to sugar the pie. I don't know what I'd say to him. While he was inside, locked away safely for fourteen months, I pushed the divorce through, cashed in all the bonds he'd put in my name for security reasons, sold the house and the cars, and gave away the pool table to the kids next door. I had some more surgery done, took a short but expensive trip to Europe and came back basically broke but feeling great. I talked Bob into letting me get the Kennel Klub for twenty thousand dollars down, and he said yes, but that they had to wait for the old guy to die first. In the meantime, I could help sort out the paperwork.

Five thousand dollars is all I have left to show for ten years of marriage. Five thousand dollars and a million scars, most of which have been cunningly concealed beyond the hairline. Looking good keeps me feeling good. And that's important.


Pauline's developing a drug problem, I'm going to have to have another talk with her. A month ago it was two days in the hospital because she'd had what she called "a slice of cake." Cocaine, Acid, Ketamine and Ecstasy. Jeez, she's lucky to be alive. No self-respect, that's her trouble, which isn't uncommon with overweight girls. Lose your figure, lose your mind, eh? And she will keep hanging around with that Victor, even tried to bring him over here last night, but Bob wouldn't have any of it. Threw him back into the taxi before it left the driveway.

"Haven't you caused enough fucking problems in this family!" he yelled. He winged a snowball at the cab, which went off-target and hit one of the blue firs. It took us hours to calm him down after that.

He's right, though. Not that I have anything against drugs *per se* – I mean I should talk – but it's just that these new designer chemicals the kids are mucking around with nowadays are bound to cause serious brain damage sooner or later. Look at Victor: he's a mess. *I try everything out myself before I'll sell it to anyone.* As if that's something to be proud of! He should carry a health warning like on a pack of smokes. *Warning! Look what this shit can do to you.*

Then Pauline went and threw more money at him for another little bag of that Alpha-Four garbage. I can't understand her. She spent the entire first night either passed out on the couch or hugging the toilet bowl, and she goes back for more of the same? I know she's two weeks late with her period but that's no way to behave, trying to force it out. She should count herself lucky she can still carry an egg; there are many of us who would kill for that ability.

Charlie's empire has crumbled. He used to run distribution for the Ring-Riders, coast to coast – a highly lucrative career, with a finger in a dozen very sweet pies indeed. He made a huge pile off the smack and the blow, kept the two of us in style and paid for my surgery. It was a risk, sure, but Charlie's spent his whole life on the wrong side of the law. Drugs were just another business venture to him.

Up until they caught him with fourteen grams of cocaine stuffed up his asshole, they had let him off reasonably lightly. Nothing more than a month inside and the rest deferred or suspended. It had all been fairly run-of-the-mill charges: break and enter, a few robberies where he pleaded that he'd just "gotten in with the wrong crowd," and God knows how many cheque-kiting scams. It was the drugs that did him in. Once they got him for the evil white horse, he was a marked man. Mention his name to any officer and their eyes will light up as if they've just won the sweepstakes.

This last time Charlie was incarcerated for smuggling cigarettes across the border in household appliances, for Pete's sake. It may not sound like much, but business was, as Charlie joked, "s-smokin'!" Tax on a carton at that time was so high we made a cancerous profit. He reckoned he'd get off with a slap on the wrists and a warning, seeing as this country was built on tobacco and he was only following in the footsteps of the founding fathers. He didn't reckon on the government getting so worked up over losing their tax dollars. They threw the book at him. I guess I helped. I wasn't too impressed with his temper in those days. I just wanted him to stop shouting.

About a month after they nailed him, they lopped the tax off cigarettes anyway, killing the trade in contraband cigarettes. I bet to Charlie, stuck in a cell, it must have felt as if they did it out of spite.

He should have stuck to heroin. At least he'd have known why he was in prison.


I had to call him eventually. I told myself that maybe I just needed someone to talk to, someone who knew me well. Sure, there's all this family, family, friends and more around me, but even though they've been so kind, they aren't mine. And it is the season. I kept thinking about him, sitting in a halfway house having a rotten Christmas all by himself. What harm could a phone call do? It's not as if I never wanted to see him again. I'm not made of stone.

"Isabella? *Isa-fucking-bella?!*"

I could hear the shock in his voice. Disbelief. Hardly surprising, as the last time I talked to him was through a lawyer.

"How are things, Charlie?"

I suppose that wasn't a very sensitive question to ask. After all, I could guess what his situation was like and I deserved the ragging he gave me for asking. And how he raged! He laid into me with a blue-streaked trowel. What could I do? I told him I was sorry as best I could and wished him Happy Holidays. He laughed at that and called me his little gopher. That was better. More like the old Charlie.

Little gopher. Suddenly, I saw myself back on the prairies. Back in the little registry office in the heat of summer, the dry air prickling at the back of my knees, the little pillbox hat slipping off my head and into the dust when he wouldn't kiss me. He had the same laugh then.

"Mr Jarvis, you may kiss the bride."

"Kiss the bride, are you kidding?! Look at her, the little gopher. Go for yer hat, my darlin'! Ha-ha-ha!"

It was the laugh from the cigar-and-steakhouse days. He and the boys would sit in that corner booth, crack jokes, drink round after round of fifteen-dollar-a-glass malts, plan their jobs, make bets and offer me up as a prize. That laugh included me in his secrets; not like the other one, the fake, insecure laugh that he used to beat me up to.

"So you called me up to gloat, is that it?"

"No, Charlie," I assured him, lowering my voice as Marg came into the kitchen. "I wouldn't do that."

"Sure you would, you ugly old cunt."

I blushed and Marg gave me a sudden look while she filled a plate with date squares. I smiled but I could feel the corners of my mouth twitch. I can't help it; it's my generation, I guess. That word always makes my lips pucker like an old hen's. The *C* word. And he knew it.

"Charlie … Charlie, don't …"

"Don't what?" He was enjoying himself. "Call you a cunt? But you are. A capital fucking *C* Cunt, super Cunt special, that's you. Cunt."

"I'm going to hang up now, Charlie."

"Can't take it, can you? You never could."

"I have to take the dog out."

Marg left the kitchen, giving me a grim nod of support. I wished she would mind her own business. It wasn't what she thought. Charlie started on one of his routines, accusing me of being a lush, a whore, a slut who'd pork any slimeball if I thought there was a free drink in it. I'd heard it all before.

"Charlie …"

"You can't leave well enough alone, can you? You have to call me up and dig your claws in. Haven't you got any fucking brains left? Or did the fucking plastic surgeon accidentally take those out when he …"

"Charlie, no, Charlie, I'd …"

"Scab-picker! That's what you are! A fucking cunt-flapping scab-picker."

"Charlie, no." I looked down at my hand. For some reason, I must have opened my purse and taken out one of those lottery tickets Cherry Beach had thrown in my face. There it was, staring up at me: *Turkey Dinner for Two at Honest John's Steakhouse.*

"Charlie, no … Charlie, *listen to me* …" I swallowed hard, my throat dry. "Charlie, I'd … I'd like to see you again."


The only time I'd really won anything was in grade eleven when I played baseball at The Golden Horseshoe Summer Camp. I was an ugly girl. My nose sort of droobled around my face, pulling my lips and chin along with it. I was slim, though. Slim and athletic, with large hands. They stuck me on the boys' list where I passed muster for games against away teams. I was their star pitcher.

"Earl" they called me, which sounded much like "hurl" when shouted. I'd step up to the mound, wrap my big hands around the ball with a slip of secret spit and hit 'em with my best.

"Pitch him OUT, Earl!" they'd cheer. "O-U-T spells OUT!"

My specialty (and the reason I was on the team) was what I called my "Wild West" – a spinning bullet of a ball that looked as if it was about to shoot ya smack in the head between the eyes. Scared the living bejesus out of many a kid, let me tell you. I even hit a couple.

Then Mr Sheppard disqualified me from the team for being a girl. I think he was jealous, or perhaps it was my ugliness; he never would look me in the eye.


Honest John's Steakhouse doesn't normally allows dogs in their dining room, but seeing as we were the winners of a free turkey dinner, they turned a blind eye, thank God. I'm not sure if they'd have let in a Schnauzer or a Great Dane, but Carlo's no trouble. They even gave him a bowl of water.

They put us at a table in the corner, partly curtained off from the rest of the restaurant with heavy velvet drapes. Charlie wore a checked suit I never would have thought him brave enough to wear in public, one of those ties with a hula dancer on it, and his hair stunk of Brylcream. He'd lost a bit of weight while inside and he wasn't wearing his ring. I don't know what I had expected.

"Did you have to bring that ugly fucking rat?" Charlie was being his usual self. "Don't let him wander into the kitchen. They might pop him into the vegetable pot by mistake."

He laughed. I joined in. He glared at me. He hates my laugh.

"I remember this place from before it opened," he said, tucking his napkin into his collar. "It used to be a fucking meat packers."

The waiter came and there was a bit of trouble over our order. Charlie wanted surf 'n turf and kicked up a fuss when he was told that we had won the turkey dinner and the turkey dinner we were going to get. The waiter was quite nasty about it, but in the end, Charlie got what he wanted.

"I've already had five turkey fucking dinners this season, you dumb faggot!" he shouted after him. "And I'll be damned if I'm going to come to Honest John's Famous Fucking Steakhouse and not have the dish that put you on the fucking map!"

"There's no need to be so hostile," I told him, glad that we had been seated in the corner, hidden from most eyes. "He was only doing his job."

"I wasn't hostile, I was verbal," muttered Charlie. "There's a difference. You have to teach these fruit who's boss."

He gave me a look to let me know what he meant. I knew.

The meal was late in arriving, and by the time it reached the table we'd drunk the equivalent of our free meals. I have to admit, I was still drinking at the Bloor cost-per-gallon calculations and I was nervous. Things weren't going so well.

"It's just like you to worm your way in at Al and Marg's," he said. "I can't believe you did that while I'm stuck at the fucking hostel. They used to be *my* friends."

"You were inside at the time, Charlie. Anyway, you've only just started at the hostel."

I shouldn't have got him started on that subject. The halfway house was, in his words, "a fucking weeping sore on the scabbed asshole of the universe." Everything was made out of rotting cardboard, covered in grunge, and infested with roaches. It couldn't have been that bad, but he did go on.

"I can't even have a proper shower because the stall at the end of the fucking corridor either dribbles a piss-stream of ice-water or sears your fucking skin off with a torrential fucking boiling downpour."

"I'm sorry to hear that Charlie, I ..."

"And if you make it through that fucking torture, the chances are ten to one your fucking towel and keys have been ripped off from the peg outside by some criminal element these places are fucking filled with."

To hear him tell it, it was worse than prison.

"How are Al and Marg by the way?" he asked, shifting topic and waving a prawn about on the end of his fork. "I take it the old bugger didn't manage to close them down, eh? Do they have anything for me?"

I told him things were fine, that Pauline was looking after Grandpa now and that the business was no longer in jeopardy since the lawyers realized that Grandpa was senile. I told him the kids were staying with Jane for Christmas and how Bob was thinking of moving into casinos. I tried to be as superficial as possible, just glossing over details as fast as I could. I didn't feel comfortable talking about the Bloors to Charlie. I knew he was after a job and that I could have given one to him right then and there, but I certainly wasn't about to tell him of my interest in the Kennel Klub. He'd flip his lid if he knew about that. My life wouldn't be worth living. I'd surely end up back in the institution.

"We should drop by for a drink after," he said, carefully. "They must be doing their Christmas thing. Got the poker game going, right?"

"I don't think that would be a good idea, Charlie."

He held my gaze for a long time. I tried to laugh it off, but that only made it worse.

"Not a good idea?" He leaned back in his seat. "Why wouldn't that be? Here I am, Charlie Jarvis, good friend of the fucking family, who just spent fourteen months out of circulation, so to speak. So tell me: what's wrong with me paying them a visit? I've helped those bastards out on numerous occasions, we all know that."

"Yes, I know, Charlie, but ..."

"I suppose you've filled their ears with your stories about me, haven't you?" He leaned forward as if to take my hands across the table, but I pulled them out of the way. I didn't like his smile.

"No, Charlie, I never …"

"I know what you done, you mealy old cunt." He spoke slowly. "I know what you done."

From beneath the table, Carlo started to growl. I guess he must have picked up on my fear and was doing what dogs do best when it comes to protecting their masters. I tried to shush him. Charlie was in no mood and one kick could do some nasty damage to an animal that size. But Carlo wouldn't rest.

Suddenly, Charlie held up his hands, palms to his ears. A flood of memories came back to me then with that one simple gesture. Years of living in his shadow, sleeping next to his snoring bulk, waking up with the sheets all over, eating across from his Neanderthal manners; the arguments, the fights, the pain; the months where I tried to block him out of my life, tried to pretend he didn't hurt me when he grabbed my hair, and tried to tell myself that I was single. Perhaps if we'd been able to have kids, things might have been different. Now he was holding his hands to his ears again.

"I'm sorry, Charlie, I …"

"Will you shut that fucking animal up? It's driving me mental!"

I peeked under the table. Carlo had backed himself into the furthest corner, behind Charlie's leg, so I had to push back my chair, bend down and crawl under to get at him.

"Shush baby, Mama's here." I held out my hand but the growling continued. "Come on, baby."

All the time, Charlie kept saying things like "Get that fucking rat away from me" and "Make him shut up," and shifting his legs around, only making things more difficult. It was only a matter of time before Carlo nipped him in the ankle.

I don't know why, but I started laughing.


Back at my rooms in the basement of the Bloor house, I fed Carlo before sorting out my own problems. I locked myself in the bathroom and wept while I ran the tub so that no one could hear me. Then I checked out the damage.

Never laugh at Charlie Jarvis. I should have known that. Not even from under the table. He doesn't take kindly to being laughed at.

Never has.

I wiped a path through the condensation on the mirror and saw it wasn't too bad. A black eye. A split lip. Some of the sutures behind my right ear had given way and the cheekbone implant had slipped, but that's always happening.

Mirror, mirror, on the wall …

I could hear him upstairs, doing the old buddy-buddy routine with Bob and Al. Clinking of glasses and loud guffaws of laughter. Fake. All of it. Fake.

Everything. The whole world. From start to finish. I was sick of it.

If I was built of stronger stuff, if I had some mettle to stand up to him, perhaps I could have worked Charlie's talents to our mutual benefit. At least mine. I could hire him out, take advantage of his violent streak. Live the life of Riley. But it'll never happen. I've never been anything but weak in Charlie's eyes.

He never saw my Wild West Ball.


I get these headaches occasionally. I know they're brought on by depression but I won't take valium like Marg. I don't believe in mixing. Usually, they go away after an hour or so. This one didn't. It changed into something worse. Not pain, but a kind of numbness creeping down my neck, bone by bone, taking me over, turning me into stone, into rock. A big, black rock.

There was a knock on the bathroom door. A flighty rappity-rap-rap. Marg.

"Bella? Are you all right in there? Bella?"


I rejoined the party upstairs just as the poker game took a short break. The drapes had been pulled open and a view of the city skyline dominated the room. It had stopped snowing and a million coloured lights were sparkling all the way from downtown.

It felt as if the furniture had been moved around in my absence, but of course it hadn't. It was the same wide expanse of golden carpet, the same couch, the same pictures on the walls. Even the TV was still playing *It's a Wonderful Life*. Nothing had changed.

"Ah, no!" yelled Charlie. "She's brought the fucking dog with her!"

Everyone laughed and I joined in. Marg put a hand on my shoulder.

"Don't take any notice," she whispered, handing me a margarita. "They're all drunk."

"Cheers."

I don't know how long I sat there by the TV, it felt like years. I know that I must have joined in the conversation, or at least part of me did. Bob was going on about moving to Casinoville and Charlie started on his Graceland stories. It was like being outside of myself, watching from another place. Every now and then I'd look up at the window and see the reflections of everyone having a gay old time. Family, friends and hangers-on. Merry Christmas. Drink up. Help your selfish.

"How about a mince tart, Bella? Have some nuts."

"No. Thank you."

"You have to eat something."

"Pour me another one of these then." I laughed.

"There she goes again," announced Charlie from the other side of the room, referring to my laugh. "The turkey special. Gobble-gobble-gobble!"

Bob slapped him on the back. "It's good to see you again, Charlie."

"Likewise, you old bastard."

"Starting up the business again, now that you're a free man?" Bob jangled coins in his pocket and rocked on his toes. "Ever thought of moving booze instead of smokes? There's a healthy market for it now, you know."

"No location, I'm afraid, Bob." Charlie shrugged. "I'm fresh out of real estate."

I tried to send Bob a look to say don't mention the Kennel Klub, but I knew it'd be offered. I have to give him credit, Charlie had done a wonderful job weaselling his way back into the family's good books.

"You can have the old Roxy as soon as Grandpa croaks." Bob gave me a repulsive grin. "That is, if Bella will sell it to you. Ha-ha-ha."

Thank Christ there was another ring at the doorbell just then. Fresh partiers arriving, no doubt. I heard a car honking in the driveway. Carlo started licking my ear where I'd tried to hide the latest suture problem, so I wasn't really paying attention when Pauline came in.

She was out of breath and still stoned out of her mind. She was in a panic, pumped so full of adrenaline that she had a wild-eyed focus. Marg sat her down on the couch and gave her a generous brandy. The womenfolk gravitated around her, cooing and clucking. I remember thinking "oh no, she's given herself another abortion."

Pauline took the Chivas Regal bottle from Marg's hand and poured herself another. We all waited for some form of announcement.

"You," she said, looking directly at me. "I have to talk to you."

She'd done something stupid and she needed me to back her up, I could tell. We played that Woody Allen nodding and pointing game for a while before I got sick of it.

"Just tell us what we're going to find out anyway, Pauline," I said. "You may as well."

"OK. Grandpa's dead."

The room went silent. The news was a surprise. Not entirely un-expected, but a surprise nonetheless. Everyone politely lowered their heads a few inches, or shuffled their feet a bit, thinking perhaps that they were doing the proper thing in showing a respectful silence for the dead. My first thoughts were about the club. I couldn't tell if old Mr Bloor checking out like this was good timing or bad. Especially with my ex-husband in the room. There was bound to be talk.

Charlie broke the silence. "So what's the bad news? Ha-ha!"

Pauline took another two fingers of brandy while Charlie let us know how funny his joke was.

"Brock's gone missing," she answered, quietly. "Smashed the door down and there's blood on the stairs."

That shut Charlie up.

Marg knew better than to ask Pauline if she'd even bothered to look for her son. Instead she wanted to know why he'd been left alone. That was when Pauline gave me that worried look again.

"You can't leave Brock Bloor by himself," chastised Marg. "We've been through this before, Pauline. And Grandpa doesn't count as a baby sitter!"

In a flash, I saw what Pauline wanted me to say.

"Cherry Beach left Brock by himself?!"

It wasn't that much of a lie. I knew that there had been, at one time, a sitter arrangement between them. But Pauline's been on a binge for the past three days and any deals with Cherry Beach have to be re-newed every twenty-four hours. Everyone knows that.

"Don't tell me Cherry Beach just left him with Grandpa?!"

Pauline's face went smooth as a balloon and she started to weep. The Chivas Regal had kicked in, giving everyone a chance to breathe.

What a to-do! Suggestions and questions filled the air. Al passed a flask of double malt around, while Marg, against Bob's wishes, wanted to call the police.

"This is family business, Marg."

"Yeah, call the fucking cops!" wailed Pauline, getting hysterical. "That fucking freak of nature ripped off my *Louis Vachon* luggage!"

Marg and I moved Pauline to the other room to lie down. We kept the door closed for ages and squeezed the full story out of her. At that point, I could have made a priest confess where he'd buried the choir-boys.

Knowledge, they say, is Power.


When we came back out, everyone started talking at once, wanting to know what had really happened, what they were going to do, suggestions as to where the kid might have gone, etc. Marg got into an organizing frame of mind, rashly put a call through to the lawyer and wanted to know who was going to pick up the old man's body. The car keys were miraculously found and the menfolk started arguing amongst themselves about who was going to do the driving.

"Are you sure he's dead, Marg?" asked Al. "I mean, mightn't Pauline have been mistaken?"

"Not by the way she tells it," said Marg.

Someone argued that Pauline had seemed rather high to them, which prompted Bob to snort in derision about the rotten-apple side of his family. The conversation got heated. I may have even put in my two-cents' worth, I can't remember. One of the lesser-acquainted-with-the-family visitors was quite shocked, but none of it surprised me. Old Mr Bloor's death didn't surprise me. Brock's running away didn't surprise me. Nor did Cherry Beach's transformation into the scape-goat of the night. Even Pauline getting so upset up about losing her *Louis Vachon* bag didn't surprise me. It was all shockingly predictable, knowing the individuals involved.

Of course, Charlie had the answer to all the problems. While Bob and Al were picking up the stiff, good ol' Charlie-Boy Jarvis was going to get hisself a posse together, go look for the kid, maybe rough up this Cherry Beach character while they're at it, if they could find her. Him. It. Whatever sex it was, he'd fucking well find it. Teach it a lesson. Since he'd lost a couple of rounds of poker it was Charlie's way of helping pay Bob back for the evening. Charlie-Boy Jarvis vowed, of course, to cover costs. Now *that* was one smart move on his part and I had to hand it to him.

"Whadya think Herman, you still renting your muscle these days?" He turned to his favourite crony and reached into his lumpy pocket as if for cash. "Wanna make a quick five hundred bucks?"

If I hadn't known that he was bluffing, that he didn't have a roll of bills in his pocket, that it was a pickle wrapped in a napkin I saw him stuff in there on the sly – well, if I hadn't known *that* – then I would have wondered where Charlie's negotiations were putting me in the big picture. Out in the cold, I bet, holding the short straw again.

I *did* know, however. I knew the creep was broke and I saw my window of opportunity.

"Oh, Charlie," I said, as if reminding him of a well-known fact. "I do the accounts now."


Knowledge, I say again, is Power.


Bob and Al are hovering at the door with their coats on, neither one willing to make the first move out of the house. They aren't too keen on dealing with the authorities and a dead body in the state they're in. They would much rather be coming with us to find Cherry Beach. They keep asking Marg what they should expect to find when they get to the apartment.

"Apparently his pacemaker flipped off," says Marg, clearing up some plates from the buffet table. She looks over at me for corroboration. "He was probably watching one of his programs, you know, the one where they tell you to put your hand on the screen?"

There is a stifled giggle from the corner. One of Bob's cousins, I believe.

"You mean ... you mean he was zapped by Christ?" Al's having trouble keeping a straight face. "Blown away by Jesus!"

We all laugh. A nervous relief kind of laugh. Charlie raises his glass. "Feeeeel the power of the Loooord!!"

Boy, do we ever get a good hoot out of that one. A real scream. The whole room explodes, we can't help ourselves. Tears roll down Marg's face. I know I must be chortling away merrily, myself. Even so, I can't help feeling sorry for the old bugger.

No. Not me. I can't feel anything. It's too funny to feel anything.

I look up. My cackling reflection in the window is a monster. A grotesque sham of a woman, lit by the golden lampshade and the flickering fireplace. And all around her, family, friends and hangers-on, their laughing faces distorted. Plasticine skins stretched over jutting bones. And inside? Nothing.

The creature in the window stands up. It's all hollow pretense. A barrier of glass that prevents us from ever getting near to ourselves.

I can't stop myself. Something grips me tight, controls me. I think it might be Charlie, but it isn't. It's me. I swing my arm back ...


I'm standing at one end of Main Street. Charlie-boy Cowboy Kid's at the other, in a crimson shirt and black Stetson. Bowlegged in the dust we stand, twenty paces away from each other. It feels as if I've been here forever.

I reach for my gun ...


In a distant room stands a woman in a red dress. Her face looks familiar. She holds a small lapdog in the crook of her hand ... that stupid, yapping fucking little dog ... she takes a stance, as if preparing herself to shoot from the hip ... takes aim at the end of Main Street ... at the golden, sparkling land beyond the glass.

*Pitch him OUT, Earl! O-U-T spells OUT!*

For the first time in days, I've got a craving for something sweet.

# 4 ... sunshine and security

Since Cherry Beach never intentionally breakfasts before noon, she's going to stay up all night to keep a morning appointment. For both Cherry and Liberty, this is unquestionable logic. According to its answering machine, the Lotto Centre is only going to be open between ten and one the next day. Cherry fears that she won't stay awake long enough. She may have to see Victor for help in the matter. She's already put in a call to his pager.

It's around four o'clock in the morning. Twenty minutes of being cooped up in her tiny room in the Belt 'n Buckle with Liberty and Rose is more than anyone could be expected to take in one lifetime, despite the attraction of room service. Luckily, the Thò Bò Vàng, a cross-pollinated exploration into Asian cuisine, two doors down the street, stays open twenty-four hours and – more importantly – is hospitable to early morning time-killers, on the proviso that something is purchased. Even though she can now afford everything on the menu twice over, Cherry orders her usual – #12 and a Special 99 – a plate of deep-fried spring rolls and a pot of vodka-laced green tea. Liberty goes for the Buddha's Feast, which would take any lesser vegetarian at least three days to guzzle their way through.

They sit in the corner booth at the back, the one with the large circular table and the worst view of the TV at the bar. They can hear the clicking tiles of an eternal mahjong game being played behind a bamboo curtain to their right. A heavily gelled fluorescent light punctuates this hidden activity by sputtering on and off as fortune takes it. A gang of kids have taken over the video machine in the corner.

A strip of flypaper hanging on the wall hasn't caught a single fly, although there are at least a half a dozen ready and able victims buzzing around the restaurant. A moth flutters around the paper, never touching it, almost acting as a sentry, warning others not to come too close. Cherry takes this a reminder that She who has dominion over creepy-crawlies can't be far away. 'Tis the season, after all.

Rose is no longer with them. She went home, saying that she wasn't feeling too well, after helping drop off Cherry's belongings at the hotel. The warehouse studio was history. First, Phoebe the roomie had been persuaded to take Rose's side, and then there had been the long-dreaded phone call from Robert Bloor, the head of the Bloor Empire, informing them that things were "up in the air" as far as the Kennel Klub was concerned and not to bother coming into work any more. The New Year's Eve Party was still on, since tickets had been sold, but for all intents and purposes, the Kennel Klub was being closed down, and did anyone know where that fucking Cherry Beach was hiding out? Nobody had grassed, but Rose thought it best if Cherry moved on; she didn't want the Bloors setting foot in her studio. At the Belt 'n Buckle, there had been an argument with Liberty over the use of the car (Rose wanted to make sure she could get to her family over the holidays), a nasty exchange about money, and then glum silence. When Cherry had invited Rose along for a bite to eat, she knew that the offer wouldn't be taken up.

So Cherry and Liberty went for spring rolls, installed themselves at their table and pulled out the *Louis Vachon*. Liberty works her way through more tickets. The scrapings fill up ashtray after ashtray, making them unpopular with the waiter. Cherry's muscles still ache from her marathon scratch-a-thon in the bathroom. She's agreed to give Liberty 10 per cent of everything – not including pop and pizza, of course.

Silver dust is getting into the scrambled tofu and bean sprouts, but Liberty doesn't seem to notice. She's scratching tickets and sorting the winners into piles on the table around her dinner plates. She keeps track of numbers on a napkin with columns of little ticks, neatly crossed in gates of fives. Hundreds of them. Liberty's face has taken on a greenish tinge, with golden reflections from the tickets wobbling across her brow, as she toils away. She is so engrossed in her new addiction that she hasn't dipped into her glue bag for hours.

While Liberty busies herself, Cherry scans through some newspapers she found by the door. She's looking for something – anything – that might give her an inkling about how dangerous it might be to cash in *XXXmas* lottery tickets at the Lotto Centre: a convenience store hold up perhaps, a daring break-in at Lotto Headquarters, even a highway pileup involving the delivery truck … nothing. Perhaps the papers aren't current enough. Perhaps the tickets haven't been missed. Yet.

Finders, keepers, she keeps telling herself. She hasn't done anything illegal.

The decision to risk going to the Lotto Centre to cash in a couple of the big winners is, however, not arrived at without discomfort. Cherry is understandably nervous, but they can't keep on pulling Operation Corner Store forever.

"They'll have just come back from their Christmas vacation, right?" argues Liberty, chasing a sprig of broccoli around her plate with her chopsticks. "And they'll be looking forward to a few more days off. Three hours? They won't be concentrating on their work."

Cherry has to agree that this sounds reasonable. It's the party season, after all, the Festival Week of Santa Calamity d'Oopsidaisy, and no one is going to be paying proper attention. It would be asking for trouble, however, to saunter in with a sackful of every ticket worth more than two hundred dollars; that would beg too many questions which neither Cherry nor Liberty are prepared to answer. So far, they have uncovered one twenty-five-thousand-dollar ticket, a fifteen-thousander and quite a few tens.

The more they discuss it, the more they realize that time is getting on. And the later it gets, the more obvious it gets that they might as well do it properly and cash in as many tickets as they dare. Even the big one, should they find it. Fuck it. Go for broke.

Victor arrives with no warning, as he so often does, and insinuates himself into the booth next to Liberty before either of them has a chance to stuff the tickets under their coats. He is, as usual, ripped out of his tree. He can't get his arms out of his coat, so he abandons the struggle, and wears it off the shoulder.

"*Bon Soir.*" Victor tries to get the attentions of the waiter as Cherry tries to get the attentions of Liberty. *Put them away.* Liberty rolls her eyes as if to say that Victor is so out of it that it doesn't matter. *Put them away yourself.* The menu arrives, a laminated card the size of a baseball bat and likely to do as much damage if Victor continues to wave it around with such abandon.

"Help yourself to a spring roll," offers Cherry.

"Buddha's Feast?" suggests Liberty.

"Nah. I need sugar right now, thanks. Glucose."

"Desserts are #40 to #57. Halfway down on the back."

After much musing, Victor risks his life with a #44 Special Thò Bò Vàng sundae, a milky green and blistering pink ice-squeamish beverage served with parasol and fruit rind in a tall glass that's been through the dishwasher three billion times and now has the opacity of a bathroom window. Someone should tell Victor that the number four is considered extremely unlucky throughout the East. Then again, maybe he already knows. He likes to live on the edge.

After a couple of slurps, Victor becomes slightly more coherent.

"Spare a smoke?"

"No way."

"Honest, Banje-girl," he whines, helping himself from Cherry's pack, "you're tighter than a choirboy's ass. What happened to your inheritance?"

Cherry tries to ignore him, but she can't pull her eyes away from his cigarette, as he burns his sundae parasol.

"What's this? What's this? More lottery tickets?"

"Hmmph."

"I wanna do some!" he squeals, like a kid wanting to help Mom in the kitchen. "I wanna!"

Liberty throws him a few to shut him up. Unfortunately, as becomes evident all too soon, Victor is so high, he may as well be scratching his balls. He has to be led step by step through the whole process, which takes up too much time, and becomes doubly infuriating when he wants to keep the winners for himself.

"It's mine," he insists. "You gave it to me, I scratched it, it's mine, mine, mine. Five hundred dollars."

"Keep it, then," says an exasperated Liberty after trying to rip it out of his fingers. "But no more, OK? Put them in their proper piles. We're following a system, here."

On the next ticket Victor scratches away at the wrong side. Then he tears a hole in another, going clear through to the table. He misses the bonus tree pot on half a dozen more, sorts a whole bunch into the wrong piles and then, once forbidden absolutely to play any more on no account again ever, starts dipping a ticket into his sundae – to see if it will melt, presumably. Like his brain cells.

"Stop it, Vic, for Chrissakes, smarten up," warns Liberty.

Victor stops abruptly, giving Liberty a strange, dissociated glare.

"Ale-ex," he whines. "You're spoiling the party."

He pouts, catches sight of his reflection in the mirrored walls, and then accentuates his pose to borderline pornography.

"What are you on, darling?" Cherry asks nicely. "Remind me to stay clear of it in the future."

"Alpha-Four," says Victor in a mechanical-demon voice. "It's new!"

"What?"

"Dimethoxy-Propylthioamphetamine. Do you want some? Sixty bucks a hit, but I can give you two for a hundred."

Cherry folds her newspaper and tosses it onto the ledge of the booth. "If I buy half a dozen, will you go away?"

Victor pulls a sour face. "So, are you girls lookin' or are you wasting my time?"

Cherry thinks for a second.

"Got any uppers without the shakes?" She suspects she's requesting the impossible. "Something to keep us awake until noon? Something for dealing with the authorities?"

Naturally, Victor can provide them with exactly what they need, no problem, and produces his pill canister to prove it. What he doesn't have, he boasts, he can get to them within a few hours. He sorts through half a dozen different capsules and pills, laying them out on the tabletop, chasing one around Liberty's plates.

"Combination's your best bet," he decides, coupling up the pills. "You could take your driver's exam on these. Your basic methamphetamines and beta-blockers. I use 'em for court appearances. Take the speed now, drop the blocks a few minutes before you need 'em. Four bucks a piece"

"Give us a dozen."

"That's forty-eight dough-la's, sister." The mathematical part of Victor's brain clearly works efficiently under any drugged circumstance.

"But you've already taken five hundred bucks of ours," Cherry reminds him.

"Yeah, yeah, yeah," drawls Victor. "How much did that ticket cost ya? Two bucks? So make it forty-six."

Fine. So that's the way he wants to play it. Cherry tosses him another couple of dozen tickets from her purse – to make up the price of the drugs. They all have torn corners.

"Scratch those," she mutters, preoccupied. "And keep them away from us when you're done, will you?"

She swallows a pill without any liquid, enjoying the trace of chalky residue down her throat. She stashes the rest of them in her purse. Liberty grabs a pill, sniffs it, pretends familiarity, then she too tucks it into her mouth. They are both too experienced at this game to react to the bitter taste.

Victor breaks into a little trumpet voluntary. "Hey, look at this! I'm a winner!"

"Impossible," says Cherry. That's a losing ticket. It has a torn corner.

But Victor isn't about to be discouraged. He congratulates himself, toasts himself, sprinkles himself with ice-cream sundae from the end of his straw, thanks an unseen deity, who may or may not be seated next to him, and swivels the ticket around, pushes it centre stage so that Cherry can see.

"Impossible, huh?" he gloats. "What's this then?"

He points with a damp finger to the bonus area, freshly scraped at the bottom of the *XXXmas* tree. He's right. He's a winner: the lucky recipient of a weekend's car rental, courtesy of A-Plus Rent-a-Car.


It can't be. It shouldn't be. But it is. A ticket bought from a corner store – a ticket with a corner torn off – is a winner. That changes everything. Well, a few things. Like how many possible jackpot winners have they thrown away to date? And how many more chances are being discounted on the erroneous theory that the only winners are in the *Louis Vachon*?

"We're gonna have to check all the ripped babies," says Liberty, swearing under her breath. "Wanna do it before or after the rest of 'em?"

"Who are you guys talkin' about?"

"Shaddup Aquaboy."

Cherry turns to Liberty. "I'll do it. You carry on with the others."

"OK. You're the boss."

Boss Cherry lugs out her stash of torn tickets gathered from Operation Corner Store and starts a-scratchin'. It's menial work and the ache in her shoulder blades returns. She imagines herself as one of those bank clerks forced to count statements at a table next to the supervisor. Soon, she has uncovered fifteen small-time winners in the stack of so-called losers. And one big prize of ten thousand bucks. Her logic shifts. She has to stop what she's doing and pinch her nose to prevent her cognition from escaping out the corners of her eyes.

This means that the Dixie find isn't exclusive, that they don't have *all* the winning *XXXmas* tickets; there are more out there in the big, bad world of corner stores and smoke shops. Other people may well be claiming their free pizzas, cashing in their ten- and twenty-dollar prizes and guzzling their free pops at this very moment. This logic, once explained, isn't lost on Liberty.

"The odds are still majorly in our favour," she insists, without looking up.

True. And what's more, the fact that others could well be turning up at the Lotto Centre tomorrow morning with their own *XXXmas* tickets worth two hundred dollars or more is a relief. It makes Cherry feel less conspicuous, more confident that she'll be able to get some redeemed without a hassle. Liberty and Cherry agree to try cashing in their top three: the twenty-five, the fifteen, and the ten-thousand-dollar ticket with the torn corner. Which should net fifty thousand dollars, thinks Cherry. Minus 10 per cent or so for Liberty, of course. Minus the two hundred dollars she paid for the warehouse space. Whatever.

At five o'clock in the morning, the late-night party shift arrives at the Thò Bò Vàng, fresh from the closing of Playland, Bliss, and other popular warehouse raves in the vicinity. High on an entire catalogue of designer togs, they scrunch up at the entrance, craning their necks and searching for empty booths. Cherry recognizes a few faces, a few outfits. Curses.

"Clear the tickets," she barks, scrabbling at the bags and sorted piles. "There's a crowd coming."

"Hey! I was working on that!" complains Liberty as Victor reaches over, snatches her napkin, screws it up and lobs it in the direction of the newcomers. Over by the cash, Paisley, in something resembling a deranged Catwoman outfit (complete with black rubber shoulder bag), jolts and looks around to see who threw the missile. Recognition is followed by a perky wave.

"Yoooo-hoooo!"

Cherry feels herself shrink inside. In vain she tries to remember the magic spell that will render her invisible, raise a force field around their booth, repel the invaders or turn the enemy into toadstools. No such luck. A procession is now on its way.

In the vanguard are Coady and Paisley, scattering promotional leaflets, invites for New Year's parties, raves and other events to all and sundry like rose petals. They are followed by the usual entourage of plastic fairies and neon goblins from the wrong side of the meadow, favoured nobility, trusted handmaidens, a couple of sacrificial neophytes and finally – in full seasonal splendour – Her Royal Heinie, Empress Estelle VII herself, in whiter-than-white faux fur with a matching headdress that makes her look like a giant puffball gone to seed. Table for six hundred, please.

Within seconds the Pride of Queens has condescended upon them, all horror-smiles and snow-damp wigs, bleary-eyed, mascara-smudged and tongues a-wag.

*Darling, Darling, Honey, Sugar, Baby, Sweetness, Douche-bag, Bitch, You cow ...*

Those who can, squeeze around the table, everyone shuffling bags and bums to make room. Her Royal Heinie and her select entourage take over the adjacent booth, settling in with the force of a caustic lavage, all glistening from the pounding of whichever underground swamp they've just emerged from. Voices are still raised unnaturally to compensate for disco-damaged eardrums. Coats are piled over the booth divides, extra chairs called for, menus are studied like tombstones, spring rolls ordered, someone spills a glass of water. Laughter.

Victor, knowing on which side his bread is buttered, deftly switches tables. His vacant space fills up immediately with two lesser children of the night, a couple who haven't risen high enough in the ranks to sit at the same table as royalty. Cherry doesn't recognize either of them.

"See you for afternoon Bingo at Dullby's?" reminds Paisley, shoving a photocopied flyer at Cherry. "It's a fundraiser, remember?"

Bingo Karaoke at Buzby's (aka Dullby's, Buzz Me's, Fuzzby's or just plain 'Eugh, do we have to go there?') is an institution. The bar houses the Royal Sceptre, Crown and Diamanté cushion in a dusty glass case by the coatcheck. Cherry has fond memories of performing her smash-hit lip-synch version of jungle medleys on Buzby's well-draped stage. Caution to all future performers: the fog-machine is on its own, unpredictable cycle, and is liable to smother your Amy Camus impersonation without warning.

"Sounds just great," says Cherry without enthusiasm, tossing the flyer to the tabletop. "I hope I can stay up for it."

Paisley takes this as encouragement and inundates her with an earful, eyeful and handful of every major event between now and the New Year. Cherry's eyes go blank. Paisley's rubberized shirt is doing a fair impersonation of the personality it encompasses: all flash and stretch, no substance. Paisley's white, white skin with its patches of sparse hair around the biceps looks as attractive as pickled testicles.

"What are you doin' for New Year's then, girl? Where you goin'?"

"I hadn't thought about it,"

"Gotta go somewhere. Come to the Mercantile Warehouse. It'll be FAB. Three DJ's are coming up from the Big Apple, and we got such a show... here, have a flyer."

Cherry's attention wanders to the handsome but volatile Zachary, the kept boy, who sits amongst the favoured entourage at the next table. He is glowering with those long-lashed purple eyes of his. O, Zachary, thinks Cherry. I know your secret. I know how old you are. Such a blatant overdose of Youth Gene is unfair, but there he is, sitting upright, drawn by a golden thread of juvenescence towards the heavens, his skin as supple as a nubile's, though his chronological age would have him peeling and sagging to the carpet. He's an ancient pearl in the oyster trough. Cherry feels a headache coming on as the blood rushes to her brain. O, Zachary. O, Zachary, you make my jaw go slackery.

"Who're you staring at, you Cheezy Bitch?"

"Cheezy Bitch! ... Cherry Beach!" Paisley gets the joke – loudly – and disintegrates into a rubbery cough.

Zachary's talking to her. Cherry gulps, strangely flattered by the attention. "I beg your pardon?"

"When am I going to get that two hundred dollars for the phone bill, girl?" Zachary's voice is a double-edged sword. "I hear you're loaded these days."

Cherry stabs at a spring roll, trying to soothe the pain in her heart with a chopstick. Zachary had smashed five of his cereal bowls in her honour six months ago and now every time they meet it's that damned phone bill. She considers squaring it up with him. But then, if she pays it off, there won't be anything left between them to masquerade as a relationship. Debts have their uses.

Still, there is such a thing as generosity of spirit and in a moment of dark relapse, Cherry catches a glimpse of her own. She reaches into her purse, counts out sixty dollars in small bills. Sixty-five. Seventy. No. Sixty-five.

"Witnesses! Witnesses!" shrieks Paisley as the money is ceremoniously handed over to Zachary. "Cherry Beach is paying off a debt!"

"Is this the infamous inheritance, honeychild?" inquires Her Royal Heinie with nail in cheek. "What are you hiding from your Auntie Ken?"

"Come on, Lib," mutters Cherry, juggling her bags and coat. "Let's get out of here."

*Darling, Darling, Honey, Sugar, Baby, Sweetness, Douche-bag, Bitch, You cow …*

"Well, it's a start," says Zachary, trailing the sixty-five dollars along his hairless chin and blowing Cherry a rare goodbye kiss. "Thanks, sister."

Cherry shudders on her way out. There's only so much incest she can take.


Waiting for the sun to rise was once an accidental daily ritual. That was back in Lotus Land, when she was no longer twenty-two but twenty-something and the arrival of the dawn was somehow more of a novelty than when she'd been five years younger. Sometime around the second or third powder-run of the evening, she'd look out the window and it would be, miraculously, lighter. By the time Apollo stuck his golden head over the mountains, the day was half over and it would be time to either go to bed or score some more drugs.

They were quite the gang back then, scraggy vampires all dressed in black, a hoard of undertakers down on their luck and on the prowl for new clients. Restaurants would mysteriously close at their approach; even instant-teller machines would shut their red-lidded eyes at them. They were refused service wherever they went, except at the hardcore sanctuaries which, of course, was where they hung out.

And the beach. They called it "the office" because everyone needs an office. They even slept there for about a week that summer, heads shaded by the logs, the sand getting into everything. That was the year they all woke up one evening with extreme sunstroke after having slept on the beach all day. They had slept right through toddlers stumbling over them, dogs sniffing through their stuff, and the sun beating down on their nightclub clothes, cooking them as surely as potatoes baked in their skins.

They didn't know what was wrong. They staggered around pitifully for a while, like a group of blind mice, squinting through their puffy eyes. Lily couldn't walk and had to be carried, first on shoulders, then piggybacked, and finally dragged behind them on a piece of cardboard. Granville retreated into poetic *absentia* more than was usual, even for him. Juan was convinced there had been something in the dope of the previous night that had permanently warped their vision. Others thought there had been a toxic spill out on the ocean during the day and they were now reaping the hallucinogenic benefits. Only Stanley, who was known to sometimes sunbathe on purpose, had some idea of what was ailing them. Since very little skin had actually been exposed, and any that had been was smothered in a quarter-inch of mortuary panstick, there was scant evidence on which to base this sunstroke theory, so it was remarkable that Stanley managed to convince them to go to the hospital at all.

They were all lumped together in Emergency, given an area to themselves where none of the staff dared go. They curtained themselves off and those who were still conscious searched the place for drugs and, not finding any, stocked up on sharps and swabs.

Lily vanished during the night in a magician's illusion. One moment she was lying on her gurney, her eyes crusting open, her mouth moaning Tom Waits lyrics as they drew the curtains around her; the next moment they pulled back the drapes to reveal an empty bed.

"We took her to the burns unit. She needed special care."

Cherry was suspicious. They never heard from Lily again. That was the year Cherry decided that Apollo has a poisonous kiss.

Back at the Belt 'n Buckle hotel room, Cherry and Liberty drop a couple more hits of speed. Liberty sits on the edge of the bed, jiggling her knee. "I don't trust that Victor as far as I can spit," she shakes out the side of her mouth. "He's going to tell them all about the tickets. You'll see."

"I wanted to hide them from him, remember?"

"Well, it's too late now." Liberty arranges piles of tickets around the bed in preparation for another onslaught of scratching. "The last thing I want to be doing is warding off club kids and drag queens."

"In a few hours we'll have fifty thousand smackeroos. Just think about that."

"Maybe a quarter of a million if I strike it lucky."

"Yeah, right."

The amphetamines coursing through Cherry's veins aren't doing much to help pass the time, or indeed, to help her relax. She tries to watch some television while Liberty rubs through a few more stacks of tickets. Nerves are very much on edge.

Finally, Cherry puts on her velour robe, which does the trick, swathing her in comfort. She curls up in a vinyl armchair and works intensely on her Cher wig. It matches a Pacific Rim medical card that she still has and which she's intending to use at the Lotto Centre if they ask her for ID. Nicola lives.

"Oh, o-o-o-o-o, OH!!" Liberty brandishes a ticket. "Fifty thousand dollars! Look! Fifty fucking thousand fucking dollars!!"

The two of them bounce around on the bed like a couple of teenagers until the manager comes to the door. That's quite the feat, getting a noise complaint at the Belt 'n Buckle.

By the time a cloudless dawn breaks, Liberty has spent over six hundred and fifty dollars on the Home Shopping Club using Rose's credit card number. And there's no more vodka.


By quarter to ten on an impossibly sunny morning, there is already a lineup outside the Lotto Centre. Having parked the Fury two blocks away, Cherry and Liberty join the waiting group of lucky winners. There are a couple dozen of them, a cross-section of just about every major demographic in the city: an old woman in a padded housecoat, a young executive-type in ski-wear, a middle-aged and balding plumber lookalike in blue coveralls. There is, however, no resemblance between these people and the cartoon caricatures of jubilant, dancing winners painted on the glass window of the Lotto Centre. Everyone in the lineup has an expression of fear. And greed. You can smell it.

"I did a polka right there in my kitchen," natters the woman in the housecoat to nobody in particular. "Just like the commercial, I tells ya."

The Lotto Centre is a smoked-glass corner of an underground shopping mall. Very corporate. The subway is to the right, a medical centre is to the left, a quartet of Victorian carollers is dead ahead, gathered around the fountain and ferns, preparing for the day over coffee and donuts. Two of them are dressed as giant singing mice, the oversize fibreglass jawless heads sitting on their laps, lending the group a definite pantomime *Guignol*. Hasn't Christmas Day come and gone? They must have contracts for the entire season.

Cherry is in disguise: dark glasses, army fatigues, Cher wig, her woolly mammoth coat – all raggedy pinks and purples – and black pumps. Mildred Pierce meets M*A*S*H*. She feels strangely relaxed. Before leaving the hotel, both she and Liberty took all of Victor's beta-blocking pills. The combination takes some getting used to.

Through the glass wall of the Centre, a bank of computer terminals and the frizzy silhouettes of bad perms can be seen. A man in a blue uniform unlocks the sliding door and the lucky winners lurch forward into a roped-off, snaking pathway.

"Man with a gun," says Liberty, nodding her head towards the security guard. "Not a good sign."

"Help yourself to coffee!" shouts a large woman in a purple cardigan. "It's free!"

"They're going to try and sell us real estate," whispers Cherry. "Real estate or steak knives, I just know it."

Liberty grunts, coughs, and almost falls over. Cherry understands. Victor's special cocktail is like surfing on alternating waves of nausea and apathy. Every so often great surges of tension build up in the small of the back, the nape of the neck or the calves, suddenly bursting through with a shudder that dissipates before it has a chance to properly establish itself. Satisfying it is not. It's like being titillated into a post-orgasmic snooze.

"Keep our place, will you?"

Cherry leaves the lineup, almost walks right into a mirrored pillar, helps herself to a plastic cup of powdery, sweet coffee, peruses a rack of leaflets and spends twenty seconds watching a video of handicapped children playing basketball. *The Lotto Corporation supports a variety of worthwhile charities.* When she returns to Liberty, she is engrossed in the information brochure on the *XXXmas Scratch'n Win* game.

"Where's *my* coffee, you selfish cow?" Liberty is getting the jitters again.

"Over there, by the fire exting…"

Her voice trails off. Her attention is caught by the headline in the brochure.

"Oh my …"

*First Prize: Half a Million Dollars.*

"So?" Liberty shrugs blankly and goes in search of coffee.

Cherry watches her go, but her thoughts are elsewhere.

Half a million dollars? *Five* hundred thousand? Not a quarter million, not two hundred and fifty thousand? Oh shit …

Cherry checks. Sure enough, three of the four winners she is about to present have *$250,000 Jackpot!* across the top in the familiar, glaring type. The other ticket, the one with a torn corner, reads *$500,000 Jackpot!* The typeface is identical, making the differing numbers hard to spot. Cherry didn't bring the other torn-corner tickets with her, but it seems fair to bet that they'll all have *$500,000 Jackpot* splattered across their faces.

Forgeries? Two differing games? Cherry scours the information brochure for any sign of two separate jackpots but doesn't find anything. What will happen if she presents the $250,000 tickets? How many alarm bells will go off? Did she bring enough cash with her to post bail?

Liberty is coasting on a wave of good humour when she returns with her coffee. She dismisses the problem as no big deal, that one hundred thousand dollars is worth trying for, that they've stayed up all night for this and she'll be hornswoggled (that's what she says: *hornswoggled*) if she's going to be duped out of her chance, especially since the torn-corner ticket is a measly, wimpy ten thousander.

"We'll say we were given them as Christmas presents, OK? They can't do anything to us. It's not like we printed them up ourselves, is it? Don't worry."

In a hectic, whispered argument, Cherry tries to be the voice of restraint, but Liberty isn't having any of it. What's the point, she maintains. Where's Cherry's fighting spirit? Eventually, Cherry agrees to risk all four tickets if only because her anarchic sensibilities have been challenged. Cherry feels as if she's dancing with the Devil, but Liberty assures her that she'll step in and save the day if they run into trouble. Obviously, she is on an invincible phase of her drug trip.

"I'll skewer the fuckers!" she smiles, brandishing her made-to-order knuckle duster that fits over her right hand. "Don't you worry 'bout a thing!"

A wave of complacency ribs up her body and Cherry surrenders herself to the fates.


"Congratulations, you're a big winner. Do you have any ID with you? Wow! Two winners! Isn't *that* lucky? Ha-ha-ha."

"Hold on a second, we have a couple more."

"Oh, wow."

The girl has hair so badly teased it could almost be described as taunted. With wide eyes, she takes the four winning tickets totalling one hundred thousand dollars and stares at them, laying them out in a line on her side of the partition. Then she punches something into a computer. Cherry feels her heart trying to beat against the drugs in her system. She fails to produce any adrenaline, so her brain takes over. The result is an asymptomatic paranoia.

Nothing is said about the discrepancy in the jackpot headlines.

Documents are bandied back and forth. Cherry hands over her Pacific Rim health card in the name of Nicola Beach. As far as she knows, it could still be current. She never loses any information from her mental Rolodex.

"This is out of province."

"Ye-es. I live on the West Coast."

"Oh. Just visiting?"

"For Christmas," nods Cherry. Liberty nods too.

More keypunching, followed by a yellow form pushed toward Cherry across the counter. All very friendly. "Can you fill this out for me, Nicola?"

Cherry grabs the allocated pen, fights with the attached cord and begins an exercise in creative writing. Halfway through, she glances up at the woman in the housecoat, who is laughing loudly and nervously as she goes through her own questionnaire.

"Oh my! You people want to know everything about me, don't you?!"

The form completed, Cherry shoves it back. The male or female boxes still anger her, even after all these years. It's a question that she's guaranteed to get wrong.

At least she's sure of getting the skill-testing question right. Fourteen.

"Did you take a photocopy of your tickets?" asks Miss Tease. "It's a good idea, you know. In case of any complications."

Complications? What kind of complications? "Er … no, I didn't," admits Cherry. "I didn't think it necessary."

"Well, I'm sure it'll be ju-uust fine." She smiles bitterly, checks the paperwork, rips off the copies, clips, folds and fastens it all with such speed and dexterity that it threatens to turn into an origami flamingo. She points Cherry in the direction of a lounge area by a magazine-strewn table. "Would you care to take a seat? We just have to run a security check, it shouldn't be too …"

A beep from her computer terminal grabs her attention.

"Hold on a second."

Cherry holds a second, holds her breath, holds her water. A sickening sensation claws at her stomach. She can smell the lining of her nose.

A fleeting puzzlement crosses the girl's face. She picks up three of the tickets, leaving the one with the torn corner. She examines them, flips them over, scrutinizes the small print. She retreats to consult her supervisor. Cherry's tongue refuses to detach itself from the roof of her mouth.

Miss Tease returns, the smile on her face replaced with one ten times worse than the one before. "No problem," she says, as if Cherry had voiced one a moment ago and she'd just waived it away. "The Major would just like to have a word with you. Our charity representative, Major Harbord. Okidoki?"

Cherry wishes she could panic. A charity representative would like a word with her? She nudges Liberty to be on her guard. The security-man-with-a-gun at the entrance is sitting, bored, on a stool. Between him and Cherry there are at least three hurdles of rope and two dozen people to clear in any bid for freedom. A camera blinks its red eye from up in the corner. Liberty finally looks worried, obviously thinking along the same lines as Cherry. *Do we make a run for it? Do we have enough energy? Do we wait?*

"Okidoki," agrees Cherry, in a strained voice. "Okidoki."

Cherry and Liberty are escorted by Miss Tease into an airy room on the other side of the security door, upstairs, and across some open-plan offices. Liberty is descending into a personal drug nightmare, muttering dire warnings of doom as the shakes start to rack her body. Cherry nudges her to shut the fuck up, but Liberty is beyond earthly contact and there are no more drugs left. Now, when it seems she most needs it, Cherry's security system is immobilized.

Major Harbord is a small Rubenesque man in his twilight years. He has childbearing hips, wears a moth-eaten mustard cardigan and combs the only remaining double strand of white hair across his pate. He looks like an apple gone soft in the corner of a fruit cellar.

He sits at one of three light-wood, upholstered chairs around a low coffee table by the window. An oil portrait of a serious man with a grey goatee hangs on the wall, scowling over the Major's shoulder. There is something lopsided about the Major that Cherry can't quite place, until she catches a glimpse of a salmon-pink plastic ankle as he stands to greet them. He has been fitted with a prosthetic limb.

At first there is an awkward silence. Whatever or whoever the Major was expecting, it certainly wasn't Cherry and Liberty.

"I'm sorry," apologizes the Major in a high, reedy alto. "I thought you were someone else."

"Me too," jokes Cherry.

Another uncomfortable few seconds makes it clear that they don't share the same sense of humour. The Major stutters, consults his notes and tries to cover his embarrassment.

"Nicola, then, is it?" He motions at the chairs for Cherry and Liberty to sit. The arrangement is calculatedly informal, almost friendly, but it's ruined by Liberty, who refuses to sit, choosing instead to hover uncomfortably around the desk, rummaging about in the pockets of her leather jacket. No, not your glue bag, thinks Cherry. Please, no.

"I'm Major Harbord." He's regained his composure and hands Cherry a business card. *Associated Benevolent Christian Charities Inc.* An address in a swank area of town. "You must be quite excited, eh? One hundred thousand dollars. That's a lot of money. Lucky you." He gives Liberty a worried grin and hands her a business card too. "Would you care to sit down, girlie?"

"No-thanks-I'll-stand."

As if to prove her independent non-girlie status, Liberty takes a whiff out of her glue bag as casually as if she were wiping her nose, then stuffs the bag back into her pocket. The scent of solvents wafts across the office.

Cherry shrugs. Silence.

"Well," says the Major, shaking off his incomprehension and flipping through a dog-eared file on his lap, at the top of which are the processed ticket forms from Miss Tease. "Well, well, well. This is most unusual, you understand, most unusual." His voice scrapes the wax from Cherry's eardrums. "Usually we get all our big winners within the first month of play, but you never can tell with folks, you know. They're as strange as strange can be."

He laughs. Cherry joins in, politely. Liberty cackles deliriously.

"Tell me," says the Major, interlacing his fingers and leaning back in his chair, "are you one of those people who believe that you not only have to have the right ticket but you have to scratch it at the right time for it to be a winner?"

"I beg your pardon?"

"Some people," he explains, pedantically, with his lopsided smile, "some people believe that the value hidden under the ticket's play surface can magically and mysteriously change right up to the very moment of scratching." He laughs again.

Cherry shrugs. It makes sense. In this world, nothing is for sure. One theory is as good as another. Heck, these days you never even know what sex anyone is until you take off the wrapping. Who can understand the machinations of Lady Luck? Or Santa Calamity, for that matter.

"Why do you ask?"

The Major holds up the old file folder. "Oh, I just wondered why you waited almost a year to cash in your winners. We'd almost closed the file."

A year? The tickets were from last year? Cherry feels her jaw drop.

"Luckily they're still good up until the last day of December. A few more days and you'd have missed it, eh?"

A year old? That would explain the jump in the jackpot figures: the prize had doubled from last year's game. It doesn't even begin to explain, though, how a bag of practically stale-dated tickets suddenly found themselves in the Dixie Laundromat.

"They … then … then they're still valid?" stutters Cherry.

"Ye-es." The Major is cautious. "But you're coming in just under the wire."

"Fine!" spurts Liberty. "Let's get on with it!"

The Major ignores this outburst and jerks his head at the portrait behind him.

"Our Chairman, the Admiral Bedford Bernard," he says, donning a pair of reading glasses, "would consider me very much remiss if I didn't tell you a little about our work before I authorize this cheque for you lucky people."

His timing is perfect. At the split second he mentions "cheque," one seems to materialize in his fingers. Cherry spots a row of attractive-looking noughts, before the cheque is whisked out of sight and stuffed back into the file.

"Are you aware of our work?" The Major produces a photograph album and flips the pages. Cherry's heart sinks. "The ABC Charities? This is Monica." He indicates some snapshots of a sickly looking girl. "Monica desperately needs a heart transplant. And here's Peter – isn't he a sweet little laddie?" Peter looks like a malnourished imp. "Peter has to spend half his life on a kidney machine."

Cherry's eyes glaze over. Her mind wanders as child after under-privileged child passes in front of her eyes. *And this is Frank – Frank was born both male and female but we couldn't give him the fucking operation he* really *needed because we don't approve of things like that.* As far as Cherry is concerned, the collection of pictures is nothing short of kiddie porn.

"Of course, any donation you make is tax-deductible." The Major places his hands together as if in prayer. "And you're under absolutely no obligation."

It's a scam. Catch the happy winners before the cheque gets handed over and hit the guilt button. Buy Monica a new heart.

"Well, to be honest," says Cherry, "I could use it all."

"One hundred thousand dollars?" The Major beams, exposing plastic teeth. "Aren't we being a bit greedy, Nicole?"

"Not at all. I have some debts to pay off." She pulls out a Camel to bolster her bravado.

"This is a non-smoking building," he screeches.

"I'm so sorry to hear that," retorts Cherry. She lights her cigarette and blows a volley of smoke at a potted plant. "Will that be all, or can we have our cheque now?"

The Major glares at her. Glares at the cigarette. Glares at Liberty.
"I'm afraid I can't do that."

"What?" Liberty lurches forward. "What did you say?!"

"We can't release the cheque."

"That's what I thought you said." Liberty's knee is beginning to shake.

"You failed the skill-testing question. Fourteen was last year's answer."

"So?" Cherry's eyelashes open to their fullest, innocent extent. "These are last year's tickets!"

"Where did you get them?" asks the Major suddenly. "Where did you get these tickets?"

"What about the ten grand one from this year?" demands Liberty. "Can't you release the cheque on that one?"

"That ticket is mutilated. Invalid. One of our hidden security features got torn off."

"Jesus!" explodes Liberty.

"Please. Keep your voice down." He takes a breath. "Where did you get these tickets?"

"Fuck you! Nobody tells me what to do, you fucking cocksucker!"

Like a magical abracadabra, at the mention of the word "cocksucker," the outer facade of the Major cracks open, revealing his inner dragon. He rises to his feet as the blood surges up his neck, his mouth opens like a hissing salamander's. Cherry buries her burning stub in the soil of some fern or another and stands, ready for action. Liberty is already screaming enough for both of them, heaping on the abuse with well-honed ease.

"...you frigid old pig farmer! ... fucking fascist! ..."

Now, that's not nice, thinks Cherry, no matter how accurate the epithets may be. The truth, which is both distasteful and pathetic, is that the Major is just another social manipulator masquerading as a philanthropist. Yes, a fucking fascist. Cherry can just imagine him at one of his Associated Benevolent Christian Charities board meetings, reporting on how many lucky winners he managed to bilk out of their hard-won cash that month. And of how he'd declared their prizes worthless if they'd declined to make a donation. He had never intended to give them their money at all. He had been hoping to get it all back, maybe placating them with a trip to Mexico or something.

"Give us our fucking money, you cancerous old testicle!" Liberty is on a roll. "We're not leaving until we get our cash!"

"Don't think I don't know your little game!" he shouts back. "Where are the rest of the tickets, eh? You've got the bag, haven't you? Where are the tickets? What have you done with them?!"

Cherry's brain flounders. He knows. The Associated Benevolent Christian Charities know about the missing tickets.

"What about them?" she interjects quickly, cutting Liberty off mid-cuss. Maybe they can make a deal.

"We want them back, of course." The Major is wild-eyed with indignation. "They shouldn't be circulating!"

"Are you offering a reward then, you poncy little prick?" Liberty doesn't realize that her continued invective is damaging any possible negotiations.

"I'll give you five hundred dollars for them," announces the Major. "You should think yourself lucky that I'm even considering it for people like you."

"People like you?!" Liberty explodes. "What do you mean, *People Like You?!*"

"Five hundred dollars?!" exclaims Cherry. "Is that all? You must be kidding!"

"Take it or leave it."

"You rotting toadstool," snarls Liberty, her lip curling with distaste.

Screw the money, thinks Cherry. It's going to be hard enough just getting out of here one piece. Or two pieces, if she includes Liberty.

The Major has made a decision. He strides awkwardly over to his desk, the prosthetic leg swinging, and snatches up the phone to call security.

"Patrick? In my office! Now! …"

Too late to abort the call, Liberty sweeps the phone, along with a pencil holder, a stapler and other sundry items off the desk with a loud crash. She brandishes her right fist, fully dressed in brass, in the Major's face.

"You're going to regret that, sir!" she snarls.

"You've done something terrible to Angus, haven't you?" he grates back, undaunted by the provocation.

"Angus? Who the fuck is Angus?"

Cherry's mind races, trying to think of a way out of this mess as Liberty runs down the list of abominations she would like to perform on the good Major's personage, leaving very little to the imagination. Cherry checks out her escape routes. The window? Risky. The door, through which Patrick, the security guard, is going to burst in a couple of seconds? Curses. This is it. They're trapped. And Liberty's self-control has vanished.

Cherry spots a connecting door to another office, half-hidden behind a potted fern. It's their only chance.

"C'mon, Lib," she says, grabbing the file folder containing the cheque from the table. "Let's get outta here!"

But Liberty doesn't want to be budged; she's having too much fun. She's become an immovable, ungainly lump of spurting blasphemy. In exasperation, Cherry puts all her weight behind a monstrous shove that sends Liberty blundering towards the door.

"Come on, you dumb dyke! This way!"

There isn't a second to be lost. Their getaway plan announced, Cherry reaches the door at the same time as the Major, both their hands grasping the doorknob in a complicated Masonic handshake. Liberty adds her bulk to the mess. There is a short, ugly struggle, with papers and fern branches flapping all over the place, but Liberty and Cherry are by far the stronger, they peel the Major's fingers one by one from the handle. They fling him backwards to the floor.

Cherry doesn't even look back.


They stumble through the office next door and then briskly walk back through the offices of the Lotto Centre, down the stairs, back through the main security door which is – luckily – a one-way contraption and, finally, back into the main lobby and the promise of freedom. They encounter no security guards, no screaming sirens, nor flashing red lights. Cherry shoves the slimming folder into the waistband of her fatigues. Liberty pauses for another massive hit of glue, transforming herself into a shaking, tweaking mass for a few valuable seconds. Cherry does her best to steer her towards the door.

"It's time to leave," she mutters. "We have to go. Now. Fast. Come on, Lib, you can do it."

Too late. Someone grabs her elbow. She spins around to come face to face with the security guard. Where had he sprung from?

"Not so fast, lady."

Cherry tries to shake him off, but his grip is too tight. She looks around for Liberty who seems to have vanished. Shit.

She flaps her free arm in an effort to escape, succeeding only in making things worse. Consternation reigns. The security guard pulls his weapon and the woman in the housecoat starts laughing. Another guard appears, running, from the rear of the Centre to join his colleague.

"I've got this one! You get the other one!"

"Which other one?"

"Crewcut and leather jacket! He was right there!"

"He?!" screams Liberty – outraged – suddenly jumping out from behind a mirrored pillar, a fire extinguisher in her hands. "I'm no fucking HE!!"

That's it. Liberty's flipped. She's prancing about from foot to foot like a prize boxer, brandishing her weapon. FOR ELECTRICAL AND CHEMICAL FIRES. Security guard number one, in a fit of good manners, starts to stammer his apologies, while his partner, realizing the impending disaster, stupidly releases Cherry and tries to edge towards Liberty. Bad move.

Liberty takes a step backwards, pulls the pin from the extinguisher, gives the whole thing a shake as if it were a can of whipped cream and squeezes the trigger, aiming the nozzle right at the guards' faces.

*Pfzzzzhh!*

An expanding jet of creamy foam blasts into the enemy. They are pushed backwards at least three feet. Their faces are obliterated with solidifying guck.

Cherry rallies every last ounce of her wits, dives out of the way of the spraying white foam, and crawls as fast as she can under the guide-ropes and between the feet of the winning public. She reaches the door, surfaces, pushes past a crimson-vested mouse-caroller, and sails into the freedom of the mall as Liberty's war cry echoes behind her.

"Scrambled tofu, ya fuckers! Scrambled fuckin' tofuuuuuu!!"

# 5 ... hard times

"*Shitting Hell, the car's been towed!*"

Liberty comes to a screeching halt and stands in utter dismay, squinting into the unbearably bright sunshine at the parking space which, up until a short while ago, contained her Fury. Tracks in the dirty slush betray recent activity and, about fifty yards toward the horizon, the tow-truck carrying her car turns the corner onto a one-way street to oblivion. Two more trucks are hitching up other offenders.

Cherry, bringing up the rear (there's only so fast you can run in heels), yells after her. "The tickets!"

"What?"

"The tickets are in the car! The *Louis Vachon!*"

"Shit!" Liberty kicks a parking meter. A crust of snow sprays onto the sidewalk. "I don't need this! I don't need this!"

Cherry glances behind her. A security guard rounds the end of the block.

"They're on to us!"

"Scrambled, boiled, fucking, poached!"

There's no time to waste bemoaning the situation. Cherry yanks Liberty by the elbow just in time to stop her pulling the glue bag out of her pocket, and steers her off the street towards a shadowy gap between two buildings. They careen down the narrow passageway, twisting and galloping sideways to check behind them. No sign of the guard. He must have missed the turning, but it won't take him long to figure it out. Slipping and sliding they run an obstacle course of frozen slush, potholes in the snow and some wicked icicles poking down from a fire escape.

"I ... could ... just kill you!" huffs Cherry, holding onto Liberty's jacket wings. "About to snort up when we're under attack!"

"Must be Victor's drugs," pants Liberty over her shoulder. "My timing's all fucked."

They burst out of the dim alleyway into a jam-packed street, slap bang crush into the congested heart of the Boxing week sale crowd. The morning sun beats down in stripes between buildings, bouncing off scarves, hats, shades. Stroboscopic woolens, acrylics, leather, quilted nylon, rabbit fur, and every so often a sprout of hair or frozen skin. People, people, everywhere people. Families, brothers, parents, uncles, kids and dogs. Some clans proudly carry their cardboard boxes of electronic equipment, while others wait in line to do the same. There is a huge lineup outside one music store, three deep and roping around a corner. Sleeping bags and camping stoves betray how long some of the pilgrims have been waiting for their complimentary CDs.

Cherry and Liberty scramble along the sidewalk, trying not to slip on the ice blisters and searching for a place to hide. It's not possible to dodge into a store – there's an obvious wait to get inside, thanks very much. They scurry past a giant window display of a hundred television screens all showing the same image: a blurry photograph of a little blond girl with pigtails. *Missing Child.* Finally, they find a bricked recess where they can duck out of sight behind a dumpster. They're safe for a few seconds, long enough to get their breath back.

"Make-over time."

Cherry pulls off her wig, turns her woolly mammoth coat inside out. It isn't officially reversible, but the brown shot-silk lining is a lot less conspicuous than the bright purples and pinks. Now the coat looks like a shiny fat suit.

"So what am I going to do?" Liberty surveys her leather jacket.

Cherry grabs the discarded wig, tucks the mass of curls into the cap and jams it, netting side out, over Liberty's crewcut skull. Instant Rasta. In the dumpster, Cherry finds an orange crate and an old pizza box.

"There we go. Come on."

"What?"

"Follow me. Hide your face. Act normal."

They return to the street, hiding behind their "purchases," blending in with the other happy box-toting consumers. A few yards away, the security guard is pacing with an annoyed expression, looking this way and that. He's covered in flecks of hardened foam that make him look as if he has a nasty yeast infection. They walk right past him, almost close enough to reach out and tickle him under the chin. He fails to recognize them. At the end of the block, Cherry gives her pizza box to some kid who tries to sell her a chocolate bar.

The come-down from the drugs is not pleasant. Colours become harsh, especially in the sunlight – jagged, painful. Liberty starts to panic when her glue bag no longer provides the lift she requires.

"I need something, bad," she complains. "I've gotta come down from – gotta change – *this*."

She dashes into a smoke shop, emerging seconds later with a can of butane *Liter-Gaz*. She pops the top, rips the adapter with her teeth and starts sucking back the fumes directly into her mouth.

"Shit, man, we're fucked," she blurts, a skin of frosting creeping over her lip. "This is bad karma. We're gonna be on News at Six. We're fucked."

"Will you just shut up?!"

Cherry finds a phone booth and leaves a message on Victor's pager to meet them back at the hotel in a couple of hours. That should be long enough for things to cool down and they'll need a little something to help them crash by then. Liberty is losing it big time; she's starting to see CSIS agents behind every garbage can, and if they don't get off the streets soon, the paranoia's going to spread to Cherry. The descent from beta-blocked Hell is pitiless. Cherry's eyeballs are flinching.

She tries to hail a cab, but is prevented – bodily – by Liberty who screams in a hoarse whisper that the police can trace cabs so easily and they all have radios, little green men sitting on their dashboards, and fuck it, they all belong to some weird cult. And don't even think about taking the subway with those subterranean cameras.

"You're always seeing them on CrimeStoppers, running through the turnstiles," she rasps. "Caught on tape and broadcast all over the city. We're fucked, man, I tell you. There goes my parole." Liberty starts to hyperventilate.

"How's about a drink? A few tequila shooters should calm you down."

"Washnegabarru di ffuggh."

"What?"

"Cabbage am kiroulli bastards."

Liberty isn't making any sense, not a jot. No matter how slowly or emphatically she speaks or how close she pushes her mouth into Cherry's face it all sounds like bubbling garbage. Communications have broken down.

"Crak a boodle pupwad tofu!"


Mercury, the god of communication, is particularly hostile toward those born into the care of Santa Calamity d'Oopsidaisy. It goes with the territory. For as long as she can remember, Cherry has been plagued with misunderstandings, crossed wires and erasures. There are whole sections in the scrapbook of Cherry's life that have been torn out, ripped from the spine, tossed in the incinerator, obliterated. The winged messenger throws guano into her ears, stymies the cognitive process with a twist of his caduceus. In times of crisis, Cherry can practically count on grabbing the wrong end of the stick – the end with the snake heads.

Take, for instance, the Halloween when she accidentally got herself locked inside one of those stolid, prison-like Art Deco-ish apartment buildings downtown. That had all been a fiasco from beginning to end. They were intending to rent a car, drive the three-hundred-and-thirty-odd miles to the Fright Ball of the Year and generally were expecting to whoop it up valiantly in the *Ville de Party*.

"I'll pick you up in half an hour," said her roomie and best friend at the time – dressed as the Invisible Man – on his way out the door. "I'll buzz you."

Ten minutes later, Cherry remembered that he couldn't buzz her – the phone was cut off. Deciding to go downstairs to wait in the lobby for her ride, she discovered that her friend, the invisible man, had inadvertently flipped the deadbolt when he'd left. She didn't have a spare key and there was no latch on the inside. The door was at least three inches thick with years of sturdy gloss paint. The lock withstood picking, even from an expert hairpin twister such as herself. Some trick but no treat.

Banging on the door and yelling for help was a waste of time; it was one of those buildings where that kind of behaviour was the norm. Cherry knew it well. She had worked her way through every available couch from the basement up and, by then, was banned for life by the management. Her roomie was not far behind. He was nearly two months in arrears with the rent and hydro, and had only just staved off eviction with a couple of postdated cheques. Cherry's status in the building was, therefore, tenuous to say the least.

She spent a couple of hours standing at the door in her Ann of Gangrene Gables costume, with her eye pressed up against the peephole, watching and waiting for the invisible man to come down the hall and rescue her.

"Where has that little fuck gone to? He'd better not have left without me."

In fisheye distortion, she saw a few witches, a couple of vampires and a staggering Joan of Arc with a moustache. Begging for help only sent people even faster on their ways – except for the Joan of Arc, who stopped for a while, head turned to the heavens in transcendent bewilderment. Eventually Cherry gave up trying to communicate with Saint Joan through the door, went into the kitchen and fixed herself a Bloody Mary before tossing her pigtails into the sink.

"Face the facts, girl," she told herself. "You've been left behind."

Halloween was ruined. She was five floors above street level and trapped. One peek outside at the howling wind convinced her not to try any Emma Peel escape shenanigans. There was no balcony, just a nasty sixty-foot drop or so from the window to the laundry-room level in the basement. It was too risky considering the way her luck was running.

At least she still had cable television and half a bottle of vodka. She turned on the popcorn machine and settled on the couch to wait for the invisible man to return.

"I said: Two for Screen 2 please. You do accept these here, don't you?"

"I don't think so, sir." The attendant curls his lip at the excrement that dares to beg admittance to his fine establishment. OK, thinks Cherry, so the *Liter-Gaz* is a tad conspicuous, but there's no need to act like a prick just because you have a uniform one step up from a burger boy's.

"We haven't had a scratch and win promotion here for a lo-ong time."

Right. Of course. Last year. Cherry flips the ticket over, searches blindly amongst the small type before triumphantly stabbing her nail at one particular line.

"Look! They're valid up until the end of the week!"

It's right there in black and white, but don't you know it, the manager has to be called over for confirmation, which he eventually gives when confronted with such irrefutable evidence, and they are in. For free.

"This is a family show, you know," the attendant spits after them. "You'd better not cause any trouble."

The audacity! Cherry gives him a withering look, one of her "I never forget a bad attitude" looks. Then she immediately wipes him from her memory banks. Swoosh. Gone! He might as well never have existed. That'll teach him.

Screen 2 is down the hallway to the left, according to the instructions given to them by an adenoidal youth who has been at his job two weeks too long. Consequently, after loading up with snacks, Cherry steers Liberty up the escalators and to the right. Screen 5. The theatre is empty, dark. Slides of Hollywood Trivia are being projected onto the screen. The perfect chill pad.

They make themselves as comfortable as is possible in the back row, Liberty swinging her legs over the seat in front of her, head against the partition, can of *Liter-Gaz* clenched between her teeth. Her eyes glaze over. Cherry shuts everything out, calms down, cools out. Grabs a few z's.

Breathe. Breathe.

She is nudged awake after only a few minutes.

"Kids!" whispers Liberty, finally coherent. "We're being invaded!"

Cherry moans and rouses herself. Sure enough, the place is filling up with five- to seven-year-olds. Not a single adult can be seen; this must be the holding tank while Ma and Pa shop the sales. Cherry groans as the laughing chatter grows louder.

"What do we do? Should we stick it out?"

The film starts – an animated version of yet another Hans Christian Andersen story or something. Rumplestiltskin with singing mice. The kids don't seem to be watching it. Popcorn, paper airplanes, screwed-up napkins and ice cubes are flying through the air. It's a party, but Cherry isn't in the mood.

"Come on."

She drags Liberty down the aisle and out the emergency exit.

"I was watching that!" There's no pleasing Liberty. "Now I'll never know how it ends."


On the second day of captivity on the fifth floor, Cherry started tossing paper airplanes out of the bathroom window in an attempt to draw attention to her predicament. *Help! Trapped on the 5th Floor!* She needn't have bothered. Peeking over the sill while balanced on top of the laundry basket, she saw that there was too much other camouflaging litter left over from Halloween – trails of toilet paper and other carnival crap in the trees – for hers to be noticed. She felt like Joan Crawford in *Whatever Happened to Baby Jane?* The wind and rain assumed the Bette Davis role, carrying her pleas for help into the tree-tops where they are probably still caught to this day.

There were a couple of close calls. A man out walking his dog picked up one of her airplanes, but he didn't bother to open it up before winging it into the air for Rover to catch and mulch in his jaws. Another time, some tiny bobble of a woman chased one down the street.

"Yes!" screamed Cherry, waving her hand frantically out of the window. "Up here! Up here!"

Clutching the unfolded page of the TV guide that bore Cherry's lipstick scrawl, the woman went into a phone booth and ten minutes later a police car drew up outside the building opposite. With a sinking heart, Cherry realized she'd forgotten to write the address on the paper.

The police car drove away without anyone ever looking up in her direction. She watched the whole thing, the shrugging shoulders, the squinting looks at every building on the street except hers. She could almost hear the conversation. "Damn kids. Must be a Halloween prank."

She emptied the bathroom cabinet out of the window before realizing that her situation was hopeless. At that time of year no one would take her seriously. She may as well have been tossing eggs.

Not long after she gave up on the whole prospect of being rescued, a pigeon came and sat on the windowsill, almost as if in mockery of her attempts. It was an emissary from either Santa Calamity or Mercury, she was certain, but she couldn't decide from which. It was creepy. It just sat there, cocking its head first one way then the other, staring at her with its little pink eye, a cruel smile twisting along its beak. She went into the living room, closed the drapes and tried to ignore it.

After the popcorn gave out on the second evening, she ate her way through the meagre remnants in the fridge: a crust of bread and a jar of pickles. Finally there was only a head of wilting cabbage and a bottle of catsup left. Oh yes, and a box of baking soda. Ballerina diet.

Cherry kept eyeing the air vent in the bathroom, set high in the wall above the clawfoot tub, wondering how long it would take to slim down enough to squeeze through. It was about two feet square and (like most fittings in the apartment) painted over to such an extent that the original wrought iron *fleurs-de-lys* were almost unrecognizable. Lowering herself out of the window on knotted bed sheets began to look like the only way out, except that she was convinced by this time that there were hundreds of pigeons waiting to peck her eyes out should she make the attempt. And the duvet cover and the handful of towels available to tie together wouldn't have gotten her far.

What with all that time to herself, her mind began to wander. Inevitably, in her darker moments, Cherry confronted the question of whether she was going crazy. Her life was so different from those around her, her understanding of reality so removed from what so manifestly was, that in this time of stagnant crisis, it began to get to her. If she had been made of stronger stuff, she would have flung herself to the street below and put an end to it all right there. Instead, she watched reruns of *The Prisoner* and fell asleep on the couch.

On the fourth day she was awakened by a pounding on the door. Once she had ascertained that her heart wasn't trying to escape from her ribcage, or that the pigeons hadn't somehow managed to break into the apartment, she crawled over to where the noise was coming from.

"Mmmphi rubble bumpht!"

Somehow she managed to translate the muffled voice that reached her through the door, but then, she'd heard that pattern of syllables many times before in her life, in many different accents. It was the manager of the building. The rent cheque had bounced.

It's still blindingly bright outside. Liberty and Cherry cut through the park. There is a peculiar smell of summer, the dustiness of a polluted August in December. The temperature is positively balmy. The sun is so hot the sidewalk is dry, and the melting snow is caked with dirt. Fallen leaves left over from autumn emerge from piles of blackened ice, their brittle brown skins reaching for the sun, disintegrating into powder at a touch, in imitation of a commercial for hand lotion. A few plastic shopping bags flap about in the mild breeze like morose sea-gulls. Some of the many folk out to work off their Christmas gluttonies swelter uncomfortably beneath new scarves and hats while others ride around on bicycles taking full advantage of this hiatus from the cold. Fledgling in-line skaters in brand new skates file by, half-squatting with their inexperience.

Cherry has given up trying to get ahold of Victor. She's stopped at every phone for the past few blocks only to get an out-of-service recording. Maybe he's been busted for dealing over the airwaves again. Maybe Santa Calamity has zapped his pager.

"Let's go back to the hotel."

"Let's get my car out of hock."

Cherry and Liberty stroll along in mutual disagreement for a while, dazed, disoriented by the sunshine, unable to decide in which direction to go. It gets too hot for the woolly mammoth coat and the Cher wig (either inside-out or rightside-in), so these accouterments get carried along like errant children. Thank god for sunglasses! The shades afford some form of night vision at least.

They find themselves in an unfamiliar area of town, discover a cemetery that presents itself like a secret evergreen garden behind a row of houses, sit on a bench, finish off their popcorn and listen to the birds debate the arrival of spring. If it wasn't for mankind's regimented calendar, the birds might have a point. As it is, the sun laughingly joins in with the argument, purposefully confusing the issue.

"Aw, look," coos Liberty, pointing to a tiny little gravestone. "Someone buried their dog next to them."

"Hmmph."

The effects of the drugs have levelled out, although there is a definite feeling of disassociation from the world. From her place on the bench, Cherry feels – for an instant – suspended above her body, removed from her problems, looking down upon herself as if through other eyes. This could be the onset of a nervous breakdown, she tells herself; she's heard as much. It could be the ghosts of dead people in the cemetery cajoling her morbid spirit to join them. It's probably the drugs.

But as much as she tries to uncover any hidden message from her psyche, nothing is revealed. Life is silent. Everything hurts: her lungs, her head, her pride. Part of her wants to run back to the Lotto Centre, demand that they cash her winning tickets and damn the consequences. She feels sure that she'd been subjected to discrimination. Another part just wants to stay sitting in the warm sunshine on that bench in the cemetery, clutching her purse to her stomach, watching the sparrows, thinking of tossing them a few dollars to get themselves something decent to eat instead of golden-topped corn.

"How much will it cost to get my car out of hock, do you know?"

Cherry ignores the question; she wouldn't respond even if she knew the answer. Liberty is beginning to grate. Instead, she flips through the folder she nabbed from the Major's office. Sheet after sheet of authorizations to deduct moneys from winning cheques – that bastard sure knows how to bilk 'em. Photocopies of tickets, carbon copies of forms and a log of winners and amounts stapled to the inside cover. Casting her eye down this list, Cherry sees that the jackpot hasn't yet been claimed. Good. That means it's still likely to be in the *Louis Vachon*.

What is she thinking? There's no way to cash it in. The Major was offering a mere five hundred bones for the safe return of *all* the tickets. It's so disappointing, thinks Cherry. Especially since the tickets are technically still valid, albeit for only a few more days. There's nothing she can do. The only solution she can think of is to find a lawyer and get them to sort it out, but the mere idea makes her skin crawl. Or she could take it straight to the top of the Lotto ladder. What was his name again? Admiral Thingy, the scowling Chairman of the portrait. It's a possibility. She commits the address of the ABC Charities from the business card into her mental Rolodex for future reference, should she need it.

"Hey, look!"

In the back of the file there's the cheque that had been waved momentarily in her face.

*Pay to the Order of Associated Benevolent Christian Charities Inc. Ten Thousand Dollars.*

The slimy cheats. It hadn't been for her at all. It had been one of their own claw-back cheques, with which they had hoped to scoop their losses straight back into the guzzling needs of lung machines and heart transplants. With a grim smile, Cherry realizes that even though there's no way on God's earth that she could cash the damn thing in, there is at least some compensation.

She burns it.


The air vent in the bathroom wasn't too small to accommodate Cherry once she'd been starved of cigarettes for a few days. Reaching it to get the cover down, however, was a problem – she'd used most of the furniture to barricade the door against the manager's bogeymen and the laundry basket didn't reach. Finally, she tipped the couch into the tub, tilted it up against the wall, making a ramp to the vent. She bent a spoon and splintered four fingernails unscrewing the grille, but unscrew it she did and forced first a garbage bag of essential Cherry-stuff and then herself into the confining space, losing a shoe and scraping her ankle in the process.

It was ridiculously tight, dark and dusty in the shaft. Inch. By inch. By painful, slow inch she wriggled forwards behind her bag of essentials. Progress was almost nonexistent. Behind her, she could hear an electrical whine at the door – probably a drill of some kind. She wasn't going to stay and find out. No. She was on her merry way; the invisible man's bounced cheque had forced her into action.

She couldn't see her nose in front of her, she kept hoping the shaft wouldn't suddenly dip down and drop her six stories into the garbage chute. Her mind was in such a state that she believed something like that could happen merely by her thinking it. Careful what you think – it might just come true.

For what seemed like hours, she crawled into the dark void. Her shoulders only just fit, her elbows and knees were getting raw. Eventually, the narrow passageway turned into one slightly more spacious, enough so that she could lift her chin to catch a glimmer of light up ahead, around the edges of her garbage bag. She could crawl faster now, although her entire left side had gone numb from lack of circulation. She passed further turn offs which were as small as the original claustrovent, so she ignored them, she just gritted her teeth and hoped for the best, worming her way towards the light.

Finally, she reached the grille which, as luck would have it, pushed away easily. The screws had rusted and her travelling beauty parlour dropped out of sight. Phew!

She squirmed forwards and stuck out her head to see whose bathroom she was about to break into. A blast of wind and rain hit her in the face. Oops.

The view was magnificent. She could almost see the lake.


The car pound is, suspiciously, one of the hardest places to get to in the city. It's down by the water, beyond the industrial district, next to a wrecking yard. How convenient. By the time they arrive, the afternoon is still sunny, but the temperature is plummeting. Cherry's pinched toes are grinding themselves into numbness. She would much prefer to be on her way back to the hotel, but lacks the appropriate diplomatic skills to get through to her companion. Liberty hasn't said a word to her for blocks.

The one-storey, prefabricated hut that acts as the administrative offices for both the towing company and the wreckers is the size of a large billiards table. Security is at a maximum even as they approach: closed-circuit cameras, sliding metal gates, razor wire, floodlights. Out front, there is a parking lot, complete with warning notices as to when and when not to park. *One hour maximum.* As she trudges the final stretch towards the office, Cherry notes the unspoken implication: Got any more cars we can take? A couple of tow trucks bearing fresh kill pass them as they approach. Welcome to the world of the vehicle vultures.

The office is divided into two unequal sections by a thick sheet of what looks like bulletproof glass. One side is reserved for the comfort of the staff, while the other – for the angry public – is about the size of a telephone booth. Cherry squeezes inside, after Liberty. It's hard to breathe and there is only enough room to reach into a purse or back pocket, pull out a wallet and push money through a turnstile embedded in the window. Two people are lounging in the relative luxury on the other side of the partition: a girl of about sixteen, with blotchy purple hair, is sitting at a computer and a heavy, bearded biker in full leathers who is banging away at a coffee machine. They both smoke furiously – the stress level of the job must be high. At least they have enough room to swing their arms. Heck, if they pushed their desks to the wall, they could stage a puppet show.

On Cherry's side of the transparent iron curtain, every square inch of wall space is taken up with notices, all of them quoting dollar figures:

$160 basic charge to get your vehicle out of hock; $40 per diem for storage; $20 to recharge a dead battery; 15% exchange rate on the American dollar, etc., etc. Never having owned a car, let alone claimed one from this prison, Cherry realizes she has stumbled across an underground empire of legalized pirates, kissing cousins to the trolls and gnomes who inhabit the deeper recesses of the woods where – as your mother warned – you are never allowed to roam.

"She's cute," says Liberty, eyeing the girl at the computer. "Nice piercings."

Yeah, right, thinks Cherry. That's all they need right now: a love interest.

"Excuse me." She raps on the glass. "Hello in there."

With jaded boredom, the girl slopes towards them. Liberty pushes forward, licking her palms to smooth her crewcut. Coifed to her satisfaction, she places both arms firmly on the counter, framing the speak-a-fone grille, effectively squishing Cherry into a corner of the compartment. The girl arrives, tossing her head like some purple piebald pony. She wears a necklace of candy-coloured letters spelling out HAZEL.

"Hi."

"Hi, yourself. Hazel, is it? Or is that your girlfriend's name?"

"It's mine. Can I help you?"

"That depends."

"Oh yeah?" Hazel smiles, shyly. Blushes.

For the umpteenth time in the last few hours, Cherry wishes she'd taken a cab back to the hotel instead of trailing along with Liberty like a spare set of boobs at a lesbian wedding. At least she'd have more elbowroom; maybe she'd have even showered, dined and sampled some of Victor's sleep aids by now. The things she does for her friends. She must be stacking up those karma points for sure.

"Liberty?" says Hazel, checking out the driver's license. "Your name's really Liberty? Cool."

"Stands for absolute freedom, you know."

"Let's just get the car, OK Lib?"

Liberty ignores Cherry, too intent on her new conquest. "What can I say? My parents were hippies." She props her head on her elbow, casually wiggles her fingerstub in greeting. Hazel's interest is piqued by the deformity.

"Ow, did that hurt? What happened to you?"

At this prompting, Liberty launches into a variation on the story of how she'd lost her finger, this one involving a Doberman pinscher and a Harley-Davidson. Usually an avid admirer of creative histories, Cherry groans and clutches her purse to her stomach, raises her eyes to the ceiling and starts slowly counting to a thousand.

"But that's dangerous!" squeals Hazel at one point. "You could have lost your entire arm!"

Cherry smokes three cigarettes in a row. This prison-visit love scene has gone on long enough. She huffs, she puffs, edges closer to the window and gets kicked smartly in the shins.

"Liberty …" She is about to say something cruel and heartless. Instead, she bites her tongue and retreats back into her corner. If she says anything right now, much as she'd love to, she might just get a pummeling for her troubles. Liberty is fast becoming a first-class annoyance, and as Cherry lets her mind wander over the events of the past couple of days, she comes to the conclusion that life, as she knows it, will be much better off unaccompanied by her bodyguard.

Friendship, for Cherry, has always been a transient entertainment.


The invisible man finally turned up, five days after his departure, to find his apartment under siege, the door ripped off its hinges, furniture everywhere and a hermaphrodite jammed in the air vent. Upon interrogation by the management and police, he denied all knowledge of Cherry's existence – he'd never seen her before, and certainly couldn't explain why she'd been in his apartment. He had been out of town for Halloween, he said, and knew nothing, knew nothing, knew nothing.

Cherry, once they'd extracted her from the building's respiratory tract, pleaded no contest to a deferred charge of mischief. She was given six months' community service. Nine weeks before her time was up, she skipped town, changed her wig and her name, and to this day has problems keeping her cool in confined spaces.

On occasion she has bumped into the invisible man in one club or another, the circuit being what it is. He may as well not take up any space at all. She can't even remember his name.

The long process of retrieving the car from the pound finally nears completion. It's taken nearly forty minutes and the sun has finally had enough, sinking out of sight behind the wrecker's yard in a magnificent visual headache. Cherry realizes that she hasn't slept in – how many hours is it now?

"There you go," says Hazel, referring to her computer screen. "Aisle K. That'll be six thousand dollars. Cash or credit card?"

"Six thousand …?"

"Just joking," laughs Hazel, pleased that she's managed to pull one over on Liberty. "It's only two hundred."

Oh, ha-ha, thinks Cherry.

"Babe." Liberty nudges Cherry painfully in the ribs, tugs on her purse handles. "Babe, will ya pay the young lady for me?"

Cherry has never liked being called babe. Never.

"What with?"

Liberty is suddenly worried, tries to hide her concern from Hazel. "You did bring the money, right? Don't say you left it at the hotel!"

"Just joking, *babe*." Cherry swings her purse onto the counter, dislodging Liberty's elbow. "Oops, sorry! Let's see … I *think* I've got enough here."

She knows full well that she does. She'd set aside five hundred dollars for that day, leaving the remaining six and a half thousand or so safely hidden back at the Belt 'n Buckle. Five hundred dollars to cover emergencies like, maybe, bail or bribery. It's a good thing she came prepared.

She counts out two hundred happy, smiling bucks into the little hatchway. Then she rifles off a couple of hundred more and hands it to Liberty. Along with the two hundred for the car and the two hundred for the deposit on the studio that comes to six hundred in total. Ten per cent of six thousand.

"There you go. That should cover everything." She stoops to rescue her Cher wig from the floor, stuffs it into her purse, then opens the door, letting in a cold blast of air. "I'm off to find Victor."

"Hey!" For the first time in what seems like hours, Liberty shifts her attentions away from the window. "Cherry?!"

"What!"

"Wait up 'til I get the car back."

"No, thanks. I'm off."

"Don't be stupid, Cherry."

"I think," says Cherry, trying to rein in her temper. "I think I'm in the way."

"I'm just being sociable, for Chrissakes." Liberty turns back to Hazel. "What time you get off work, doll?"

Hazel turns to consult the clock on the wall behind her, clearly not bothered at all by being likened to a plastic plaything.

"Half an hour."

Cherry holds out her hand.

"Give me your keys," she sighs. "I'll go wait in the car."


"Lousy, bug-eyed lesbians!"

Cherry curses without thought or consideration as she wanders through the pound looking for the Plymouth Fury. She's miserable and it's cold, despite the anger that fumes through her gritted teeth. Aisle K is a fair distance, but she can do with the hike.

Those two lovebirds were making her nauseous. The cooing and the laughing, the oggle-eyes and the sparkle, sparkle. It was all too much for a Natural Born Spinster such as herself. It's just as well there was a glass partition preventing them from furthering the course of their desires. Young love. How repulsive. Cherry trudges along, indulging in a poverty of spirit she hasn't known for at least six months. Unseeing, she passes Aisle E, Aisle F ...

She is beyond tired. She's exhausted. The kind of exhaustion that's gone over the edge; she knows she'll be unable to sleep without pharmaceutical help. It's no longer possible for her to tell if it's snowing, or whether she's seeing spots before her eyes. It's imperative that she get in touch with Victor, otherwise she'll be hallucinating herself into an iceberg and she'll forget who she is. And right now, after years of gender-hopping and alias-flipping, she's happy being Cherry Beach, thank you very much. It's taken her long enough to arrive at an identity she can feel at home with.

"Ruddy dykes!"

The search for the Plymouth Fury in Aisle K turns into something not unlike trying to find someone's plot in a graveyard. You know it's around here somewhere – you've even gotten directions from the curate – but you still have to look at each and every slab to find the one you're looking for.

There it is. A ticket's been slipped under the windshield wiper –

another sixty dollars for the parking violation. She leaves the yellow slip where it is. Liberty can deal with that one herself, she thinks, as she opens the door and gets behind the wheel. The seat is cold, the inside of the car quiet. Everything stinks of grease and gasoline.

"Crazy glue-sniffin' muff diver! Why does everyone think copulation is the goal of all?!"

She turns the key in the ignition to warm up both the engine and the interior, feeling like a grave robber. *I'll go sit in the car*, she'd said. Screw it – now that she's here, she doesn't want to sit around in this outdoor mausoleum for half an hour waiting for *them*. She could end up in the wrecker's yard before they arrive. She has a better idea. She'll drive back to the gate and idle the car outside the office where they can see her.

The *Louis Vachon* is in the back seat, half obscured by chip packets and candy wrappers. She swings it over to the front and stabs at the chunky pushbutton transmission on the dashboard that reminds her of a kitchen blender. Drive. Reverse. Pulverize. The Fury gives a pneumatic splutter before lurching off slowly down the wide lanes between the cars, towards the exit. It's a while since Cherry's driven a vehicle, so it takes a minute or two to get the hang of navigating the old boat.

As she trundles around the corner to the homestretch, she spots something out of the corner of her eye. She brakes, pulling the car to a halt. Reverses. Rolls down the window. Now isn't that interesting ...

It's a van.

Nothing special about that. There is a handful of vans and trucks scattered throughout the yard. But this one in particular catches her eye. It's a white van with a cartoon bulldog painted on its side, along with the name of the business: Dixie Wash 'n Dry Coin-Op Laundromats.


The ticket on the van's windshield is dated from the day of her lucky find. The time of the infraction is not long before the Laundromat door closed up for the night. The van is locked, and the grimy windows don't let her see much of the inside. Some papers are scattered on the passenger seat, a few cardboard boxes are just visible through the back windows.

A pigeon flies by so close Cherry has to move out of its way or risk losing her lashes. Its pink eye glints at her as it passes. She feels a prickling nausea climb the back of her nose. It means something – all of it. The van, the pigeon, the tickets. There's a message here, waiting for her to grasp it. But it's unfathomable. She can't figure it out. Communications between the required sectors of her brain have broken down. Mercury has wiggled his caduceus in her face again.

Stymied, Cherry returns to the car.


"Hey! Let's go for a spin along the waterfront!"

"You can spin my waterfront any time, babe."

"Mmmmm!"

"Cherry, turn off here. We'll go linger by the lake for the little lady."

Cherry glances in the rearview mirror, omits to turn, continues on the road back to civilization. That she's been roped into being Liberty and Hazel's chauffeur while they scrapple for the apple in the back seat is bad enough, but being ordered to take a detour for the sake of some libido-boosted twat has turned her bitter to the core.

"Hey! I thought I said …"

"We're going back to the hotel, Miss Daisy." Cherry floors the gas. "Got an appointment with Victor, remember?"

"He'll be long gone by – whoa! That was a red light!"

It's the only colour I can see right now, thinks Cherry, weaving her way at high speed through three lanes of traffic beneath the Expressway. If Liberty wants to make an issue out of it, then she can fucking well drive herself.

"Aw, c'mon, Cherry. Just a little jaunt along the lakeshore?"

"You guys got any barbecue chips in here?" pipes Hazel.

Cherry pulls into a gas station, screeching the tires.

"I won't be a moment," she says, grabbing the *Louis Vachon*. "I have to go use the little girl's room."

Hazel's voice rises, muffled from the back seat. "Can you pick us up a pack of chips? Barbecue flavour?"

A scrunched up two-dollar bill pokes its pink head between the seats. Cherry snorts and ignores the proffered money. She isn't going to pick up a pack of chips for anyone, let alone Miss Hazel. She isn't even really going to the washroom – that was just an excuse to get out of the car. She gets out, slams the door and stands there for a second, listening to the sounds of Liberty and Hazel doing the equestrian special in the back.

She breathes deeply, letting her lungs fill with city air. She's got better things to do than play chaperone to a couple of lubricating fiends. She lights a cigarette and starts walking, ostensibly towards the filling station.

A knocking on the window pulls her attention back to the Plymouth Fury. The back window rolls down and the two-dollar bill juts out at her again.

"Barbecue?"

Oh, why not? thinks Cherry, swiping the bill. She takes a last drag on her smoke before flicking the still-lit stub through the crack in the window, effectively lighting the fuse on the Fury firecracker. Barbecue? There you go. With the interior saturated in flammable substances, there's probably about ten seconds or less before the whole thing explodes. She walks away, faster this time, veering out onto the side-walk, pretending not to hear the yelps and screams behind her. She can feel each step bringing her closer to freedom, each step turning Liberty, Hazel and the Plymouth Fury less visible. As if they had never existed.

Fifteen yards down the street, she chances a look over her shoulder. Black smoke billows from the car, the back door is open, and Hazel is making a stumbling bid for safety. Liberty is prancing around the vehicle, flapping away at the flames with her leather jacket. Bet she wishes she had the fire extinguisher now.

"You come back here, Cherry Beach! I'm warning you!"

Cherry continues, picking up speed, striding up the street, her eyes peeled for a taxi.

"I'm going to count to ten. You come back here!"

You do that, thinks Cherry. Count to ten. Count to twenty. Count to fucking three billion. She's lost friends in less time than it'll take Liberty to count to five.

"One … two …"

Perfect timing. An empty cab turns the corner. Cherry grinds her teeth and flags it down. Two seconds later, Liberty is obliterated from her mind – the invisible woman – and Cherry is on her way to hunt down Victor for a well-deserved refuge from the day's events.

It's been a hard day.

# 6 ... for the good of others

Victor's pager is no longer working. His old cell-phone number still gets rerouted to the police, and all other roads tonight lead to Buzby's and Bingo Karaoke, where Victor simply has to put in an appearance if he knows what's good for him. He wouldn't dare call himself a true drug dealer and pass up the business. Unless, of course, he's having more fun somewhere else.

Bingo Karaoke at Buzby's is a fundraiser for the local AIDS hospice. The Karaoke section has been taken over by drag queens who've turned it into a fascinating lip-synch-to-a-backing-track-event. They mouth the words while all their friends in the audience sing the words (mainly the same large smiling lesbian near the front). Grooming counts for a lot if the grand Karaoke prize of a getaway spa weekend is to be won. To be honest, there aren't many contestants and most of the crowd is treating this singalong-with-Barbra as something to be endured between the bouts of Bingo.

Ah yes, the Bingo. This perennially favourite portion of the evening is offering a two-thousand-dollar kitty. Cash. So it isn't surprising that every hard-up soul in the community who doesn't have a family to go to for the holidays has turned up – which includes the squeegee kids from outside the burger joint, the skinheads, the Goths, the rave kids (still going strong from last night) and half a dozen single mothers on Prozac from the housing project across the street, complete with toddlers. Onstage, stuffed into the corner, a blue Christmas tree suffocates beneath red ribbons. Three veteran mascots of honour, sipping at bottled water and nodding off on morphine, are installed in wheelchairs by the stage where one might expect an orchestra pit to be. All told, the crowd numbers a few hundred, give or take the odd Christmas cracker. Another great turnout for Buzby's, assuring them the title of Fundraiser of the Year – again. There's something to be said for packing them in.

On the dance floor, trestle tables are wrapped in Christmas paper and decorated with dishes of dusty peanuts and pitchers of beer. Two-buck Bingo cards are being sold by such wandering glamour superstars as Paisley, who squeezes up and down and around the people, chairs and tables, wares held aloft. Chatter and smoke fill the air, and get tangled in the dripping decorations: icicles of menthol-lite conversation, garlands of roll-your-own gossip. This is the gambling grotto of charitable delights.

Her Royal Heinie, Empress Estelle VII, is hosting the event. Including her earrings and tiara, she must weigh over four hundred pounds. Her fur-trimmed gown could double for a parachute, although it's clearly intended to evoke images of White Christmas and Bing – as in Crosby. Oh, Bing-O, Bingo. No matching cap for her Majesty tonight; she has a ballroom chandelier cleverly ensnared in her platinum wig. Every time she moves her head it sounds as if a waiter has dropped a tray of glassware. She is stationed centre stage at the only working microphone of the evening. As usual, her mouth is running a mile a minute, as flighty and as nimble as an epileptic shrew as she calls the game.

"Under the G for Gayboy – hold onto your assholes everybody – *fifty-two*, the number of cards in the deck unless you're playing with only half the usual amount like that table over there, in which case I'll let you guys off with twenty-six and you *owe me a beer*."

Cherry enters more or less unnoticed. It is only when she pushes through the crowd to scan the faces that she get spotted by the eagle eye of Her Royal Heinie.

"Hey folks, didja hear the one about Cherry Beach who thought she'd won a million on the scratch and win?" Cherry tries to ignore the room turning around to stare at her. "Turned out it was just a bad case of crabs!"

A roar of laughter, scattered with applause, erupts from the crowd. Cherry acknowledges the recognition with a tight smile and a demure wave. The fifteen seconds of fame pass and the room settles down to some serious Bingo action. Cherry wanders the aisles, her Victor antennae on full. The French table mistakes her for a waiter and tries to order a fresh pitcher of beer. *Bon soir, bon soir, bon soir.*

Sugarbush, an aging drag queen who ought to know better than to wear floral-print organdies after Halloween, flags her down.

"Someone's looking for you," she wheezes, all lemon-wedge smiles. "Bad suit, flashy tie. Ring any bells?"

No, it doesn't. Cherry feels a slight perturbation. Sugarbush wouldn't normally talk to her unless she felt it was important.

"There's a price on your head." Sugarbush checks her makeup, as if it would a) make a difference, or b) make the conversation more clandestine. "Fifty dollars, I hear."

"Well, I'm looking for Victor," explains Cherry. "When we all meet up, we can have ourselves a party."

"Looking for your drug dealer, Cherry, my sweet?" Her Royal Heinie booms into the microphone. "I understand he's waiting for you back at the hotel."

"Hotel?" Cherry plays dumb. "Which hotel would that be, Ken?"

"Your hotel, you dizzy thing," continues Her Royal Heinie, Cherry-picking. "The Belt 'n Buckle, isn't it? Room 301, isn't it? Did I hear you say something about a party?"

The French table erupts with a chant of "*Parti! Party! Parti!*"

"Hmmph." Brilliant. Now the whole world knows where she's staying.

Her Royal Heinie continues with her impromptu standup routine. "Where d'you get the *Louis Vachon*, sister?" It comes out as a sneer. "Oh, I'm sorry! I should have known better. It's just a cheap imitation, isn't it? Ha-ha!"

"Oh, grow me a new set of tits." Cherry turns on her heel, tired of all this crap, tired of the extended family, tired of being nice to everyone, tired of herself. "And I'm not your fucking sister."

The moon is full – actually it's two days shy, but it's still bloated enough to trigger Cherry's internal clock. Thanks to Dr Lyndhurst, Cherry no longer has all the requisite bits and pieces to menstruate, but she feels the loss as sharply as if she were still intact. Every twenty-eight days she is haunted by phantom menses like the itching toe of an amputee. Sometimes it can last for a gruelling four or five days. Great Diana, the lunar goddess, still keeps the monthly appointment. The curse. Liquid ginseng helps.

The fantasy of acceptance has haunted Cherry from that first moment of bleeding back in the Monaghan bathroom. She always knew she was different, knew somehow that hers was a path strewn with more pain and confusion than most. She wasn't so much desirous of changing this as claiming recognition for it. She dreamed of one day entering some elite collection of biological rarities, some delicious menagerie of oddities maintained in comfort by some eccentric millionaire, loved for her ambiguity, restored to the hermaphroditism that was her birthright. Once she came close to realizing this dream, at the Rawhide Ranch. Now that, too, has passed.

The times of the carnival sideshow have gone. There is no room in the modern world for ambiguity. There is no place for the truly exotic, except perhaps in the domain of the impoverished. We no longer venerate our variables. They must seek their own rewards.


Back at the Belt 'n Buckle, Coady, the callipygian messenger boy, is waiting in the lobby. He is in Egyptian eyeliner and a midriff-revealing powder-blue top. The steroid treatment is beginning to arch his spine. Soon he'll have to wear a neck brace – that is, if he can figure it out between his mood swings. As soon as he catches sight of Cherry, he launches into a fugue of hand-giggles.

"*Buenas tardes*," he sings. "I'm subbing for Victor." He reaches into his pocket, pulls out a handful of crimson-and-cyan capsules. "Here. On the house."

Thank the Gods! Never one to look a drug-horse in the mouth, Cherry takes them with the air of doing Coady an immense favour before he scatters them. Oh, all right then, if you insist. Cherry picks out four, swallows two, pockets the rest. Smiling her big-sister smile – meaning thanks a bunch, little brother, now bug off – she heads for the elevators. Unfortunately, Coady proves harder to shake. He follows right behind and rides with her up to the third floor. As they get out, he hits all the buttons on the panel inside the elevator – a juvenile prank he does merely out of form, not because he gets any joy out of it. At the door to the room, Cherry tries once more to get rid of him.

"Thanks for the pharms, Coady, sweetheart." She even kisses him twice on the cheek. French style. "Gotta crash now. Bye-bye."

Coady nods, vigorously. There is an urgency to his eyes that Cherry hadn't noticed before. An edge. He's watching her too closely.

"What's up?"

Coady looks down at his sneakers and shuffles a bit. "Oh, nothing."

Cherry stops, her key in the door. "Then beat it, will you? Girls have to get their beauty sleep."

Coady gives a shrug. "You working New Year's Eve at the Kennel?"

"I quit," snaps Cherry, finally opening the door. She staggers in and flings her bags onto the bed before turning to deal with the annoying Coady who's craning his neck into the room, hoping perhaps for an invitation (which he isn't going to get) to come in for a drink. "I don't work for those assholes any more. Nightie-night."

She closes the door firmly in his face.


Look at this pathetic hotel room. Hardly the domicile of someone who has just come into a fortune, is it? Howard Hughes wouldn't be caught dead in it. It's all the same shade, the same smell. Stinky carpet, nicotine-stained wallpaper, the TV in the corner. The whole place is wilting like soggy cardboard. Cherry shrugs off her coat and collapses into the chair.

A few tickets have spilled onto the bed from the guts of the *Louis Vachon*. Big deal. Each and every one is worthless. The Major must have them all flagged in the computer by now, warning memoranda have more than likely been sent to all outlets in the city, along with descriptions of the two bandits on the rampage, trying to cash in last year's Lotto tickets. If she turned them into the Associated Benevolent Christian Charities, she could get five hundred bucks. Ha! Five hundred bucks! No. The festive spree is over. Time to count the winnings, lick the bruises and call it quits.

Using her nail file, she unscrews the back of the television set. It's still there. Ahhhh.

Including what's left of the day's spending money in her purse, she has six thousand, five hundred and thirty-five dollars. That's all that's left. It's a decent amount, but it ain't a hundred thousand, that's for sure. To be tempted with such riches and then to be deprived of it at the last moment makes the six grand seem much, much less than it is. Sure, there had always been the possibility that the Lotto Centre wouldn't honour the tickets, but somehow, Cherry feels that it's personal. If she'd become a plumber, an accountant or perhaps a bank teller, instead of a superstar of the club circuit, then doubtless there wouldn't have been a problem with the tickets. The bitch-deity manipulating her fortunes is no benign benevolence – dangling a golden carrot in her face and then whipping it away before she's had a chance to sink her teeth into it. Santa fucking Calamity. She who taunts the greedy with her Russian roulette wheel, she who spins the barrel, pulls the trigger.

Curses.

Cherry punches the wall. Twice. *Monarch of the Glen* crashes onto the dressing table.

"Fuck!"

Cherry wishes she could cry. Just weep. Instead, she attends to practical matters and convinces herself that she's landed on her feet again. She skewers six-and-a-half-odd thousand dollars – in twenty dollar bills, tens and the occasional fifty – with a kilt-pin, runs the spike through Her Majesty's face, and fastens the resulting wad into the secret pocket of her purse. She then shoves the *Louis Vachon* bag under the bed, pulls the drapes closed against the offensive moonlight, makes herself comfortable in her chair and watches about thirty seconds of some inane soap opera before a crushing wave of narcotic bears down on her shuddering frame, burying her in a velvety black, suffocating nothingness before she has a chance to realize what's hit her.


Back in the early days of exploration in the Big City, when the world was as full as the moon and the possibilities were inexhaustible, when Cherry had the genitalia of both sexes still reasonably intact, the search for others who were like her drove her into the darkest reaches of the night. Drag queens were the first ambiguous creatures that she came across. At the tender age of seventeen, they seemed fearsome role models.

It was acceptance, of sorts – an ego free-for-all where the main rule of the game was to blast your own trumpet as loudly as possible while trashing the competition. Any pretense of caring was smothered under layers of panstick. Cherry dove into the deep end and survived – nay *thrived* – amid the drag queens.

They fed her and clothed her, taught her how to walk in high heels, showed her how to create breasts from bags of birdseed. She has a lot to be thankful for.

When asked, she said her name was Pat, or sometimes Graham, but she was soon dubbed Black Cherry, from the sour candy that she favoured. She enraptured the Royal Court when it was discovered she was truly neither one sex nor the other. Here was an oddity! A truly tuckable cock (distorted as it was). And when Cherry lost enough of her inhibitions to show off the trick that she had, up until then, kept to the privacy of her bathroom explorations, she blew their minds.

"Wow! Tuck 'n Fuck!"

"You should get a zipper put in girl!"

"You could make a fortune!"

Which was what she had in mind when La Grande Dame Rachel found her and asked her to come stay at the Rawhide Ranch, a converted stone farmhouse on the outskirts of Cowtown. A true hermaphrodite – an *intersexual*, as Rachel put it – could become *très riche* indeed in the right environment. The wooing lasted two days before Cherry said *oui*.

She was flown half a continent away from familiarity on a first-class ticket, was met at the airport by a limousine and then driven the twenty miles in the dark. When she got there, they stripped her, tied her to a stake in the yard, hosed her down and kitted her out in a training harness. She was given a stall to herself with a trough and a bucket in the corner. A blanket was thrown over her shaking flanks and she was locked up for the night with the rats.

"Ah, ma petite Cerise, que tu est ma pouliche précieuse!"

It took two months to break Cherry in, during which time she learned the tricks of the trade, so to speak, along with a sputtering of French. *Moi, je parle français comme une vache anglaise.* Rachel herself showed her the ropes, teaching her the difference between a strike with intent and a wasted whack that brought no pleasure to anyone. The constant stream of businessmen who came to spend a week, ten days, or longer at the Ranch expected the best. They'd paid through the nosebag for it, after all.

"This is for your own good you miserable worm! Hup-si-daisy!"

Submission, mostly. Flagellation, whips and spurs, with a few other fetishes thrown into the *mélange*. The Rawhide Ranch boasted twenty-two rooms of specialization. There was the room of the one-way mirror, the mud room, the courthouse, the jail, the saloon, the schoolroom and sixteen other carefully decorated and fully functional set pieces. It was a bordello of such dedicated purpose it could make an open wound weep with gratitude. Rachel lived in the coach house, the furthest possible distance from the fully equipped dungeon and the isolation tanks in the barn.

Rachel ran the whole s/hebang; she was the hostess, the Lady Sheriff, the Madame, the undisputed Queen of Rawhide Ranch. She required her breakfast tray brought to her in the morning, the covers turned down for her at night. Punishment for transgressing any of the many Rules of the Ranch were, perversely, an opportunity to make some extra pocket money. There was always someone willing to pay to watch.

Cherry soon earned herself preferential treatment. She made Deputy. She got to hold Rachel's ashtray – a position of great honour, and Rachel left such long roaches! She learned how to cheat at euchre without getting caught. She saw to the needs of the most demanding guests.

During Cherry's eleven-month stint at the Rawhide, Rachel never allowed her to be deflowered by either client or ranch hand. Cherry remained, technically, a virgin, although her most popular performance onstage in the saloon involved a complicated display of self-violation to the accompaniment of a solo violin, an artistic *pièce de résistance* that proved too painful to repeat more than once a month.

Rachel is gone now, lost to the cause. She returns in dreams, restored to health, the KS lesions gone, vibrant, brimming with the same generosity of spirit that she'd extended to Cherry in those first days.

"Stay as long as you like *ma chère. Chez moi, c'est chez toi.*"

The saloon, where Cherry slept on the divan, had silk-papered walls the colour of dried blood, a golden piano, and a ceiling painted with gamboling nymphs, in the centre of which a fan lazily stirred the marijuana-drenched air. Statuary, tapestries and other works of art were crammed amongst lace and draperies. On the table presiding over Cherry's head while she slept was a small ebony statue of Anubis, the jackal-headed god of Khem, whose features could never quite be discerned. He stood beside a set of those stacking Russian dolls.

"*Matryoshka, ma Cerise*," said Rachel. "They're called *matryoshka*."

On the other side of the saloon wall there were six binding cages, of which at least one was always occupied. Rachel called them her *petites momies Égyptiennes*. Cherry called them "hummies" due to the noise they made through their bandages as they fought off the rats.

"You may want to wear earplugs, *ma Cerise*."

But Cherry found it soothing. She imagined it was the smallest doll in the *matryoshka* singing her a lullaby. She adored the Ranch, adored Rachel, adored the attention, the leather harnesses, the wigs and the corsets. Golden times spent in the cast of the moon. Cherry would have stayed forever had Rachel not succumbed to KS in her lungs. The Rawhide Ranch was foreclosed by its silent partners.

A year later the farmhouse was taken over by a group of monks who now produce honey and a highly potent liqueur, reminiscent of a julep. No evidence of its former glory survives. The dungeon, so they say, was stripped and its contents burned in the courtyard. The mud room was converted into an apiary.

Rachel never made it onto any AIDS memorial, and no acknowledgment was ever made in conversation or otherwise that she or her ranch of delights ever existed. Cherry was present at the final moment, watching the room readjust itself to accomodate Rachel's passing. It was like Lily's vanishing trick of years before in Lotus Land, but without the hospital curtains. Death made itself visible by an indefinable absence. Cherry has even lost the double-snake ring Rachel pressed into her hand from her hospital bed two days before the end.

All that remains is the dream, which is always the same: Rachel, smiling without using a single muscle in her face, a smoldering reefer clenched between her teeth. Perfect lacquered brows, hair as slick as a glossy catalogue, every follicle either in place or removed. Breasts as proud as silicone *vol-au-vents*. The baritone voice of authority for every VIP, the husky tone of familiarity for every daughter welcomed into the fold.

"Stay as long as you like, *mes chères*. *Chez moi, c'est chez vous.*"


A telephone rings. Stops. Voices. Sleep …

The devotees of Diana, the votaries of the Moon are, by necessity, virginal. They hunt by night in the silver glades, their bows drawn, their vows intact. Pure of vision and intent, their desires are uncluttered by the pull of the flesh and they are thus able to concentrate on the kill. Death is the substitute for reproduction. It is a clean focus. The hunt is sacred.

Abstinence provides a pleasure understood by few. When entered into voluntarily, it's a position of strength. The only person Cherry has ever had intercourse with is herself, onstage at the Rawhide Ranch saloon: glorified masturbation whereby she fucked herself over royally. Her violation was "in-house," so to speak, and, consequently, she still regards herself as a virgin. She can still run through the forest with the best of them. Or so she tells herself.

The Easter before Rachel died, Cherry missed two months. Fifty-six days without bleeding, it had her worried. She started having stomach and lower abdominal pains which wouldn't go away; something was pushing against her prostate or whatever she had remaining up there. She spent two days clutching her abdomen with a persistent screaming blue-ball erection, followed by two more nights writhing on the couch in the parlour, moaning at the statue of Anubis, unable to work, or even to hold an ashtray. She thought it was a hernia. Rachel figured differently and had airline tickets booked to Hogtown by the Friday and an appointment with Dr Lyndhurst at the Trinity Surgical Rehabilitation Unit.

Someone more skilled than the Ranch's resident vet was required.


Cherry wakes with a jolt. A dream of jogging along a verdant forest pathway suddenly vanishes as her foot lands in an unexpected pothole and her stomach jumps into her ribcage. Her heart pounds inexplicably.

It is dark outside, and the TV tints the room with a flickering light. The soap opera is over, replaced by an infomercial soliciting funds for starving children in the Third World. There's a crumpled depression on the covers of the bed showing where someone isn't.

"Hello?" Cherry levers herself out of the chair. She feels sluggish, unresponsive. Her left hand's fallen asleep. "Lib?"

The whining of children from the TV mingles with the unmistakable sound of someone having sex in the next room. Since the walls are so thin, they should have at least installed one-way mirrors, thinks

Cherry. Or a glorious viewing hole.

She looks around the room, pulling her eyes into focus, then sits on the bed to turn on the table lamp. At the very moment she looks at it, the telephone rings, startling her. She lets it ring twice more to allow her nerves to stop jangling.

"Hello?"

Nothing, not even a dial tone. She shakes the receiver.

"Hello?"

Still nothing. She pushes one of the chunky white buttons along the base of the phone. There is a buzz, a crackle and a ringing.

"Front desk, may I help you, no?"

"Er ... did a call just come through to this extension?"

"Couldn't tell you, sorry, yes."

"Thank you." Cherry hangs up slowly, lost in an unattractive sense of foreboding. She sits for a few seconds, holding her head in her hands and trying to shake the willies out of herself. Then she looks up.

Her purse is on the floor by the window. It's lying on its side, clasp open, mouth gaping like a dead barracuda.

The pin's gone from the secret pocket and so's the money. Not all of it. There's a two-dollar bill left as a memento. No! She daren't believe it! With mounting shock, Cherry dumps the entire contents of the purse onto the bed and scrabbles through it, somehow hoping that six and a half thousand dollars will materialize out of the tubes of lipstick and the complimentary sachets of perfume. No such luck. A plastic pencil sharpener shaped like a die falls to the floor.

She's been robbed.

Fearing the worst, she lifts up the bedspread and peeks under. The *Louis Vachon* has gone. Santa Calamity has been busy while she was asleep. Cherry peers under the bed in the faint hope that the tickets have all fallen out or that the bag has somehow hidden itself behind a leg of the bed. Nothing. Just a long-dead mouse, covered in dust balls.

"Jesus fucking Mary and Joseph!"

Curses. Curses. Curses.

Her dreams evaporate instantly. The world is back to how it was: cruel, impersonal, unforgiving, expanding from the sleepy stiffness in the back of her head, spinning outwards, stranding her in its epicentre, moneyless, friendless, despised and destitute from one too many adventure.

What a loser. Typical.

She sits on the bed and starts slowly putting everything back into her purse, a heavy sigh for each item. She is too despondent to be relieved that she still has her Camels. Without thinking, she shoves a cigarette between her lips and scratches around for a match. The lovers in the adjacent room build towards climax. Wait a minute …

They're not next door. The noise is coming from the bathroom. Cherry freezes, snaps her head in the direction of the heavy breathing and moaning. Yes. Definitely the bathroom.

The door is closed and, as she looks at it, she can see the strip of light along the bottom flicker from the shadows of bodies in motion. She puts her ear to the door and is rewarded with a pocket of intimacy.

"Fuck, I'm gonna cum … I'm cumming … yeah … !"

It's Victor. Cherry's hackles rise.

"Police!" she rasps in a cracked voice, her fear sputtering momentarily through her bravado, her voice unrecognizable even to herself. Santa Calamity must have sent the fucking cockroaches to crawl down her throat while she was asleep.

"Open up!!" She bangs on the door, authoritatively. "Police!!"

Silence.

Does she hear whispered voices? A hurried consultation? A shuffling of feet? There's the sound of the sash-window being opened. She's got them on the run – damn, they're trying to make their escape! The light at the bottom of the door goes out.

Cherry swallows, her mouth dry. As quietly as she dares, she wraps her sweating fingers around the doorknob. With the speed necessary for such an ambush, she twists the door open and fumbles around with her spare hand for the light switch. The bathroom springs into bright light and the vermin scurry into their dark hidey-holes. Pink shower curtain. White porcelain sink. A gust of cold air. A few bills of varying denominations flutter about the floor.

"Aha!"

Victor is halfway out of the window, one leg up on the sill, his knee pushed up against his cheek, trying to squeeze himself through. His face is as white as a dress shirt, his eyes like two loose buttons, his glasses askew. In expectation of the police, his hands are held aloft by his ears, palms facing Cherry. Shaking. He's half-clothed, his pants pulled up hastily, caught around his thighs, his pimpled buttocks getting a light sprinkling of snow.

"Ch-Cherry, hi."

"You bastard!"

Without thinking, Cherry rushes him, meaning to drag him back through the tiny window. She'll teach him a lesson or two. As she takes a step toward him, however, she catches a hint of an expression on his drug-addled face and realizes that – of course – Victor isn't the last one out. There's someone else in the bathroom. On the other side of the pink shower curtain. Behind her.

Too late, she twists around. Something hard hits her over the back of her head, followed by a spray of broken glass and the gush of stinky liquid. She loses her balance and falls to the floor, twisting her ankle and banging her funny bone against the edge of the shower stall. Ouch.

"Take that, pig!"

There's blood everywhere. No, it's not blood, it's cough medicine. She's been brained with a bottle of *Dr Buquough's* finest expectorant which, she can now testify, hurts a damn sight worse than it tastes. She tries to lift her head up, but an unseen, buzzing force in her skull stops her. The back of her throat prickles and as her vision fades, she sees a pair of blue jeans pass by, tiptoeing over the broken glass. Red and white sneakers. Her eyes close against her will.

"Ow man, I've cut my face!"

She hears the gremlins of the night make their bumbling escape through the window, onto the fire escape, Victor trying all the while to explain to his friend that Cherry Beach is not, in fact, a policeman.

Then she is aware only of her breathing and the plaintive cries of the Third-World children in the other room.


Doctor Connable Lyndhurst was a tiny old woman who specialized in sexual curiosities and psychiatric disorders. Sunday, Monday, Tuesday she worked at the Queens Quay Mental Health Centre, while Wednesday, Thursday, Saturday she worked in the Trinity Surgical Rehabilitation Unit. Fridays she visited family. She must have been over ninety and well under five feet. She had white, white hair and wore her spectacles on a black cord around her neck. Her clothes were made to measure. Other than that, Cherry has nothing nice to say about her and would feign disinterest if asked.

Dr Lyndhurst, however, was intensely interested in Cherry (or Nina, as she was then calling herself), so much so that Nina/Cherry felt depersonalized in her presence, as if she'd lost all control of her own identity. Nina lied profusely about her history, imagining for herself a rich family background and manufacturing a fable of being locked away in an attic room for her entire childhood, hidden from the world by a family determined to keep her existence a secret. Dr Lyndhurst had come into her life via Rachel, so a certain level of mystique was demanded.

"But who performed the surgery, Nina? Who sewed you up?"

"My mother was an expert seamstress."

"Ah, your mother. Tell me about your mother."

There wasn't anything to tell.

"My mother was an Aztec princess belly dancer. The family didn't approve."


Cherry opens her eyes. For a moment, she can't quite figure out what she's looking at. Then she realizes. It's the floor around the back end of the bathtub. When the hotel had painted the place, they'd obviously just come in with a paint bomb and sprayed the shit out of everything with the same repulsive shade of beige. Including the cockroaches. Hundreds of the little fuckers are all painted over, stiff, immovable, crowding the crack between the linoleum and the wall. Dead. All of them. Antennae motionless, tiny heads and thoraxes sealed with the lava of paint. Close enough for a kiss.

The image remains after she closes her eyes.


A shadow has substance insofar as it retains the form of that which cast it. Distinct, yet part of the same. An ovum, at the moment of penetration by a sperm, becomes a mirror of that which caused it, if only for a split-egg-second. All the knowledge of the Universe is contained within that moment when the zygote is formed. The breath of God.

But which god? In Cherry's case of self-impregnation, it was as if she had cast a shadow across her own womb.

"Don't be silly. Of course you can't keep it."

The worst thing about Dr Connable Lyndhurst ("Connie" to her friends), was that she, in all her years, had never experienced intimacy, not even with herself. She lived vicariously through her patients while exercising her sadistic instincts over them. She was as dry as a scrawled prescription, as sympathetic as a pharmaceutical company.

"I'm giving you something for the pain, Nina. You may need it after surgery."

Need it? *Need* it?!

"But I was hoping ..."

"We can't allow you to carry the baby to term. For your own good, you do understand, don't you?"

Cherry nodded but she didn't understand at all. She didn't want to understand. She wanted to be special. She didn't care if her baby had two heads and six arms, she just wanted the chance. She couldn't put it more succinctly than that. Dr Lyndhurst told her she was being selfish, and in the same breath, assured her that abortion was a simple process – she'd be in and out in an hour. Nothing special.


Someone is at the door. *Rappity-tap. Rappity-tap.*

Cherry cracks open an eye. She is lying in a pool of what is likely a mixture of cough syrup and blood. How long has she been here? Her right eyelash is coming loose and the side of the bathtub has grown warm where her cheek has pressed up against it. The painted cockroaches are still a few inches away from her face. A cold wind puffs through the window.

She pulls herself painfully to her feet and braces herself against the doorjamb, feeling like a demented Bambi on ice and probably looking just as stupid. With the change in altitude, a moiré landscape of grey-and-white checks appears before her. She shakes off the nausea and surveys the scene of her accident. What a mess. Glass, blood and cough syrup are everywhere. Her beautiful Cher wig is lying dead on the floor. The dangling tail of the toilet roll is sodden. A few bank notes of minimal denominations are littered around. Thirty bucks or so.

*Rappity-tap.*

"Hold on!"

She squints to avoid *Dr Buquough* dripping into her one good eye, scoops up her wig and the loose cash, stumbles into the main room, bumps into the chair and makes her damaged rumba-dance tour over to the door. She jams the wig over her head, giving her that Slut leaning against the Bedpost look. Some of the cough syrup is drying into lumps that are going to be as hard to get out as chewing-gum.

She opens the door, forgetting to put the chain lock on first.

"Oh fuck."

"Jesus Christ, what *is* that?!"

Crowding the hallway are Cocktail Mama, Whatserface, and not one, but three large men in bad suits, one of them in supersonic checks with a hula-hula tie. They're all pie-faced drunk and the hula-hula tie-guy is clutching a baseball bat. They can't believe their eyes. Neither can Cherry.

And now: This.

Staring at the thousands of tiny squares of the suit, Cherry feels as if she's about to lose consciousness again, but she manages to pull herself back from the edge with a rumbling snort and a couple of blinks.

"Can I ... can I help you?"

"Cherry Beach!" crows Cocktail Mama triumphantly, intoning the name like a death sentence. "What the hell did you do with my fucking baby?!"

"Is this the one, Pauline?"

A nod. A few grunts.

"That's her, all right," sneers Whatserface. "Go get her, boys."

"OK then."

The hula-hula girl on the tie seems to take a step forward, hips swinging her grass skirt – dancing *La Cucaracha* – and dragging the bulk of bozo behind her. Cherry sputters something inane, "What's this all about?" or "Now what am I supposed to have done?" as the baseball bat wings its way towards her.

It catches her behind the knees, brings her to the floor with a shudder. Strangely, it doesn't hurt. She notices a cigarette burn on the carpet.

"That's it, Charlie, you show her!"

The bat is poking into the shoulder blades now, with nasty, insistent jabs. Cherry tries to crawl back into the room, realizing there is no escape. They follow her in, feet kicking away, boots making pointed contact with her hips, her ribcage, one in her face. Voices accompany the smell of shoe polish and dirty snow.

"This is for your own good, you know that, Cherry, don't you?"

"What the fuck did you think you were doing?"

"Leaving a six-year-old kid all alone!"

The pounding pauses for a breath. The ridiculousness of it all hits Cherry with more force than any of the actual blows. Someone has been telling naughty stories about her and, judging by Whatserface's wicked cackle, she has a good idea who that someone might be.

She chances a look up. Bad move.

From her angle on the floor, it seems to Cherry that it's the hula-hula girl on the tie herself who is swinging the baseball bat. The eyes glint, a wicked smile twitches away at the corners of the mouth as the weapon whistles through the air towards her. It is more this illusion that catches Cherry full force on the side of the skull ... her hearing suddenly skips, like a tinny radio station ... the grass skirt turns red ... a gown of crimson ... she hears laughter ... a million miles away as if from the distant mountain top ...

She feels a sudden release of pressure. Her brains bubble through her nose. Her eyes fill with singing tangerines.

Curses. There goes another pair of lashes.

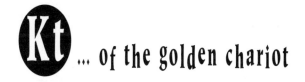 ... of the golden chariot

Things fell into place last week, the moment I got the call that Alpha-Four had come to town. I can't remember when that was exactly, so it makes no difference except that from then on, I knew there'd be no turning back. The time had come. Full steam ahead to the next level. Head of the pack, that's me: flying out in front, blazing the way for the others to follow, wind in my face, stars above me, frozen earth somewhere far below with the sleeping children. Man, it takes the breath out of you. It's beautiful. This is the only way to die.

For years I've been trying to find the right drug to go out on. It's been a kind of personal quest before deterioration takes hold. Call it vanity, but I couldn't bear no crumbling hospital room, no feeble rotting away, losing my looks with raspy breaths, emaciated hopes and boring old painkillers. I never lived that life and I've got no intention of ending up that way. Out with a bang! I'm gonna jump across the void with my fists flying. Charge the fucker head-on, baby.

Seven hits and out, that's the magic formula. Start off virgin, keep expanding the dose by one in a sacred pyramid: one the first time, two the second, three the next, and so on. The seventh time you let it take you. This way the drug never loses its edge, you never slide backwards, never end up hooked on the shit, never turn the wondrous into the mundane. Never eke out the end of your life chained in misery to an escape hatch that won't open properly. The magic number seven. The seventh hit of seven has got to do it.

Obviously your common or garden-variety dope could never fit that bill – not acid, coke, smack, E, K, ups, downs or roundabouts – I've done them all too often to be able to take the seven-step program with any of them. Not that I have any complaints; they've served me well. I've had my CAKE and eaten it, too.

I'll be honest. I'm a plastic raving party groove fiend. Victor, the vinyl Banje-boy, that's me. Always have been, always will. Toss me into a sweaty warehouse filled to the sprinklers with a couple of thousand bottles of dancing mineral water and I couldn't be happier. *R.I.P.* Ripped In Public. That's me in the middle of the pit, flapping my arms trying to get higher. Every once in a pink moon I'll catch a warm air pocket and float upwards through the clouds, for days on end, soaring into a Jonathan Livingstoned Seagull Nirvana. Until last week, though, I hadn't found the right stuff to stay up there.

Hey, there's little else in this shitty existence worth chasing other than this lofty chemical Bliss Quest. Once an admission like this is made – that the pursuit of happiness involves drugs and lots of 'em – then the rest of Life is easy. Extend the Weekend, live on Welfare. Heck, you don't need to eat! You can go for weeks on the right regimen of amphetamines and a pack of instant noodles. The trick is to evolve your body to deal with the situation. Drug programs work.

Oh yeah, and sleep. You have to get some sleep in there.

Look at me. It's taken years to achieve this level of toxicity. I've got the only regenerative liver in town thanks to hepatitis A, B, C, non-P, Q, R, and all the way to secret formula hepatitis X-Y-3, I'll bet. Normally this would be lethal, but because I've consumed, over the past twenty-four years, such a large quantity of *Krafty Dinner Noodles with Cheezy Type Flavor* (which, I maintain, is also the common antidote to AIDS), I have developed into a kind of *Überdrügemensch*. Go ahead and laugh. I'm having a great time, stuck in my tree in the middle of fucking nowhere talking to the gods.

The way I see it, most people don't get to experience this level of spiritual advancement until after they're dead. Bonus. I get to practice. Look, there's no point in being scared of the big bucket. Heck, you may already have kicked it; most of the population have and don't know it. Let me tell you a little secret: Death is not what it's been made out to be. It's only a transition from one reality to another. The deal is that you can't come back. Nobody ever sends a postcard either, do they? It must be way too interesting to waste time on mundanities like that. Count me in.

So you can imagine my relief when the A-4 came through. Alpha-Four: a blue-green powder that's an improvement on Dimethoxy-Propylthioamphetamine Hydrochloride – or so I'm told. It's from the phenethylamine family, so it's like a key to parts of your brain you never knew existed. Even though it only lasts a few hours, it's certainly one of the most intense substances I've ever known to affect the reality structure of this existence, I kid you not. It blasts fucking holes in it man, tears it to shreds. Much like ketamine, Special K, it edits out whole chunks of your life – but way stronger. In the gaps you get to participate in another dimension. Truth. Sixty bucks a hit. A grand will get you two dozen. You do the math.

On my first hit, at work at the Gentleman's Quarters last week, I thought I'd never come back. Even with my experience, it had me worried for the first few minutes, scared even, but I soon realized that as fast as the discomfort of being ripped into two dimensions accelerated, so did the neat stuff. After a while, you go to a place where you can feel safe. You know, like keeping the balance. Just breathing was like manipulating the hub of the cyberuniverse, my body was the very centre of Adam Kadmon, my lungs the rippling branches of a rain forest, my spine an elastic palm tree. And the visuals! I thought this is it, Victor my boy, all seven steps tied up in one, you've slipped through the cracks and you ain't makin' it back after this. I had to jack-off under the showers for ever, had to bang my head against the tiles to come down to earth.

From then on things kept falling into place.


The second hit and I met Alex. We were in the chill lounge at Playland, the kids all hanging loose, dropping in and out of K-holes. I decided to share the turquoise. I love those kids, especially the ones who've realized that they really are immortal.

We took it in our drinks, so there were a few minutes to wait before it kicked in. I'd dropped a double dose, of course, so I was a tad on edge. Nobody quite knew what to expect. I'd riffed a bit on the strength and so a few kids decided to split some hits amongst them. Pauline took a whole one, as did three others, and I made over two hundred dollars, so I was set up for the next round.

Alex appeared out of nowhere. It was as if he'd stepped out of the shadows and into my face. He was the one. The one I'd given up waiting for. I knew it instantly and so did he. He sat down next to me, punched me on the leg. Kismet.

I was looking at his elbow when the drugs took hold. I think he may have been trying to reach for his drink or a smoke, but anyway, his arm was right in front of me and I became transfixed. The angles of the bone jutting out from the muscle glistened with perfection. The skin seemed to breathe in a digitized rhythm with my own, transformed by beads of sweat into succulence. Edible.

It was there and so I bit.

"Wow!" He turned to me, grinning. "Do that again!"

"Yummy bum-holes!" I teased.

No one can tell me it wasn't consensual. I don't know what pickle the management had stuck up their ass, but they had no reason to throw us out. We were only playing, you know, like puppies. No tongues or genitalia flying around at that stage in the game, just a bit of a tussle. We didn't mean to knock over a whole table of drinks – it was an accident, I swear. I wasn't even aware it was there and, to be honest, I'd edited it out of my reality. All I could see, touch, smell, hear and taste was Alex.

Alex, Alex, Alex, Alex, Alex.

We fooled around in the alleyway, on some industrial loading dock, ankle-deep in snow, with groups of joint-smokers looking on. I couldn't get my nose out of his armpit and he had somehow gotten himself jammed up into my Skivvies. I jizzed into the snow while he dumped his approval into my cloth.

Then, hoisting our pants back up, I gave him my pager number and left for work.


There's a small town to the south which keeps jumping into my mind. A flash and there it is: gas pumps, farmhouses, antique dealers, garden supply stores, no school for big kids, you have to take the bus. Everyone looks the same. Men and women, kids and dogs alike. The girls curl their hair until they get married, when they let it go flat. They wait for their first baby then chop it all off. As soon as they hit menopause, they start to grow it again, sit around in the Legion all year, drink pitchers until, eventually, everybody's hair curls grey and falls out. Men and women. It ain't my idea of a good time.

The church has a graveyard that backs onto fields that never rotate crops in sequence because the land changes hands too often. I spent a lot of time in that graveyard, playing alien monkey-boy in the crook of the old oak, dreaming of crop circles. I dropped my first hit of acid up there. Now I have this thing about trees. Yeah, Hickey Stick, Canada, is the town where I grew up, threw up and left.

I wasn't born there, though. Probably would have stayed there if I had. No, I emerged into an artificial world on the third floor of Saint Nick's Hospital in the Big Smoke, and so it was back into the Big Smoke I always knew I would return. Don't think anyone was at all surprised when I left home. Who cares? I wasn't looking back. I had other things to think about. School. University. Oh, I had plans and I was smart. I always knew that. Had my sights set on anywhere but home, and still do. But lately, old Hickey Stick, Canada, keeps jumping into my mind, not clear or sharp, but jumping into my mind nonetheless. It's been a while.


OK, so I blew school. I started working at the Quarters as a way to put myself through, to try and better myself, honest. It was part of this deal I'd worked out with my Ma but, of course, I spent the five hundred dollars she sent me in less than a weekend. I told her that the Gentleman's Quarters was *A private health club for men*, which is what it says on the door, so it isn't a complete lie. It's the *Open 24-hours* line that gives the game away. And if you look on the price list, the rates are higher after the bars have closed. Hey, as far as my Ma is concerned I've got a job that will put me through college. Linguistics Schminguistics. All I've managed to put myself through is K-hole loops. I've become quite the vitamin consultant at this private health club for men.

I guess I've always been able to sniff out the action. Figures, eh? Like a pig on a truffle hunt I just dig around in the muck and sooner or later I'll always get what I'm looking for. Like when I first arrived, I can remember just walking the streets, feeling my skin tingle beneath my clothes as the prospects walked by. It was late May. I hung out in Laundromats and Coffee Shops, begged for spare change on the one corner and lost my mind on the other. My libido, however, never could stay put in any one place, preferring to put in appearances wherever and whenever the mood struck it. I had a four-way sex drive in those days, although I always seemed to end up at the same damned burger joint at five in the morning to lick my wounds and compare bruises with the other kids.

I was making money, so I wasn't complaining. I'm still not doing bad, but if I'd been like Gerrard (who can clean and prep a room in less than fifteen seconds), I would have a degree by now. Then again, if I'd been like Gerrard I could have kept my ass in one place longer than a month. I could have kept my hands clean, the holes out of my socks and I could have made my coworkers fall down with lust for me every time I brushed by them, because if I'd been like Gerrard, I'd have been blessed with skin that makes you want to lick it at fifty yards. I also would have had manners.

But slaving in the chlorine pits all night long, cleaning lard off the mirrors and picking condoms off the floor six or seven nights a week isn't all jealousy and frustration. Mostly it gives me an appreciation for my down time and now, to be honest, I've given up all pretense of grabbing myself an education. I pick my shifts, spend my money on exploration of the soul. Fuck the schooling. Besides, I've seen where the graduates end up – at the Quarters. Sometimes as often as four or five nights a week.

The first time I went there it was for a cheap place to spend the night, and rumour had it that a smart kid could turn himself around a couple of hundred dollars if he hit on the right guys. The suits are in disguise at the Quarters. Everyone wears a towel. You've gotta be able to spot the Rolex watch, the civil-servant diamond ear stud, the pricey cologne. Some of them are obvious – heck, desperate – walking around the wet area with a twenty tucked under their key elastic and a roving, dark eye searching for the tricksters in the deck. First dip into Our Lady of the Perpetual Waters and I got lucky. I met Mr Favour Central, ended up with five guys in the party room smoking crack from a pipe made out of a broken lightbulb and from that point on, my passport to Funland got a VIP visa stamp.

It was weird at first, that world of towel-draped flesh where no one really made any attempt to hide their hard-ons beyond, occasionally, an embarrassed smile. I never thought there were that many fags in the country, let alone under one roof. Don't talk to me about sexual orientation. Who needs a map? Most guys I know are happy to get lost in a dark corridor once in a while. It's easier to pay ten bucks for a locker, or fifteen for a room, and joust around with another guy, party a bit, knock back a brew or a couple of hits of Vitamin C. No chance of anyone getting pregnant. No chickadee hanging around your neck like some concrete Saint Christopher, wishing you well just so long as you carry the kid. No wonder I switched.

Hits number three and four took me to a place I'd rather not think about. Alex vanished, to be replaced by Pauline who just isn't the same thing, no matter how hard you try to let the drugs help you imagine otherwise. The triple and quad levels, which you'd think would have been liberating, actually held me in a kind of vice-grip, a comatose hiccup, if you will. I think it was because I was snorting the shit, which brought the buzz on real fast, but once that was over, all I could do was sit and melt in anguish.

I was obsessed with breaking through the mental barrier to the land of enjoyment, but the physical side of things just wasn't being cooperative. I was stuck upstairs in the Kennel Klub for the longest time – it might have been forever – watching Isabella going on and on about what a bad influence I was. Her face, man. That was a preview of Hell in itself, like that stop-motion plasticine animation on the music channel where the guy's head bursts into snakes. Pauline saw it too, but she was more mobile and was able to escape the horrific vision. Me, I attributed my paralyzed state to working off some karmic debt – probably something to do with the kid.

I got a glimpse into the pit of the dark side sitting there on the Kennel Klub couch. Everything went flat, lost its dimensions. I kept dipping into a suffocating blackness where all I could hear were whispering voices in the shadows, fragments of family: Dad and I playing street hockey, my Ma crying at the dinner table, the growling of Dobermans guarding the gates of freedom. But try as I might, I couldn't break through into that other dimension. My body refused to go. It was like being stuck in neither one place nor the other.

As I came down I couldn't shake Pauline. She really wanted to get into my pants, but I wasn't having any of it. I've stopped with the pussy three years gone, and she knew that, but it didn't stop her from trying. She called me evasive, in denial. Responsible behaviour is what I call it. Women are too easy to pass things onto, even if you take precautions. Look at Brock. Condoms can break. Oh boy, she was still trying to hold that one over me. I kept telling her she's got no proof that the kid's mine. No proof at all, the slut.

I took her back to my pad and fucked her in the kitchen, no sweat, mainly mechanical to shut her up. I should have slipped the rubber over the handle and slammed the door in her face; she wouldn't have known the difference. I couldn't even look at her, kept thinking of Alex, kept glancing at my pager to see if he'd called me yet. You could say the romance has gone from between me and Pauline. I couldn't even turn it into a sort of goodbye, it was so twisted.

I got rid of her when she tried to drag me back to her family poker game. Thank Christ for that; I was beginning to despair. In the cab over, she'd told me she was pregnant again and didn't we make the perfect couple. I saw where that was heading, right enough. No way. She was only two weeks late – she'd told me as much earlier on – so I knew it was all a load of crap.

We create our own destinies, I'm sure of that, and if you're filled with self-loathing and doubt, then that's how it's going to end up. It's better to pull all your monsters from under the bed, have a good long look, then dump them as quickly as you can.

My pager went off as the cab left the driveway. Onwards and upwards.


I must have slept because I remember waking up. The sun was streaming in through the window of a strange bedroom. We were on a waterbed, the three of us, and I can't remember how I got there. Butt-naked with Alex and this girl, Helen, who I recognized from the scene. Our limbs were all tangled together, so it must have been some groove we'd gotten ourselves into. When I checked my coffin stash I found I was down to three hits. We'd lost ten, so I figured I'd done the five for number five, given a few more away and blanked the whole experience out. Maybe it'll be waiting for me as a gift in the future. I hope so.

Even though I'd missed out on my trip, I was still buzzing. The walls were jumping around, shifting in the sunlight. But it was one of those highs you can function on, where it feels like you can do no wrong – like the tail end of a cleaner-than-clean acid trip modified with percs.

I needed to hustle if I was going to get the final supplies in. We were ten short, plus whatever Alex felt like doing. He knew he had a free ride if he wanted it. We discussed it over coffee, Alex and I, Helen, and this cheezy rocker guy, whose apartment it turned out we were in. It didn't seem at all like we were riffing about death, it was so cool.

"It's your choice," I told Alex.

"Does it make a difference?" he asked. "I mean, to your trip, if you're the only one doing it or not?"

"Hell, no."

I explained about the seven steps, and the transference of reality planes. Everyone got off on that. We could have been chatting about the weather it was so casual. I felt inspired by this, so I pulled out the old pill bottle and we planned our day.

"How much do you need?"

"Only a few hundred dollars," I said.

"What about this?" asked Alex, picking up my winning Scratch'n Win ticket from where I'd dropped it on the floor. A free car rental. "Can't you cash this baby in?"

"Hey man, no way," I said, grinning at him. "That's our lucky car rental! Let's go claim ourselves some wheels for the weekend!"


Suddenly certain people keep showing up in my life. It feels like synchronicity, but of course, it's much more complicated than that. Cherry Beach had been doing this lately; it was as if our lives were intertwined. I'd gone the whole fall without seeing much of her and now here she was, appearing like some Goddess, dishing out the favours: first my beautiful Cadillac, which was like a gift from the sky; and second, that wad of cash to fund my last two steps to seventh heaven. I'm just sorry I won't be able to pay her back this time around.

I regard Cherry as one of my soulmates. A true spirit, she's never done me over. I remembered she was doing well financially and I knew she'd want to help me out, conscious or not. At the Thò Bò Vàng I had wished her well on her court case or whatever it was she'd needed those beta-blockers for. The chances were high that she'd be after a perc or a Nabilone to take the edge off the speed when she was done. And I have unlimited supplies of that shit. I've got a whole medicine cabinet full of dead-man's drugs and Cherry's welcome to 'em – for a price. The only thing was, I couldn't remember where she was currently staying. She's like that, never in one place for longer than a couple of weeks. I tried a couple of numbers with no success. I wasn't about to call up the fucking Bloors, though, I've had enough of them for this lifetime.

As luck would have it, Cherry paged me just as we were picking up the car. I didn't have a valid license, so Helen put the rental in her name, which surprised me. I didn't think she was old enough to drive. My pager was going on the blink again – it's always doing that these days, it seems. Just before it died, though, it came through with Cherry's message to rendezvous at the Belt 'n Buckle in a couple of hours, so we went for a joy ride in our new automobile to kill some time.

There had been very little choice of rentals in the lot, a bunch of Hondas and the like, but we were all immediately drawn to the beaten-up tan Cadillac in the corner. It was our chariot, full working cassette player, shiny cream seats and a full tank of gas. We rode around in the glorious sunshine of the day, blaring *Otis Redding* and *Flying Lizards* tapes that Helen had in her backpack, all of us high on bennies. It seemed appropriate – a Cadillac and bennies. A couple of classics. Beans and cornbread.

We stopped off at the Minute Mug for a coffee and a snack where we bumped into, amongst others, Coady, who tried to break our mood with a glum story about losing his job at the Kennel Klub. Like no one had seen that one coming. Give me a break. He still had a shift at Buzby's, didn't he? What was he complaining about?

Coady eyed Alex with a jealous gleam. "Is this your new poke then, Vic?" he kept asking. "Is this your new poke?"

Coady and I used to have a thing going for a while, so he knew damn well he was pushing my buttons. He thought he was being cute, but it fell flat – unlike his chest, which I couldn't help noticing was over-responding to steroids. He kept thrusting his new-grown tits in my face, as if I hadn't noticed them. Coady likes to think he's one great mass of sex appeal.

"What are you on, Vic? It's that A-4 stuff, isn't it?" Then he started whining, "Drop me a hit, will ya?"

I was not about to waste one of my last three on that piece of trash. Out of the goodness of my heart, however, I gave him a gift of a handful of extra-strength Mogs. I told him they were downs, which they are in a way, so I wasn't completely lying. I just didn't tell him how strong they were. Hopefully he'd drop them during his shift while he was carrying a tray of bottles. Serve him right. The ingrate didn't even say thank you.

"Mind if I tag along?"

I was in too good a mood to tell him to fuck off and I didn't want to appear a grinch in front of the gang.


We got to the Belt 'n Buckle way too early, so we dropped into the bar for a drink. I sent Coady out into the lobby to wait for Cherry's return while we ordered up a few lines of shooters. Peppermint schnapps, fuzzy navels, test-tube-babies – that sort of thing. Everything was fine until we hit the Pernod. That was a mistake. I should have kept clear of that shit. Before I knew it, I was barfing in the can, and Alex, who'd followed me in to make sure I was all right, caught the wave and sprayed the urinals with a layer of his own puke. Some leather queen who was faking a piss got all uptight and pulled a hissy fit, threatening to call the management. That set us off laughing like a couple of jackals and I swallowed my guts the wrong way.

"What, like barfing isn't a bodily function?" Alex wanted to know. "Isn't that what washrooms are for? Or is this one reserved for sex?"

"It could be," I suggested, pulling him into the john and fighting back a liquid burp. "Quick, before he comes back."

I've always loved the odd grapple in a tearoom. It's the threat of being caught that turns my crank, although at the Belt 'n Buckle, the chances of any reprimand are slim. This time, however, was a new one on me. Rainbow showers. I'd never gotten off while vomiting before. Puking always ended any romance; this time, it *was* the romance. Something triggered between us – tears rolling down our cheeks, sniffling noses, sucking, churning, weeping, retching, crying, blasting as we fell, knees and elbows catching us off balance, to land in a heap on the stinking floor of the john.

We lay there in each other's arms for hours, our pants around our ankles, too stupefied to move. It was cool in a freaky kind of way.

Later, back in the bar, after we'd cleaned up a bit, Coady told us that we'd just missed Cherry, that he'd given her some of the pills I'd given him earlier. I didn't like the gloat in his voice, like he knew they hadn't been normal downs and was playing my own game back at me.

"Fuck you, Coady, you asshole!"

The front desk couldn't get an answer and I think they were suspicious when I manufactured an emergency. They let us in though, with a passkey, then turned heel and split when they saw Cherry flaked out in the chair. I guess they didn't want to be responsible for waking her up.

But Cherry proved impossible to rouse, her constitution being what it is. She even hissed at us when Alex tried to shake her shoulders. I checked her eyes. She was way under.

"Jeez, what did she take?" quipped Coady. "Those can't be normal downs."

"Mogadon," I snapped, pushing him out of the room. "Charles Sobraj used it to knock out his victims in the seventies. Seeya!"

Alex was already going through Cherry's purse, doing a bit of Beach combing.

"Money – shit, look at all this money!" he mumbled, pulling a kilt-pin out from a wad of cash and stuffing the loose bills into his pockets. "Never thought drag queens carried around so much. No wonder their purses are so huge. How much did you need?"

He tried to stuff a wad of bills in my mouth, so we ended up having a bit of a fight – nothing serious, more like a pillow fight than anything else, but we did use our teeth. I wanted to make the best of it, so we dropped a couple of hits of vitamin E to power our loins.

It certainly helped kill the time.

Then Rose turned up, looking for her girlfriend, so we moved ourselves into the bathroom, taking the cash with us for safety.


I remember a flash of coming to in a taxicab with twenty-dollar bills all over the place, blood on our hands and our clothes covered in crud. I looked up through the haze of ecstasy and saw that the driver's license number was 777 and he had a little plastic kewpie doll hanging from his rearview mirror.

It was one of those moments you don't want to discuss. Ever.

We came down from the E to realize that we must have mixed it with some ketamine by mistake and fallen into a K-hole. We hadn't lost all our money and we found our way back to the Cadillac. Things were still on track! We managed to hit my connection as they were leaving for dinner and we got the sweetest deal: twenty hits for five hundred bucks. Alex gave me the weirdest look over the exchange. I knew he was thinking of joining me on the final jump. I didn't dare say anything one way or the other. Fuck, I'm only responsible for my own life and even then I have problems.

He was quiet on the drive back through town, sitting sideways in the front seat, his head against the window, his feet in my lap. We'd patched up the cut on his chin with a Band-Aid, but he kept sucking on his finger where he'd done some damage with the bottle.

"I can't believe I mistook a drag queen for a policeman," he said finally.

"Cherry Beach isn't a drag queen," I assured him. "Just tragic. Don't worry. I don't think you'll need a tetanus shot."

That cheered him up. At least enough to kick me in the balls.


We dropped the next round at the Gentleman's Quarters. I felt a need to be in familiar surroundings, and we both needed somewhere to clean up. We were kinda messy by this time. Alex took three, saying that he took three the time before and three was his number. I took my whole six.

We didn't have to wait long. We were in the laundry room putting our clothes through the cycles, much to the annoyance of Gerrard, who wanted to get fresh towels up to the front desk. I was sitting on the washer when mine kicked in. I thought the vibrations were going to send me to the moon. I could have sworn the room exploded.

We floated down the Nile in Cleopatra's barge and ended up in the Jacuzzi. The scenes kept changing with no prompting, somehow shifting us from one to the next. We found ourselves on the roof, looking out at a humming, orange city with snowflakes whispering dirty things in our ears. That was where we had our first Big Screen Kiss and I saw the credits start to roll in Panavision.

We loaded into our golden chariot – the whole gang – and went for a spin. Helen, Zachary, Paisley, shit, I can't remember who else. A party had gathered around us. I saw everyone I ever wanted to see, they just popped up out of nowhere, or else we popped there. I hadn't planned it that way, but that's what happened. Or else I created it all. Odds are even on either score.

We came to, stone-cold sober, in a transit shelter to the north of the city that was filled with Hasidic Jews. Me and Alex together, we snapped out of it as one. He was wearing my shirt and I his jeans and not much else. We just looked at each other, staring. I had no idea who on earth he was. Nor he me.


The universe, I say, is mental.


Fuck, it's cold out here. Keeping myself warm by smoking cigarettes. I think my arm is broken. My glasses sure are.

Crazy, ain't it? I still haven't gotten it together to get my glasses fixed, though I could have had them done twenty times over by now. New frames is what I need and Coady keeps telling me he can lift them easy enough if I let him know which style I want, but I don't want to be owing that piece of street trash anything, so I'm not asking. I don't want that queen holding anything over my head, even frames for eyeglasses. So for the past year I've been peering through the crack in the left lens, but I've learned to adapt. Now half of it's fallen out. Hell, who wants to see the world as it really is anyway? I have my own fucked-up version which works just fine. It's like I'm looking through a spider's web.

The final hit is taking its own sweet time to kick-start the old neurons. I can feel a slight stoking going on in my internal combustion engine. This is it. Number Seven. Hold onto your balls. Come on, come on. I'm waiting.

Maybe it doesn't work in these temperatures. Minus twenty-seven with the wind-chill factor, that's what they said on the radio a couple of hours ago. That's downtown, back in the Big Smoke, so out here it'll be a darn sight colder. Probably somewhere in the minus thirties.

I completely forgot about running the engine on a five-minute cycle: five on, five off, like my Uncle did one winter when we got stuck on the trails. Now who's tragic? No one's gonna drive by here, that's for sure. No one's gonna fly in with the rescue team for the likes of me. It's not too bad. I'm only noticing the temperature in waves. I can deal with that. I can adapt.

Sometimes I have to be alone, you know? It gets too crazy in the city, all those people milling around, screaming, laughing, bumping into each other. Sometimes I gotta get myself some space. Air. I may seem like the original party animal, but that's only part of the portrait. There's a spirit side as well, I believe that. It connects deep down, speaks to me in a way that I can't really hear, but I know when it's speaking all right. It pushes me away from the crowds. It sits me down quiet for a while in a field in the dead of winter to chill. *Yea, though I walk through the valley of the shadow of death.* Maybe it was my spirit that drove into that ditch, smashed through the fence and broke my fucking arm.

Pedestrians should be banned from the fucking highways, man. I couldn't believe it. Maybe it was a hallucination, but I could have sworn that I saw this stupid goof stumble right out into the middle of the road in front of me. Just a flash of a red coat and I was off through the fence and into the ditch. Hallucination. I'm expecting some more, soon. Come on.

Snow's died down. It's too cold for snow. Bet the instant-teller booths are filling up with bums downtown, right now. Bet the Quarters is packed with the holiday crowds – the boys coming back from the family Christmas, screwing their heads back on, trying to forget. Even at five in the morning, they'll still be at it. Make the porkin' last boys, you never know how long you've got left on this planet once you've eaten Christmas Dinner back at the family homestead. Momma might have poisoned the stuffing to teach you not to leave the nest again.

I guess I must have been aiming for Ma's house when I set out tonight. Can't clearly recall. I must have turned onto the highway going south without thinking, because I found myself pulling into the rest stop, buying a hot chocolate and a box of donut bits. Mixed myself up the last seven hits into a turquoise Bavarian Creme in the washrooms, then sat in the parking lot and ate the whole box. Slipped back onto the highway with a snapshot of the kitchen back home pasted on my mind. The holidays call the children home. Shit, I don't know what I was thinking. I was so keen on laughing at the joke of walking in and surprising them all that I clear forgot to fill up with gas.

Once I got out of the car I was glad, you know. I gasped at the cold when I first stepped out. It was like jumping into a swimming pool. I could feel the cartilage in the back of my throat the size of a frozen whalebone. But it was only a temporary discomfort. It's refreshing outside in this air. The car had started to give me a headache with the stench of exhaust seeping in through the floor, under the snow, even after the tank was empty. It was closing in on me; I had no choice. Outside gives way to the night, the stars, the frosted air, the blackness and that amazing 3-D space, like you're at the Planetarium, and I know I've done the right thing. The car isn't going anywhere. It's stuck and the axle's broken. Fuck it, it's only a rental.

I found my tree beyond the edge of the field. It's an old oak, just like the one in the graveyard I used to hang in. Soon as I saw it I knew where I was heading. There's only so many opportunities that Life hands you. It's time for me to get back to Nature. Tidy up the loose ends.

My clothes are folded down there on a tree stump; I couldn't get them off fast enough. They're piled up properly with the shoes on top, the socks rolled and tucked inside them like in a regular Boy Scout handbook. I'm glad I'm out of them and back in my own skin. It feels cleaner, somehow.

Neatness. Now that's something I've always prided myself on. Mess I can't stand: not figuratively, not literally. There are some, I know, who would say that my whole life has been one big fuck-up, one big shitpile of irresponsibility. Like Pauline. But that's all because I'll never screw her any more. Not properly at any rate. I stopped dating women the moment I tested positive, didn't I? Now that's neat. That's responsible.

But Pauline can't see that I keep my distance out of respect. If I was a true shit, I'd be spreading my bad news all over, right? But Pauline, she can't see beyond the drugs, beyond the HIV, beyond the labels, beyond the death sentence. She looks on Life as one long struggle to escape Death – what a waste. What a waste.

Look. Life unfolds; it shifts in one direction and then to another, a pulse, an ebb and flow, if that's what you want to call it. And that window of opportunity only presents itself for so long before the pendulum takes a swing away from you. You've got to grab onto it at just the right time if you want to escape.

Everything is so crystal clear, so sharp-edged, so neat and tidy, packed into little boxes, stacked on a tree trunk, ready for the movers. I can't feel the cold any more. I keep looking at the branches hanging heavy with their load of snow and they keep threatening to turn into something else. Reality is what you make of it. Mine has a road leading out of town, a road winding its way up into the stars, like for reindeer to follow and over the moon. The road never ends. The scenery changes, that's all.

I'm outta here. It's all been a fuck-up from the get-go. Small town cage kept me holed up for so long that I blew my chances before I'd even had a decent bash at them. Ma fed me a line of bullshit along with the *Krafty Dinner*. She poisoned the special sauce and thought I wouldn't notice. And Dad would trip me up on purpose whenever he started to lose at street hockey. The world isn't what they taught me. I know better now. Hockey doesn't make the man, and love doesn't make the world go round. Never could stand hockey. Not ice, not street, not field. I never fell in love. Not once.

Aha. Here it comes. I can feel it, finally. This is it.

Merry Christmas and a Happy New Year everybody. Santa's just around the corner. Seriously. I can hear the jangling bells of the reindeer. They're getting closer, rounding the top of the rise. Here they are.

Next step of evolution, here I come.


I don't know what happened, but it's beautiful. The sun came up on the slopes and I'm no longer where I thought I was, after all. The frozen field opened out upon itself like a blossoming chrysanthemum – transformed from the glistening snow into a lush, green meadow. Neo-colours, like in the illustrations of the Bhagavad-Gita. Long grasses wave gently in the early morning breeze and flowers dot the slopes where a golden cow is wandering towards me.

There's a woman astride it. Her red cloak is spread out over the rear end of the cow, and she lopes, lazily, from side to side, with the rhythm of her ride. I know she's looking at me. Her eyes are fixed on mine. I know her face but not her name. The bells around the cow's neck are jangling in a cloud of insects.

She pulls up below the tree. The branches now bursting with heavy, sweet blossoms. The cow lowers its head as it comes to a halt. It scrapes a hoof against the trunk, then looks up at me.

Sitting between its horns, just kinda floating there, is a little pink baby. All shiny, like a star, or as if it's been dropped in glycerin. I don't understand.

The woman looks at me and speaks without moving her lips.

"You can't just vanish," she says in a voice I can't quite place. "We have to make a swap."

I lift the child from between the cow's horns, hang it on a branch in the tree. It seems the right thing to do.

Then I swing down from my perch like the alien monkey-boy and jump up behind the woman and pull her cloak around my skinny white bones. The flesh of the cow is surprisingly cold and smooth. I expected it to be hairy but it isn't. It's smooth. We jerk forwards. Upwards. I can feel a breeze in my face. A scent of jasmine, honey, wet grass.

Mistletoe.

# 7 ... nothing to lose

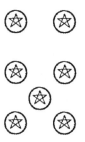

The hospital wristband says Angus Dobson, whoever that is, and it won't come off, it won't. The powder-blue nylon has stretched as far as it's going to and has turned into a wire of lethal properties. It can't be slipped off *à la* Houdini's handcuffs. Cherry takes her knife, wipes a gob of raspberry jelly onto her toast, saws through the wristband and frees herself from the final shreds of hospital bureaucracy. That done, she attacks her All Day Breakfast with renewed vigour.

It's one of those reptilian winter days: no sun and a cloud cover of lowering green drained of vitality, an eternal dusk relieved only by sweeping curtains of freezing rain. A panhandler works the strip outside the restaurant window, petitioning every prospect with an unheard request and a cup held out beneath dripping noses. It's cold and miserable, but Cherry doesn't care. She's free. And now, at almost four o'clock in the afternoon, she's enjoying an All Day Breakfast Special Number One: eggs scrambled, sausage, white toast, coffee and orange juice. There is a bale of French Fries instead of potatoes, but at this time of day the choice is limited to fried or boiled. She has escaped from Saint Theobald's Hospital with her addictions intact and has so far enjoyed three uninterrupted cigarettes. The last one is still burning in the ashtray. She's not really smoking it. It's for *ambiance*. She douses her scrambled eggs in catsup and pepper to hide the little bits of hamburger and nibbles on her jelly-spread toast.

The bruise on the side of her skull keeps making itself known with searing spasms that start at her nape and reach over her forehead and into her right tear duct like giant fingers gripping a bowling ball. There's a burst of pain every eight to ten minutes, which means she's getting better. Up until a few hours ago she had still been getting visual fireworks every time she changed position.

The breakfast tastes strange. Her stiff jaw makes it hard to chew and swallow food. She has too much time to savour the flavours. Maybe she put too much pepper on her eggs. Maybe there's a Life message in all of this.


"(nggh) Where am I? (nggh)"

That question, with all its asinine wounded Hollywood pretensions is one that, evidently, still needs asking on occasion. How many movies, how many hospital-bed scenes have been played out starting with that one line? How many times has Cherry eagerly awaited the answer, prepared to shift her reality to accommodate the response?

"You're in the Trinity Surgical Rehabilitation Unit."

"Shhh. Don't worry yourself. You'll be fine."

"You're lucky to be alive."

"I thought it was supposed to be a routine procedure. In and out?"

"There were complications."

"What kind of complications?"

"Dr Lyndhurst will explain. Now, try not to exert yourself."

The doctors were always explaining – never with any conviction and always after the fact. They could go on for hours, justifying why this piece had to be removed or why that bit no longer worked as it used to. And they always used the multiple pronoun mask of "we," abdicating any responsibility and implying that they were above being questioned.

"We had to make a decision. The fetus was lodged against your bladder."

"What have you done to me?!"

"We can't keep opening you up all your life, Nina."

Cherry has never been impressed with postoperative justifications.

"You should have installed a zipper! Why didn't you give me a fuckin' zipper?!"


Waking up in hospital. It's like spending a night in jail: everyone should do it at least once in their lives. For Cherry, it had been a while for either experience – a couple of years – but the impact was still less than if she'd been an Emergency Room virgin. She'd had a moment of cognizance in the ambulance, a glimpse of swinging rubber tubes and medical equipment in a subdued green light and a vague memory of someone repeatedly asking her what her name was. Not much else. She was, therefore, at least on some level, prepared. By the time she was able to stay awake for more than a couple of minutes, able to close her eyes without that catherine wheel of pain in the centre of her skull forcing her into unconsciousness, well, by that time, she'd already incorporated the Emergency Room into her dreams and tangled the saline drip with the ties of her hospital gown. She'd also accidentally ripped the IV tube out of her left wrist in a flailing dream of cockroaches crawling up her arm.

"How was I to know you'd stuck that thing in me? I was out cold!"

"Mr Dobson, will you keep still!" complained the nurse as she retaped the needle into a new site. Cherry feigned sleep; small talk would only have gotten in the way and her jaw hurt too much for chitchat. No, any future communication would have to be done ventriloquist-style and kept to the point. Which was a shame, because she would have loved to have found out who this "Mr Dobson" was. Papers must have gotten mixed up. Was Mr Dobson the moaning child at the far end of the corridor behind the curtain? Was he the roving drunk with his pants around his ankles who kept bugging her for cigarettes and loose change? Or was he lying on a slab in the morgue with someone else's name tagged on his toe?

Tentatively exploring her wounds, Cherry discovered her skull was bound, but not in an attractive turban; rather, she'd been kitted out with a lumpy girdle of a bandage, with tape stretched across the bridge of her nose. Something reeked of disinfectant and her eyelashes had been completely removed. There was further damage. Badly bruised ribs, aches and pains all up and down her left side, and a gauze dressing covering a mystery wound on her right elbow. Nothing insurmountable.

The true horror, however, was the discovery that her clothes hadn't made it through the maelstrom. Not her woolly mammoth coat, not her fatigues, not her pumps – not even her training bra or panties. Certainly not the wig. She was draped in one of those backward, verge-of-privacy garments which they hadn't bothered to tie up, leaving her bare ass sticking to the rubberized mattress. Try as she might, she couldn't quell the suspicion that a crowd of curious nurses had checked out her genitalia while she'd been unconscious. They must have seen her surgery, but still insisted on calling her "Mister." Really. One glance could have told them she was a "Mzz."

She was destitute. She had nothing. Not even her purse with her smokes. She kept asking, but with the efficiency that is borne on the wings of attending angels, no one could enlighten her as to where her belongings might be.

"My stuff!" she lamented. "Didn't I come with stuff?!"

No answer.

Someone was going to pay for all this.


The charges:

Wanted for grand larceny, theft, stealage, burglary, plunder and gross opportunism: Victor fucking Logan, the cocksucker. Last seen high-tailing it out of the bathroom window with a fortune in lottery tickets and nigh on seven thousand dollars in cash (minus a two-buck tip). Dead or alive.

Wanted for aiding and abetting the above, and assault with a cough-medicine bottle: unidentified street scum in blue jeans and red-and-white sneakers.

Wanted for squelching on accommodation arrangements and for creative blame-throwing: Cocktail Mama, aka Pauline Bloor. For grievous bodily assault with a baseball bat and polyester fashion crimes: El Bozo in the toupee and Hawaiian tie. And for allowing the aforesaid mob to set foot on the third floor of the Belt 'n Buckle Hotel in the first place: the front desk. Punishment: death or rent rebate.

For impersonation of a drug dealer: Coady. For impersonation of a child: Brock Bloor. For illegal broadcast of confidential information: Her Royal Heinie, Empress Estelle VII and the microphone at Buzby's.

For exploitation, kiddie porn and fraudulent withholding of prize moneys: Major Harbord, the Lotto Centre and its scowling Chairman of the portrait.

For suspicion of having a fingerstub in the whole affair: Liberty Hanna. Plus new girlfriend. Or old girlfriend.

And finally, for masterminding the entire fiasco from start to finish: You Know She.

Ladies or gentlemen of the jury, have you reached a verdict?


It was Frère André who'd taught Cherry how to make the best use of her time in a hospital bed. He was in a position to know. He'd been in traction for two years, both legs broken in over two dozen places, kneecaps removed, his spine trampled into the shape of the concrete steps on which he'd been attacked. That's what you get when you cross the Saturn Ring-Riders.

"Imagination, *tapette*," he'd say, out the side of his mouth. "Fantasy is the cure for all pains, all losses."

Stuck in the bed next to Frère André for two weeks while she recovered from a bashing she'd received from a Subaru packed with teenage yobbos, Cherry soon learned that Frère André's imagination got its biggest reward from watching her respond to his stories of bikerland practices. His eyes would sparkle as he relayed tortures employing kitchen appliance, creative uses for a plumber's snake and – he was an expert on this one – the most effective means of eliciting the greatest amount of fear from his imaginary victim.

"My brothers went about it all wrong in my case," he said. "They just went about their business as fast as they could. Didn't get me worked up about it. I don't think they got any enjoyment out of it at all. They should have chained me to the latrines for a year – that would have sorted me out. Ha-ha."

His theory – and Cherry had reason to believe that he'd had considerable practice – was that you should always lay the score out in the open, slowly lead your victim through the details of what you're about to do to them, so that the full impact of the upcoming torture is understood before you do it. Then do it. This method, according to Frère André, is guaranteed to be twice as effective as simply rushing through to the end. Any extra twists you think up on the spur of the moment can always be thrown in – grace notes, as it were.

"Give them a glimpse of freedom, *tapette*. Make them believe they can escape, that they have a way out. Then slowly close the door on their fingers. Ha-ha."

Sometimes he would laugh too hard and his traction weights would come off their pulleys and the nurses had to come running to prevent his spine snapping from the sudden loss of pressure. Cherry spent a large amount of her time imagining herself standing at the foot of Frère André's bed.

"I'm going to remove these weights, one by one," went the fantasy. "And then, you see this wire here? I'm going to give it a bi-ig tug. Want some Demerol? Oh dear, I'm sorry, André, we're fresh out of painkillers. How about some amphetamines to boost the experience?"

Oh yes, Frère André had taught her how to exploit her imagination well. Hospital stays were almost something to look forward to.


Saint Theobald's Emergency Room doctor, when he finally deigned to put in an appearance, was a disapproving world-weary asshole of the highest sphincter. He didn't have time to dirty his fingers with what he viewed as a drag queen who'd gotten into a cat fight and was now sullying the corridors of his hospital, and he said as much. He screwed his face up into his notes and conducted his examination two feet away from the gurney, getting the nurse to do all his work – and even that was cursory.

If Cherry had been someone else, she wouldn't have been treated like this, she was certain. If she had been – say – the Angus Dobson she was supposed to have been, or the Angus Dobson who had made some father a proud man and who had gone on for a stellar career in – say – the Fire Department or even the Police Force, well, if that had been who she was, things would have been different. She wouldn't have had to lie to the doctor about how her accident had happened for one thing. But seeing as Cherry was – not altogether unhappily – still Cherry, with all the prejudices that entailed, it was her fate to endure the injustices of her treatment.

"What happened here, then?"

"I fell downstairs. I was drunk."

"Nurse, isn't this patient supposed to be on a drip?"

"Mr Dobson keeps taking it out, doctor."

"Mr Dobson, you have to keep the needle in your arm. You're

dehydrated."

"So get me a fucking drink. Vodka tonic."

They gave her an aspirin derivative for her pain and when she complained that it wasn't strong enough, they informed her that they couldn't take a risk, what with the head injury and the drugs and alcohol she'd consumed.

"What alcohol?" asked Cherry, all innocent and wide-eyed. "What drugs?"

"Do you want me to show you the lab results?"

And that was the end of that argument. Besides, she had problems opening her jaw wider than a few millimetres.

Typical, she'd thought. Here I am, a gallstone's throw from one of the city's best-stocked 24-hour medicine cabinets and I can't get my mouth around anything stronger than a 222.


Imaginary confrontation number one:

"Eat! You miserable little prick! Eat them all up!"

"Y-yes master ..."

"*Mistress*. Yes, *mistress*," corrects Black-Hearted Cherry, Mighty Ruler of the Universe, pushing handfuls of multicoloured pills into Victor's mouth. "Say it like you mean it, you worm!"

"Ow! Ow!" Victor strains at his bonds as she pulls her fingernails across his drug-stuffed cheek. *Scratch'n Win*. "P-please ... no more!"

"What was that? Did you say something? Don't speak with your mouth full!"

Fade to next sequence ...


The earthly representatives of Saint Theobald, in their ineffable wisdom, decided to keep Mr Angus Dobson in overnight for observation which, in actuality, meant abandonment on an impossible-to-adjust gurney in a corridor near the Emergency Room. For hours, Cherry was ignored. There was, however, plenty of entertainment to keep her amused, even apart from her sadistic fantasies of what she intended to do to Victor once she got her hands on him. The hospital was in full seasonal swing: traffic accidents, drunks, enigmatic screaming, general depression, gloom and – like a *divertissement* from all this misery – a young man with a Christmas tree ornament stuck in his mouth, sitting patiently reading a magazine.

This young man – it didn't take Cherry long to discover – had a nearly full pack of Ultra-Lite cigarettes in his breast pocket. He was in no position to smoke them, so Cherry befriended him, milked him of the weak tobacco slowly but surely throughout the night. Finally he gave her the whole pack just to get rid of her. She broke off the filters, but it wasn't that much of an improvement; it was still like sucking on a mattress.

In her search to get some decent clothing on her flapping back, Cherry made a nuisance of herself at the nursing station, argued with an overworked administrator, grilled the ambulance boys beyond their smirking endurance, and was eventually rewarded with a black plastic bag of clothes which had the tag: *Dobson, Angus.* Inside the bag she found a stiff pair of oil-stained green overalls, a pair of salt-stained black shoes, underwear which certainly wasn't hers, a yellowing shirt flecked with suspicious brown spots, and a separate paper bag of woolens so steeped in blood it could have been tossed in a butcher's window amongst trays of liver and ground beef and sold to a housewife for $1.92 per hundred grams. These are not my things, she thought, distressed. I wouldn't be caught dead in these.

"I think there's been some mistake."

"You're Angus Dobson, aren't you?"

"Well, actually," admitted Cherry, "no."

"Why not?"

There was no answer to that without getting into a deep philosophical debate, so Cherry swallowed her persona and reluctantly accepted the bag of belongings as hers. She still didn't recognize any of it. The bump on the head must have made her forget herself. Himself.

At the bottom of the bag was a manila interdepartmental envelope containing Angus Dobson's personal effects and stapled to the outside of this was a yellow carbon copy of a filled-out form. Acronyms abounded. Things like *P-VRI* and *NFTV*, which she soon learned stood for "Pedestrian-Vehicle Related Incident" and "Not For Television" (for when the nature of an accident is considered too gruesome for the evening news). At the bottom of the form three ominous letters in a circle stood out: *DOA.* Cherry was familiar with what that meant.

"See?" she barked triumphantly, "I'm dead!"

"No, you're not," replied a paramedic, "but you will be if you don't leave us alone."

"But this says I'm dead. Dead On Arrival."

The envelope was snatched from Cherry, the form given the once over before being brusquely handed back. "You didn't have your health card with you when you arrived, did you?"

"Probably not."

"Well then. Consider yourself lucky you got any treatment at all."

She weaseled the story out of them. It turned out to be a not uncommon practice when patients didn't have any coverage, to use the health card number from a recent unclaimed corpse. It was a humanitarian white lie to ensure treatment for all, she was told. The paramedics were begrudgingly proud of revealing this bureaucratic loophole to her. The particular misfortunate who had provided Cherry with health benefits – one guy gleefully informed her – had been run through by a snowplough attachment on a streetcar a couple of days ago.

"Smashed their glasses. Went straight through the eyeball. Brains all over the street."

Feeling less than thankful for the subterfuge, Cherry gave in and wandered back to her gurney with Angus Dobson's chattel. She couldn't bring herself to put the shirt on – it had to be blood that was spotted all down the front – and the underwear were only to be worn in case of dire emergency. The overalls could almost be interpreted as stylish if she ignored the dark stain around the collar, but the nurses wouldn't let her put them on, saying that the drip got in the way.

She rifled through Mr Dobson's envelope with a repulsed curiosity. There was a large ring of some twenty or thirty keys, a broken candy cane still in its twisted wrapper, a handful of varying-sized screws, a tampon (now what was *that* doing there?), $22.37 in loose change, a snotty grey handkerchief and, loose at the bottom of the envelope like a visiting card from the Devil himself, something that made her heart skip a beat.

A bloodstained *XXXmas Scratch'n Win Lottery* ticket. Possible jackpot: $250,000. A quarter of a million. One of last year's tickets.


How had that gotten there? Those blasted tickets were going to haunt her if not to her grave then certainly to Angus Dobson's and beyond. There was no escaping them. The unwinnable lottery, the warty finger of fate, the unlucky lucky-find. She'd found herself in some loop of destiny that was going to taunt her over and over with its fake promise of wealth. Santa Calamity had it in for her.

She didn't dare scratch the ticket to see if it was a winner. The date made it probable, almost certain, but every time she brought one of her last remaining nails close to the surface of the play area, she'd shake uncontrollably and start to pass out. Angrily she shoved the offending ticket into a pocket of the overalls and tried to forget about it.

So there she sat on her gurney, with a bag of dead-man's clothes in her lap, feeling like the Grand Auntie of Idiots. She spent her time bemoaning and bewailing her losses: of her clothing, of her identity, of six and a half thousand dollars, of the lottery tickets and of the occasional period of consciousness. Few times in her life had Cherry ever been deprived of so much in one lump. Strangely, it felt good.


Imaginary confrontation number thirty-eight.

"*Et voilà – la cerise!*"

Renowned gourmet chef, *Madame LaPlage*, places her signature finishing touch on her *crème brûlée du pédé méchant*, a dish that has garnered her the accolades of the crowned heads of the underworld. The table of criminal dignitaries bursts into applause as the presentation is made.

"*C'est fantastique!*"

"*Délicieux!*"

"*Ach, mein Gott, himmliche! Was ist* – how you say – der secret ingredient?"

*Madame LaPlage* raises an eyebrow. The secret ingredient is hers and hers alone. She's not telling a soul. Anyways, who would believe that it would be such a simple thing? So simple and she has so much of it laying around.

Time.


"How long are you going to keep me here?"

The second question in the hospital-bed series. It's a question Cherry no longer asks, since it never – *never* – gets a true answer.

"We're going to keep you here until you get pissed off with waiting and leave."

No doctor, nurse or orderly has ever uttered these words. Cherry, however, just doesn't have the patience to see anything through to a mutually agreed-upon conclusion, and she always ups and goes before the official release date, leaving a cabinet of open files behind her to be closed at the discretion of the staff. She is sure there are some hospitals where she's still presumed to be sneaking a smoke in the washrooms, and others where reports are still being filled out about her by doctors and nurses who couldn't care less that they've lost contact to such an extent that they don't even know that their patients have gone.

*Still unresponsive to treatment. Recommend continuation.*

It's the time thing. Abraxas, Chronos, Thoth, or whichever god it is who controls the Universal Clock, never got to program Cherry properly. Her digital display is blinking permanently at twelve. Unprogrammable. Unrecordable. There is no "log in" time next to her name in the Akashic Records, an oversight that can't be rectified until she "logs out," and that could take forever at the rate she's going. Until then, she is left to thrash around in overlapping sequences, one escapade blurring into the next, the past and the future indistinguishable.

Call it temporal disorders of the nightclub variety. Add at least an hour to any rendezvous. Subtract a week from any relationship. Multiply by months for any realization to sink in. Divide by years to achieve a level of maturity.

In the meantime, keep on going. Doesn't Chronos ultimately devour his children?

The night had been interminable. She had tried to sleep, but approximately every hour, depending on other people's emergencies, a nurse would come and wake her up to take her vital signs. That is, if Cherry was there for her vital signs to be taken, because Cherry kept getting up, pulling out her drip, gathering her hospital gown about her and wandering around the corridors in search of a place to have a smoke without someone screaming at her to butt out. She needed to smoke to be able to think. To indulge her revenge fantasies. The washrooms, it didn't take her long to discover, had smoke patrols. Outside was way too cold – minus twenty, someone said. The staff canteen proved only good enough for two cigarettes and half a cup of machine-expelled coffeestuff before they found her.

It was the height of indignity. On top of kicking up a protracted fuss over Cherry taking her tubes out, her passing out, her wanderings and her lack of manners, no one would allow her to smoke. Every attempt to soothe her nicotine addiction had been met with a "We should be lying down, shouldn't we?" or a "What are we doing out of bed?" Questions that Cherry could answer on her own behalf, but not for them.

Some things never change.

A tattoo, they say, is forever. Frère André was covered in them from his twelve-year stint with the most notorious biker-gang in the country, the Saturn Ring-Riders: a group of hardcore reactor trouble-makers who kept crime-story newspaper-clipping scrapbooks for their grandchildren. It was a reputation that required constant upkeep. The Ring-Riders kept rumours flying in every province across the country about their initiations and rituals. Switchbladed chickens and junkie orgies – the stories were always sensational, but not all of them, as Cherry was assured by Frère André, were false.

"The Ring-Riders have no connection with the Mob," he maintained. "That story is false. The initiation ceremonies, yes. The Mob, no."

They had no need of the Mob; they were their own. Indeed, Frère André had spent half a dozen years as their Angel of Death. On his right arm, he had a tattoo of a seven-pointed star for every "judgment" he'd performed on behalf of his brotherhood. He boasted five stars in all, but you could only see three, due to the bandages.

The rest of his skin art – what could be seen of it – reflected a deep connection with the Roman Catholic Church. Cherubim floated around his ankles, the feet of Jesus could be seen, nailed to their crucifix, peeking through the body cast just above his navel. Saints and apostles blessed his neck. Every exposed piece of flesh had some form of sanctified design. Even his head was crowned with a circlet of thorns, visible in the bald patches. He was said to have the Stations of the Cross down his back and graphic depictions of the Seven Deadly Sins around his crotch. If he ever died, his pelt would surely make it into a Museum of Religious Art, depending, naturally, on how he died and the moral leanings of the museum curator.

"Never get a tattoo with writing, *tapette*," he warned, as if Cherry was contemplating it. "Leviticus, Chapter 19, verse 28. It says 'marks' but it means words. Never put words on your body. Only symbols and pictures."

It sounded like good advice.

"What about brandings?"

"Oh, those are fine."

"What about Chinese?"

Frère André thought for a moment.

"I guess that would be OK."

Cherry was relieved. She bears three pieces of "artwork" on her body. The cigarette burns from the Pongos up the inside of her thighs is one. That could hardly be described as language. The double *R* monogram that identifies her as a Rawhide Ranch alumni is another. The third is in Chinese. It isn't tattooed on her, but it's just as permanent – it's embossed on her implant. She once got a friend to translate it for her.

*Manufactured in Beijing.*


The plastic-wrapped meal masquerading as breakfast, served at the crack of dawn, tasted of stale urine. A young intern with the complexion of sour yogurt visited Cherry and asked her how many fingers he was holding up. He checked her eyes with a flashlight, felt for lumps in her throat, asked her if she'd had any dizzy spells or thickenings of the tongue, scribbled away on her chart and was gone before Cherry could punch him in the face.

Hours later she was visited by a spiffy young woman who wanted to know if there was a history of mental illness in Angus Dobson's family and asked three times what day it was. Cherry had no idea on any of these counts and, unfortunately, that seemed enough to prevent her from being pronounced fit enough to be discharged. Instead, more tests were ordered, just to be on the safe side. *Hey Baby, Take a Walk on the Safe Side.* After a short but heated exchange about the necessities of dangerous living, Cherry was advised to think about getting in touch with some professional help. That did it. Cherry, who'd always viewed possible insanity as something to look forward to in her old age, just couldn't hack it any longer.

In the women's washroom, she sluiced the blood out of the bag of woolens. She rinsed through sink after sink of dark, rusty water, which slowly got clearer until she had resuscitated a lavender scarf, a very pink balaclava and a pair of mittens, one ruddy, one tawny. She dried them all under the hot air machine, hitting the button over and over until the warm wool stunk. The scarf and balaclava, although still a tad damp, were quite serviceable and would stand her in good stead in the freezing temperatures outside. The mittens had shrunk in the wash, and were too ugly. The overalls, about three inches too short, made her feel grimy from the waist down and the underwear was tight and scratchy. She decided to leave her hospital gown on underneath everything for added warmth. The contents of the manila envelope were transferred back into the pockets from whence they presumably came: the keys, the money, the loose screws and the candy cane. The tampon, Cherry tossed. The days when she needed to carry *those* things around with her were long gone.

She squeezed into Angus' shoes and teetered out into the corridor, mightily aware of the bruises all over her body and of the bandage poking out from underneath the pink balaclava. The spiffing woman who would have had her committed was still chatting at the nursing station, so Cherry had to wait until the coast was clear.

Humming a little Gershwin tune to herself for immoral support, she waved goodbye to the poor lad with the tree ornament still stuck in his mouth and managed to sneak through the seeing-eye double doors into the real world without anyone stopping her. It was way too early in the day to start visiting anyone. No one she knew would be awake for hours yet. Paradoxically, wandering around the freezing streets, she felt – for the first time in ages – as if she were actually doing something constructive with her life, even though she felt empty, had nowhere to go, had no one to see and nothing to do except to savour her perversely laconic anger.

She hit a drugstore and stole herself some fresh lashes and a pair of sunglasses.


Breakfast. Cherry takes a long ostrich pull on her cigarette before impaling another sausage. The bursting of the skin as the tines penetrate the meat deflates her mood. The lack of sleep is getting to her. She chews away, slowly, until breakfast is done. She mops up the last bits of catsup from her plate, smokes a handful of cigarettes, reaches the huffing-waitress level of the bottomless cup of coffee and tries to decide what to do. The waitress keeps glaring at the bill on the table as if she suspects that Cherry doesn't have the money to pay for it. Everyone in the restaurant studiously avoids looking Cherry in the eye.

Her head is a constant surf of pain – the bandages could take a while to come off – but am I still *attractive*, Doctor? No. She looks like a beaten-up Chevy in the back of a used-car lot. Olivia de Havilland in *The Snake Pit*. Disappointment and dilapidation from her lost fortunes and misfortunes respectively have left their marks. Worse, she has only seven cigarettes left in the pack.

Eventually, Cherry pays her bill. She checks her cash situation. $16.30. Yay.

She tosses two dollars to the panhandler outside the restaurant when he asks her for money "to get back to the hospital." She stuffs her hands deep into her pockets and sets off. It's almost five-thirty. People should be waking up around now.

The freezing drizzle is almost soothing. She contemplates hailing a taxi but decides that she'd better economize if she wants to keep herself in smokes. There's no knowing where money will come from next. She trudges through Chinatown, down through the housing projects and across the park, making up stories as she goes. Eventually, her fingers go numb, much like her mood. By the time she nears her destination, she is a twisted combination of angry melancholia and curdled philosophy.

The world is a second-rate bonanza. Reach for the top prize and someone will chop off your fingernails, rip off your eyelashes. Strive for the great and you'll get the mediocre more oft than not. It's a shame, but there it is, thinks Cherry. Some people are born winners and some, losers. The rest of the population, herself included, fall in the middle, neither winning nor losing but making do with partial dreams, maybe hopes, and sometime lovers.

There is only one point to life, she concludes as she descends a familiar flight of stone steps: staying awake for it.


Zachary doesn't open the door to his basement apartment at first, leaving Cherry cowering under the icicled porch. Finally – after repeated poundings – the door opens to the width of the chain. Zachary's gold-flecked purple eyes peek out at her. He checks her up and down.

"Ye-es?"

"Do you have a moment?" Cherry swallows hard, realizing that the moment Zachary has already spared her is filled with distrust and antagonism. "Can I come in? It's really gross out here."

It seems an age before Zachary takes the chain off the door and lets her into the hallway. He tries to keep her there, with the boots and the umbrella stand, but after carefully removing her slushy shoes, wet balaclava and scarf, and unbuttoning her overalls, Cherry slips past him into the living room and flops herself down on the futon-couch. Zachary patters after her on bare feet. He's in pajamas of spotted flannel, his hair loose, cascading around his neck, over his eyes.

Cherry choses her moment to dramatically remove the sunglasses. Zachary is vastly unimpressed.

"I must be crazy letting you into this apartment," he says. "What happened to you? You look awful. Is that a hospital gown underneath there?"

"I need a favour."

"I was afraid of that," mutters Zachary in a martyr's tone, shuffling off towards the kitchen. "I'm making espresso. Do you want one?"

"Mmmm," agrees Cherry, casting her eye over the coffee table, which looks as if it's nursing a hangover, "and a glass of water, perhaps?"

Party debris. It's recognizable instantly, even amongst the florid Christmas decorations. The ashtrays are overflowing with a thousand and one shades of lipstick butts, garlic-dip traps on the floor gather sprinkles of pine needles from the tree, that has, for its part, attracted a congregation of dead beer bottles beneath its branches. Drug paraphernalia and garlands of tinsel litter the side tables, videos and compact discs are spilt all around the sound system. It looks as if there's been quite the crowd making the old merry-merry.

At the centre of the coffee table there is a small, ornate Persian-style mirror, lying face up, bearing the residue of a turquoise powder. A fifty-dollar bill, rolled up and tucked in on itself lies diagonally across the mirror in a perfect snapshot of North American drug use. It could be an album cover for a seventies rock 'n roll band.

"I see Victor was here," says Cherry, as nonchalantly as she dare, pitching her voice to carry to the kitchen.

"Ye-es." Zachary shouts back, dismissive. "They all came over here after the tubs, and … *Fuck! Shit!*"

The espresso machine malfunctions again. Cherry recognizes the distinctive sound of the filter coming loose and coffee grounds being forcibly expelled all over the kitchen in a spray of steam. A few seconds later, she hears the smash of crockery as Zachary defuses his annoyance. After a while he returns, serene and calm, carrying two glasses of water.

"I knew I should never have woken up this morning." He seats himself in a leather armchair and picks at his toes, massages his ankles. Starts rolling a joint. "I hope your turning up on my doorstep isn't an omen?"

Cherry daren't answer him. Surely he's joking.

"So what's the story?" he asks eventually. "You can't stay here you, know."

Cherry sighs. She feels too comfortable to start dredging up her sordid escapades. She'd rather watch Zachary in his pajamas. If she hadn't seen the birth certificate, she wouldn't believe his age. He still looks cardable. Perhaps she could try (once again) to squeeze his secret out of him? But her bruises remind her that she has a mission. She takes a deep breath before launching into her story.

"You heard about the lottery tickets, right?"

"Some." He splits open a cigarette to add tobacco to a healthy heap of marijuana. "Didn't you and Liberty get your hands on a pile of scratch and wins? Word is they're stolen, right?"

"They are now. Victor swiped them." Cherry chooses her words carefully, looks Zachary right in the eye. "I have to get them back by midnight Sunday, or I'm dead. D-E-A-D."

Oh, that little remark certainly grabbed his interest. It may not seem so by the way he finishes off his rolling – sealing the paper with a swipe of his tongue, a twist, a trim and a lubrication of the spliff with a dipstick plunge into saliva-puffed mouth – but his interest is definitely piqued. You can see it in the shadow of a wrinkle around his eyes.

"Oh yeah?" Zachary lights the joint, blowing a blue jet of sweet-smelling smoke into the air. "What's that supposed to mean?"

"I have to find Victor before *they* do," Cherry continues with a grim smile, squeezing a wince from the bruise on her head at the word *they*. "They're none too pleased about losing their investment. They tried their best to beat Victor's name out of me, but I kept my mouth shut."

"They …?" He pulls a parting toke on the joint before handing it over. "Investment? Beating? Who are you talking about?"

"I was baby-sitting," explains Cherry, puffing away like a sputtering muffler. "Bikers. The Saturn Ring-Riders. Know them?"

Sure he does. Everyone knows about the Saturn Ring-Riders. Anyone who's been around has heard of them, and Zachary's been around since the Great Flood. Cherry watches him click through the mental connections. The Saturn Ring-Riders are up to their studded denim necks in any illegal activity worthy of their reputation. Drugs, prostitution, pornography, corruption, smuggling, extortion, government logging contracts, etc. And gambling, naturally. Lotto tickets. Click.

"I didn't know you were involved with the Saturn Ring-Riders."

Cherry smiles enigmatically and plays her trump card. "I was their property for years, didn't I ever tell you? Look-see." She unbuttons the side of the overalls and shows off the Rawhide Ranch branding on her buttocks. Double R. It doesn't stand for Rolls Royce. Neither does it stand for Ring-Riders, but Zachary needn't know that.

"The initiation stories are true." Cherry buttons herself back up and strokes her bandaged head. "That's probably why they weren't too hard on me. Respect for a brother."

Warning sirens must be going off in Zachary's head; he's known Cherry long enough to be wary of her fables. But the branded proof is sitting right there before him. And she looks bad enough to have been beaten up by bikers – she looks worse by the second, if the truth be told. Before Zachary has time to delve too deeply into Cherry's double R past, she spins him a tale of her torture, pulling back from the details, letting his imagination fill in the blanks. He falls for it.

"Shit! That's really heavy. They didn't follow you here, did they?" Now he's starting to get worried. "Because the last thing I need in my life right now is the Saturn fucking Ring-Riders ..."

"Oh, you're safe hon. Don't worry." A dramatic pause before she continues. "But I wish I could say the same for Victor."

"Wha–? What do you mean?"

"What I mean is that I hope he doesn't try cashing in any of those tickets or anything stupid like that. The Riders have the city posted. Locked up tight. He'll be dog meat if they catch him."

Zachary sighs over Victor's imminent grave. He knows full well that the first thing Victor will do is try to cash in the tickets. If only he knew where Victor was, he says, he could warn him of the danger he's in. But he doesn't. Last he saw of him was the night before when Victor and his new friend were stoned out of their minds, rabbitting on about visiting Victor's folks for the holidays or some such foolishness. Zachary says he could make a few phone calls and find out ...

"Good idea," says Cherry a tad too quickly. Oops.

Zachary looks at her sharply, holds for a beat. Age and experience snap in. Now he's suspicious.

"They didn't – they didn't put you up to this, did they, Cherry? Did they?!"

Too late, Cherry realizes the trap she's stumbled into. The more she denies it, the more Zachary is convinced that Cherry is hunting down Victor for the Saturn Ring-Riders. She's doing their dirty work for them! Nobody could withstand their biker brand of torture. Of course she gave in to them. Of course she ratted on Victor. Of course they made her go find him.

"You're a fucking snake, Cherry Beach!" Zachary's eye twitches, one of the early signs of a mood getting the better of him. "You'd sell your best friend down the river to save your own skin. I know you!"

"I don't have any friends!" counters Cherry, trying unsuccessfully to maintain her calm. "I was born under a cursed planet."

That could be true. It would certainly explain a lot.

"Exactly! No. No! Don't try to misdirect me. Fuck!"

Zachary's hands are flying into the air, stretched, taught – he'll have to break something soon if Cherry doesn't cool things down. And he's so stubborn with his anger. The man smokes way too much dope.

"I swear to you, it's the truth," she says, grabbing Zachary's hands and looking earnestly into his eyes, feeling her swoon glands kick in. "I didn't rat on Victor. I swear I didn't. You have to trust me on this, Zach."

He glares at her, his eyes betraying his peculiar mix of stoned hostility and macho vanity. *I know you're in love with me and my youthful beauty and you know that nothing will ever happen between us. Never. You know that. But I ... like the attention ...*

He says nothing, frees his hands from hers and takes a long toke. Holds his breath. Exhales. Shooting her a bitter look, he hands her the joint and turns on the television with the remote. Sports.

During a commercial break the conversation resumes.

"You can't stay here, you know that."

"So you keep saying."

"But you can't. I want you to be sure you understand that."

"Uh-huh."

Cherry drags herself up off the couch, goes to the kitchen where she fixes the espresso machine. That should keep him happy for a couple of days.


During her shower, as she washes the stench of hospital from her and lets the pounding water sluice over her neck, a laugh erupts. It isn't the kind of laugh anyone would want to suppress. It's a wipe-clean kind of a cackle, an evil-witch-in-the-mirror snort-a-rama, a bilious guffaw-fest. She hopes the water drowns out her noise.

"Ha-ha-ha!"

Zachary has bought her story hook, line and bathroom plunger. She blows dear old Frère André a nice big thank-you kiss, imagining it winging its soggy way to where he's probably still lying in his hospital bed. Thanks bro', much obliged. And it looks as if she might actually manage to track down Victor by faking concern for his safety. If that happens – and once she's finished with him, natch – then maybe she'll consider getting a seven-pointed star tattooed on her arm ...

"Ha-ha!"

Congratulations are in order. She's successfully twisted things around to her own advantage. Mere hours ago she was completely destitute, without a friend in the world and now, here she is ensconced *chez* Zachary: fine coffee, multicable television and a never-ending supply of marijuana. This is the fifth time she's wound up on his doorstep in the past two years. It's beginning to feel like home. Whatever that is.

"Ha!"

The laughter turns hollow. It empties itself out, leaving nothing behind. Zilch. An intolerable void. Whatever humanity she had left to lose, she's lost it.

# 8 ... pocket money

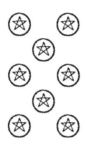

"I've got to go now. Bye."

Zachary hurriedly hangs up the phone, when Cherry, draped in a giant black bathsheet, emerges from the bathroom. She ignores him and nurses her elbow. Then she pretends to be as interested as he is in watching the muted television.

Zachary is uncomfortable. He keeps stabbing a fresh cup of espresso across the table. His mouth is drawn tight, the muscle beneath his eye twitches down his cheek. He looks younger than ever – about sixteen. You'd think he'd be pleased that the machine has been fixed.

She sits down next to him on the couch and rubs her scalp dry with a corner of the towel, paying extra attention to the eternal damp spot behind her ears. For a while she listens to his heavy breathing. He seems unsure of himself. He sparks up another joint to help get the language flowing.

"Would you …" the words come hard and slow. "Are you …?" He tries again. "I can't believe I'm saying this, but …"

Silence. Cherry shrugs and gives him her helpless smile. He seems such a poor, awkward lad. She feigns interest in the hockey.

Suddenly, Zachary finds his syntax rushing out of him.

"I appreciate your fixing the espresso machine for me, Cherry. You may not think it, but I really appreciate it, so thank you. And I'm sorry about what I said to you earlier about …"

"I'm in a bit of a bind," prompts Cherry, gently, "until Sunday, midnight."

"Well, I guess you can stay here until then." Zachary's head jolts a couple of times after this announcement, as if in disbelief. "But I don't want you using the phone, OK?"

Cherry respectfully agrees to the condition. It's taken a lot of effort on Zachary's part to blurt all this bullshit out. It could even cause him to age.

"I don't suppose," adds Zachary with sudden acidity, "I don't suppose that there's any point in mentioning the phone bill?"

No, there isn't. Not now.

"Excuse me."

He gets up, shaking with the energy required to check his anger, and leaves the room, clutching his cup, his knuckles white. A few seconds later there is the distant sound of a smash, followed by a "Fuck!" Cherry nods to herself. Zachary's so predictable. She calculates she has five days – seven at the outside – before he runs out of things to break and then she'll have to move on. Who had he been talking to on the phone to make him change his tune? He could never have come up with that apology on his own.

Ten to one Zachary had found Victor. Cherry picks up the phone, hits the asterisk button and looks at the display screen. *K. McKee.* Aha. That's Her Royal Heinie's number.

Zachary comes back in with a quilt and other bedding which he drapes over the back of the futon-couch. He taps a pillow with his fingers.

"Until Sunday night, OK?" he says, before vanishing into his bedroom and putting on loud satanic music.

Sunday night. Well, it was a partial truth. Sunday at midnight is when the tickets become worthless. Stale-dated into the New Year. Other than that, it's an arbitrary deadline that Cherry wouldn't mind extending. In fact, the chances of Victor coming out of hiding after Sunday are pretty high, especially if he thinks that by that time

Cherry will have been beaten to a pulp by the Saturn Ring-Riders. Ha! She smiles to herself. It's a waiting game, isn't it? Who can hold out the longest. Well, she's played that game before. She can wait forever.

To the sound of a screaming guitar coming from Zachary's room, she makes up the bed, folding out the futon with practiced ease – one of modern life's required skills. She hangs her towel over the railing at the foot of the frame, rearranges the cushions and pillows, fluffs up the old quilt then slips beneath the covers. Naked, except for a Band-Aid on her elbow, she snuggles herself into a cocoon. Soon she is fast asleep, her hips nestling into the familiar hollow between the lumps of the futon, her mind singing along to the lyrics of a heavy metal song that she hasn't heard for years.


Community Service, as organized through the courts and the Mount Pleasant Rest Home for the Elderly, had to be the most tedious torture ever devised for the punishment of the not-so-hardened criminal. It involved sitting in a room full of geriatrics watching MTV without sound, listening to Sister Sharon tell everyone stories about her dog. Hour after hour after hour of puppy tales. Sister Sharon was the administrator, and she sat at a desk beneath the television. You could tell everyone wished it would just fall off its ledge and squash her flat. It was an old set. It would have done the job.

Her dog, Mr Phipps, wasn't allowed in the home for reasons of hygiene, but Mr Phipps' picture was everywhere – on the walls, on her desk, even on the door to the men's washroom. His one-time "girlfriend," a vicious-looking Yorkshire terrier, was on the door to the women's can. Mr Phipps was one of those boring, I-look-like-every-other-kind-of-dog dogs. Black snout, pointy ears, beady eyes. Hair. Vaguely brown, depending on the photograph. Sister Sharon had an album close to hand at all times. Woe betide anyone who asked to look at them. She had a twenty minute story to go with every snapshot.

"... And this is up by the lake, two summers ago ... Look carefully, you can see Mr Phipps swimming! That's his nose just sticking out the water ... To the right, there, see ..."

This was how 80 per cent of the time was spent doing Community Service at the Mount Pleasant Rest Home. The remaining 20 per cent was allotted to helping the residents go to the toilet, accompanying them down the hall with the washroom key, and then – depending on the robusticity of the bowel or bladder in question – helping them make themselves presentable for the TV lounge again.

"I hope you like cleaning up feces," Sister Sharon had joked on the first day. "You'll get used to it."

Which was an absolute lie. It was possible to numb yourself to it, but never, not in a million lifetimes could Cherry ever get used to it. Nor could anyone else who was on the program with her.

There were five other miscreants assigned to Community Services, for crimes committed, charges deferred, and freedoms bargained for. They were all forced to sit in a lineup of chairs against the wall. The person in the chair nearest to the door was "up" – which meant that the next expedition to the toilet was theirs, followed by approval and a dog story from Sister Sharon when they handed over the washroom keys. Everyone would then shift one chair to their right and the whole process would start over. Sometimes two patients had to be taken at once and, rarely, a major accident would require everyone's help. On these occasions everyone would return to the seat they had just occupied, feeling, somehow, that someone had escaped their fair share of toilet trips. That was exactly the sort of mindfuck it played on you.

If it hadn't have been for Rose, Cherry would have gone mental.


Rose St James was (and still is) one of those children of the night who can, under close scrutiny, pass muster as a standard-issue human being. She pays her taxes, possesses credit cards, knows how to dress, and keeps a healthy relationship going with her parents. If it wasn't for her long-term association with Liberty Hanna, there would be little to distinguish her as alternative, subversive or otherwise deviant from the norm.

If Cherry has gone through her life being subjected to the taunts and whims of Santa Calamity d'Oopsidaisy, then Rose has spent hers under the watchful eye of Saint Scott the Free and Blameless, patron saint of those who cheat and get away with it. Rose was the girl in high school who called in the bomb threat, put Vaseline on the door handles in the gym, left the toilets locked from the inside, sold dope and pornography to the kids, and tortured frogs. Teachers thought the sun shone out of her asshole. She wore a metal tag: *Head Girl*. She still wears it, although its meaning has changed somewhat outside the structure of school. Had Cherry known Rose during those formative years, one of them would have undoubtedly killed the other.

That Rose was stuck doing Community Service at the Mount Pleasant Rest Home was no aberration. Liberty had strayed from the path of monogamy and Rose had "put the other bitch straight," which is to say that she drove her out to the sewage treatment plant, frog-marched her up onto the catwalk, and made her jump in.

"I gave her a choice," Rose said in her own defense. "I told her she could jump or I could push her." The kid jumped, ended up in hospital with permanent liver damage, and Rose got off with twelve days of Community Service to be carried out on weekends.

Sister Sharon never twigged to the fact that it was Rose who was slowly emptying the narcotics cupboard opposite the washrooms. You'd think she could have figured it out by a simple process of elimination, but no. You'd think she'd have been smart enough to separate the wash-room key from her ring of other important keys so that temptation was removed. Once again, no. Sister Sharon deserved what she got.

"I'm going to get that fucking dog if it's the last thing I do," whispered Rose to Cherry one afternoon. "Just you watch. I'm gonna get that Mr Phipps. I know where she lives."

Rose was no selfish creature, Cherry had to give her that. She shared her drug haul with everyone. It made the dog stories less invasive, the emptying of colostomy bags less gruesome, the entire punishment of waiting in the chair line less tedious. Sometimes, however, someone would melt down in their seat and fall to the floor in a rubbery heap. That – as Mom and Pop might say – was a dead giveaway that the kids have been getting into the medicine cabinet.

Anyone caught falling off their chair would automatically get extra days added to their sentence. They were threatened with urine analysis. It became a game to see who could best hold their drugs, which got more and more addictive as the weeks blurred past. By the end of Rose's time at the rest home, Cherry felt as if she needed three more weeks in rehab.

"Hey, you should meet my girlfriend," said Rose as they made their farewells to each other on the steps of the Mount Pleasant Rest Home for the Elderly. "She'll be picking me up in about five minutes. I hope she brought that Mr Phipps."

Cherry is awakened by the sound of a garbage-can lid crashing down the steps outside, followed by a frantic pounding on the door. A dog starts barking. The doorbell rings. More pounding. It's nearly five in the morning. Cherry wraps herself in the quilt, drags herself to the hallway, still half asleep. Standing on the porch is Coady, with a couple of friends lurking in the shadows. He's not at all surprised to see her at Zachary's.

"Hi, Cherry. Victor here yet?" The chipper little bastard.

"He doesn't live here, you know."

"Neither do you, but we heard …" One of his friends nudges him in the ribs to shut up.

"Who is it?" calls Zachary, emerging from his room. "What's going on?"

"Chemical-seeking monsters," announces Cherry as Coady and gang push their way into the apartment. "Want me to sic the neighbour's dog on 'em?"

The arrivals crowd around the coffee table, as high as buzzards, as low as sewer rats, sitting with the tippy-most edges of their asses on Cherry's freshly abandoned nest, their knees jiggling, their mouths chewing, the cold smell of night drifting off their coats. They pass around the cigarettes and smoke with their gloves on.

"But we heard he was here," complains Coady. "Fuck, man, I've got a big order for him."

"Try the fried chicken place down the street," suggests Cherry dismissively, hating to get into a conversation about Victor in case she suddenly starts turning blue in the face and spitting poisoned ice cubes.

"I think he went to his folks for the holidays," says Zachary in a tired, sane voice, obviously thinking that the cooler he appears, the sooner they'll be gone. "He had a rented car, right?"

"Right," echoes one of Coady's friends. The blond one with a Band-Aid on his chin.

"Hey, I know you," says Cherry, suddenly transfixed by a pair of red-and-white sneakers. "You. Blondie. What's your name?"

"Alexander."

Zachary reaches for the phone, dials a number.

"Oh, Alexander, is it?" Cherry languorously lights herself a cigarette while she rolls the name around her tongue. "Well … Alexander. Correct me if I'm wrong, but I seem to remember last seeing you in a certain bathroom at the Belt 'n Buckle, committing an offense with a bottle of *Dr Buquough's*."

Coady and the other kid think this is hilarious and burst into a fit of giggles. Cherry shuts them up with a withering glare. This is no floor show. Zachary gets through to his party on the phone.

"Hi, it's Zach ... yeah, I know it's nearly five ... can you tell me why Coady is over here with a couple of shaking gerbils looking for Victor? I thought you said ..."

Zachary listens to an explanation, while Cherry stares at Alexander, waiting for an admission.

"You don't happen to know what happened to a bag of Scratc 'n Win lottery tickets, do you, Alexander, sweetheart?" Cherry leans forward, grips him by the kneecap, squeezes into the muscle.

"We split up," says Alexander in the smallest voice imaginable. "I don't remember much. I lost my T-shirt."

"C'mon, honey, you can do better than that."

"You mean the money?" asks Alexander, wide-eyed, lip trembling. "The cash? I dunno, it disappeared. We lost track of it. Honest – ouch! – OK, we spent some of it, but somewhere during that night, the rest of it vanished. Along with Vic. We were really stoned, you know."

Cherry isn't interested in the money, although she wouldn't say no to six and a half thousand bucks if it were offered her. To be frank, she'd written the cash off as soon as it was gone. It's the bag of tickets she's interested in, or so she maintains. To keep up her pretense of the Sunday deadline, she has to pursue the bag. She's beginning to convince herself that she wants it more than she wants Victor.

"What happened to the *Louis Vachon*?"

"*Louis Vachon*? What's a *Louis Vachon*?" sing all three gerbils in chorus.

By the time Cherry has described the intertwining *LV* logo, Zachary has finished his phone call and she has come to the point where she believes that not only does Alexander not know where the bag is, but also that he's never seen designer luggage in his entire life. Really. What are fags coming to these days?

It takes another twenty minutes, two joints and four Extra Strength Tylenols before the late-night visitors leave. Zachary slams the door behind them, sighs heavily on his way back to bed.

"Zach?"

"Goodnight, Cherry."

"Zach, who were you talking to on the phone?"

He doesn't want to tell her.

"Kenneth," he finally admits – meaning Her Royal Heinie. "I thought you wanted to find Victor. I was asking around earlier, for you, OK? Coady was over there and he must have gotten things mixed up, I guess."

"Zach!"

"Do you have a problem with that?"

"Zach! Nobody's supposed to know I'm here. Word could get out. I can't have the Saturn Ring-Riders knowing I'm here. It could be fatal!"

"I know," mutters Zachary vanishing into his bedroom. "I want to make sure you're not here beyond Sunday."


"Mr Phipps, is that you? Mr Phipps, what is wrong with you?! What are you doing here?! *Mr Phipps!!*"

Sister Sharon's voice got higher and higher as she pitched herself into hysteria. Liberty, Rose and Cherry, hiding in the alcove in the corridor, had to hold onto their noses to prevent themselves from bursting into uncontrollable laughter.

"Mr Phipps, what have you done to yourself?!"

Sister Sharon must have lost her last remaining brain cells years ago if she couldn't figure out that Mr Phipps couldn't possibly have given himself a haircut and dye job. He wasn't making a statement. Not one of his own, at any rate.

"Liberty, this is my good friend, Cherry Beach," said Rose as they bundled into the Plymouth Fury. "Cherry, this is my lover, Liberty. Keep your paws off, OK?"

Liberty held up her fuchsia-stained hands in defense. "Hey, c'mon Rose. I don't go for drag queens. You know that."

"Cherry's no drag queen."

"Trannies then."

"Cherry's no tranny either," said Rose, archly.

"Oh, give me a break," growled Liberty, turning to Cherry. "What've you got down there, then? A dick or a cunt?"

"Neither," replied Cherry as politely as she could. "They gave me a valve."

"A *what*?!"

"A valve. I asked for a zipper, but they wouldn't give it to me."

The next day, Cherry dons a Cinderella persona and drags a damp rag over a few surfaces. Zachary has done a U-turn on his agreement; he's threatening to call the police to get Cherry out of his apartment, out of his life. He can't be serious – it's only Friday. Furthermore, he's got a ton of dishes to drop kick before he really makes good on his threat.

Not that he hasn't almost worked his way through a complete twelve-course setting already. At least he's being tidy about his destruction; he's been hurling his plates, cups, saucers and bowls out the back door. His kitchen leads onto a small yard surrounded by a ten-foot-high concrete wall, and this yard is now a porcelain charnel house, the walls covered with little white stars of execution, the snow crusted with broken china corpses. Skeletal remains of a relationship.

The six-hundred-dollar genuine collector's edition hand-painted Elvis Presley commemorative plate, however, still hangs on the living-room wall. When her reluctant host goes for this prized plate, Cherry knows it will be time to leave.

Cherry alphabetizes his CD collection, cleans the bathroom mirror to a sparkling finish and disposes of a dustbunny she finds under the sink. She is just about to start on the heavy stuff (vacuuming, dishes, garbage, the living room, etc.) when she is stopped by her nasty headache and has to lie down and smoke more of Zachary's pot.

She isn't avoiding the work, she genuinely wants to help out but she doesn't dare risk it with her injuries. Fuck it. If the road to Hell is paved with chores undone, then Cherry Beach is sailing down the gutter of indolence.

In the early afternoon she cooks a meal. She spends the remainder of her money on exotic ingredients. The finished result: a tuna casserole with fresh coconut, olives, endives and oysters. It tastes of soap.

When Zachary graces her with his presence he rarely talks. That he enjoys Cherry's admiration is obvious, even though he pretends otherwise. He manages to exude a martyrlike broken-heartiness, as if he doesn't want to hurt Cherry with rejection while ignoring her or berating her at the slightest provocation. He revels in Cherry's agony.

For Cherry, however, it's the ideal love affair. A grunting familiarity, a thinly disguised hostility, the sharing of an occasional joint, and no sex. Aggravated stagnation. Perfect.

What more could a girl ask for?

"Found a new place yet?" demands Zachary. "Still here?"

Other than a permanent headache, she's on the mend. The bandages are off and she's managed to borrow a T-shirt from the bottom of Zachary's closet, but that's as much as she got from him. He drew the line at any further robe appropriation and flew into a smashing rage when he caught Cherry with her hand in his underwear drawer. Really. She wasn't after his fountain of youth, just some Skivvies. She had to steal his swimming trunks when he was out of the house on an errand. She hid Angus Dobson's old, scratchy briefs in the garbage. Zachary won't need his trunks until summer, she reasons, and by that time, she should be long gone. The overalls aren't too bad, now that she's wearing them with the top sloughed off, the seat pulled down, and the arms wrapped in a knot around her waist. But the shoes pinch something terrible, especially without socks, so she leaves them off except when she runs to the corner store to get cigarettes.

To pass the time, she sneaks through Zachary's bedroom whenever he's out of the apartment, searching for a secret something – a diary, love letters, or other such *billets-doux*. She should be so lucky. All she finds is a stack of bondage porn mags and gun catalogues beneath the bed which she couldn't be less interested in. The best find is an eight-by-ten glossy photograph of Zachary taken by a local celebrity photographer about twenty years ago. Dorian Gray in a jockstrap. It's worth sighing over for a few minutes, but not worth stealing from its place in the back of the closet.

She calls Her Royal Heinie half a dozen times to find out whether Victor's put in an appearance on the circuit yet. But he's still missing, presumed to be at his folks, wherever that might be. No one can remember. Time is running out; the little shit can't stay in hiding forever. Sooner or later he's going to have to come out and party.

She also throws out a feeler for any work that might be had at clubs and restaurants. Bartending, hosting – shit, she'll even lower herself to bussing if that's all there is – but not at the Kennel, thanks very much.

"What's the rush?" asks Her Royal Heinie. "Isn't Zachy-baby looking after you?"

"I should be so lucky."


Zachary doesn't understand money. He's never had to. For years his needs have been taken care of by men of means. He is, in the parlance, a kept boy, putting in appearances with his patrons a few hours a week, in return for which he never has to worry about finances. Or, it would seem, aging. Hooking keeps him young, he says. Cherry doesn't envy him nor hold him any malice. He has the looks to do it; it only makes sense to exploit them. It does, however, make things difficult when Cherry tries to explain her cash situation. Zachary's spent so long in the Land of the Kept that he simply doesn't comprehend.

"What do you mean you don't have any money left? What happened to it?"

"I've already told you. I was ripped off."

"Then you'd better get yourself some more. I don't know. Get yourself a job or something. Hit the streets."

"Come on, Zach. Not all of us are as good looking as you, you know."

For that flattery he loans her twenty bucks. Pocket money.

"You're a parasite," he announces, getting up from the couch with his dope box clutched to his breast. "You're a fucking moth in my closet. I want you out tonight and I want to count the silverware before you go."

Cherry sulks as she watches him huff out of the room. She hears another cereal bowl hit the wall.

"Count your fucking silverware," she mutters to herself. "But don't count your dishes. You'll only upset yourself."


The moth, according to Cherry's Encyclopedia of Entomology, leads a riskier life than the butterfly. Its antennae are covered with tiny hairs which not only heighten its olfactory abilities, but also make it susceptible to the slightest breeze. It's a nocturnal creature, which may guarantee it a fun-filled nightlife on the one hand, but also exposes it to the dangers of the dark side on the other. During the daytime, after a night spent gorging itself on mink and fox stoles, the sated moth sleeps with its wings spread open – dreaming, in all likelihood, of being a butterfly. Butterflies may be trivial but they're no fly-by-nights.

When Cherry met Zachary for the first time, she'd been his moth. She was drawn to his youthful flame, desperate to burn her wings. She spotted him as soon as he walked into the restaurant. Her antennae sprung to attention and she flew into action and despatched a tray of courtesy drinks via the waiter to his table. By the end of the night, she'd found a new place to crash for a couple of days. Somewhere to rest with her wings in the sun.

She kidded herself that the reason Zachary had let her stay on his couch was because he was – even in the slightest way – in love with her. She could easily imagine it, and oh, how she wanted it to be true! Venus had awoken within her, climbed on a pedestal and waved her magic wand. A chemical reaction had been triggered and there was nothing Cherry could do to change it even had she wanted to. For the first time ever, she entertained the possibility of sexual union with another.

But it was not to be. She may as well have been invisible. The bounty of Venus was not for her. Zachary had made that plain.

"I hope you don't want to sleep with me. I think I'd kill myself."

"Not at all, sweetheart," said Cherry, swallowing her pride. "I don't have sex. Not my style."

She hung up her love for him in the closet of desire and chewed away at his pelt in her dreams. Venus descended from her mound, hung her head in shame and went home alone.


A dozen or so times that day, when Zachary isn't around, Cherry takes the bloodstained, demon-seed lottery ticket out of her pocket and stares at it. She still hasn't scratched it, still can't bring herself to do so, still finds her heart pounding at the thought. The dried smear dulling the face of the otherwise shiny ticket is strangely evil, a blight spreading across the Christmas tree.

There are only a few possible ways that ticket could have gotten into Angus' things and they all involve coincidence, something that Cherry is learning to loathe. It is remotely possible that Angus could have come by the ticket honestly, that he'd bought it from a corner store a year ago and just kept hold of it, waiting (as the Major had said) for the right time to scratch it.

It's more likely, however, that the ticket did, indeed, come from the Dixie stash, and Angus got hold of it either before or after Cherry had appeared on the scene. If it was *after*, poor Angus had stumbled across a ticket that Cherry had missed and it was further proof that the tickets were bad luck. If it was *before*, then Angus had stolen the tickets. Or not. In any case, it was all coincidence, all too horrendous, and every time she thinks about it, Cherry's head starts to throb.

She plays absentmindedly with the other things from Angus' death envelope. There are seventeen keys in all, including two for a vehicle, a Ford. She eats the candy cane. It crumbles in her mouth.

Then Cherry gets stoned. She's happy watching TV, intoxicating herself into a petrified lump to rival those in the futon. Marijuana makes the tobacco last longer – kind of like hamburger helper. With THC in her system, all she can think about is why the numbers of the cable stations don't match the channels on the remote. Zachary has an illegal cable descrambler, so hundreds of channels are available at the push of a button. It's an escape of sorts, but it's hardly healthy.

She's fascinated by Floyd Burley's tie on the News. How come it matches the tie of the prime minister? They must have known. Then she watches reruns of that vampire Mountie series starring Gervais Wynford, trying to recognize city landmarks beneath the set-dressing. She finds herself watching commercials. There's a lot of detergent ads. Washers and dryers. Stained garments going in, brilliant ones being hoisted out. Closeups of the molecular structure of soiled cotton. Bright colours keeping to themselves. Fluffy kittens bouncing around on the softest of soft fabric softeners. And everywhere, bubbles, bubbles. The world is obsessed with cleanliness and Cherry is having trouble breathing. She finds a news channel and watches disaster reports for a while. Pileups on the highways, airplanes bursting into flames, flash floods, snowstorms, casualties of war, that kind of thing. Santa Calamity is busy the whole globe over.

The news turns to local events.

*The lucky winners of this month's lottery …*

Happy smiling faces clutch giant cheques. She flips the channels looking for preferable choices. Aha. Here's something she can deal with: The Psychic Network, hosted by none other than that financially beleaguered, bleached-follicle wonder, Elka Zelda!

Entertainment at last. Cherry settles down to watch the badly acted scenarios of the luck of "real" people. There's the long-lost son finding his mother, the gal who gets the promotion, the guy who wins the car. Urban legends in the making. Some of the actors seem to be drunk. Cherry even dares to imagine herself in the studio audience, cheering at the inane platitudes and lovey-dovey advice that Elka Zelda's professional psychics are doling out to the multitudes like so many soggy loaves and fishes.

*So you see my darlinks, Fate has somezhink vuuuunderful for all of us! I uuurge you to pick up zhat phone right now and let my vuuuunderful professional psychics help you vizh youuur problem.*

Cherry falls asleep. She's developing a crick in her neck from this fucking futon.

The calibre of a couch is seen through the eye of the sleeper. Its prowess – or lack of it – is revealed via the astral plane. Zachary's futon isn't exactly the Rolls Royce of couches. It's as lumpy as a sack of coal, and far too short. Cherry's feet are obliged to dangle over the end, so her dreams are filled with Eros, hopscotch, or Julie Andrews skipping over the hill. Or she has to scrunch her head up against the armrest, forwards for visions of Quasimodo or backwards for Saint Theresa's ecstasy. Definitely, she's slept on better.

"Get up!"

Cherry opens her eyes. She'd nodded off on the couch. It's completely dark. Angus Dobson's overalls have been thrown over her head.

"Get your things together and get out!"

"Zach? What's this?" Cherry feigns innocence and bewilderment, disentangling herself from the overalls. "What's the matter?"

It doesn't take her long to figure it out. The room is filled with smoke, a thick, plastic stench that hangs in the air like smog. She's fallen asleep with her cigarette lit and now there's a crater-burn the size of a hamburger in the futon. It's wet where water has been dumped on it.

"Are you trying to burn the fucking place down?!"

She looks at Zachary pityingly. It was an accident. Standing just behind him, in the smog, her arms crossed, is Rose. Oh, great. That's all Zachary needs – an audience.

"Hi, Rose."

Rose nods.

"I can't believe I let you stay here!" Zachary flaps.

"Oh, calm down, sweetness. You're getting overwrought. Act your age." Cherry folds the overalls, strokes its stained threads. "The flames are out. There's not too much damage. Let's talk this over. How about some coffee? Let me fix you a nice cappuccino."

"Out! Out! Now!!" Zachary strides over and literally pushes her off the couch and onto the floor. "Get out!"

Cherry protests that she has nowhere to go, but Zach isn't having any of it. The age comment was too much. He chases her around the coffee table, bombarding her with bullets of unstoppable accusation.

"You smoke my drugs, you eat my food, you drink my Scotch, you wear my clothes, you zone out in front of the TV instead of helping around the house, and now you try to burn the place down ..."

He picks up his water bong and hurls it at her. It misses by half an inch and crashes to the floor by her elbow. He follows it with an ashtray, which glances off her shoulder and spins off her hand. Her last fingernail – the last bastion of identity – breaks off

"Ouch!"

"And now I find out you've been lying through your teeth to me about the fucking Saturn Ring fucking Riders!"

"What do you mean?"

"Those weren't bikers, Cherry, that was the Bloor family posse teaching you a lesson for jamming out on your responsibilities. You're lucky you aren't in jail."

"What?"

"You left the old man dead in his bed and the kid got out while you were supposed to be baby-sitting."

The Elvis plate hits her full in the face. She hadn't seen it coming out of the fog. Suddenly, the evil, blank eyes are three inches from her own, the full-painted lips zooming in for a deadly kiss. *Love Me Tender.* The bridge of her nose buzzes with a warm, dry pain. The plate doesn't even break.

"Get your fucking miserable ass out of here now!" Zachary's hands rear up around his head in exasperation. He stands like a lion rampant at the doorway and turns to Rose. "She's all yours. Take her away."

"C'mon," says Rose, helping Cherry into the overalls. "You and I are going for a little ride."

Meekly, Cherry dusts herself off, looks around for her stuff, checks her pockets, realizes she doesn't have anything other than what she's wearing and the things hanging up in the hall, and follows Rose to the door. She feels shanghaied. On her way out, she sneezes twice into the snow on the doorstep. Her headache clears.


"Two bits a pocket, ten bucks for the game." Rose hands Cherry a cue and starts chalking up her own. "Your break."

Cherry lines up her opening shot. "I don't have any money."

"OK, then, we'll play for the Truth."

Perfect timing. Cherry completely misses, hitting the cue ball with a dry, echoing crack which reverberates all the way up to her elbow. The ball wheedles pathetically along the green and comes to rest against the cushion without having struck so much as an attitude, let alone another ball.

"I meant to do that," she confesses.

"Take the shot again." Rose is being magnanimous. Overly friendly. What *is* this, thinks Cherry, tennis?

The last ten minutes have been like a game of Go Fish. On leaving Zachary's, Rose shovelled the captured Cherry into the burnt-out shell of the Plymouth Fury that was – miraculously – still functioning. It stank of burnt plastic and a carcinogenic scar ran down the back door below a cracked and smoked window. Cherry didn't know whether to act surprised at the state of the car or to acknowledge that she at least had some knowledge of its condition. In the end she held her tongue.

"It was delivered to my doorstep by a tow truck," said Rose, expertly reversing out of her parking spot. "There was a note on the windshield. *Ask Cherry.* Now what do you suppose that meant?"

"I haven't the faintest idea."

"Any clue as to where my girlfriend might be right now?"

"Do I look like the lesbian information centre?"

"You look like a mess. Let's go for a game of pool."

Which was Rose's way of getting at the truth.

Liberty hadn't been home for four nights. No explanation, no phone call, no message, no nothing. Which could only mean one thing: she'd found herself a piece of ass. Obviously Cherry was involved in some way or other. A relaxing interrogation on the racks around the green would get the truth out of her. They went to the Kennel Klub. Rose still has her keys and the game is, thanks to a couple of loonies swiped from the cash register, free.

Rose pulls a pitcher of amber beer from the taps and carries it, along with two glasses, over to the pool table. Once again, free. The percs of the job. Or the ex-job.

The Kennel Klub is in transition. The work lights are on and a handful of Bloor hired-hands are lugging cases of liquor in through the back from a rental truck idling in the parking lot. A cameraderie of male discontent grumbles in the background. Blasts of wind keep gusting into the club every time the double doors around behind the back of the bar bang open. Cherry thinks she recognizes a couple of the guys from her assault at the Belt 'n Buckle.

"What's going on here?" She tries to keep her face turned away from the action over at the bar. "Is that alcohol in those crates?"

"Smuggled," elaborates Rose with a knowing shrug. "The old dog's now a holding tank for smuggled booze. I can't think of better camouflage, can you?"

Cherry's second attempt at the break is a doozy. The castanet explosion of balls turns a few heads of approval from the case-toting lads. Cherry sinks two balls, one of each.

"Table's still open," she smiles, indicating that it's Rose's turn.

"Whose rules are we playing by?"

"Yours, Rose, yours." Cherry lifts her beer in acknowledgement of who's running the evening. "Cheers."

Rose spreads blue chalk over the web between the thumb and forefinger of her left hand before taking her shot. She flips her ponytail out of the way as she lowers herself to the game level. She's a serious player. As she proceeds, methodically, to wipe Cherry's butt, she talks about how her holiday plans have been ruined. She was wanting to spend a few days with her parents, but Liberty's disappearance and the Kennel Klub's closing down had fucked those plans.

"I'm driving down tonight, with or without Lib." She strides around the table, figuring out her next shot. "I've had my things packed for the past four nights. Gotta be back here for tomorrow, though."

"What? I thought the place is closed?"

"They're having a blowout New Year's Eve Farewell Party," mutters Rose as she sinks a complicated combination. "Everyone and their dog's going to be here. With a bit of luck, I could make back in tips the wages they owe me. Twelve in the corner."

An hour later and with another pitcher under their belts, the score is even. Rose's tactics are working. Cherry's actually having a good time. Loosening up. Dropping her guard.

"Four nights away from the marital bed, eh?" Cherry slurs, racking up a fresh game. "That's quite the dalliance. Hazel must have a talking clitoris or something ... oops ..."

"Hazel?" Rose pounces on Cherry's slip immediately. "Who's this Hazel? Hazel? Where does she live?"

"I don't know where she lives." Cherry's voice is small and distant.

She feels as if she's speaking out of her cheekbones. "I can show you where she works, though. Your break."

"Screw the game," says Rose, pulling on her jacket. "Get your ass into the car before you waste any more of my time."


There's a hive of activity down at the towing yard. The bashed-up carcass of a tan Cadillac is centre stage – front wheels hoisted in the air. A crowd of trolls gather around it. A police cruiser is parked to one side, and a uniformed officer is taking notes.

"Well, look who it isn't!" says Rose, pulling up and braking with such force that Cherry almost goes through the windshield.

She follows Rose's pointing finger through the darkness. Sitting on the step of the rig, in partial silhouette, is a familiar figure in a black leather jacket, her nose dipped into a small plastic bag. Floodlights reflect off the short bristles of her crewcut. Liberty.

"The jammy cunt," swears Rose, reaching under her seat and grabbing a crowbar. "C'mon."

As Cherry tags along behind Rose, the wind spits in her eyes. Liberty looks up as they approach. Something in her expression diverts Rose's anger. The crowbar falls, forgotten, to her side.

"Whassup?"

"Game's over for Victor," says Liberty, after a short swallow. "It's gotta be."

Cherry swallows. Rose stops short.

"Come again?"

Liberty explains, telling her story in a flat, distracted voice. She'd started work at the towing company, she said, seeing as her job at the Kennel Klub was fucked. Fine. No problem. Fifteen-hour days, overtime after eight and a half, time and a half after twelve, and double time on holidays and weekends. Anyways. They'd gone out on a call from the police, south of the city to haul back an ALIEN.

"No-no-no, not an ALIEN," says Liberty, correcting herself. "An OTHER. Off The Highway, Emergency Related."

"It was a rental you know," mutters Cherry. "He won it."

Liberty ignores her and continues with her tale.

"So we get there and this blunted Caddie has crashed through the fucking barrier – *wheeee!! ka-ploewie!* – right bum-fuck in the middle of this field.

"Police, ambulance, tracking dogs everywhere. They'd managed to trace some just-visible footprints leading away from the crash site that ended at a tree. That's where they found Victor's clothes, socks, shoes, ID and shit, neatly piled up on a stump. They couldn't find no pants, so they figured he must have been wearing them, only they couldn't figure it out 'cause he'd left his BVD's behind."

"So where'd they find him?" asks Rose.

"They didn't." Liberty holds up a small plastic kewpie doll. "I scored this from up in the tree. It's got really fucked eyes. Look."

Cherry shudders, reminded of Brock's warning about the soul shrinking. Victor must have told a whopper.

"Yup. That's Victor," she nods. "Must have been pretty cold to shrink him down to that size, eh?"

Liberty gives her a curled-lip glance of disapproval. "It was more than thirty below, Cherry. There's no way he could have survived the night. There was nothing for miles around."

"Oh well." Cherry is philosophical. "They'll find him in the Spring."

Along with the *Louis Vachon*.


The police leave the towing yard and everyone disperses. It's too cold to be standing around in the snow chatting about death. Rose remembers the crowbar in her hand. Liberty is still coming out with maudlin Victor stories.

"Where's Hazel?" Rose interrupts.

"Oh, she's inside …" Liberty spots the crowbar. "Oh come on now, Rose. There's no need for that."

"I think we need to have a little chat." Her ire is returning. "You didn't even call me, Lib. Guess she must be some hot little number, eh?"

Liberty rolls her eyes, pulls herself up from where she'd been sitting on the step of the tow truck. She lays a restraining hand on Rose.

"She's really quite sweet. I'll introduce you."

"I'd like that," says Rose sarcastically.

They start to cross the yard towards the office.

"Wait in the car, Cherry," snaps Rose, tossing her the keys. "This is girl talk."

"Wait in the car, Cherry," mimics Cherry as she slams the door of the Fury. "This is girl talk."

She blows a raspberry at the retreating figures of Rose and Liberty. She watches them vanish into the small prefabricated building. She sighs and slips the key into the ignition so she can turn on the heater. It's all so tedious.

Here she is, destitute, homeless, wigless, still limping from being attacked less than a week ago, and now she's sitting in a stinky car waiting for a trio of dykes to sort out their extramarital affairs. If it's not all sorted out in thirty seconds, it'll be three hours.

Time passes. The heater reaches its thermostat level and cuts out. She glances in the back seat, wondering if it's worth taking a quick lie-down from it all, but Rose has her bags packed, taking up most of the space. A couple of burgundy leather bags, the size of small pigs, and a shopping bag filled with wrapped gifts for the family. At the other end of the seat, under a blanket, there's the lump of another bag. Cherry flips off the cover.

Life is filled with revelations. Things lost resurface in the most unusual places.

It's the *Louis Vachon*. *Quelle surprise!* So it had been *Rose* who'd stolen it from under the bed at the Belt 'n Buckle. Well-well-well. How much longer before the tickets are worthless? Just over twenty-four hours. How much had the Major promised for their safe return? Five hundred dollars. Compared to nothing, which is what Cherry has now, that's five hundred dollars.

And the keys to the Fury are in the ignition.

# 9 ... treasure hunt

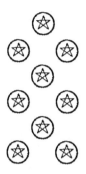

The mental Rolodex was never intended to be consulted while screaming down the expressway at a hundred clicks plus. For Cherry, the task of dipping into her memory banks and coming up with the address of the Associated Benevolent Christian Charities Inc. is exacerbated by that fact that it's been a while since she's been behind the wheel of a speeding vehicle. And the Plymouth Fury, thanks in part to its burn-out condition, responds erratically to every command. After one particularly hair-raising swerve towards the median, Cherry risks a glance in the mirror.

Rose and Liberty in the tow truck are gaining on her. She can see the distinctive high-beams and flashing yellow lights weaving through the traffic about two hundred yards behind her. Shit. At least they didn't stop to take the dead Cadillac off of the rig, so that slows 'em down a bit. If only she could remember where she was supposed to be going, she might be able to shake them, or at least form some kind of plan. As it is, she is overcome with a sense of breakneck futility, hurtling into the evening traffic, pedal to the floor on a suicide mission.

She prays that she won't run out of gas, cause a ten-car pileup, get pulled over by the cops or, worse, get caught by her pursuers. She doesn't have time, however, to figure out to which deity she should be appealing, let alone what she'd do if she was graced with an answer; it's tough enough just responding to her own earthly reflexes – and the Fury's. Thank heavens she wasted all those years playing pinball and video games. It's sure paying off now.

The expressway is crowded with vehicles that are, for the most part, keeping to their lanes and observing the speed limit, giving Cherry ample room to screech and veer around them. For a while, a businessman in a sportscar who's taken umbrage at her manœuvers, challenges her to a race, pulling up beside her and giving her the eye. Cherry keeps her foot to the floor and ignores him. Rose and Liberty are about twenty seconds behind her. She has to lose them.

She wishes that a black hole could open and swallow them up. Invisibility. Others have managed to achieve it. She knows it has to be possible. Victor is a prime example. Sunburned Lily on the West Coast is another. With a bit of luck, Rose and Liberty will be a couple more.

A gap appears in the traffic to her right, leading to an off-ramp. It's practically a 90° turn, the angle approaching the acute by the millisecond – dangerous in the extreme but what other choice does she have?

She winces as she hauls away on the wheel and careens across three lanes of speeding cars. Horns blare and vehicles swerve wildly out of her way. Someone shakes a fist at her as she sails across their prow, flat on. Feeling like a crash test dummy, she doesn't wave back.

The Fury misses the exit ramp by a few feet and cuts over a bumpy section of snow-covered grass before depositing her back onto solid road. She made it! The tow truck, caught in her snarling, honking wake, veers onto the hard shoulder and misses the exit. Phew!

Liberty attempts to reverse, but the Cadillac won't allow it. They can only go forwards. And there's a ditch.

Cherry soars up the ramp, over a bridge and, before long, she hits a tangle of major intersections. She could go anywhere. There's no way Liberty and Rose could follow. She's free.

Of course it is at that very moment that the address of the Associated Benevolent Christian Charities bursts through the mulch and into the foreground of her mind. *The Priory. Saddlestrap Way. By*

*Appointment Only.*

She looks around her at the signs for Highway this and Shopping Centre that to get her bearings. Damn. She's going in completely the wrong direction.

It's nearing ten o'clock when Cherry finally pulls up outside The Priory. She stops for a moment before turning through the gateway in the high hedge. The Priory's in a swank area of town on a street famed for having no numbers. The houses are few enough to be known by their first names. The place is daunting – affluence is never any good at hiding in the dark or under snow. Through a dark, yawning gap pinpricks of light can be seen through a lace of branches. Cherry turns the wheel, feeds the gas and negotiates the Fury between stone pillars set into the hedge.

*The Priory. Associated Benevolent Christian Charities Inc.*

As she passes through the portal, the car triggers a hidden switch and the grounds burst into a zillion lights. Looped through the trees and snowbound shrubs that line the driveway, ropes of multicoloured bulbs twinkle and blinkle their Merry Christmas greeting to new arrivals. The house is suddenly illuminated by floodlights, like an oil tanker exploding on the horizon. An electric Santa and reindeer buzzes away on the roof. The Fury lurches forward and a wheel catches against the snowbank.

The Priory is a red-brick mansion at the end of a winding driveway. It has pretensions of being a few centuries older than it actually is. The flickering carriage lamps are fake, the latticed, leaded windows prefabricated. Most likely it was built in the fifties and is thus only a decade or so older than Cherry herself, although as she pulls up in front of an imposing oak door, she feels ancient.

With the *Louis Vachon* firmly in hand, she climbs out of the car onto scrunchy snow, and slams the door behind her. A dog barks from somewhere inside the house. Light snowflakes gust around her bare ankles as she aims for the stone stairs. Her limp has almost disappeared. On the second step she spots a coin, half obscured in the frozen drift. A lucky penny. *See a penny, pick it up …*

The door is opened before she even touches the glowing orange button set into the frame. Of course. They would have known of her arrival from the massive burst of Hydro-waste. It's the Major. A small

Band-Aid is stuck on his shiny pate. His eyes glint as he peers into the night.

"Good evening," he says politely in his high, reedy voice. "Dixie, no! *Heel!*"

This last is directed at a full-size bulldog, a brown and wrinkled brute whose pea-pod doggy erection is visible even in this light. Dixie? As in *Laundromat* Dixie?

"I've come for the reward," says Cherry, breathless. "I've brought the tickets."

"Tickets?" echoes the Major, sharply. He scrutinizes Cherry and shifts to one side to see her more clearly. Recognition, then Hostility. "Oh. You again. You didn't bring your friend, did you?"

"No." Cherry almost falls down the stairs in an effort to avoid the dog which sniffs her shoes suspiciously. "Not this time."

"You were wearing a wig before." The Major is satisfied that he's figured out the difference in Cherry's appearance. "Why are you wearing Angus' things?"

"I haven't missed the deadline, have I?" Cherry holds up the bag, ignoring the question. "Five hundred dollars? You promised."

The Major accepts this information with a slow nod, letting it settle into his neck. His bottom lip juts pinkly from his face. He flips a switch by the door and the thousand twinkly fairy lights behind Cherry go out. The hall lamp bumps brighter.

"You'd better follow me," he says, pulling the dog away from the door to let Cherry through. "The Admiral will be glad to see you, I suppose." He gives Dixie a slap on the rump. "Come on, old boy."

Cherry is led through corridor and room after corridor and room, each stuffed to the picture rail with antiques. On every side are carved tables, statuettes, and furniture of every type imaginable: wing-backed, armed, stuffed, Queen Ann and Chippendale, Chipperfield, Barnum and Bailey. The Major hobbles past drop-leaf tables, curio cabinets, Tiffany lamps that sprout like mushrooms, grandified lawn jockeys, velvet footstools and – yes – couches, divans, and *poufs*. In room after room, dark walls are riddled with pictures, mostly in heavy gilt frames and surely all originals. Serious faces of cracked and peeling gentlemen in frock coats. Austere women in dusty silks. A winter skating scene looks like a window in need of a good cleaning. Occasional watercolours of flowers and birds. A couple of framed needlework samplers and, Cherry notes with a touch of repulsion, a case of mounted butterflies.

They continue their wordless trek. The only constants are the chunky Spanish-style chandeliers that hang from the ceiling and the blood-red carpet, worn in patches. The whole place smells damp and fruity, like a dark and welcoming restaurant, the kind that serves strawberry ice-cream with a fan-shaped wafer for dessert. *Right this way sir, I'll see you to your table. Smoking or non?*

Glazed, Cherry is finally ushered through an open door and into a small, windowless, circular room that smells of lemon. After the long journey, she feels as if she's at the hub of the house – the very centre of the Priory's universe.

The room is nice, neat and sterile. The walls are bare and bright. Two modern mauve chairs and a couch are arranged at jaunty angles to each other. Everything is still covered with the plastic wrappers from the showroom. A computer sits on a desk unit. From the screen, the face of a young Asian child smiles forlornly at Cherry. A high-backed *La-Z-Boy* chair of pink velour is by the computer and a hand pokes out, clutching the mouse. A plume of smoke rises in a languid curl. Dixie rushes ahead, pushing past the Major's prosthetic leg, determined to reach her master first.

"We've got the tickets back, sir!" shouts the Major, lifting his voice to a higher alto than normal. "I told you they'd come back!"

A grunt comes from the chair. The screen changes to another child. This one is crouched in the gutter of a Third-World slum, eyes pleading at the camera.

"It's that transvestite who attacked me the other day," continues the Major, overenunciating. "Calls himself Nicola, I believe. He's brought the tickets."

Cherry is pushed forward to where the Admiral can see her. And she him.

Two globular, fishlike eyes peer out at her from a skeletal form wrapped in a plaid blanket. Shrewd grey eyes. The Admiral must be nearing his century. He's a good deal older than his portrait, but still imposing. His skin sags from the cheekbones, his goatee is a coarse, white whisper of its former self. He is smoking an oval cigarette screwed into an amber medicinal holder. Dixie is now curled up at his slippered feet.

"Whassat you say? Speak up, man!" When he talks, he clenches down onto the cigarette holder with his teeth, leaving scant space for his words to escape.

The Major repeats himself, leaning forwards on his plastic leg.

"Transvestite, eh?" ponders the Admiral, his attention still on flipping through images of impoverished children on the screen. "What did they do to your hair and eyelashes? Is that hormone treatments?"

Cherry isn't listening. She's captivated by the array of unfortunates on the computer.

"I asked you a question, laddie!" snaps the Admiral, somewhat annoyed. "If nothing else, you're hard of hearing! You and that Angus would make a great pair! Couple of the fucking century!" He splutters into a spongy laugh that continues for some seconds before petering out into raspy breathing. He medicates himself with a quick pull on his cigarette.

"This isn't a transvestite," he snaps dismissively. "Believe me, I know what a transvestite is, and this isn't one of 'em."

Cherry nods her thanks, warily. The Admiral poses with the cigarette in his hand, his thoughts apparently distant for a few seconds.

"Bathsheba!" he shouts suddenly, eyeballs bulging in his skull. Dixie's ears prick up then fall flat again. "Bathsheba!"

"No, I don't think so, sir," says the Major, after a second of embarrassed silence. "Bathsheba was the wife-of-Uriah and the mother of Solomon-the-father-of-wisdom. You're getting them confused again. Can I get you another Scotch?"

He picks up the empty tumbler from the Admiral's desk and vanishes out of the room. The Admiral yells after him to make it two. In the ensuing silence. He shrugs at Cherry.

"I know you aren't Bathsheba," he leers, revealing craggy yellow fangs. "I just said that to get rid of him."

Cherry thanks him, carefully. She tries not to show too much tooth or crack her lips into an expression of anything. She starts believing that the more like a statue she behaves, the better her chances are of escaping out of this grandma's house without being devoured by the wolf.

"Well?" The Admiral removes his cigarette from its filter and stubs it out in the overflowing ashtray. "What have you to say for yourself?"

"I was thinking," says Cherry, slowly, "I was thinking that you had at least another three minutes left in that smoke, if you must know."

The Admiral passes his cold, clear gaze over Cherry. Whether he is amused or not is impossible to tell. There is no trace of antagonism, none of the usual cultural repulsion she is accustomed to from men of his social ilk. He sees with the eyes of royalty, through costume, through race, through gender, through language. Cherry feels violated.

Leaning back in his chair, the Admiral proclaims his diagnosis. "I knew you weren't a transvestite. You're a fucking opportunist."

Cherry's heart quickens. She goes on the defensive. "What do you mean by that?"

He offers her a cigarette. "You're wearing Angus' clothes. I take it you smoke. All gamblers smoke. Sit."

Dixie's ears twitch, recognizing the command. The canine brain does some calculations, a couple of muscles flicker in the shanks and then subside as Cherry lowers herself onto the plastic-swathed couch.

"Angus is dead."

Cherry surprises herself. She wasn't meaning to part with that information unless she had to. The Admiral says nothing.

"Our papers got mixed up at the hospital," continues Cherry, pulling at her pant leg, trying to expose less ankle. "He was knocked down by a streetcar."

The Admiral glances at her sharply.

"Obviously you didn't see Angus, did you?"

"No."

He nods, as if a problem had been solved. "Where's the body? What do you mean when you say the papers got mixed up?"

Cherry shrugs and sniffs. "Do you want the whole story or just the condensed version?"

"Just don't make anything up."


The Admiral twists another cigarette into his filter. He seems unimpressed by Cherry's convoluted story of how she and Angus got mixed up at the hospital.

"Aah. Yes. The world is full of such accidents, such coincidences, such tragedies." A pause while he lights his smoke. "So. You have the tickets. You were expecting a reward?"

"I believe five hundred dollars was the price."

"Did you notify the authorities?"

"Only the Lotto Centre."

"I see."

The Major returns with a tray bristling with cut crystal. "How goes it?" he asks cheerfully in his boyish voice.

"Angus is dead," says the Admiral.

The way he says it, verging on glee, strikes Cherry as malicious. It's as if he's hoping that the Major will drop his tray of glassware from the shock. But the Major is too good a man to lose control of break-ables, even in the face of bad news. He slides the tray gingerly onto the side table.

"Oh dear," is all he says. "Oh dear."

"The body's at Saint Theobald's and, I believe ..." the Admiral looks to Cherry for verification, "I believe that the paperwork has been, shall we say, suitably obfuscated?"

Cherry agrees.

"And our good friend here tells me that *he* was knocked down by a streetcar."

"No, not me," corrects Cherry. "Angus."

"That's what I said!" snaps the Admiral. "You said *he* was killed by a streetcar, yes?"

"I suppose so."

The Major seems to take great cheer from this. In fact they both do. There's no hiding their relief. Cherry finds it all a little gross.

"Excellent, excellent! Well then!" says the Admiral, and then chang-ing the subject and gesturing to the *Louis Vachon*, "Those are the tick-ets? All of them?"

"Are you kidding?" Cherry acts affronted. "Do you know how hard it was to keep ahold of any of them in the circles I travel in?"

A triumphant smile breaks out on the Admiral's face as he turns to the Major with a supercilious "I-told-you-so" expression. The Major's cheeks grow shiny as he tries to sink into his cardigan.

"I know – I know I should have gotten rid of them," the Major mutters. "I just thought it was less ... less *final* somehow. With the tickets still in existence, we could always recirculate them in case of an accident."

"Ye-es," agrees the Admiral. "And that's exactly what happened, isn't it? Only the accident was that they *did* get recirculated, you fuck-ing moron. Don't say I didn't warn you!"

"Oh get off your high horse, you old goat!" snips the Major, thor-oughly peeved. "How was I to know what was going to happen?"

"Don't talk to me like that, you pansified old ponce!"

Cherry smokes a complete cigarette while the couple argues. It's touching in a way. She could hope for such a relationship when she reaches their age.

"Excuse me?" she ventures, standing up to stub her smoke in the ashtray. She picks up the *Louis Vachon*. "The tickets?"

"What about them, laddie?"

"Do you want them or not?"

"Of course we want them, you dolt!"

"Then where's my five hundred dollars?"

The Major sighs, reaches for his wallet. Must be nice, thinks Cherry, knowing that you have five hundred bucks sitting around in your pocket at most times. He counts off a stack of fifties onto the desk.

Cherry smiles sweetly, hands him the bag. She reaches for the cash, but, quick as a flash, the Admiral puts a restraining hand on the bills. He wants to check the goods first. Then she'll get the money if everything's in order. He nods at the Major, who has dropped to the floor and is unzipping the bag. A moth escapes from the mouth of the bag, sending Cherry's stomach a-flutter.

The Major pulls out the contents of the bag. Cherry's heart sinks.

A leather harness, a bag of carrots, a bottle of baby oil.

Oops.

A pair of surgical rubber gloves, a length of chain, a packet of wooden clothes pegs, a long purple dildo that flops out of the bag like a live eel. Double oops. Wrong bag.

With sickening clarity, Cherry remembers. *Loo-wee-wa-chon.*

That must have been what Liberty meant when she'd told Cherry not to let Rose see the *Louis Vachon*. It almost matched the bag in which she kept her sex toys.

Now that she knows the error she's made, Cherry can see that even the printed monograms on the bag are wrong. *LW* instead of *LV*. It's a cheap imitation imitation.

The Major looks up, horrified. "What is this? Some kind of a joke?"

"I guess this means I don't get my five hundred dollars?" asks Cherry, just to make sure. She needn't have bothered. The money is already on its way back into the Major's wallet.

Suddenly the lights in the room jolt and dim. The computer screen pings out. Dixie springs to her feet and bounds, barking, out of the room.

"More visitors," snarls the Admiral. "What a night! We should have printed fucking invitations."

Could that be Rose and Liberty? Surely they hadn't traced Cherry to the Priory. Cherry vaguely remembers that Liberty had one of the Major's business cards in her pocket from the Lotto Centre. Had she had the presence of mind to realize where Cherry had been headed? Perhaps it's just a dog wandering through the gate and triggering the electrics. But Cherry doesn't feel like taking any more chances tonight. She's already fucked up bad enough.

"I have to go now," she smiles. "That'll be my cab. Is there a back way out of here, by any chance?"

Silly question and one that, by the looks of it, isn't going to get her an answer.

"Nice to have met you," she continues, nodding and bowing her way to the door. "OK, bye-bye now."

She trots back through the corridors and rooms, negotiating the furniture with varying degrees of success and trying to remember her way out. She finds herself in unfamiliar territory. A multibranched candlestick on a sideboard appeals to her gothic sensibilities and she grabs it as a potential weapon, or just for some appropriate atmosphere.

Room after room opens up to her flight. An oriental sanctuary, octagonal and lacquered in red. A room that contains nothing but an electric organ, three levels of keyboards bristling like ivory teeth. Another where the furniture is covered in white sheets as if in storage. Still another that has an inflatable sex-doll slumped pinkly over a black leather Ottoman, looking remarkably like Cherry with no clothes on. Rooms that smell of orange peel. Rooms that smell of dust.

Is there no end to this house with its collection of rooms stacked one inside the other like *matryoshka*? Blood rushes through Cherry's body. She has the suspicion, with every room she crosses, of encountering a trace of herself coming through a door in the opposite direction. She dashes through the mansion of her psyche – each room a different version of herself, another personality, another name, another couch.

Move on. Keep on running. Don't stop. Don't.

Finally, at the end of a kitchen area and a twisting scullery/utility room filled with stacked cardboard boxes, ancient water tanks and what looks like a mediaeval electrical generator, she finds the back door. She knows it's the back door because the Admiral is standing there in his dressing gown and slippers waiting for her, his cigarette clenched between his teeth. He must have taken a shortcut.

"You needn't have bothered," puffs Cherry as she pulls up. "I can see myself out, thanks."

"The candelabrum if you don't mind." The Admiral thrusts out a withered demanding hand. "It's an heirloom."

For a split second Cherry contemplates bopping him over the head with it. She's in such deep shit already, what's one more corpse? She probably wouldn't get away with a self-defense plea, but insanity would be easy to prove. Then she thinks of the prospect of spending the rest of her unnatural life in a prison for the criminally insane. She hands over the precious heirloom.

The lights lurch back up to their original level with a buzz. The Major must be at the front door.

"Got to get that generator fixed," mutters the Admiral. "You don't know anything about generators by any chance, do you?"

He tilts his head towards the massive machine huddled in the corner next to a stack of wooden crates. It looks like the engine of an old submarine: all dials, valves, plugs and piping. A burgundy sports bag sits on the floor nearby.

"Some other time," Cherry apologizes. "Gotta dash."

She starts to negotiate her way around the Admiral to get to the door, but he blocks her way. He smiles menacingly. Flicks the ash from his cigarette.

"I couldn't let you go without giving you a token of my appreciation," he says, pushing a ten-dollar bill into her hand. "It was worth it to see the expression on his prissy face. I haven't had so much fun since the fucking Depression."

"You're nuts." Cherry stuffs the money into her pocket. "Make it twenty and I'll give you a real thrill."

The Admiral wheezes. His chicken jowls wobble with amusement. For a moment, Cherry thinks she's going to get another ten bucks just for the joke.

"Go fuck yourself!" he finally sputters, opening the door for her. A gust of cold snow blows into the house, tweaking at the corners of his dressing gown.

"Been there, done that," quips Cherry by way of farewell, and steps into the darkness to freedom.

Santa Calamity d'Oopsidaisy, patron saint of the inattentive and clumsy is having the time of her life. She loves this town. It's given her quite the reception and the party's not over yet.

She's in an exuberant mood, one could almost call it Devil-may-care. The New Year approaches. Her Grand Finale is always the best. This time around she has big things planned.

She has her work cut out for her. Fates to snarl, destinies to collide and lives to sabotage. The wasps are getting anxious and the Sacred Bovinity is griping for a night off. Cherry Beach is surely but one project among thousands, although recently, she who currently goes by the name of Miss Beach seems to be garnering more attention than others. Perhaps, even, privileges have been bestowed. It's hard to tell. Santa Calamity is notoriously secretive about things like that. She won't even show her face in public. Not without a mask.

Only one thing's for certain. Her farewell blowout is going to be messy.


It comes as no surprise that the Fury breaks down ten yards from Dixie's Wash 'n Dry Coin-Op Laundromat – the source of all Cherry's troubles and delights over the past week. A needle-fine snow is gusting horizontally as she clambers out and slams the door behind her. Her ankles prickle.

Someone's trying to tell me something, Cherry thinks as she trudges the short distance along the street. There's a pattern in all this madness.

The door to the Laundromat is locked, the lights are off. She tries to peer through the glass but cannot see a thing, just a few shadowy machines. She rattles the handle, pushes against the lock, but to no avail. It won't budge.

Now what? She plants herself on the doorstep, shoves her hands deep into the overalls' pockets and leans against the pillar to get out of the way of the sharp snow.

Her fingers touch Angus Dobson's keys. She jiggles them around, in an effort to keep warm, perhaps, although she can't be generating much heat. Suddenly, she stops. The *keys*?

She tries one and, of course, it doesn't fit. Not even close. She was dumb to have even thought it in the first place. Extending her stupidity, she continues, trying the second, third and fourth keys on the ring. She revels in her brashness as the door remains steadfastly locked.

Nearing the end of the bunch, at the point when she's about to call it quits and go find a two-dollar cocktail, one of the keys slips into the lock so neatly, so smoothly that it might actually have been designed for the job. Like a porn flick slam fuck the key penetrates the secrets of the lock. Cherry inhales deeply to avoid any further mental interruptions and twists the key.

Barrels slide, tumblers fall into place. The lock turns with a generous click. The door is open.


Inside there is the stench of Hell. Something is rotting and the floor is spotted with puddles of dark, sudsy water. She wrinkles up her nose, holds her hand to her face and tries to breathe as shallowly as she can in small, quick gasps. Streetlights shine through the windows. No one has been in here for a while.

One of the top-loading washers has some abandoned laundry half-pulled out of it. In the dim light it looks like a drowned animal with matted, soaked fur. A cat perhaps, or a skunk. Another machine clicks loudly every few seconds, some internal timer stuck on a perpetual cycle. Out of service notices – *Broken, Not Working, Don't Use* and so on – are everywhere, scribbled on scraps of paper and the backs of cigarette packs and stuck on the machines. This is a dead Laundromat.

Cherry sploshes her way down the aisle to the far dryer, the dryer in which she had found – it feels like years ago now – the bag of tickets. She stands for a moment in front of it, her mind buzzing. Then her hand moves without bidding and opens the circular door before she has a chance to stop it.


Cold and as empty as a memory.


What am I doing here? Cherry asks herself. Returning to the scene of the crime? Trying to get back out of the mess the same way she got in? What was she expecting – the bag to be there? Or, perhaps, another? She must be crazy. Certifiable.

Her feet are soaked. The water is cold and clammy. She wishes she had a pair of fresh warm socks. A quick search through the machines proves even that coincidence beyond her reach. Then she starts craving a cigarette. Burning tobacco might even relieve the air quality. Wait a second – isn't there an ashtray around? Maybe that nice long butt she'd left on her first visit is still there.

It is. And more have joined her collection of Camels in the circular dish. She sorts through them, trying to find some of decent length, ones which aren't too damp and soggy. She stops. Shudders. What is she doing! Sorting through your own cigarette ends for reincarnation candidates is one thing, but picking through the stogies of complete strangers is quite another. Who knows what evil lurks in a filter? Good heavens, there could even be menthols hiding in there! Still shaking at her own recklessness, Cherry lights up one of her prodigal Camels.

The match hisses and gives off a flash of blue as it hits the floor. The flooding is not as bad here as near the entrance, but still enough to extinguish a flame.

She sucks on her fag-end, trying to keep the ember alight – the tobacco's a bit damp. She strikes another light, gets her cigarette burning like a torch in Frankenstein's castle, then tosses the match to the floor where it lands on the edge of a curling linoleum tile and stays lit.

For a second. Two seconds.

*Hsss.*

What can happen in two seconds? Small things, usually. You can swallow a morsel of food, walk a couple of yards, dial the operator, lose a friend. Not much. Or – less frequently – greater things can happen. You can win a bet, fall in love, witness God – or you can see something you'd never noticed before. As does Cherry in those two seconds while the match dies at her feet.

The ashtray has wheels.


The house whose address is painted in red on the underside of the "ashtray," turns out to be a one-storey cardboardesque shack set back from the road, one in a row of similar dilapidation. Green tarpaper peeks through the snow on the roof, the walls are covered with a raised pattern of industrial grey intended to resemble quarried stone. A strip of imitation red brick runs beneath a window where a telephone line has been stapled into place up the wall and over the sill. Patches have been slapped on haphazardly, like destination stickers on a suitcase. It's a three little pigs kind of house: one puff and it will collapse into a pile of dust.

A faded pink plastic holly wreath frames a cast-iron knocker on the otherwise utilitarian door. A yellowing bulb lights the porch, creating purplish-grey shadows. Cherry negotiates the mobile "ashtray" up the wonky stone steps and knocks on the door.

Not that she expects an answer but she'd seen the curtains twitch on the hovel next door as she'd trolled her way up the snowy path, so she knocks for the sake of appearances. She waits ten seconds then works her way through the bunch of keys until she finds the right one and jiggles the lock. It's a simple Yale; she could have used a credit card, had she (or rather, Angus) had one.

After groping around uselessly for a light switch, she finds that the insect flying around her face is actually a pull string with a fluffy tassel. A tug on the string and two rooms and a kitchen area fade into view, lit by a 40-watt glass-domed lamp in the ceiling. The place has a dusty chemical smell, as if it's just been sprayed for roaches. There's a hint of juniper berries and incense. A day-by-day calendar hangs on the wall, the tear-off block displays December 23.

Welcome to Angus Dobson's domestic wasteland.

It's clean, in a practical, sparse way. A cot, made up neatly with rose-patterned sheets and a brown blanket, takes up an alcove. A heavy wooden table, used as a desk and smothered with yellow gloss paint and papers is on one side of the room, a well-stocked workbench on another. There's an old Underwood typewriter and other strange machines of the same era in the kitchen. There isn't a single couch in the house. In the main room, a wooden chair stands beside a wire-legged television set, an impractical position for viewing TV, surely. A miniature Christmas tree, not much bigger than a saltshaker, shares the top of the television with a brass water buffalo statuette and a mint-green transistor radio. A red bobble-fringed shawl is pinned up at a strange angle. The walls are papered with vintage automobiles and fake pine. Cherry hazards a bet that there's fish wallpaper in the washroom. If there is a washroom. One thing's for certain: Angus had an abysmal sense of style. But then, she'd already surmised as much from his clothing.

The smaller room may originally have been designated as a bed-room, but Angus has been using it as a workroom – it's filled with machines in varying states of repair and there doesn't seem to be any adequate lighting. Washers, dryers, vending machines of all kinds and sizes huddle together in the dark. Cardboard boxes of stock – pop, snacks, powdered drinks and, to Cherry's delight, cigarettes – are in one corner and shoeboxes of parts in another, some of them bearing labels. GROMET'S, BOULT, COIN EXEPTORS, RESISTAR'S and, tantalizingly, MISTLEANIOUS. Cherry recognizes the script immediately; it's the same as that on the walls of the Dixie Laundromat.

She sorts through the stock, horrified to discover her choice of brand is limited to a half-dozen or so that she would never dream of smoking. Peter Johnsons are the closest to anything real. There is an inordinate number of light menthols. Most of the packs are crushed.

It doesn't feel as if she's breaking and entering, although techni-cally that's what she's doing, even though she has keys. Since part of her has been Angus for a few days now, she feels that she's merely ex-ploring an undiscovered part of her own personality. She looks over the dim room full of machines and shakes her head. Angus the Dixie repairman had lived in a strange world. This sad little house filled with stalled activity and quotidian existence is completely unexpected. Alien.

The "ashtray" fits right in. It has come home. She was surprised that it had still been in the Laundromat, that no one had noticed it up against the wall, with its handle hidden amongst a tangle of water pipes. But then it was really only the wheels that gave it away, and as Cherry had stubbed out three of her own butts on it, it had been per-ceived as an ashtray by those who had followed.

It wasn't, of course, an ashtray at all. It was one of those coin col-lectors used to safeguard quarters collected from the cash boxes of washing machines and dryers. A portable strongbox. Angus must have been collecting his night's cash when he had stumbled across the bag of *XXXmas* trees in the dryer.

Had he stumbled across them or had he stolen them from the Admiral? Duh! He'd hidden them himself in the dryer, hadn't he?

Only something must have gone wrong. Something must have made Angus run out of that Laundromat and onto the street, spewing tickets as he went, obviously in too much of a hurry to worry about his coin caddy and thousands of dollars' worth of lottery tickets left behind in the Laundromat.

It's all making Cherry's head spin. She could use a drink.

She checks out the fridge in the kitchen for alcohol. Juice? Milk? Nope. There's nothing but a can of lichee nuts and a few tubs of yogurt, so she settles for a glass of water. Her eyes wander while she lets the tap run. Hanging above the sink is a framed black-and-white photograph, the kind usually seen in community newspapers. It shows a group of sombre men gathered before a large banner, handing over a giant cheque for One Thousand Dollars to an Asian girl who looks more than a bit lost among the dignitaries. The photograph must be at least twenty years old, faded with time, but preserved behind glass and obviously in pride of place above the dish soap.

The banner in the picture is from the Associated Benevolent Christian Charities, and the proud-looking man in the foreground with the distinguished goatee streaked with grey, is a younger version of the Admiral. *Admiral Bernard, Chairman*, says the caption.

The identity of the little girl is also written there in black and yellowing white. Cherry feels as if maggots are hatching in her brain.

*Angus?!!*

It explains why their papers got mixed up at the hospital, how the Admiral knew that Cherry hadn't seen the body, why Angus had a tampon in his pocket. Her pocket.

Angus Dobson was female.


The answering machine – an old chunky TAD-86 – has thirty-seven messages. Cherry hits *Playback* and settles down to listen to a tape filled with distraught voices. The very first message confirms Angus' gender.

"Miss Dobson, this is the Hospital. The pop machine in the nurses' lounge is malfunctioning ..."

"We have a burst water pipe in the basement ..."

"Angus, the generator's gone, can you get here today ...?"

"Hi. My name's Adelaide Simcoe and I got your number from the Yellow Pages ..."

"The damned refrigerator's on the blink again ..."

"The cigarette machine's jammed ..."

And so on.

About five minutes into the messages, one jumps out at Cherry.

It's the Major's thin and reedy voice, definitely upset.

"Angus, you forgetful girlie, you left your tools behind. The Admiral – well, the Admiral's been asking for you. Can you drop by *immediately*. Thank you."

Thereafter, all of the messages get more frantic. Machines are breaking down, requests are repeated in rising tones of desperation, complaints begin about Angus' tardiness, five more high-pitched "Angus, Angus" pleas on behalf of the Admiral and finally, a group of nasty, vindictive threats from people whose laundry days have been ruined by malfunctioning washers and dryers.

At the end of it all, Cherry switches off the machine and sits in silence. She lights another stale Peter Johnson cigarette and smokes half of it before stubbing it out.


*You left your tools.* Cherry sits up suddenly, realization creeping up her spine. What had Angus been doing on that last day of her life? She had been doing her rounds, hadn't she? Collecting the money from the machines, making repairs if and when necessary. For that, she'd have needed her tools. Or rather, her bag of tools. Except that …

Cherry sighs. Angus had been no thief. Or at least, she hadn't been an *intentional* thief. The whole damned thing had happened – not surprisingly – completely by accident. Victims of Santa Calamity, the whole lot of them.

It was obvious, now that she saw it. When Angus had been at the Admiral's earlier that day working on the generator, she had left with the wrong bag.

The green bag instead of the burgundy bag which is still sitting in the Priory kitchen. Now how could Angus have made such a simple mistake like that? The lighting wasn't that bad at the Priory, even with someone coming up the drive.


The lock on the strongbox is easily opened by one of the small keys on Angus' loop. Inside is a good six-inch depth of quarters. The cash situation is getting decidedly better.

Cherry finds a strange machine of beige plastic on the workbench. It's not much bigger than a breadbox, certainly much flatter.

It's filled with gullies and racks and has a flattened funnel at one end, a series of notched, vertical gutters at the bottom. It's a coin sorter and there's a stack of brown rolling paper beside it. Now here's something she can deal with.

She sets to work. After a few attempts, she gets the hang of it, figuring out how to insert the paper into the little gizmo, pull the lever and produce a perfect roll of quarters every time.

She continues rattling the coins through the machine for what seems like hours. She feels as if she was born to do this. She's beginning to warm to Angus Dobson.

Three hundred dollars. Enough to buy herself a new outfit. Get out of these dead-man's rags. Dead-woman's weeds. Whatever.

Four hundred dollars … a massage and a face peel … five hundred … a leather corset … six hundred and thirty dollars … matching boots … and an argument with the bank teller when she tries to cash the quarters in for bills …

With just under seven hundred dollars in coinage rolled up in their brown paper shrouds, Cherry takes a break, lying down on the cot for a few minutes. The scent of crisp cotton sheets folded neatly beneath the brown blanket and encasing the single bolster is a strange, virtually unknown smell to Cherry. It reminds her of the days back when she had her own room as a teenager at the Monaghans. She scrunches her head satisfyingly into the pillow and takes a little rest. Just a couple of minutes. The sound of clanking coins remains in her ears like an aftershock. The keys in her pocket gouge into her thighs, so she empties her pockets and passes out.


Santa Calamity trudges into her temporary lodgings, her boots still wet from the Laundromat. She's tired, her work is far from over and she isn't getting much help from that good-for-nothing beast. She gave it the night off and what does it do? It goes and gets drunk with the new valet. It just goes to show that you can never depend on the Bovinity.

She finds her servants in the back of the warehouse, crowded around a computer, playing a game of *Death! Doom! & Destruction!* As she enters, the monitor flips to a lava-lamp-style screen saver.

"I thought I told you guys to keep working," she snarls, sitting in a chair and lifting a foot for the mice to help her off with her boots. "I come back and you're playing games? What? Did you honestly expect to win!"

A moth flutters to her shoulder and whispers in her ear. Our Lady of Perpetual Disaster's eyes light up and a smile spreads across her face. She seems pleased and calms down.

Her boots off, stuffed with newspaper, and drying out before the electric fire, she gets up to check the computer. A studious bookworm moves out of her way.

"How you guys liking it here?"

"Couldn't ask for better thanks!"

"What's this?" Her finger traces across the screen filled with numbers, magnetically attracting all the sevens as she points to an entry. "What in the name of my devil is this doing here?" She stabs at another. "And this? ... And this!"

The bookworm reads out the entries pedantically.

"*The Top Ten Disaster Movies of All Time. America's Funniest Home Videos ...*"

The ants stutter, trying to explain but to no avail. The crickets shake in her boots, over by the fire, trying to make light of it all. She who sprinkles bugs in the Web, however, is not amused.

"Destroy them!" she orders. "Remove them from the catalogue! If necessary, get that cow to help you. *I will not be homogenized!*"


In Cherry's dream, she wakes up in the little house. The place has been repainted in designer colours, remodelled, and has a fancy swimming pool in the garden. It's a glorious summer's morning. A gleaming *Dobson Repair* van stands in the laneway ready for the day's work while bluebirds sing and the sun jives in the sky as in a cereal commercial. Still wearing her Madame Butterfly kimono, she drinks her coffee by the edge of the pool and sorts through her mail.

A postcard from the Big Apple catches her fancy. It's a picture of the Statue of Liberty, complete with the infamous slogan:

*Give me your tired, your poor*
*Your huddled masses yearning to breathe free.*

She flips it over to read who has sent it to her.

*Dear Angus: Wish you were here. Hope you can make it. Love, Victor.*


Cherry wakes with a start with one thought on her mind: she has to find the missing tickets. Not to cash them in or to claim any reward; it's too late for that. She could return them to the Laundromat. Or perhaps she could burn them, yes, or dump them in the lake, but, at any rate, get rid of them before the New Year arrives. She feels it's her responsibility, somehow. She was the one who'd found them; only she can get rid of them. And the one thought she cannot shake is that she has to do it. By midnight.

It takes Cherry a few seconds to figure out where she is. The heat must have gone off during the night because it's freezing. Outside, a grey daylight fills the strange little house with a gritty reality. It's Sunday. She has no idea what time it is.

The clock in the kitchen says it's quarter past seven in the morning. Cherry suppresses a shudder. She feels like a vampire.

She finds some instant coffee and makes a half-decent beverage, although there's no milk, just whitener. Cigarettes taste awful in combination with the hot beige liquid, so Cherry contents herself with just sniffing the nicotine from a freshly opened pack. She warms her fingers against her cup. Eventually, she finds a pair of mittens stuffed in a drawer. They match the pair she'd abandoned at the hospital – One red, one green – except that they haven't been through a bloody accident and a shrinking wash.

Eight o'clock. She has sixteen hours and counting. Cherry reminds herself of her mission. Ah yes. The *Louis Vachon*. Where is it? Who has it?

It wasn't Victor, she realizes now. Victor's hands had been empty when he'd climbed out the bathroom window. He'd shown them to her. He, or Alexander, had taken the money – that much was common knowledge. And then they'd lost it. The idiots. How can anyone lose six and a half thousand dollars?! No. Those two were too dumb to even look under the bed.

It wasn't any of the Bloor set. They'd come a-knocking on her door *after* she'd noticed the loss. Nor was it Liberty or Rose. That was the *wrong* bag. And it wasn't the Admiral or the Major. They're still offering a reward. Maybe.

So. It could have been Coady, or Paisley, or any one of the club kids, drag queens and others who'd heard her hotel room being broadcast at Buzby's. Like Sugarbush, for example? Or Her Royal Heinie herself? Zachary even? Cherry feels nauseous, shakes her head in confusion. It could have been any one of them.

She rescues Angus' keys and her things from the bed, stuffs them back into her pocket. A stick of gum, a handful of quarters, an invite to a New Year's Party. She lights a cigarette. It sure is hard to smoke wearing mittens, though ...

"Duh!"

With sickening realization, Cherry twigs to the truth. She knows where the bag is. Coady? Paisley? Her Royal Heinie? One of her minions? Zachary? What's the difference? They all know each other; they practically live in each other's pockets and everyone knows everyone. In the club world, the rule is *one* degree of separation. Two, if you don't count one-night stands. If any one of them had swiped the *Louis Vachon*, it would still end up in the same place.

At the Royal Court House.

But how to get it back? Cherry's mouth tightens unpleasantly. Those fuckers. She's going to have to trick them out of it, that much is clear. Spin them some tale, ply some disguise. But what? She can't use the biker gang story; they're wise to that one. It's a challenge. Her Royal Heinie has so many flies buzzing in her web of servants, it's going to be tough to break through it.

Money. She's going to need money. Everyone loves money. How much does she have? Just under seven hundred dollars in rolled quarters. Surely that won't be enough ...

She reaches for the phone. She has an important call to make. There's only one way to find out how much she's going to need. And that's to ask. She glances at the clock in the kitchen. 8:30 a.m.

Treason always has its price.

Santa Calamity d'Oopsidaisy is giving her final speech of the season to her cast of thousands. Her festival is gearing up for its finale and she'll need all the strength and cooperation she can get. She who swaps bags and bodies when your back is turned congratulates her servants on a job well done.

"Well done, moths!" she says. "Well done, roaches!"

It's a pep talk designed to inspire her minions to new heights of devastation. Everyone will have to pull their weight if the show's going to finish as she would like. Even those blasted pigeons will have to clean up their acts. Santa Calamity wants the Gods in Olympus to sit up and take notice and for that, she can't have any dissension in the ranks.

In the corner, the Sacred Bovinity chews away at its cud and smiles to itself as its Mistress lays out her plans for the assembly. Through lazy long-lashed eyes it watches as roles are assigned to each player in the game. It flicks away a fly with its tail.

"Pay attention you," it lows at the fly.

The briefing session continues. Watches are desynchronized.

"Just make sure that *they* don't see you," warns Our Lady in conclusion. "Remember guys: Play Safe. When in doubt, ask a spider."

The wasps are buzzing to get in on the action. One of them displays its stinger in an overzealous attempt to show how well-prepared it is.

"Soon, my darlings," purrs She who pulls the back ends off of bees. She closes her eyes and leans back in her chair for a quick snooze. "Soon."

# 10 ... pay dirt

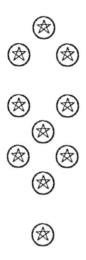

On the final night of the year, Mercury has plummeted, fallen from the grace of heaven to twenty below. His disgraced fingers probe the core of winter; it is an obscene, detached rape. Cold. He eats away at you from the inside and doesn't give you a second chance. His message is simple: not everyone gets out of here alive.

The Kennel Klub has opened its doors for the last time. Crates of smuggled booze are stacked into a fifteen-foot-high fortress at the end of the bar – not even the crowd who've turned up could possibly exhaust the supply. And the place is packed, thanks to the potent combination of a New Year's Eve, a gibbous moon, and the imminent death of a nightclub. Every vampire in the city wants in on the kill.

The place is jammed to the mirror ball. Cherry needn't have worried about sneaking past the coatcheck, needn't have concerned herself with her disguise. If it could be called a disguise. She is resplendent in a whorling lycra pantsuit of merbromin-germicide green, family-room orange and refugee purple. No pantie-line for she isn't wearing any. Her bell-bottoms flare out beneath the knee to almost cover a pair of cork wedgies. Her new wig hangs in a curtain of scarlet down to the small of her back. She has a new set of nails, each finger painted a different colour of the acid rainbow. She looks and feels like a shattered kaleidoscope. Disguise? That'll be the dark glasses. To cover the rings of exhaustion.

She's been a busy girl. It's a good job she woke up so early for it's been a full day. She was relieved to finally get out of Angus' overalls and chuck them in the garbage. She'd made good use of them and squeezed the last drop of lucre from those world-weary oil stains.

Fourteen hundred dollars, that's how much she's made in one day, above and beyond the cost of her new outfit, gas, taxi to the car pound to pick up the Dixie van and the fee to get it out of hock. But, lucrative as it has been, one day of fixing other folks' machinery has been enough to last her another few lifetimes. As it is, she's going to have to drink an extra pint or two from the Waters of Lethe to forget it all.

It's amazing how much people will pay to get service on a holiday. The answering machine had provided her with her list of suckers, while Angus' client list on the desk had provided her with the missing addresses. It was simply a matter of spanner work, making the rounds, screwing the rubes for as much as she could get.

"If you want it fixed today, you're going to have to have cash, ma'am."

Cherry had applied her Mr-Fix-it skills to over two dozen wayward appliances. She'd kicked the shit out of the vending machine in the nurses' lounge, replaced a fuse in Mr Woodbine's basement, coaxed Dr Chester Belsize's garburator back to health and removed a dead mouse from the motor in Mrs Adelaide Simcoe's refrigerator.

"Is that it? I could have done that myself."

"Yes, but you didn't, did you? That'll be two hundred dollars, ma'am. Thank you."

Fourteen hundred dollars for a day of running around. If she hadn't run out of time she would have made even more, and she hasn't even touched the quarters waiting for her in half the vending machines. They can wait. She has enough.

One thousand bucks. That's what her stool pigeon had asked for – the price for committing treason and helping her to the *Louis Vachon*. That leaves her four hundred in the black. Or fourteen hundred dollars, truth be told, if she can get away without paying the ransom.

Things are definitely on the upswing. It's about time.

With an hour to go before midnight, the Kennel Klub is shaking its patrons into a final debauch. There is at least one busload of kids in pastel T-shirts and pants wide enough for hang-gliding. The leather jacket and army boot crowd is out in full force – pierced body parts and tattoos roving in packs, looking for trouble. The hat and glove set hold court around the tables, sipping exotic cocktails. The denim pigs hog the pool table and the pinball machines while the cashmere fairies keep looking around for the video-porn they're so used to in the other bars. Littered all over the floor are streamers and confetti, paper hats and noisemakers – and broken glass by the bucketful. People are now drinking straight out of the liquor bottles – there's so much of it around and it's so cheap.

Both washrooms have healthy lineups. Consumption is high and the promise of cross-fertilization is in the air. It's a sexy crowd, a *dangerous* crowd. The superstars of the evening are those who have the most potential for evil. Everyone wants the old year not only dead but tortured into oblivion.

Cocktail Mama is working the coatcheck while Whatserface is standing behind the cash register with El Bozo of the Hawaiian tie. They both have their arms folded across their chests and they wear matching *Happy New Year* tiaras. He looks shocked; she looks heavily sedated. Clearly, they weren't expecting such a crowd. Rose is working her ass off, unloading a crate of whiskey onto the shelves behind the bar between serving customers.

"Oh, it's you," she says when she pours out Cherry's vodka tonic. "Liberty's going to kill you. Do you know how long it took us to find the car last night?"

"Where is she then?" asks Cherry snarkily. "I believe she owes me six hundred dollars."

"Oh, she'll be here," warns Rose. "Soon as she finishes work. You're dog meat."

It's more than a threat. It's spoken as a *fait accompli*.

"Happy New Year," says Cherry, working her way back to a spot where she can keep an eye on the door.

She keeps checking the newcomers, scanning the multitudes for her date, who hasn't shown yet, she's certain. Every so often she raises her dark glasses for a better view, flutters her multicoloured lashes a couple of times before lowering the anonymity visor again. It shouldn't be too long. It's just past 11:30.

Sugarbush approaches, sloshed out of her chintz.

"Did you hear?"

"No, what?"

"They found the kid."

"Oh, that," lies Cherry with the ease of a professional. "Yes, I heard that."

"Uh-huh. Turned up in Santa's grotto in the mall. They've got him chained up in the coatcheck in case he tries to escape again. I mean ..."

Sugarbush carries on talking, her voice drowned by the music, obliterated by Cherry's boredom filter. Tuned out.

With less than twenty minutes to spare 'til midnight, he appears, a vision in white vinyl pants, the *Louis Vachon* slung over his shoulder. Cocktail Mama is chasing after him, wanting him to check the bag, but she gets shrugged off. Arms wave. Shouts are exchanged. Then he spots Cherry and weaves his way toward her.

"Made it." He arrives, breathless, before Cherry, and hands over the bag. "Here you go. A thousand bucks, right?"

He's here. Cherry can't believe her luck. The idiot has come. And he actually brought the tickets with him. He must be missing a few brain cells, but then she already knew that. Cherry makes sure that the tickets are real this time and not another Case of Fallacies. They're there, although the level of tickets inside the bag is seriously depleted.

"Did you find the jackpot?"

"No-o." He's a tad hesitant. "Not exactly."

"Right," says Cherry, zipping up the bag, feeling a wave of relief sweep over her. "Congratulations Zach, you just made Loser of the Year."

She starts waltzing towards the exit. That had felt good.

"Hey!" Zachary is taken aback by the affront. "What about my thousand dollars? I went out on a limb for you. Fair play, Cherry!"

"Hey!" yells Cocktail Mama, pushing her way through a crowd of kids. "That's my *Louis Vachon* you've got there!"

"Oh right, fair play." Cherry feigns sudden remembrance. "Here.

Play this!" She reaches into the bag, fishes around in the pile of tickets, finds one near the bottom and tosses it back at Zachary. It's already been scratched. "Good luck."

Zachary, Paisley, Coady, Alex, Her Royal Heinie, Empress Estelle VII and all the rest of them who've ripped her off, played her for a fool, can go play with themselves until the cows go home for all she cares. Not that they need any encouragement. Especially Zachary. How could she ever have found him attractive? Mutton dressed as lamb. At forty-two, he should have more self-respect.

Suddenly Cherry feels a pain in her leg. She looks down. Brock has his sharp little baby teeth sunk into her calf. She tries to shake him off as if he were a humping dog.

"Get ... off me! You rabid whelp!"

Cocktail Mama approaches, pulls her attack-brat off its quarry. With some difficulty. She's flushed in the face.

"That's my bag," she says, yanking on Brock's collar while tucking a strand of hair behind her ear. "You stole my fucking bag, Cherry Beach."

"So what?" retorts Cherry. "You stole three weeks of my life."

There's no getting past her and Brock, so Cherry spins on her wedgie and takes off in the other direction. Cocktail Mama gives chase, but Cherry has a good head start.

Mr Carroll could not have imagined a stranger quadrille around the dance floor. In the lead is Cherry Beach, like a giant dodo, lolloping along in her screaming pantsuit, barging into the serious dancers, clearing a swathe of destruction across the dance floor. Zachary follows, helping the wounded back onto their feet, slowly realizing that this White Knight approach isn't helping him gain any ground. Then comes the Duchess, Cocktail Mama, more focused on her goal than Zachary, her beach thongs flapping on her feet, her happy-face Cheshire-cat T-shirt puffing and sagging with the exertion. She brandishes a bottle of Chivas Regal in the air, either as a weapon or to help her gain momentum. Stumbling up the rear is Brock, the white rabbit, hip-hopping after his mother, a bandage on his leg unraveling like Ariadne's thread.

Approaching the homestretch back to the bar, Cocktail Mama catches up with Cherry, ditches her bottle and latches onto the bag. A tight bunching of leather queens opens up like a relaxing sphincter (with the usual accompanying complaints). A widening arena develops as gleeful onlookers gather to watch the first juicy fight of the evening.

It's more a tug o' war than a fight, a grunting spin around the fulcrum of the *Louis Vachon's* stretching handles with Cherry on one end and Cocktail Mama on the other. Someone spills a drink on Cherry's shoulder.

"Give … give … give," huffs Cocktail Mama, trying to get a better purchase on the floor with her beach thongs. "Give!"

"Oh, all right then … if you insist."

Cherry feels her fingers prickle as if she's being stung by a thousand wasps.


Roll back a few seconds. Cherry hates pointless arguments and always has, especially since she discovered that getting her own way could also include graceful retirement from a situation. A loss is a win if you treat it as such. There is nothing worse than extenuated stalemate – except, of course, in matters of the heart, where that is the aim.

Such a waste of time is this game with Cocktail Mama, who, like a pit bull terrier, is determined to get the bag away from Cherry. Not because of the tickets inside it, but because the bag originally belonged to her. Different values for different folk. After a week of chasing thousands of dollars – the $250,000 Piedish in the Sky – it's a shock to find Cocktail Mama so concerned over a cheap reproduction piece of luggage. It's all so pointless – which is one reason why Cherry releases her grip on the handle.

The other reason, of course, is that she was beginning to lose the circulation in her fingers. Or that's what she will always maintain. The less said about the invisible wasps, the better.


Cocktail Mama isn't expecting Cherry to let go. She has all of her bulk behind the struggle and Cocktail Mama is a big girl. She's gearing herself up for a slow but sure victory, the grip of her beach thongs giving her, perhaps, the winning edge. The expression on her face, therefore, as she goes flying backwards through the parting crowd is a mixture of triumph and dismay.

People scatter. Cocktail Mama lands with such force against the bar that the old cash register is dislodged from the counter and comes crashing down upon her head. Right down on her skull. The sharp corner of the till gouges through the left temple, deep into Cocktail

Mama's brain. The cash drawer opens like a sprung trap. Coins fly into the air.

*Ka-ching-a-ling-a-Ka-chunk!*

For a fleeting second, Cherry sees a *Fata Morgana* of someone she thinks she recognizes, superimposed over Cocktail Mama's face. Someone ... she can't place who. The tired creases around the mouth, the lazy eye that never quite looks at you and the goldfish mouth that opens and closes without thinking or saying anything. It reminds her of someone.

Get a grip, Cherry tells herself. This is no mystic flashback. Chill girl. Cut to a commercial. If this is some prime-time thriller, then this would be the perfect place for the schlock-horror, big-chord end of the act. So where's that commercial break? Where is it?

Cherry's first clue that this is more than sanitized TV violence is the blood that starts to pour out of Cocktail Mama's wobbling mouth, a thick torrent of blackcurrant syrup that gobs down her chin and onto her T-shirt. The club smells of burned toast. Rajah Sultana, up in the sound booth, provides an oblivious groovy soundtrack to the gurgle of blood and the death rattle of coins dribbling out of the cash drawer onto the floor.

The smell of burning increases and Cherry's legs sway, dancing with the stream of blood that drip-drip-drips to the beat-beat-beat of her tom-tom heart. The nauseating buzz in her brain segues into a jungle-acid Cole Porter remix that rips into her vision, blots out the light, invades her fingertips.

Sightless, she suddenly feels so relaxed, so floaty, so warm and fuzzy, cuddly, cozy and bubbly, tra-la-la ... *In the still of the night ... When the world is in slumber ...* That's funny. She doesn't remember taking a valium.

Hello, floor.


Cocktail Mama Pauline Bloor is dead. The life rushed out of her body as the blood swept out of her mouth. Woosh. Gone. Cover the mirrors.

She who snarls the lives of others has pulled off a big one. This is her finale and it's spectacular. An accident engineered out of the minds of dragonflies.

In that moment before losing consciousness, Cherry sees the club adjust itself, the way a place does when Death arrives. It's a peripheral wavering of reality, a slight rotation along a different axis and the universe shifts onto another plane. Sorry, Cocktail Mama didn't make it through this one.

Oops.

Cherry comes to, maybe four or five seconds later. Rose is slapping her face.

"Now look what you've done!"

"Me?" groans Cherry, adjusting her wig, checking that her eyelashes are still there. "I haven't done anything."

The music has stopped. Finally. Rajah Sultana got the message. Everyone stands around awkwardly as if pasted on paper – thin magazine cutouts in a scrapbook collage of horror.

In the quiet, a car honks its horn and revs noisily from somewhere down the street. A distant reminder that the world continues to buzz unabated out there.

*Bzzzz.*

Taking advantage of the temporary hiatus in the world of adults, Brock appears out of nowhere, runs up to the corpse of Cocktail Mama and starts pulling away at the handles of the *Louis Vachon*. Cocktail Mama refuses, even in death, to give up her grip. The Bloor tenacity.

"Mine!" shouts Brock, yanking away. "MY BAG! I saw it first!"

Rose glares at him. "Someone get that child out of here."

*Bzzzz.*

Brock is pounding with his little fists now, trying to bash Cocktail Mama's hands into relinquishing their hold. Then he starts picking away at the individual fingers. No one makes a move to stop him, the only barrier preventing him from getting the bag is Obstinate Mother Death.

But Santa Calamity hasn't finished with her bag of surprises.

*Bzzzz. Bzzzz! Bzzzz!!*

The revving, honking car has been getting louder and louder. Now it's upon them. Coming through the wall.

In the rending of mortar and moment, everyone forgets about Brock committing an indignity to a body. In less time than it takes to roll another set of eyeballs or choke back another cocktail of surprise, the child and his dead mother are abandoned as the centre of attention.

Chaos. People scrabble for safety and dive for cover. The wall behind the bar buckles and splinters. A signed eight-by-ten of Bessie Smith jumps to the floor, followed by a couple of bottles. Another resounding crash and the wood gives way with a deafening, bursting roar. *Smash! Smash!* Shelves of glassware shatter into fragments, the neon beer sign fizzes, crackles and finally swings from its wire. *Smash!!*

The front end of a particularly infamous Plymouth Fury appears behind plasterboard and lath. It's forcing its way through the double doors from the parking lot outside, its horn screaming electric-blue murder, its driver yelling at the top of her lungs as the car roller-coaster rides a path of destruction, front wheels finally coming to a spinning, smoky halt over the edge of the bar.

"Scrambled Tofuuuuu!!"

The fake exit – a well-used trick of the vaudeville stage or the sawdust ring. She who choreographs the drunk's totter and the pedestrian's stumble must have cut her teeth in the circus. Just when you think she's gone, she's back with a flourish of trumpets.

*T-daaaa!*

I'm not gone yet. Didja miss me?

There's a moment of silence as the dust clears. And now: This. Who could have ever imagined as they were dressing for the evening that the last night of the Kennel Klub would include death, destruction and a Plymouth Fury being driven through a wall? Ding-a-ling-a-ling. Out with the old. In with the new!

Liberty extracts herself from the wreckage, a look of highly stoned triumph on her face. The driver's door falls away from its hinges. She waves her totem kewpie doll in the air, yells an incomprehensible encouragement to the gods and gives the Spirit of Anarchy reason to live on into the New Year.

Without realizing what she's doing, she gives Cocktail Mama a playful kick in the ribs.

"Hey-hey-hey! What d'you think of *that* then?! Pretty fuckin' cool or *what*?!"

She sneezes. A glob of mucus lands on Cocktail Mama's face. And Liberty, drawn to the burst eyeball now streaked over with her expectoration, finally notices that something is wrong.

"Killer!"

No one responds. They're all too busy watching, wide-eyed, as the corpse slowly lilts over to one side ...

The cash register teeters and falls from its macabre perch with a resounding crash. Liberty takes a step away from the mess that was once Cocktail Mama. There is a collective holding of breath.

Suddenly, released from the stopper of pressure that had been sitting on it, the corpse of Pauline Bloor shudders. A column of air that had been sitting bottled-up inside the diaphragm rushes up through the windpipe and reflexes are triggered. Fingers peel one by one away from the tacky brown handles of the *Louis Vachon*. Her beach thongs flap away on her feet as her legs twitch like the trotters of a freshly slaughtered pig. Cocktail Mama's final thoughts come rising out of the mouth as if the pause button on a tape deck has just been released.

"... *Take* ... *The* ... *Fucking Bag* ... *You Stupid* ... *Cow* ..."

Brock Bloor is the first to bovinate himself. He doesn't need to be told twice. He takes the bag.


Cherry chases the child up the circular staircase, her wedgies slowing her down. Screaming past a grooving Rajah, she flies into the VIP lounge, but she is too late. Brock has defenestrated himself, the *Louis Vachon* vanishing after him through the window as Cherry enters the room. The window is tiny. Memories of air vents and the invisible man prevent her from following. Damn. She's trapped.

She slumps into Whatserface's chair. Curses. She had wanted so much to personally escort those damn tickets into oblivion before the New Year started. She had turned it into her personal mission – an irrational one, she now concedes. What difference does it make? They're all worthless, aren't they?

Just like her. Every time she tries to do something it fucks up, leaving a trail of destruction behind her. The opposite of the Midas touch. Better to not do anything at all, better to petrify into a lump of inactivity, better to never attempt to achieve a dream. Not for Cherry Beach. Frank Metcalfe. Whoever. The deck is stacked against her. Abandoned by the gods for eternity.

Whatserface has left the television on. The city's New Year's Eve celebrations are being broadcast live from Mackenzie Square, the site of the old city hall, which is swarming with anxious participants awaiting the impending countdown. Traffic has been stopped for at least six blocks around to make room for thousands upon thousands of people converged on a temporary stage in the middle of the square where a giant clock counts down the few minutes that are left to a year that many hope will be a damn sight better than the miserable one they've just endured.

Cherry is reminded of a phrase of the Major's. *Some people believe that the value hidden under the ticket's play surface can magically and mysteriously change right up to the very moment of scratching.*

The logic is screwed, but it's just as good as any other when you're dealing with the wiles of Lady Luck. Santa Calamity. Bathsheba. Loki. Queen Mab. Whatever name she's using these days. Now is as good a time for a big bonanza winner as any. In fact, everything points to *Now* being a particularly excellent moment indeed.

Cherry takes out the bloodstained *XXXmas* ticket from her purse. Was this one the big winner? The quarter-million jackpot? The one that Angus had taken to her grave with her, the one that Cherry had miraculously rescued. She sighs. Time is slipping away even as she ponders the question. Certainly the ticket won't be worth anything after midnight.

Over in Mackenzie Square, the countdown starts. There's a close-up on the giant clock, celebrities (including actor Gervais Wynford of vampire Mountie fame, and the Mayor) are gathered around it, wrapped in their goose-down anoraks and beaver-fur earmuffs. Fake tanned faces smile grey at the cameras, shouting puffs of breath into the cold night air above the noise of the crowd.

*This is the moment*, thinks Cherry, it has to be. She chooses her nail: the citrus one, middle finger, right hand. Her cursing finger; it seems appropriate. So what if there are only seconds left before the *XXXmas* game is invalid? The game has changed. No longer is she scratching for the prize – now she just wants the satisfaction of knowing. Of finishing up her tournament with Santa Calamity d'Oopsidaisy.

She looks down at the ticket. Horrors! A wasp the size of a small radish is crawling across the bloodstain, feelers waving, tail ominously raised.

Without thinking, Cherry rushes to the window where she shakes and shakes the ticket in the night air until she is certain that the insect has to have gone. She returns, heart beating, to the television.

"Ten … Nine … Eight …"

$250,000 is revealed.

"... *Six ... Five ...*"

A second $250,000. All she needs is one more. Despite the fact that the ticket will be stale-dated no matter what, she feels her pulse quicken and prickle. That old gambling fever kicks in. Outside the club, a few car horns start honking, jumping the gun on the new year.

"... *Four ... Three ... Two ... One ...*"

She scratches the last ornament from the tree and blows away the latex residue. A strange panic grips her stomach. Her mouth wobbles, simultaneously impersonating both expressions of the Greek tragedy-comedy masks. A tear springs from her eye. A tear of joy. Of sorrow.

There it is. A parting shot from Santa fucking Calamity. The bitch is always one step ahead. $250,000. Jackpot.

Irredeemable. Worthless.

Typical, thinks Cherry as she slips the ticket into her purse. Fucking typical.

"*HapiNOOyear! HapiNOOyear! HapiNOOyear! HapiNOOyear ...!!*"

The crowd in Mackenzie square bursts into cheers.


Emerging from the VIP lounge, Cherry sees that the club below has transformed into Pandæmonium: imps dancing in the fires of Hell, malevolent spirits feeding off misfortune, maintaining a front of Puritanical shock while all the time revelling in the Chaos. A regular shindig in Bedlam. There hasn't been so much excitement in one place since Halloween.

The police have arrived and are in the process of cordoning off the exit. For some reason they have Whatserface and her bozo boyfriend in handcuffs. They're being led away, the Happy New Year's tiaras still on their heads. Cherry smothers a guffaw and retreats back into the DJ booth as police boots stomp up the circular staircase. Time to leave.

"I demand my phone call!" screams Whatserface over the crowd. "I know my rights! Charlie! Cha-aa-arlie!"


Wriggling out of the window and onto the fire escape is not just a tight fit, it's a swimsuit squeeze. Cherry would have better luck trying to hide in a mailbox. She inches her buttocks over the sill, almost dislocates her shoulder ...

"Ow!"

She snags the crotch of her pantsuit on something sharp. For one terrifying moment, Cherry thinks she'll be caught there for the cops to find her, one leg in, one leg out, straddling the window ledge, the unidentified barb pinning her in place. The fear of being found in such a compromising position, however, spurs her on to freedom. Her pantsuit is not so fortunate. Cherry may be free, but a small triangular rip of her costume is left behind, snagged on what turns out to be an exposed nail. Cherry's valve is exposed to the elements. This is no time to be prudish, she tells herself, flying down the metal stairs, concentrating on not twisting her ankles on the steps. Besides, there's no one around to see.

The cops must be out front. She can see tracks in the snow where Liberty battered her Fury through the wall. Light from the club spills out of the hole and into the parking lot. A pizza delivery car drives by. Wet snow begins to fall. The sound of cars honking their horns for the New Year fills the air.

Cherry turns the corner of the alleyway at a slight jog, the wind whistling up her plastic valve. *Toot-toot-toot.* Never mind, it's not far. For once, she knows exactly where she's going.


It's time to say goodbye. Farewell. *Auf Wiedersehen.* The party season is winding down, the damp cloth of the New Year wipes the slate clean, stops those dates from piling up on top of each other. Our Lady of the Sacred Bull is pulling on her driving gloves, preparing for the long haul home. She adjusts her flight goggles. A million cockroaches have been sacrificed and the spiders outdid themselves this year, as did the wasps and the ants, although the pigeons weren't as cooperative as they might have been. Ah well, she's paid them all off. Her servants have been rewarded for playing their part in her pageant; their next reincarnations have all been approved. The Golden Bovinity changes its sex one last time while it can, before growing a hump for the long journey home.

"I wish you wouldn't keep doing that," says Santa Calamity. "It makes me giddy."

Of course she gets no answer, just a long-lashed stare of weary superiority. Really. Some creatures act way above their station.

"Oh all right!" snaps She who once sat at the High Table of Chaos.

"If you insist!"

She reaches into the folds of her crimson cape, unfastens the large pin she'd hidden there and tosses it to the ground. A flutter of paper follows, escaping from its prison, merging with the snow, tossed on the wind, weaving its way back into the stories of *they*.

"There. Are you happy now?"


The sign saying *Men Only* doesn't apply to drag queens. Never has, never will. Since time immemorial, the Gentleman's Quarters has – unlike some other bathhouses in town – allowed transvestites, gender-fucks, aliens and party superstars to congregate in the appropriately named TV lounge on the second floor for a two-dollar fee, on the proviso that they keep away from the wet area and don't upset the accountants. Up in the lounge, they gather around the video games, drape themselves on the easy chairs, bicker up a storm, sharpen their tongues and proposition wayward young men with teasing catcalls. The Gentleman's Quarters is a three-o'clock-in-the-morning institution. Rumour has it that it was once home to a famous writer whose ghost still wanders the hallways, spouting short, pithy prose on the glories of bullfighting.

Cherry doesn't wish to be announced to the crowd in the lounge, so she pays ten dollars for a locker at the entrance window. A fleeting wrinkle appears on Gerrard's forehead, but he still buzzes the door open, hands her a towel and – after a moment's thought – a condom.

"Locker #22 by the showers. I don't want any trouble, Cherry, all right?"

Cherry smiles sweetly at him. She's tempted to blow him a kiss but thinks better of it. Instead, she manages a gruff "thanks Gerry." Holding the towel in front of herself as a figleaf, she winds her way through the labyrinth of corridors and up the stairs, excusing her way around the usual towel-draped customers, the occasional leather cowboy in chaps (no underwear, not a stitch) and the giggling gaggles of tourists.

As she rounds the corner to the TV lounge, voices rise in a thick vapour of sound. Familiar voices. Well, what do you know? It sounds as if they're all here, forfeiting their New Year's Eve parties at the Mercantile Warehouse and Bliss to rally around their beloved sovereign in her hour of need.

There they all are: every thieving queen in the city worthy of the title, scratching away as if her life depended on it. Paisley, Sugarbush, Coady, Candy, vampire Goth attendants, dates in towels, pixies, elves and gnomes ... everyone right up to Her Royal Heinie, Empress Estelle VII herself, sitting on her throne beside the Christmas tree, daintily scratching away at a ticket with her royal nail file. It's like a sweatshop, so intent is everyone on the task at hand.

"It's gotta be here somewhere!" says Coady, sucking his thumb between tickets. "It's gotta be!"

"Hey, watch what you're doing!" says an angry dwarf, who, along with Paisley, is chopping up a cocaine carbuncle on the video table. The lights from Ms Pacman bounce off their eager faces. *Gobble, gobble, gobble.*

Cherry stands, unnoticed, assessing the scene.

"Aach!" splutters a Goth, shaking a hand frantically in the air. "There goes another nail!"

Everyone has a good, knowing laugh at this. A couple of hecklers respond with "Welcome to the club, girl!" and "Save it for your coffin!"

Paisley, one finger pressed against a nostril, finally notices Cherry standing there, watching. Eyes widen, the jaw drops while teeth, still aching from an onslaught of cocaine, continue their grinding motion with nothing but air to chew on. Paisley nudges Coady mid-snort, motions with a flick of the head at Cherry.

"What *now*, girl? Can't you see I'm busy? ... oh ..."

Slowly but surely, like pancake mix being poured onto the grill, a spongy silence spreads around the room until all that can be heard is the faint hiss of Jimmy Stewart on the television. *It's a Wonderful Life.* Cherry tenses, ready to flip.

"Hi, everyone. Hi, Ken."

Her Royal Heinie raises a finger from her throne in the corner. Her two attendants turn as one to face the crowd. A proclamation is in the offing.

"Well if it isn't our good friend, the wandering Cherry Beach," intones Her Royal Heinie, arching her mock surprise-brows. "What can we do for you, my dear? Come for a scratch? Pull up a towel."

"Are you guys looking for this?" Cherry asks, taking the winning ticket out of her purse and holding it up. Exhibit A. She walks up to the royal throne and attempts a curtsey before ceremoniously handing over her gift. "Make sure this goes to a deserving cause, will you, Ken?"

"Wha–? Where …? How …? Wha–?"

This is the closest to an admission of guilt that anyone has ever gotten out of the royal personage.

"Don't mention it," smiles Cherry, her eyes twinkling. "By the by, I hope you frame that or something. Hang it over your fireplace with the Erté prints. I mean, you won't try to cash it in, will you?"

"Oh, we wouldn't dream of it." Sarcasm is Her Royal Heinie's strongest suit.

"Good." Cherry calls the bluff. "Because you know of course that it isn't worth the tinsel it's printed on. None of them are."

Her Royal Heinie's mouth makes an O without any sound.

"You're just saying that," accuses Coady.

"Sure I am." Cherry grabs a ticket from a nearby scratcher, holds it up in the air. Exhibit B. "Have we all had a good look at these tickets? Any of you chicken hawks got good enough eyesight to read the small print on the back?"

A studious Goth makes the attempt. Cherry inspects her cuticles as the rules and regulations of the *XXXmas Scratch'n Win Lottery* are read pedantically to the assembled listeners. At the end of it all, blank faces turn to Cherry. No one has caught the importance of the date. Cherry wastes no time in educating them.

"You queens are all in a time warp," she warbles triumphantly. "Read that last part again, will you, sweetheart?"

"Winning tickets are valid for redemption up until midnight, December 31."

"And that big number after it?"

The Goth reads it out. Those who are still wearing them, check their watches. Realization slowly sinks in.

"Thank you," blossoms Cherry, looking around the room at the various expressions of shock and disappointment. "I'll treasure this moment forever. Thank you."

And with that, she spins on her heel and retreats down the hallway, leaving them to stew in their own vapours.


Back at the front desk, up by the vending machines, Cherry catches Gerrard's attention. He comes over to her, his arms full with a basketload of dirty towels.

"You wouldn't happen to have a spare safety pin lying around, would you Gerry?"

"What's up?"

Cherry reveals the ripped crotch in her pantsuit. A two-hundredths-of-a-second flash of plastic. Gerrard is the first person in years to have been given a glimpse of the notorious valve. It doesn't faze him. He can't help her out, though.

"Sorry, doll. The only pins round here get disposed of with rubber gloves."

"You sure? Even a Band-Aid would do it at a pinch."

"You know what?" he suggests. "I think there's a sewing kit in the laundry room. I've got to put this in the wash anyway. Come on down."

The moment Cherry sees the broken washing machine with the OUT OF SERVICE notice taped onto it, she feels as if a spider just crawled across her grave. Here we go again. It's not over yet, obviously.

"We're operating one machine down, thanks to Victor," says Gerrard, starting to his laundry chores. "I don't know what he did to it. Probably sat on it. Gave it a contact high." He fills a washer, empties a dryer of towels, and tosses a pair of jeans that are tangled in with the dry load to Cherry. "Here. Try these on for size."

Cherry holds the jeans up against her. They're not too bad, if a little short. She checks the pockets, pulls out a couple of crumpled fifty-dollar bills that are faded and worn from having gone through the dry cycle. In each bill there is a pinhole.

She peers into the broken washer, her heart beating with revelation. A stink of stagnant water wafts into the laundry room.

"Have you had anyone look at it yet?"

"Ever tried to get an electrician or a plumber over the holidays?" Gerrard remarks, acidly. "We've got a call in. It'll be sometime *next* year before someone shows up, I bet, and it'll cost us a fortune."

He spins the dial to demonstrate how broken the machine is. An annoying buzzer accompanies the overbalance light for a split second before he turns it off.

"I fished out those jeans and a T-shirt," he continues, "but I wouldn't risk my life seeing what else is in that cesspool."

Cherry is pulled to the grey surface of the water much as Arthur was drawn to Excalibur. Without any thought for her safety, she rolls up her sleeve and plunges her arm into the cold, exhausted suds.

Her fingers touch what feel like weeds. Soggy membranes. Pay dirt.

"Hey! Look what I found!"

Her face is triumphant as she pulls out a handful of drenched and dripping bills, squeezes the water from the wad of wet money in her fist. Twenties, tens, an occasional fifty. A sodden snowball o' cash. If memory serves her, there should be around six and a half thousand dollars, give or take a few hundred, floating around in there.

"Hand me a towel, sweetheart," she says to Gerrard. "And get the dryer ready. You and I are going to launder ourselves some cash."


Our Lady, Santa Calamity d'Oopsidaisy, Mercury's evil, transgendered twin sister, is finally leaving the city. Her festival is over; it's been one to remember, this year. The Golden Camel on which she rides carries her beyond the gates, beyond the overpacked underpass, beyond the city's welcoming floral tributes that slumber 'til spring beneath a blanket of snow. Wave goodbye to She who has rule over the lower creatures. Say farewell for another winter.

She'll be back. For some she never fully leaves, but for most, there's a reprieve. Time to count the bruises and mend some of the damage she's wreaked. She who kicks a beggar when he's down is exhausted. The faithful showed her such a good time over the past week that she'd gotten quite carried away; it had almost felt like work. Exhausting. She grits her teeth, pulls on the reins and heads North. A wasp buzzes lazily round her head, as eager for hibernation as She.

Gods willing, her talents will be appreciated and her festival will be approved for next year. Something to look forward to. She knows that there'll be future battles, that she'll have to fight to keep her misfortunate rites. Apollo, Lord of Risk Management and Logic, for one, is dead set against her and her kind. He and that other guy. Give them the chance and they'll spout an eternal diatribe against her chaotic brand of gambling, accident and fate. They are the type who would have a warm and safe and open world where wheels run smoothly, where slips and blunders are banished to a fuzzy feel-good electronic memory, assembled on video for a Monday-night TV show. A world without risk.

And where, ultimately, would be the joy in that?

# J... of all trades

These last days before Christmas and I'm on the go a heck of a sight more than the rest of the year put together. It has to do with the clumping of holidays, the pressures of families, the expectations of traditions, etc., etc. Everyone wants their Perfect Christmas – batteries included – which is nigh-on impossible given the variables. When things start to go wrong, yours truly gets the panicky phone calls ... *The refrigerator's defrosting itself and we just put the turkey in the freezer ... The pipes burst in the guest bedroom ... I think the lights on the roof just blew a fuse on the stove ...* I have to move and think three times faster than usual. Things get screwed up. So, of course, I'm charging more than triple for my services in this crush. Blame it on the time of year. Everyone else does.

Christmas. It's crazy. And it's not as if no one saw it coming. It's been building to a head since Halloween – before Halloween, truth be told – so you'd think two months would be enough time for people to prepare themselves and not get so worked up over something that's going to be over in less than a week. But people live their lives from moment to moment and always leave things until it's too late. It's a kind of collective ignorance.

I'm so busy trying to sort out other people's Christmases I never have a chance to prepare for my own. I have a wreath on the door and a miniature tree that I've had for the past ten years. I could do with some help, but I'm a one-woman operation here. I've only got myself to blame. I don't get on with other people. I never have.

*... I am like a pelican of the wilderness: I am like an owl of the desert. I watch and am as a sparrow alone upon the housetop ...*

Rootless, that's me. Like a mutant potato picked from the furrow and tossed in the bucket, taken back to the farmhouse and kept on the windowsill as a curiosity. Snatched by the neighbour's kids one spring and thence to the schoolyard, thrust into a pocket or a satchel, bounced around from hand to hand as a trophy, forgotten in some corner until my skin grows fur and my eyes mould shut. Rootless.

Only I wasn't a potato. I was a stone. A little Vietnamese pebble.

War was burning our village to the ground when my nameless mother went into labour with me on a sandbank, or so the story goes. There was an explosion – a landmine, I believe – and the soldiers delivered me into existence right there in the mud. To this day I can't think why they kept me. The blast that killed my mother not only deafened me, but also shocked me sightless. What good could I have been? But someone took me to heart and pulled me through, hid me in their pocket, no doubt, as some souvenir of the wars and smuggled me back in the quiet darkness of a backpack to this cold land I now call home.

Deaf. Blind.

For ten full years I lived my life in a sensory confinement. There was a lot of pain and confusion. Mostly I kept still to avoid an accident. By the time my ears plucked up the courage to start relaying the drumbeat of noise to my brain, I was ten years old and I'd created my own world a thousand times over, every day destroying the one I'd built before. I learned the tickling language of hand over hand and mastered the six magic dots of Braille from the invisible gods who fed me, clothed me, caged me, safe in their cloisters. Brother Hubert – he who appeared with a motorized pocket fan to announce his presence – taught me the words. *ball. nose. bible.*

My birth was translated into a parable, a story that I was told along with Santa Claus and the Tooth Fairy, Jesus Christ and the Blessed Virgin. But I like to think that I've maintained a memory of the sand-bank. An icy touch in the warm, sweet air. A breeze both sharp and damp. Blood.

The statue of Our Lady in the chapel was cold enough, smooth enough, unyielding enough to substitute for my mother. I used to lay my cheek upon her peeping toes and hug her sculpted skirts for hours until the brothers coaxed me away. *forbidden*, they'd spell out on my hand. *not good.*

*mother*, I'd tell them and they'd give me the shawl that was supposed to have been rescued from the sandbank along with me, except I knew that the fringe had changed over the years, that the smell was wrong. *not mother.* I've kept the shawl to this day, if only to remind myself of their lies. Lies are a warm and manufactured fabric. They have a changeable fringe and they'll impersonate your parents to shut you up, to stop you from pawing the hems of their idols. *mother.*

Sometime after my eighth birthday, they installed a Braille plaque below the feet of the statue. *Our Blessed Virgin, Mary, Mother of GOD. Do not touch.*

I was forbidden to raise the topic of my birth. The talking hands would slap me around the face if I so much as started on my *why?* routine. Nowadays when people ask me where I'm from and how it is that I have a name like Angus Dobson, I tell them what Father Ermanno always told me to say.

"I'm from the Land of Green Ginger."

What else could I say? The truth? That I'm not really supposed to be in this country? That I was smuggled into Saint Stephen's Orphanage under false pretenses? That even my name doesn't belong to me?

Angus Dobson – the *real* Angus Dobson – died of tuberculosis when he was three months old. I was given his name and I've lived my life as a lie ever since.

The day my hearing arrived I was sitting in a pew in the chapel with my fellow stones. I wasn't anywhere near the statue. I remember sharing a joke on the hand of my best friend, Bruce, when something hit me across the head. A rolling bead of vibration snaked its way to my brain, echoing louder and louder, invading me until it was a glorious wail, a terrifying ribbon of jumping, jagged particles ripping its way into my skull. I thought everything was going to end for me right then and there. I peed my pants.

Sound!

It took me a while to realize that all those excited waves of noise were coming from my own mouth. (I was screaming because something had struck me on the head. Father Ermanno always maintained that it was God.) Me? Making that racket? It was too much to conceive. The familiar muffled breeze that hummed through my bones when it flew out my mouth and back through the air to my ears, was a voice!

"... o ... oo ...ooo ... ooO ... ooOOW!!"

And so sound raped and blustered its way into my life, linked forever with pain. Everything hurt. But through that hurt I finally began to understand the world I lived in. I was able to make sense out of the textures, flavours, smells, temperatures and moistures that had always been obstacles in my search for food and sleep. This pain in my head called noise led the way, showed me the secrets, and I shouted back, able to respond and measure the loudness of my reactions. And boy, could I ever scream!

Bit by bit, I learned to communicate with the chattering gods who up until then had led me around by the elbow and steered me by the neck. Before, I had been a stone; now I was an animal to be dealt with, a wailing beast able to make them sit up and take notice! They could no longer ignore me. Nor I them, for I could hear them all – every last squeak – their noising, burping, sighing and growling. They were so much more than I'd ever imagined from their vibrations in my silence. Noise was everywhere. It didn't stop, not even for sleep. But I didn't mind, for I could noise them all back.

Then they made me learn a new language: speech. The greatest pain of all.

Twice a week, Brother Hubert dragged me off to the old vestry which housed the Perkins Brailler, laid my fingers on his lips, twitched his signing hand under my hand and we worked our way through the Psalms. He'd squeeze my face, form my lips and tongue to his satisfaction, and rub my throat to make me speak the words of Our Lord. Then I would read them aloud from the giant Braille Bible on his desk.

*… My lips shall utter praise … My tongue shall speak of thy word … Let thine hand help me …*

What I minded was not so much that Brother Hubert reeked of fish or that he sweated like a lump of rancid butter, or that he always grabbed me by the neck and tried to push me around the room, but that my sessions with Brother Hubert meant leaving the supper table early and missing out on television. And he was so cheerful about it! I was told that since I couldn't see the TV, I wasn't missing out on anything – an attitude I was quick to challenge, but to no avail. Every Tuesday and Thursday evening I was shunted off to the old vestry where I would endure the slobbering lips, the putrid breath and the raised dots and pinpricks of Brother Hubert's enthusiasm.

*… In my distress I cried unto the Lord, and he heard me. Deliver my soul, O LORD, from lying lips and from a deceitful tongue … My soul hath long dwelt with him that hateth peace. I am for peace: but when I speak, they are for war …*

I loathed it all, and I blame Brother Hubert's chipper teaching style. To this day, whenever I am confronted with Braille, I find myself returning to the horrors of the Perkins Brailler machine, the slate and stylus and those hated evenings fingering the Bible. And it's everywhere now – Braille – in elevators and shopping malls, handicapped ramps and emergency exits. I can't fathom it. If someone's blind, what on earth is going to induce them to run their fingers over every wall just in case there's a secret message waiting for them somewhere? *In case of fire, pull red handle.* And spelling! Why does a new language have to make the same stupid mistakes as the old one, for crying out loud!

Braille is a secret code. It creates its own hermetic order, seals you off from the rest of the world, follows its own rules, keeps you apart.


*got my hearing back*, I signed to Bruce. *I can hear now. and talk.*

*we're opposites then.* Bruce was philosophical. Bruce was born with Usher's Syndrome; his world was getting smaller as mine was getting larger.

Away from Brother Hubert I was teaching myself. I adjusted my four available senses, with my new ears guiding my tongue, my fingertips, my nose. I could lose myself forever in the squeak of a foam cup, the scuff of a footstep, the whisper of salt being shaken on a meal, the lapping wetness of a bath. In my fantasies I created a shape for the stink of a polished floor, a taste for the boom of the chapel organ, a sound for the burn from a candle.

Machinery held a special pleasure for me, the Perkins Brailler notwithstanding. I adored the smell of oil, the movement of a hinge, the curl of a cable. It was a land of mystery, a world of designated function. I dreamed of spending time in the machine shop, but I was forbidden because I was a girl; nevertheless, I dreamed of one day being surrounded by engines and automata. Instead of people.

"Angus! Angus!" jeered the other children from Brother Quentin's dormitory. Twenty times a day, and more, they reminded me that Angus was a name meant for a boy. "Ooh Angus! Angus! Give us a kiss!"

... *Behold, as the eyes of servants look unto the hand of their masters* ...

The brothers treated me well, I suspect. I was their miracle, they said, their little angel of Saint Francis de Sales, patron of the hearing impaired. I thought them all saints – yes, even Brother Hubert – capable of bringing me another miracle, for I was greedy for change, and their enthusiasm was contagious. I was their secret prodigal daughter, their screaming mutant potato.


When I was eleven I was moved out of Brother Hubert's dormitory and into Sister Hilda's. It was she who lectured me about my womanhood and taught me about our inner strength over men. Saint Stephen's Orphanage was, at that time, blossoming from the charity boom of the late seventies, and the monastic order was infiltrated by the so-called weaker sex. Associated Benevolent Christian Charities Inc. now oversaw the operation and pumped funds into our development. A new building was added around the back of the chapel with special equipment for the handicapped. Sixty new kids – boys *and* girls – were moved in and foundations for a swimming pool were dug. We were always being presented to Chairmen of Boards and Secretaries of Societies. There were telethons, marathons and bottle drives. Pricey colognes patted us on the head and lipsticky breaths asked us questions we were not allowed to answer.

"I'm from the Land of Green Ginger!"

I spent my eleventh summer answering the telephone during a pledge drive. *I'm a little blind girl*, they made me say. *Can I depend upon your twenty-five-dollar donation? It's tax deductible.*

By accident, I once got my photograph in a paper, a mistake that Father Ermanno made sure was never repeated. I was to avoid any publicity on account of my name. I still have the clipping. I think I look like an idiot – a cross-eyed, vacant-looking idiot.

Those were the days I refer to as my "blind acceptance." Five years adjusting to a world of sound. I believed everything the Sainted Brothers and Sisters told me. Why would I not? Slowly, I stopped screaming.

Until I got the gift of sight.


I prefer a sightless universe. I would be happy if I never had to gaze upon another person's face, never look at ugly skin stretched over bones or ever watch the showing off of teeth behind those fleshy strips of lip. Without sight, I had built up in my mind a version of humanity far more attractive to me than what my eyes now see. The outer shell of appearance is too gawky for me; when I close my eyes it vanishes anyway. I trust the sound of a voice, an odour, the curve of a nose, perspiration on a hand and the heat of a body. The wind of breath. Then, and only then, does humanity emerge with any semblance of beauty. Mankind is easier to deal with as a formless, morpheus god. Unseeable. A shape to fit my imagination.

Sight for me is, and always will be, a handicap. That's because I am a heathen.


*… They have mouths, but they speak not: eyes have they, but they see not: They have ears, but they hear not: noses have they, but they smell not: They have hands, but they handle not: feet have they, but they walk not: neither speak they through their throat …*


Sister Hilda gave me a typewriter for my twelfth birthday – an Underwood that smelled of grease and ink, a heady combination that made my ears pound with excitement. Not, you understand, because I was at all thrilled about the prospect of churning out letters, poems, or the occasional novel, nor because, as Sister Hilda kept telling me, it could help me get a good job as a secretary in the future. No. It was simply because it was a machine. My requests to start mechanics classes were still being rebuffed by Father Ermanno, so the typewriter and the Perkins Brailler were the closest I could get to the machine shop. Father Ermanno agreed to my having the Underwood *so that our little angel can communicate with the outer world*, a joke that infuriated me. I could communicate already. I could speak, couldn't I? I could hear. I could sign (both two- and one-handed) and I could Braille. What more did I need? But, as Father Ermanno explained, the Underwood would allow me to do something I had never been able to do successfully before: write the language that the rest of the world spoke.

I presume he meant English.

It was torture. The keyboard didn't make any sense to me after the Perkins Brailler. My fingers had to follow a different configuration – actual letters, not numbered combinations. I kept trying to add the number six before a letter to denote a capital, as it is with Braille. I felt as if I'd completely wasted my time with those fucking magic dots.

Even worse, because I was unable to read my own typing (unless I used the special expensive textured ribbon), my work was filled with errors, the existence of which I was kept ignorant of until one day when I was the object of much cruel laughter from the kids in Brother Quentin's class. *Mary, Queen of Snots*. It would have been nice to have known about my mistakes, but Brother Hubert was so overjoyed that his little performing monkey-girl could even hit the keys in some semblance of sequence that he just encouraged me to continue rather than point out my deficiencies.

When I found out my mistakes, I was livid and I brought my scream back out of hiding to infest the air. Father Ermanno marched me to the Underwood, sat me down and forced me to write an apology to Brother Hubert.

Instead, I wrote a letter to God, outlining how I'd been misled, how I'd been stolen from my homeland, kept a virtual prisoner and abused under the hands of his so-called servants. I made a point of saying that I'd been prevented from learning mechanics, a much-valued skill in this modern day and age. I closed the letter by asking for help in my hour of need or else I'd kill myself. In the silence that followed the ratchet-snarl of the paper being pulled out of the Underwood roller, Father Ermanno read my diatribe, my threat. He was touched, he eventually told me. Moved. The next thing I knew, he'd sent my letter – or a version of it – to a newspaper. *Can you believe this was written by a poor little blind boy?!* He had to have retyped the thing, for mine had been filled with not only incriminating accusations but also, by my reckoning, a load of unintelligible typo-garbage, and it certainly didn't ask for money. Donations flooded in and yours truly became an unidentified *cause célèbre*. Once again, lies. The swimming pool was finished and work was started on a gymnasium and a rose garden.

I did, however, get my wish and started classes in mechanics. Nothing demanding or dangerous for a twelve-year-old blind girl, mind you. I ended up mainly sitting at a bench feeling up an oily old engine, which was supposed to have put me off mechanics, but didn't.

Something was born within me while I sat at that bench, my fingers running over valves and pistons. It was like a little seed that took root and grew in my stomach. I had gotten what I wanted, my womanhood had beaten the men and, yes, I *was* stronger. I could do whatever I wanted! I wasn't going to be pushed around any more.

From my perspective, Father Ermanno was a bully. Brother Hubert was more subtle, but still a bully. One day I was going to run these bullies through with a giant Perkins Brailler, a massive slate and stylus. Smash their weaker male brains in with the Underwood. Punch a secret message into their flesh with a three-foot spike.

*Olé!*


When I was fifteen years old, surgery with experimental lasers became an option. Both Bruce and I were good choices for guinea pigs, since I was – officially – dead already, and Bruce's eyesight was deteriorating fast. If anything went wrong, no one would be the wiser. The money was fronted by the ABC Charities. The doctors were eager to progress beyond working on pig corneas and so Bruce and I were wheeled into the operating room. A shelf was fitted snug around my face like a toilet seat. Nurses' hands held me at the elbow, stroked my shoulders.

Eye operations, I discovered, were done under local anesthetic. I was awake for the entire ordeal, trapped in that pillory. The needles, the swabs, the smell of disinfectant, the heavy breathing of the surgeon. I can remember it all.

Three minutes into the operation, a fearsome dawn arose on my darkness. Light. A sensation I could neither control nor understand burst across me and poured into me.

I screamed.

*… Make a joyful noise unto the LORD, all the earth: make a loud noise …*

The operations were declared successful, although, had I kept my big mouth shut – as Father Ermanno said – things would have been even better. I had a two-inch scar along my nose which required seven stitches. But this was no time to grouse! Thanks to the Associated Benevolent Christian Charities Inc., both Bruce and I could see and the doctors were overjoyed. There was laughter and smiles all round when the bandages came off. Brother Hubert cheered when I identified the letters of his alphabet for him. Bruce was tired but relieved. I smiled along with them all; it seemed the appropriate thing to do. I wasn't happy though; far from it. I was in shock, complete and utter. Devastated. No one had prepared me for the light; no description could have ever prepared me for the light. Never.

The universe I had previously understood, the translation I had made in my brain of what everything "looked" like – well, it wasn't anything like the universe I suddenly found myself in. My hair was dark, my skin was light. It was a rude awakening and I had no recourse. Just my good ol' faithful lungs.

*… I prevented the dawn of the morning, and cried …*

I stopped smiling. I locked myself in my cell for two weeks and wailed. I drew the curtains against the light, refused all but the most basic foods, threw my clothing all over the floor, smashed my glasses, and sat on my cot, ripping out the pages, one by one, from the Bible that Father Ermanno had given me for my fourteenth birthday.

Messy. I couldn't believe the world was so messy. A double shadow intruded on the centre of my vision. I was told it was my nose, and I had to pretend it wasn't there. What kind of trick was this where I had to fool my mind to be able to see a world I hated? Before the operation everything had been clean and tidy. My mental universe had a place for everything; reason was allocated, even if that reason was a mystery. I had had everything under control. But with the full horror of form revealed to me, there was no escaping the chaos, no refuge from the way things jumped on top of each other, crowding space, barging unbidden into my brain through these two holes in my skull. There wasn't a single area where nothing was happening! Nowhere could there be peace from this writhing, vibrating, inundating mess.

Unless I closed my eyes.


Thanks to my timely scream in the operating room, I would never experience colour – whatever that is. I was permanently colourblind, able to see only in shades of grey or – to be more accurate – sepia. *We are not precise machines*, the doctors told me. *The body doesn't come with gauges or dials. The optic nerve isn't labelled and colour is a slightly differing experience for everybody.* The more they tried to explain it, the more I became convinced that the mysteries of the surgeon's practice are mere guesswork.

The news was hardly a disappointment; I couldn't imagine having to deal with colour on top of everything else! Father Ermanno maintained that my condition was completely my own fault.

The longer end of my spectrum – the reds and the oranges – are distorted, almost indistinguishable from black, sometimes disappearing altogether. I can distinguish tones; a dark hue is always dark. I think I must have had a memory of the colour of blood from birth because blood vibrates differently than ink or paint. Middle-range colours, like greens and blues and yellows, appear much the same to me. But I've learned to adapt; we all do. I know that the light at the top of the stoplight is *stop*, and *go* is at the bottom. Most equipment is marked *on* and *off* and when it isn't, the *on* switch is usually at the top. It only takes one trial to discover if it isn't.

There was, however, a further complication resulting from the operating room incident that I was not to discover for months. The shorter end of my spectrum had compensated for my lack of distinction in the longer. Purples appeared to me as a blinding swathe approaching white. Thanks to my screaming intervention, I came out of surgery with a fascinating ability: I can see ultraviolet.

Not that I had any idea of this. How could I? I was too busy adjusting to sight itself. I thought it was all part of the same deal. For six months, my extra ability went unnoticed.

The deck of trick playing cards belonged to Bruce. He wore a pair of special dark glasses to see the secret printing on the backs of the cards and thus determine their values. I, on the other hand, without any mechanical aids, could see JD and 2H, etc, as clearly as if they had been printed there in white – the letters sort of floated there, not quite above the surface of the card. It worked best under daylight, but fluorescent lights weren't too bad.

I wish to heaven I had kept my big mouth shut about this.

But of course, adolescence is irrepressible when it gloms onto novelty. For a couple of weeks Bruce and I cleaned up on poker games. We held them in the coffee shop just down the road from Saint Stephen's, where all the smokers went during lunch. The place was filled with truckers and other blue-collar workers who fell for the orphans playing cards in the corner. We never went too high with the bets; a couple of times some guys tried to push us over the dollar mark, but we refused to up the ante – after all, it was guaranteed income.

I spent my winnings on magazines and cosmetics and it wasn't too long before we were both caught and dragged in front of Father Ermanno to explain ourselves. As far as I was concerned it was all partly Father Ermanno's fault anyway, for having had my sight restored in the first place, and so I told the truth. I told him that I was able to see ink that normally wouldn't show up unless you had the right pair of glasses or a black light.

"Angus Dobson, I'm afraid that you've become the lowest of the low in God's eyes. You're a harlot."

So now I was a harlot. I was given a rap over the knuckles with a blackboard eraser. The welt faded after a few days, but I will never forget that condemnation. *You're a harlot.*

Bruce, who spent half an hour longer than I in Father Ermanno's office to explain where he'd purchased the evil deck of cards, walked into a door that evening and spent the next two days in bed. Or so I was told by Brother Hubert. I never believed that story.

*... He that worketh deceit shall not dwell within my house: he that telleth lies shall not tarry in my sight ...*

Thereafter, I could see it on their faces – Brother Hubert's, Brother Quentin's, even Sister Hilda's – God's Disapproval. I closed my eyes to it all. How was I supposed to have reacted? Here I was, almost sixteen years old, and all my life I'd been taught that those who were "different" from the rest of the world through no fault of their own were, in fact, "special." Except – clearly – where gambling was concerned. Unfortunately, further hypocrisies were to follow.


Bruce declined rapidly in the following weeks. Usher's Syndrome and *retinitis pigmentosa* accelerated until, within a month, he could no longer see any light at the end of his tunnel and the blacksmith shut up shop in his ears permanently. Major Harbord of the ABC Charities came and took him away one day with no explanation.

I didn't react well. Even though I had known the risks involved in our experimental operations and knew that it could as easily have been me being carted off and not Bruce, I felt betrayed. I suspected that Bruce's "walking into a door" had caused his deterioration. I cursed my so-called good fortune and tried, unsuccessfully, to make people understand that Bruce had been the lucky one.

Bruce was transferred to the Queen's Quay Mental Health Facility where he remains to this day, kept in a chemical straightjacket, misdiagnosed, mistreated and ignored. Shove 'em in a corner, turn the lights out and slam the door. But I couldn't see that in those days. I was jealous.

All my schoolwork – with the exception of metalwork – took a turn for the worse. I became withdrawn. Sister Hilda tried to blame it on my adolescence, on a phase I was going through, but I knew better. I loathed this world they had forced me into. Often, I would carry out my duties with closed eyes just to escape the madness, to find some solitude, to restore my original understanding. I would spend days at the lathe, turning screws with my eyes shut, the whine of the machine pouring into my ears, the smell of hot metal filling my nostrils, the seed of discontent flowering in my stomach. That was the only time I was happy, the only time I allowed myself to dream. Otherwise, I kept myself to myself.


One day, Major Harbord, whom I had known for years through the ABC Charities, came to visit me at the orphanage. It was all very secret and underhanded, making me feel more uncomfortable than usual. I was presented with six pieces of white paper laid out in a row on the desk and told that one of them had been treated with an ultraviolet mark that could normally only be detected by a special machine. I was asked if indeed I could distinguish this mark. He talked to me as if I was six years old.

I stayed at that table all afternoon pointing out, time and time again, the paper with the floating white $X$ on it. I would have thought that after the first couple of times I'd gotten it right that the Major would have believed me, but no. He kept me at it, trying to fool me with his tricky shuffles, or telling me to look away while he swapped the $X$ paper for a $Y$ paper, or removing it all together. Finally, hours after I'd first been sat down for this experiment, Father Ermanno left the room and the Major showed me two lottery tickets and asked if I could see the one that had a secret security mark on it.

In the top right-hand corner of one of the tickets was a small UV square. Eager to end the whole episode, I showed him exactly where it was. Strangely, I only needed to do this the once. Major Harbord tried to hide his excitement, but I could see his agitation as clearly as I could see that square on the ticket.

"I know you'd like to help out the orphanage, wouldn't you Angus?"

"Maybe."

"If you're a good girlie, you can help thousands of needy children throughout the country, throughout the world. Children like yourself. Children who desperately need operations." He leaned across the table and screeched in my face – his version of a whisper. "Don't you want to help your friend, Bruce?"

It should never, never have been put to me that way.


The first time I was taken to the printing plant, Father Ermanno came with me. I'm not sure if he knew what was going on any more than I did, but I'm positive he suspected. We were ushered into the staff lounge and kept amused with hot chocolate and rice pudding until they came to get us. I was beginning to tire of Father Ermanno's reminiscences of the Vietnam war.

I was taken downstairs, walked through security and directed to a basement room where they had tickets waiting for me in cardboard boxes. Thousands upon thousands of tickets. Official scrutineers sat at a nearby table, guarding the tickets from any shenanigans.

I was introduced – can you believe it? – as *Hilda*, and the Admiral said that I was there as St Stephen's lucky mascot to choose some tickets for supporters of the orphanage. The scrutineers knew of my coming and joked about searching me for secret equipment. I rolled my eyes at the ceiling and was sorely tempted to tell them I didn't need any.

In ten minutes I had pulled out enough tickets with UV squares in the corner to fill a large carton. The Admiral shook my hand and told me I'd done a good job.

On the way home, I warned Father Ermanno that he was a hypocrite and that God would do more than rap his knuckles for his involvement in the scam. I wasn't stupid. I knew I was pulling the winning tickets from the game.

"My hands are tied," he said, not looking at me. "My hands are tied."

A week later the Major gave me a television as a token of appreciation from the ABC Charities. I still have it, even though it flickers so much that I can never see a proper image on the screen. To me, it's just another reminder.


There was a stained-glass window in the orphanage chapel depicting the stoning of Saint Stephen, the first martyr of the Christian Church. The blood poured from his wounds, spilled onto the ground, splattered on the stones. Sometimes I would sit and watch the sunlight pour through the glass, the ghostly white patches of violet jumping among the dust mites.

*...LORD, lay not this sin unto their charge ...*


On the second ten-minute visit to that sweaty basement room I managed to get through nearly five times as many tickets as the first time. I cheated. I was so angry at the whole charade that I closed my eyes while I picked. I didn't care which ones were the winners – some of the ones I'd picked were bound to be. I bet most of them, however, weren't.

It didn't take them long to figure out what I hadn't done. I wonder how much they'd had to shell out in prizes before they'd twigged to the fact. Ten thousand dollars? Fifty thousand? Ha! I was taken by Major Harbord to the Priory to have "a chat" with the Admiral.

In that grandiose environment, I felt more than a little awed. I'd never seen so much stuff! It was beyond me why anyone would want to cram more things into their lives than was absolutely necessary. I was suitably intimidated.

The Admiral wanted to know what had gone wrong and so I told him. Why should I help ruin other people's lives as mine had been ruined? I hadn't asked to have my sight restored. I had been quite happy blind, and anyway, if there were millions of dollars being manipulated here, what was I getting out of it? What was Bruce getting?

I don't think he grasped my philosophical viewpoint but the monetary aspect hit home. What did I want most? he asked me. That was easy. I wanted out of the orphanage. I wanted Bruce out of the Mental Institution. And – as the seed in my stomach reminded me – I wanted my independence. I was old enough. Screw it, if we were talking blackmail, then I wanted my own business. Machinery.

"It's a man's world out there," warned the Admiral, sceptical of my dream.

"So what?" I countered. "I'm halfway there already, by name."

It was hard to shut me up once I got started. I may have even quoted from the Bible.

"I admire your spunk, kid. I admire your spunk."

This was how I came to inherit the Dixie Wash 'n Dry business which was, at that time, being run – badly – by the Major, more as a hobby than a real venture. For my freedom, I had to make five more visits to the printing plant. The final time, I got through all of them. I pulled all the winners from the chaff.

I figured that yours truly had paid her dues to the Devil.


*… Let us break their bands asunder … Thou shalt break them with a rod of iron; thou shalt dash them in pieces like a potter's vessel …*


Machines are more reliable than people; they have functions, applications. They don't fly into rages, they don't try to coerce you into doing something you don't want to do. Even the Perkins Brailler had its charm. Machines have a logic that begins and ends with themselves.

The touch of metal parts or the smell of dust and oil will always attract me, make me feel stronger. I remember that, even back when I had neither sight nor hearing, Brother Hubert's hand-held fan, the vibrations of the radiators, and the liquid swooshings of the toilet tanks were more real to me than people. There was a coldness of action that awed me, stirred something deep inside me. Could it be that there were personalities behind all those gears, levers, pipes and tubes that had been forced into a working relationship with each other?

I thought so then and I think so now.

Inanimate objects have a form of consciousness, I'm convinced of it. Treat them as you would have them treat you and they'll keep bread on the table.

The trick to keeping afloat in the service and repairs business is to keep the machines happy just long enough to satisfy the customer. This requires not so much knowing how to fix any given problem – that's the easy bit – as it is knowing which screw to loosen, which belt to slacken, which wire to bend, so that one month, two months down the road, yours truly gets a repair call that pays off the phone bill.

That's the economics behind my relationship with machines. I'll play dumb if they will.

… *Happy shall he be that taketh and dasheth thy little ones against the stones …*

Over the years, the Admiral and the Major have become good, if tiresome, clients. It's their generator and plumbing in the winter and their air-conditioning and lawnmower in the summer. I did their Christmas lights one year and one year only! Now they contract out. I try to spend as little time as possible in that house – the disconnected clutter makes me uncomfortable. Besides, I can't stand that stinky dog of theirs. Always jumping in my face, trying to lick me to death or hump my leg. Both the Admiral and the Major think this is humorous.

They're like an old married couple, the way they bicker all the time. More than once, I've had to settle an argument between them. Stupid things, like who starred in such-and-such a movie or who is the president of so-and-so. I couldn't care less. Trivia bores me. But they always tip me extra for the trouble of looking up an answer in the encyclopedia, which is a joke. I still can't read very well, so usually I make something up. There's no point in wondering why they can't do it for themselves; it would be way more accurate, but that's the way they are, always dependent on the labours of others. You'd think the world owed them a living.

They know I'm not their personal lackey, though, we sorted *that* one out years ago. They're well aware that I'll never again return to the lottery basement to pick out winners for them and the subject is never brought up. Every now and then I'll find myself in a corner store, looking at the tickets laid out for purchase. I can still spot the winners immediately – if they're there to be won. More often than not, they aren't, so I suspect that the Admiral and the Major are continuing their little game of stacking the odds in favour of the charity, helping needy children throughout the country. Ha!

I visited Bruce in the institution this morning, brought him his Christmas present: a bag of tangerines, fresh from the market. My day was booked solid, but I found ten minutes to sit with him in the common room.

*cigaruttts?* he asked, his fingers shaking with the drugs.

I left him with a dozen packs of slightly crushed cigarettes that I'd rescued from my machines. They're forever getting jammed in the dispenser, so it's no bother to me; I'd only end up tossing them away. I always give Bruce a few packs, but not because he smokes – at Queen's Quay, cigarettes are currency.

*… His enemies will I clothe with shame: but upon himself shall his crown flourish …*

What a day! I should take the rest of the year off and just work the Christmas season! I go through half a dozen Extra Strength Tylenols a day, but it's worth it. People are willing to pay a king's ransom for the attentions of a professional at this point. It makes up for the rest of the year. I left the Priory to the last – just before doing my rounds of the Laundromats. That generator and I have an excellent working relationship and I knew it was just the coupling that had come loose. It was a two-minute job at the most, which I could stretch to ten if I rolled up my sleeves and looked busy.

So. Yours truly gets to the Priory just as dusk is falling and I go straight around to the back door to deal with the generator. I had to clear away some old boxes and stuff to get at the problem, and then that obnoxious dog came bounding through the kitchen, all sniffling jowls and slobbering rolls of skin, its penis pointing at me like a shiny toy whistle.

"Can't you put that animal in another room while I work?" I asked the Admiral, who had arrived to see what all the noise was about.

"But he's so pleased to see you," he said, refusing to do anything. "Aren't you, Dixie?"

I could have kicked it, but instead, I sighed and fixed the coupling as fast as I could, what with that beast putting its paws in the way all the time. Then I left. I couldn't get out of there fast enough. It was getting late and the Laundromats were going to be closing soon.

I have five Laundromats in operation in the city, all Dixie machines. They're definitely not the best on the market, but they do the job, although they require too much maintenance as they age. One day I'll replace them with more efficient machines. Until then I have to put aside at least an hour every day for their upkeep.

It was at the first location that I realized my mistake. Somehow, in all the fuss and bother with that blasted dog, I'd picked up the wrong bag! To be honest, I was more annoyed that I couldn't repair the dryer than I was about being lumped with a bag of winning lottery tickets. One look at them and I could see those little UV squares jumping around in the corners. Winners.

I stood there like an idiot for five minutes, trying to figure out how I was going to unscrew the heating panel of the dryer with a lottery ticket. The colour-tone of this second bag was different to the one that bore my tools. Now that I looked closely, I could see they were quite dissimilar.

As I stared at the broken dryer I knew that I was going to keep the tickets. Cash them in and buy myself a new fleet of washing machines. Yes! This was good luck! Maybe I could afford to pay the legal fees to get Bruce out of Bedlam and move him into my place. Anything, I knew, was possible with money. I couldn't have cared less about the Associated Benevolent Christian Charities having lost a bag of winners.

*... Let the wicked fall into their own nets, whilst that I withal escape ...*

I had two great fistfuls of tickets in my hands, trying to figure out how many of them were in the bag – it looked like well over fifty thousand – when my attention was drawn to the window. The neighbourhood isn't the safest in the world, and it looked like somebody was mucking around with my van. I crept to the door and wiped a little porthole in the condensation to see out.

Two men were fiddling with my van. Stealing it! I panicked. Then I realized that they weren't car thieves *per se*. It was a tow truck and they were hitching up my wheels! Jesus! That was all I needed.

What to do? My mind blanked and for a while I did a strange little dance, juggling my keys, the bag, and the loose tickets, which were flying every which way. I tossed the bag into the broken dryer, slammed the door shut and scooted out into the street after the bastards who were towing my van.

Damn. I was too late. It was being hauled away. That's $120 just for starters. Cursing the fates, I gave chase, shedding tickets behind me as I ran, but I wasn't going to stop for them. The street was treacherous, and I slipped and slid into elbows and parcels. An obstacle course of people laden down with Christmas shopping. Fat people, tall people, small people, men, women, and those in between. I hate people.

Finally I hopped out into the road, where it was less congested and easier to keep a grip due to the recent salting. Through the falling snow, I saw my van cross an intersection mere yards ahead of me.


I heard it bearing down upon me before I saw it. In fact, I never did really see it. I didn't want to. Not the streetcar. No. Not the street, not the people, not the snow, not the city.

I felt the rumble of civilization beneath my feet. *I am like a pelican of the wilderness.* The Psalm of the afflicted when overwhelmed.

As I'm standing there, in the middle of the intersection, I realize the futility of escape, feel the inevitability of disaster. And I don't want any part of it.

I close up my eyes.


Transported. That's the only way I can describe it. One moment I'm standing in the street, chasing after my van – the next, I am standing here in the middle of a large, earthen arena under a blazing sun. People. Noise. Ahead of me, about twenty yards or more, the carcass of a dead bull is being dragged through the dust by a team of men and horses, out through the swagged and flowered vomitorium. It's a bullring! I'm in a bullring! And somehow, I'm wearing the traditional garb of a matador: the ornate embroidered jacket, the tight pants, the silken cummerbund. In my hands are the weapons of my trade. There is no time to question it all. I raise my arm in salute to the people. Cheers explode from the crowd as I turn to face my new adversary.

It's a huge, thundering beast. Its head is lowered, horns pointing right at me, eyes blazing like headlights, skin glistening like that of a machine, bearing down on me, steam escaping from its nostrils.

At the last moment, I twist aside, aim my pikes.

Without a doubt, I've made contact. I can feel one of my weapons pierce the creature's brain, running it right through the eyeball with a satisfying "pop."

The exhilaration is unbounded. Swirling. Irrepressible. Liquid flows.

*Olé!*


Colour? Is this colour?

Yes, I know now. This is blood. Red. The colour of blood. On my pikes, on my hands, and dripping to the dirt where my foe lies dead, gushing more crimson from his wound. Red! The colour of War!

And that must be blue, calling at me from way up there between the clouds, like a passing echo, scarce understood. A worm on the ground expands in segments of a purple I've never seen before. The earth counts the years in brown, its shadow hunts in grey. The kiss of golden sunshine. A woman's fertile green hat and the beauty of a boy's yellow shirt. Silver coins like beads of mercury are being tossed into the ring. Coloured flowers. Ribbons. Flags. It's a universe of all-vibrating colour.

"Yaaaa-a-aAH...!"

The crowd in the bleachers blossoms into a multihued explosion of sound and I'm swarmed by smiling faces. They carry me aloft on their shoulders to the winner's box. Pink and yellow flower petals shower across my face. A group of young men is cheering me and I cheer back, waving my cap above my head, my hair swinging loose to my collar. I am being brought to receive the congratulations of the dignitaries.

At the end of the line is an imposing woman. She is strong, with a lean neck. She wears a veil. Her black dress hugs her waist and her red shawl falls in tassels from her elbows as she stands to greet me, holding out her hand. I feel unworthy in her presence.

"That did the trick," she says. "You took my breath away!"

"Thank you, ma'am."

"Ma'am?" She lifts her veil and her voice drops. "Don't you know who I am? Angus!"

My stomach skips a beat as if it were my heart. Do I recognize her? She looks familiar, but I cannot place her. Her skin shines with a mother-of-all-pearl luster. I start to feel clumsy, inarticulate. Tired, all of a sudden, withdrawn. Oh, how I wish I didn't feel like this with people!

"I – I'm sorry?"

"Didn't you read your invitation?" she smiles, casting her eyes back out into the ring, where the crowd is melting, melting in a palette of colour.

What invitation? I feel at the centre of a spinning disc. A giant carousel with me in the middle. The sky expands, folds out upon itself, the air grows warmer. A green line of vegetation spreads along the horizon, forming like fast-growing crystals into a new vista. The bullring wavers, ripples and transforms into sweet-smelling grasses bending in the breeze. A low-flying airplane scorches overhead. I hear shouts in a language I don't understand. A pair of yoked oxen plough through a field in the distance … *Thus they changed their glory into the similitude of an ox that eateth grass* … I'm at the fulcrum of a laden, foreign terrain. A war is going on and I'm at the centre of it all.

What invitation? I vaguely remember having received something in the mail this morning – a postcard from someone I've never heard of. The Statue of Liberty. I'd thought it was just a misdirected Christmas card. Was that what she was talking about?

Where am I? Something is burning; I can smell it. A fulsome stench like autumn leaves on fire. Sharp and damp. Clouds of billowing black smoke rise from the shoreline. I hear the lapping waves against the sandbank. A group of soldiers runs through the shallow water nearby, helmets shining, weapons bristling. A woman screams. Everything swirls. Roars.

"Angus, don't tell me you've forgotten!"

… *for he remembered his holy promise … and gave them the lands of the heathen …*

Frantically fighting off my unease, I go through my pockets, my frogged and piped pockets, two of which, I discover, are just fake flaps sewn onto my little jacket. The world is still revolving around me. I empty everything into my bloodied hands, almost too tired to focus. There are a few coins, a stick of gum, a two-dollar bill, a twenty, a driver's license, a bottle of painkillers, a tampon, my keys and a couple of those lottery tickets. But no invitation. I feel giddy.

"I – I can't seem to find it. I'm sorry – so sorry," I stutter, lamely.

"Never apologize," she says, wisely. I will try to remember the advice. She tosses back her head and laughs. "Let's see what you've got."

I'm so tired. I offer up the contents of my pockets for inspection, but all I can think about is my need to sleep. The fight must have taken it out of me.

*... but ye shall die like men and fall like one of the princes ...*

She leans forward, as something catches her eye. A gasp escapes from her throat. Suddenly, she coils out her arm and snatches one of the lottery tickets out of my hand. I feel a cold breeze as her fingers graze mine. So cold.

So cold.

"Oopsidaisy!" she says. "Almost took the wrong one!"

*... for I was cast upon thee from the womb: thou art my God from my mother's belly ...*


Cold as a memory.